The Road to Mars

By: J.C.L. Faltot

For my beautiful wife, who has endured many nights of me typing
away in our bed next to her.

Acknowledgments

Much thanks to Immanuel, Paul, and Brent for pushing me to completion. You guys are amazing friends.

Credit to Immanuel for the cover art too. Thank you, sir.

Also, thanks to my good friend, Jared. Your knowledge of all things I don't have a clue on was a huge help.

Chapter Listings...

Chapter 1
The Light in the Sky

"Be careful, son."
"I will, Father."

From the Mars program, Alpha, Archives.
Marion Perriello, Chancellor, and Founder of Mars, speaking with his son,
Cale Perriello, July 12, 2049, A.D.

* * * *

A dream? No, a *nightmare*. That was certainly a nightmare he'd had. Tired and weary, Darion Wallace awoke; face up and pressed against the wall of an alley. This was not a surprise for he'd chosen this spot the night before. The nightmare was nothing new either. He'd had it several times, but never this many nights in a row. Still, it was always the same: a ring of fire spiraling downward surrounded in darkness. He never saw himself in it, just the flame. And then it was over.

In the past, he'd try to understand it. Repetition in anything was a sign of something important, but he'd given up on trying. The nightmare was actually a *good* sign. It meant he was getting close. Yes, Darion remembered, his dreams turned to nightmares whenever he was getting close. He'd only believed he was on the right track. Now, he *knew* it to be true.

He raised a hand towards the sky and outlined a single cloud. It looked like a bird, but Darion's strokes were turning it into something else. A runway; a door to the heavens. If only it were that easy. Nothing flies anymore. Except for the birds and everything that was meant to in the first place. If he could fly though, what would his life be like? Would he even need rescuing? Would *anyone*?

I'll find you, he thought. *I will.*

There was a rustle behind him and he sat up, alert. The wind? A person? Darion kept a hand on his pocket, weapon at the ready and the other he pushed against the ground to steady himself. The noise returned and this time, an orange tabby cat appeared.

"Stupid animal," he said aloud and fell on his back, resting again. Quit being so jumpy. Nobody knows you're here. Nobody even knows you're alive.

Darion repositioned himself on the pavement, breathing in and out to calm himself. His shoulders rubbed atop a few layers of thick blanket. It gave him an unorthodox yet manageable sleep. He felt the cloth and silently convinced himself he was comfortable. No. This is *not* comfortable. I hate having to live like this.

He rubbed a hand through his dark hair and pulled at the tiny bit of scruff on his chin. "Gray, gray, go away...."

Gray hair. He'd only recently started to show. Yet, the gray of this world - that had been there for much longer. Worsened by the calamity of the *Pulse*. The 'Light-Eater', the 'Dark Bomb', among other names. The force that ate energy and electricity like it were a food source. Darion lingered on the thought for a moment and then shook his head.

No more of that, he thought. Time to get a move on.

He sat up and turned to the person lying next to him: his 10-year old daughter, Olivia, who was dreaming and cooing softly. Her lightly blond hair was wrapped around her neck and shoulders like a scarf. Darion smiled. She would have liked to trace the cloud with me. She likes doing that. But, it's better to rest considering what's ahead.

"Two more days is all, sweetie," he said again. "One more if we're really lucky. I can feel it. I know it."

Another thump at the front of the alley and Darion turned. What now? The cat again? No, a taller man, dressed in a brown coat and jeans. He stumbled about, falling to one side and knocking against the alley walls. He could barely hold himself under his own power, but it was unclear if he was too weak or too inebriated. The man snorted and coughed, a vile gagging sound like he was about to vomit. Darion knew for sure now.

"Drunken idiot..." whispered Darion. I don't need this right now.

The slovenly man righted himself and belched. He was younger, lighter-skinned, unshaven and looked like he hadn't showered for days. Darion's face wrinkled with disgust as the man began a slow walk towards Darion, eyes to the ground with feet jockeying like one knew the right way and the other didn't.

How did I get so lucky today, thought Darion.

Swaying back and forth, the man in the brown jacket came within a few feet of Darion and stopped. He pressed a hand against the wall opposite Darion and took a deep breath. His eyes meandered a while before settling on Darion's. Hand on his pocket again, Darion waited. Go ahead. Nobody will see us. Go on. But, the young man seemed unaware of Darion and strode off towards the other end of the alleyway. Darion watched him closely, shaking his head when the man disappeared around the corner.

"Getting drunk off something strong, eh son?" said Darion. "Was it worth the headaches, I wonder?"

In some way, Darion felt sorry for the stranger. It was probably the young man's way of dealing with the way the world was. A way of dealing with the monsters in one's own head. He must have found the drink as a reliable ally. An ally against the *fear.*

Stop thinking about that, Darion thought. *Get back on track. Leave it alone.*

Darion removed the blanket from his legs, stood up and stretched. He combed his hair back with both hands, careful to not pull on the tiny traces of gray that crept round his ears and ran along the base of his scalp.

"That's it," he said. "Next time we're napping out in the fields, Liv. I thought there were no people around here, but I guess you can never be too careful...."

He closed his eyes and took another deep breath. The image of the burning spiral was waiting for him behind his eyelids. So he opened his eyes and shook his head of the picture. The nightmare was a good sign, but that didn't mean it still didn't disturb him.

Darion bent over and poked at something on the ground. It was a small disc; silver with smooth edges, about the size a grapefruit and flat like a pancake. It blipped and whirred like a wheel spinning when he touched it. And when it was done talking to him, he picked it up and held it in his hand. Then he pushed the center of the disc with his pointer finger and the sound of three more discs could be heard springing to life: one on the ground, another on the wall by his daughter, and one more by the back corner of their bed. Each disc detached itself from its hiding place and flew into his hand like high-powered magnets, neatly stacking themselves atop one another.

"For a moment there," said Darion, tucking away all the discs but one. "I thought that idiot could see us, sweetie. I know it's impossible but it still makes me wonder. Nothing sees through these barriers. Nothing from *this* world anyway."

Darion zipped his bag and looked about the alley. It was morning, but the air felt like dusk had settled in. No matter what time of day it was, it still felt like the night was holding on. Olivia twitched and Darion caressed the top of her head. No need to wake just yet. It's still dark out. It's always dark nowadays. Darion stood and raised the fourth disc to his face. He muttered a few words, indiscernible to anyone other than himself, and waited. The silver disc morphed into two rounded cylinders, reflective lenses at the end. Darion pushed the new object to his face and looked through.

"Where are you?" Darion said aloud. He blinked and his vision changed to see beyond the alley. He blinked again and this time, he could see past the hillside, and when he blinked a third time, he could see deep into the woods, just outside the city. There was a gravel path there and he smiled like he'd found the golden road.

"That's where you'll be," he said. "I'm sure of it."

Darion pulled down the strange binoculars and adjusted his eyes, blinking madly like he'd been staring at the sun. He'd hoped he'd be used to them by now, but he wasn't. The object reverted back to its former shape and Darion placed the disc back into his pack.

"Olivia? Sweetie? It's time to wake up...."

Olivia was already awake, though. Her eyes were open and she was staring at the wall.

"I'm sorry. Did I wake you by accident?"

Olivia nodded.

"Your hair's a mess, little lady."

She grinned. Darion used one of his fingers to push her blond hair to one side. Now, he could see her eyes clearly. They were light blue and shimmered like pearls might in a desert.

"Those eyes of yours," he said. "They're always a joy to see in the morning."

Olivia didn't smile this time. She was tired and hadn't slept well. Why her father always chose the streets rather than a comfortable bed confused her. But, she sat up and watched her father gather their things, awaiting her instructions. She was willing to help, but she knew her father would not ask anything of her. That was the norm. It was the routine she knew. When Darion was ready, he took Olivia's hand and walked her out of the alley and onto the sidewalk.

"Hungry, little miss?" he asked and Olivia shook her head, 'yes'. "Good – so am I."

They stayed close to the buildings, walking like they preferred to be seen as shadows rather than people. Darion kept his head to the ground, avoiding eyes like the plague. Drifters would want conversation, but Darion didn't. The drunk from earlier had Darion feeling extra cautious as well. He wasn't familiar with this town so he kept Olivia to the inside, her hands practically brushing the stone-laced walls. Above them, the sky was waking up. Clouds had formed but none looked hostile and packed with rain. Still, Darion moved with a purpose. He stopped only when Olivia squeezed his hand, signaling when it was best they stop for a time.

"Sorry, sweetheart. I just want us to get where we are going and get there soon. You know that, right?"

Olivia nodded. She'd always nod, even when she didn't agree, she would. It made life easier for them both. When they stopped a second time, Darion took some pictures. He loved doing that when they had downtime. That's when Olivia saw something: a tiny cloud of static. It rippled the air, crackling like a live wire. She tried not to alert her father's attention to it, but when he saw her eyes staring, he looked also. Too late. Now, he would have more reason to be upset.

"No need to be afraid, Liv," he said. "We're protected, remember? The monsters in the cloud can't hurt us."

More interference. *This place must be a hot bed for fear,* Darion thought. He searched for his coveted silver disc and when he found one, he gripped it tight. It was the oldest disc he possessed but it still worked. Olivia dared not move. That always seemed to work best.

Please don't call the monsters out, Dad, she thought. Let them lie where they are. I don't want to see them.

"Remember, Liv," said Darion, tracking the cloud with his eyes, disc at the ready. "It likes fear. It wants us to be afraid. So don't be. I'm here with you. Don't be afraid. Don't be afraid and the monster won't come out."

Olivia did as she was told. But, to her, that meant closing her eyes and singing a song her mom used to sing. That worked just as well.

Eventually, the crackle of foreign energy dissipated and Darion grinned like he'd won a fight. That's right. Go on and hide. You know I have all the tools to beat you.

"There's more to be afraid of down in the city, Liv," said Darion. "Where there's a lot of people, there's lots of fear. And what do we do when we feel fear?"

This time, Olivia didn't nod. She just stared blankly at her father. "We don't show them fear, do we, sweetheart?"

Olivia looked to the sky. The crackle of static was gone, but there was another light; one high above the clouds. It broke the atmosphere like it was careening downwards yet had the power to keep itself from crashing. Olivia held onto her father, the only witness to the strange streak of light in the sky.

"What is it, Liv?" asked Darion and he turned round. Nothing. There was nothing he could see. "Let's go, Liv. No more to see here."

Olivia sighed. The new light - the one in the sky - was gone. This was not like the other ones. It didn't sputter or hiss or cause distress. It shined brighter than the dark clouds she was used to. What did it mean? Again, she sighed. Why was everything beautiful always here and gone in a moment? This world never allows more than a few moments of beauty. She heard the words in her head and recognized them as her father's. Did she feel the same? Or was she just repeating what she'd heard so many times before?

No matter. The strange light was gone. Time to go.

The pair traveled down a side trail and onto a bridge. They walked it, stopping halfway and Darion took another snapshot with his camera. The click-click sounded ancient.

"Might as well get some more of these while we can, eh?" he said. "Who knows, maybe someone has a processor somewhere in the old city? Would be nice to see how these came out."

Olivia didn't acknowledge her father. Taking pictures seemed to hold little purpose. She'd never seen one 'developed' before. But, she often heard people talking about them. How 'back in the old days,' people could take pictures, print them out and view them from something called a 'phone.' Then they could share these pictures with other people. It all happened instantaneously and without much effort. Now, that seemed wholly impossible. So why take them?

"This city used to be filled with lots of people, Liv," said Darion. "One time it was. Now it's just an empty hole with fewer people, but just as much garbage as before. Then the Pulse hit, as you know. Those idiots. If only...."

Olivia held her father's hand tighter, but Darion carried on. She knew where this was going. Her father would always tie things back to the Pulse, the worst event in human history, or so her father would say. The story was always a little different each time. And by now, Olivia focused on listening for the inconsistencies in Darion's monologs, trying hard to pinpoint where anger was overriding truth. That's how her father was when he spoke of the Pulse: *angry*. His mood would shift and he'd begin saying things like something had overtaken him and his words. From then on, it wasn't her father talking but someone else. Something having to do with those floating balls of static always seemed to put her father in a foul mood. She knew the static hadn't been here before the Pulse. That was a truth that never changed; no matter who was telling the story.

So Olivia held on. She held on until her father was through.

"I know you may not feel like you're connected to any of this, but you are," said Darion. "And I'm sorry you've had to live through these days, Liv. I really am. But, that's how it goes, I suppose. Humanity anyway. Inheriting messes you never started and never finishing the ones you started either. Maybe one day we'll get it right."

Darion and Olivia came to the end of the bridge and waited. The old city was barely awake, save some people moving about on horses. No cars. No big vehicles on the move. *That's good*, Darion thought. The less of that, the better. There was a chatter of voices bouncing about the alleys, but they were casual. Only white noise. This was also a relief for Darion. So they entered.

The buildings of the old city were bathed in rust and cracked with old age. Darion winced, acting like the scene was hard to endure. Olivia didn't know the better and took it all in like the rust were a normative function rather than an aftermath of civilized decay. Something about human structures covered in mother Earth made her feel at home. For Darion, it was very much the opposite feeling.

"Not for much longer, Liv," said Darion. "You won't have to suffer this for much longer. Do you understand?"

Olivia nodded, this time not knowing if she should have.

Down the street, around the corner and into the lower part of the city, they went. Darion kept one hand in his coat pocket and the other firmly grasped upon Olivia's. He took note of a large building to his right. It had been decimated and made into a new shelter. That was to be expected these days. People gathered outside and inside like it was an open tent. Taller buildings were clean near their foundations but the higher they stretched, the less attractive they became – covered with dirt or something else unsightly. Nature appeared to be winning the war, not mankind's creations. Large signs hung from the sides of buildings. They were handwritten with words and arrows to direct travelers around the city. Nothing with light; *human* light. Only the sun's rays could illuminate the old city. Darion bit his lower lip, imagining what the old city would have been like at night. It would have been glorious. No need to fear the dark. What a thought.

Then Darion saw the remnants of what he knew to be an old traffic light on the corner of a street and smirked. Next to it were other traffic lights, their wires neatly wrapped next to one another. Beside them were other odd electronics, all of which were stacked neatly under the canopy of what Darion believed to be a merchant's tent.

"Nothing but relics," said Darion, stopping to observe the traffic light. Olivia didn't know what he meant by it, but she assumed it meant 'not usable.'

An elderly man, darker-skinned and uncombed, came rushing to the canopy and put a hand over the traffic light. Darion and Olivia backed away. The old man caressed the light like it was his pet or some precious medallion.

"I see you have an interest in this beautiful piece of hardware here," said the old man. His eyes sparkled over top of a scraggly gray beard. He seemed unbalanced when he moved and Olivia noticed that he smelled of something awful.

"Tell me," he continued. "Would you like to put a wager on this here? Would you like to buy one of these amazing products I have right here? You won't find anything like this in the old city. Nothing like these, I tell you!"

Darion moved Olivia behind him. "No, thank you."

Darion eyed a canning jar under the canopy. It was filled with a few silver dollars and coins made of bronze or nickel. Not a good sign. Some of the currency wasn't 'current' anymore.

"But this is the best!" insisted the old merchant. "You know what this is, don't you?" Excitedly, the old man began explaining what the traffic lights were for and what they used to do. The way he spoke, you'd think they held genies or tiny fairies with pixie dust. But, Darion wasn't impressed. He'd seen these machines work in his youth. And there was no need for them now. Not since the Pulse had struck and ripped the magic out of these old things.

"No, thank you," said Darion. "I'm already aware of... "

"Oh, so you're someone from before the darkness, are you?!" said the merchant, eyes coming ever more alive. "A fellow brother-in-arms, are ya? The *P.D.B.* era, right? Well, my friend, you will be someone who knows how important it will be to have one of these with you when the light returns! Yes, when the light returns to us all – you will want this with you! Don't you agree?"

P.D.B.

Darion knew the acronym: *Pre-Dark Bomb*. Like B.C. or A.D., it was meant to identify those who lived before the war with Mars and who were still alive today. Darion hated it though. But only because men like this merchant used it to try and connect with others. To find some common ground. To make a sale, most likely.

"The light is not returning," said Darion, defiantly. "What you're holding onto there is ancient history. The *Darklight* keeps that from happening. Just what the devil are you doing trying to sell these anyway? You should get off these streets. Find something productive to commit yourself to."

Olivia trembled. Back to the anger again.

But, the old merchant's eyes glowed. "Ah yes, the *Darklight*. That evil gift from brother Mars...."

Darion turned to walk away and the merchant continued.

"Seen it, did you?" said the merchant, stopping Darion. "Were you there for the whole thing? Did you see it when it happened? Oh, I thank God the sun still shines upon us. I thank God for that at least!"

Darion shook his head, continued to inch away, but the merchant went on. "I tell you this now," said the old merchant. He held up a finger up like he was making a divine statement. "For 40 years, the Darklight has ruled over us. It's kept us from having our precious lights. You know this. *I* know this. You have been there, my friend. But I tell you this now: *this will not be forever!* I have seen it, you see. I have seen it! The Darklight won't keep us in darkness. Our brothers and sisters on Mars have not destroyed us entirely. We will get our light *back*. So you and your little one there – you will want this when the light comes back! It's coming, I tell you. It'll be coming sooner than you think!"

Darion rolled his eyes. He knew so many like this man – the delusional, the sorry - the ones drowning in denial. Darklight, the Pulse's remnant that eats lesser light, inhabits the Earth just as the merchant claims. The alien substance brought to Earth as a 'gift' from brother Mars. Darion knew it and despised having to listen. It reminded him of what the Pulse had done. Dark minds became darker and hopeful men, became less hopeful. Moreover, and worst of all, somehow the foolish had become elevated. People, such as this merchant, would use whatever they could to draw on that shared misery of how things used to be. No doubt trusting weaker-minded people might buy into their notion of a rejuvenated future. Darion knew this the kind of man and immediately felt ashamed for even trying to speak to him. Completely lost, aren't you? At some point, the future must have become so dark that the Old World needed to reawaken. But, Darion knew better. The Old World was dead. The lights were never coming back on. The Darklight would forever make certain of that.

Still, the old merchant held out a hand like he expected Darion to fill it. Darion kept his hands tucked away, tightening his grip on one of the four discs in his pocket. He turned with Olivia, leaving the merchant behind. This man reeks of desperation. And desperate men are repulsive, if not dangerous, too.

"Well, what do you say, my friend?" asked the merchant, this time more insistent and following Darion up the street.

Something stirred in Darion. One part of him wanted to lash out and hurt this man. *Get away from me, you idiot.* He could already hear the words in his head. But, then a group of children came running down the street. They had tattered clothes and old sandals that clicked against the pavement. Their expressions were joyful and it stopped Darion in his thoughts. They passed the merchant, and to Darion's surprise, grabbed some stones and began to pelt the merchant's tent.

"Hey you!" shouted the merchant, turning back towards his things. "Get away from there! Stop that now! Monsters!"

The children were causing a disturbance and yet, Darion felt like smiling. That's what you get for trying to sell junk. The world *does* have a sense of justice after all. So Darion led Olivia away from the scene, her eyes fixed on the merchant and the children who terrorized him.

"Liv," said Darion. "Do not ever become like that. Do you understand me? That life is no better than a bottom-feeder. It's wrong and we're worth so much more than that. Do you hear me?"

Olivia grasped her father's hand slightly as if to say, 'Okay, but in truth, she was confused. To not be like the old merchant? Or the children? She wasn't sure, but she logged her father's words away like she might be able to understand them later.

The sun was getting higher and that made the smell of the city even worse. Everything seemed to reek of sewage. The air was tight and when the wind blew, Darion felt like he was swimming in the stink. There were piles of garbage in every alley and Darion made mental notes of the best spots to sleep if things came to that.

Meanwhile, Olivia was peering at every building with curious eyes. She paid attention to the tiniest of details: a half-departed sign that said, "Bank" or a logo that resembled a snake on a staff. Olivia enjoyed it most when she could recognize the same symbol from one city to another. Some were harder to catch than others, but the game kept her mind busy. Her father, however, did not delight in this game as much. But, when she saw one she thought she knew, she squeezed her father's hand and pointed.

"Not now, Liv…" said Darion and she looked up. There were two men on horses, staring down at them. Where had they come from? They looked like dark angels, their eyes squinted and cold. Were they monsters in human form? Olivia heard her father speak of them often. Were these one in the same? Olivia hid behind her father.

"Off to somewhere special?" asked one of them. His tone was deep; the type of voice one might think would belong to a demon.

Darion kept his eyes to the ground. Then slowly, he raised his head to face them.

"Just passing through," said Darion, voice shaky. *Don't give them any reason to search you*, he thought. Just stick to the basics.

"Where to then?" asked the other horseman. Darion could see the insignias on their uniforms. Lawkeepers, he presumed. Every city had its own since the Pulse. Some were horrible while others were less-than-tolerable, but there were always the decent human beings Darion found too. Those were the least. There was no way of knowing which these were so Darion kept his eyes down.

"Looking for someplace to eat," said Darion. "It's still early. There's something in this old city, right?"

The men on horses didn't say anything. They looked past Darion, at the merchant farther down the road. They said something to each other that Darion didn't hear and Darion swallowed. *What are they saying?* he thought. *Oh God, please just leave us alone. We don't want any trouble.*

Darion looked about, searching for signs of static in the air. Surely, if this were a dangerous situation, the clouds would be there. The Darklight would accumulate itself. Then he saw a purple cloud. It *was* here. Near to them and getting bigger. No, no, no… what am I going to do?

"Enjoy your breakfast," said one of the horsemen and road off, the other following him. Relieved, Darion watched as they made off for the merchant's tent. They didn't want me. They didn't want *us*, but when Darion saw them pass the merchant, Darion could see they weren't interested in the merchant. Where were they going then? To those children throwing the stones? Yes, it was the kids they were after.

Darion held Olivia close as the Lawkeepers gave chase. They scattered the children like wolves splitting a flock of sheep. And when one of the children threw a stone at the officer, the Lawkeeper took out a beat stick and cracked one of the children across the face on the next pass. The boy screamed, fell to the ground, and Olivia screamed too.

"Damned parent-less monsters!" shouted the Lawkeeper and again, Olivia jumped. "Get off the streets! If you're not here to make money then quit disturbing the people who are!"

Darion quickly led Olivia away from the scene. What a bleak sight. That child could have a concussion, or worse. Could be bleeding from the inside out with how hard he'd been hit over the head. But, Darion couldn't go back and check. No, he needed to get his daughter out of there. There were more shouts and screams, but again, Darion ignored them. Olivia heard everything.

"Come on, Liv," said Darion. "You don't need to see any more of this."

So they hurried around the corner and found shelter inside of a pub. At last, they could rest a while. Their problems were their own and Darion had no time for the troubles of others.

* * * *

He'd been wandering for a while, wanting to stop but his mouth was dry and he needed water. He stumbled around a back alley and tried to recall the events of the prior night. Where were his friends, the people he'd gone with? No, he was alone. He was always alone. He chuckled softly like it was foolish to have entertained the thought. But then again, he'd chosen things to be this way. It worked easier, even on mornings like these. Was it morning though? He looked up at the sky and saw that the sun was already up. It hurt his eyes and again, he chuckled like it was stupid of him to not think of these things before he did them. Too much drink and not enough water. Still, he was alive.

"Way to go, Jack," he said. "You made it through another scorcher."

He knew it wasn't midday, but it was definitely past morning. Had he slept? He had no idea, but he was fairly certain he hadn't. He was tired, but he wasn't without the gumption to keep moving. He paused in another alley and saw a man and a little girl, hand in hand, walking fast. They had their heads down and the man had a hefty knapsack thrown over his shoulder. A bold move, old man. What's in the sack? He decided to follow and find out. Why not?

It was hard to keep up with the pair. *You had too much last night, Jack,* he thought. Way too much. He needed water more than anything, but a knapsack could mean more than just water – it could mean other valuable things too; things that would be worth a pretty coin. So he continued following the pair, staying far enough behind to not appear too conspicuous.

He followed them into the old city, staying in the shadows. It wasn't hard. Jack was good at staying hidden. He kept close to the buildings, head down and eyes forward. The brick of the buildings were disfigured and jagged, much like him. And every so often, he'd stop and observe the graffiti that lined the older, more decrepit structures.

Die Mars.

Death to Mars.

Bring back the light, you bastards.

How lovely. Jack recalled writing some of these when he was a kid. Some of the designs had changed, but the messages stayed the same: Mars was an enemy. The majority of Earth hated Mars. But, there were always those on the other side of that feeling. Jack saw gypsies on the streets, talking about the "union of two worlds" and how "Earthlings were the real aliens." Jack thought it weird, though he longed for the strange peace these travelers without a home seemed to possess. Was there truth in their words? No time to figure that out yet.

Up the road, he saw the pair talking to a merchant. If they're smart, they won't buy from that swindler. Jack had never bought any from the merchant, but he *had* taken a few things without paying. None of the junk ever worked of course. Not since the Pulse.

He watched the pair carefully, noting how the old man became annoyed quickly. No small talk, is it? In a hurry? You *must* have something special with you. The father kept one hand in his pocket and the other on the girl. So, which of those things is more important to you, old man? We'll have to find out, won't we?

He wiped his mouth. Still dry. I'm hoping it's water you have, if nothing else.

A group of children came round the corner and immediately set to pelting the merchant's hut with rocks and stones. They yelled at the merchant, sounding like hyenas as they tormented the old man. *I remember those days*, he thought. This city hasn't changed at all, has it? The merchant cursed back at them but they wouldn't cease. The children disappeared and then reappeared, each time with more stones and more cackling.

Up ahead, two men on horseback were talking with the pair. And the *clouds*. Those strange clouds were there too. Those clouds that always showed up right before something bad was going to happen. Jack looked around like someone might see him and hid next to a building stoop. I can't be found out now. Why did I even come here? Stupid.

The Lawkeepers stopped talking and started towards him. No. They saw me. They knew who I am. They're going to come for me now. Dammit anyways. Run. Get out of here. Those clouds – I should have known. Why didn't I run?

He got low and pulled his knees to his chest. Play stupid, play dumb. Do *something* to make them not recognize you. And when they passed him he assumed his ploy had worked. But then he saw what these men, these Lawkeepers, were really after: the *children*. They didn't care about him or the merchant. They were trying to disperse the children. More men on horseback appeared when the Lawkeepers called them forth. They drove the children apart, beating them with sticks and clipping them on the heels of their horses.

The young man rose up, not thinking of the consequences. He didn't care if anyone saw him. He didn't care if these men *knew* him. He couldn't stand to see it. He'd seen it himself as a boy and knew what it was like. To be an orphan and have one's life only good for beating when someone else was angry.

Using that emotion as fuel, he ran towards the closest man on horseback and tackled him. It was a surprise attack so it worked. He then took the beat stick in hand and clobbered the Lawkeeper with it until the resistance stopped. One down.

Ha, he thought. I may be hungover but I sure gave one hell of a fight.

But, that was all he had in him. For the other Lawkeepers had discerned that one of their own was down so they turned their attention towards Jack and what followed was a harsh beating. In the midst of it, Jack's only wish was that he wasn't so dehydrated. Losing some blood or some sweat would be more costly than normal. Still, he saw the children run off from beneath the heel of one of the Lawkeepers and a tiny smile formed inside.

They got away. I guess that means something, doesn't it?

They beat on him good and when they were through, they threw him atop one of their horses. They tied his hands together and told him how stupid he was. That was all normal too. The Lawkeepers loved to badger people who didn't wear badges. At least in this city they did.

"That was real ballsy of you, kid," said one of the Lawkeepers. "Makes me want some breakfast. What do you say, Mitch?"

The other officer and several others nodded.

"Jack…" muttered the young man.

"What was that? Hey, gents. I think this orphan-saver wants to say something. Go on, speak up for everybody here."

"I said, *Jack*," he repeated. "My name is *Jack*. Not 'kid' you pricks. It's – "

A beat stick across the face silenced Jack on the spot and he fell to the ground in a heap. Way to run your mouth, Jack. He thought he heard laughter after that, but Jack imagined it was his own. Playing the martyr, am I? What good did that do for me? He looked about and saw the pair he'd been following was gone. Sonuvabitch. I come all this way just to get my ass kicked. How stupid am I?

The Lawkeepers, now with Jack in tow, made their way up the street and around the corner. The merchant chanted at their heels, going on about the darkness and the light returning. No one replied.

Overhead, a light appeared in the sky. It moved swiftly from one side of the city to the other. It scorched a small cloud, splitting the patch of white in two as it traveled. Then it broke off into separate directions – one to the north, the other northwest. And when it was gone, the cloud reformed, swirling together as if the light beam had never existed.

Jack squinted, cheek swelling up as he gazed upon the strange beam of light.

"Hey, what was - " he said, but another swing of the stick and Jack was practically knocked out. His head fell and his body went limp. No sound anymore. All was still.

And yet, high above the city, something alien had come.

Chapter 2
Incident and Irony

"This is not some training exercise, you know."

"Isn't all of life a training ground? Meant to prepare someone for what's coming? What's predestined for the one lying in wait?"

* * * *

Darion looked up and saw several men enter the pub. They were Lawkeepers and they had someone with them: a prisoner. His face was red like, he'd picked a fight and lost mightily. He staggered, head falling forward as the Lawkeepers took him to the bar side. There, they asked for ice and a dry cloth and when they were given both, one of the Lawkeepers pressed it to the prisoner's face. After a few moments, one of the men pulled the bag away and looked at Jack.

"Yep," he said, with eyes squinted. "You're gonna have a nice shiner, boy. Bet you're regretting that little stunt you pulled out there, aren't you? Those kids were causing a lot of trouble."

Jack didn't answer. He took a deep breath and pressed the ice to his flesh. It felt good. Painful, but good. The Lawkeeper leaned in again.

"I know you probably thought you were protecting them," said the Lawkeeper. "But, those kids have been causing chaos on the streets for weeks and we don't negotiate with chaos."

Again, Jack was silent. The Lawkeeper looked at Jack with sympathetic eyes, searching for some kind of sensibility tucked beneath the exterior. But, Jack wouldn't respond. He hunched his back and leaned against the bar top, looking away as if to hide his face. Yet, someone *did* see him – Darion – and he wondered how he might know this young man's face.

Is that the man from the alley? Darion thought. Couldn't be. That seemed incredibly unlikely. However, there was always that chance, wasn't there? Had this man been following them? Or was he just the unfortunate receiver of some local law enforcement? Whatever.

Darion needed to stay invisible so ducked his head and returned to eating.

But, then a large man next to Darion's table muttered something under his breath and stood. Then the disc in Darion's pocket stirred and he looked up. Olivia, too, was stirred by something, it seemed.

"Something wrong, sweetie?" asked Darion and Olivia nodded. Her intuition was hardly wrong. She sensed something was about to happen. Something bad, so Darion rushed to finish his meal and get them out of there. If the discs and Olivia could feel it, then he'd better hurry.

Meanwhile, the large man and two others approached the Lawkeepers. Their huge bodies blocked Darion's view as they stood in a line. Jack hid his face, tapped his foot on the barstool.

"Howdy," said the big one, his coarse voice scratching the walls as he spoke. "Have some trouble out there this morning, gents?"

One of the Lawkeepers spoke for the group. "Just some kids tormenting a salesman on the sidewalk. Nothing major."

The big one glanced at Jack, who was still trying to hide himself. "Kids, was it?" he asked. "That's no kid you have you with you. What's his story?"

"He was part of it, unfortunately. Decided to be a tough guy and hit one of our own. So we'll be taking him back to the courthouse. See what his story is, that sort of thing. You know how these things work."

"Course I do!" said the big one. "But I don't care about that. I really don't."

The Lawkeepers seemed to grow tense. Darion felt it from across the room.

"What *do* you care about?"

"That young man with you," said the big one. "The one holding the cold compress to his cheek. Pressing it to his face like it'll hide his messed-up mug so I won't recognize him. But, I do, *Jack.* I really *do* know it's you. Ain't it, boy?"

Jack turned slightly towards his accuser, eyes forward. "There he is," said the big one. "What the hell are you doing back in the city, boy? Didn't anybody tell you to stay away from the places where nobody wants you?"

"What do you have to do with him?" asked the head Lawkeeper.

"I'll save you the trouble, bub," said the big one. "Your boy here is wanted by the *Hunt*."

"The *Hunt*?"

The Lawkeepers, all at once, became frightened by the mention of the word, 'Hunt.' They drew closer to one another like a herd surrounded by predators. And at the center was Jack, their unlikely bounty with a hit on his head. Darion fidgeted in his chair, the disc moving ever so slightly. This was going to be bad. He needed to leave as soon as he could without drawing any eyes upon him.

"Yeah, the Hunt," repeated the big one. "So, you going to give over the kid now or later?"

The big one's words caused a few others within earshot to take notice. Two women moved away and two more left their seats. Yet Darion saw the worst of what was to come: *Darklight*. Small clouds were forming about the men. The static crackled in the air but had no sound attached to it and Darion wondered if anyone else in the room could see what he did.

"That won't be happening," said one of the Lawkeepers though his voice was shaky. "He's with us. That's all."

"Yes, it *will*," said the big one and he took another step forward. Again, the Lawkeepers huddled closer. They outnumbered the big one and his group 2-to-1, but by sheer size, the odds were even, perhaps tipped in the big one's favor.

"No, it *won't*," said another of the Lawkeepers. He moved his hand across his hip, grabbed hold of his beat stick and stood like he was ready to unsheathe a sword. "You're not one of the Hunt, so back off. This one is ours. Not yours."

The big one looked at Jack and smirked.

"You really messed up, Jack," said the big one.

"No way, Reg," said Jack, pulling the cloth from his face. "I planned it this way the whole time."

Then Jack threw the cold pack at one of Reg's men and tried to grab a beat stick from the Lawkeepers. Chaos took over. Reg's men and the Lawkeepers went at each other with whatever they had available. The confusion was enough to cause both parties to choose sides, neglect Jack, and fend for themselves. Jack tried jumping over the counter, but Reg was upon him. The large man had thrown two of the Lawkeepers away like trash and grabbed hold of Jack's pant. He threw Jack to the floor as the other men dispatched of the remaining Lawkeepers. It was over so quickly that Darion hadn't the time to take Olivia and run. On the ground, Jack howled in pain, Reg's boot crushing his back.

"Oh yeah" cried Reg. "There's some good fight in you, Jack! Atta boy!"

Reg removed a knife from his back pocket and the clouds grew thicker. Darion had had enough. Amidst the screams in the room, he took Olivia by the hand and tried to sneak out. He said only a few words to her as they kept their heads low, headed for the door. But, before they made it through, Olivia stopped. She tugged at her father, eyes turned towards the fight. Darion saw Jack on the ground, afraid and grimacing in pain. The clouds were swarming towards him. These men - they were not going to take him hostage. Reg was going to *kill* Jack. The Darklight clouds would not be clustering like this otherwise.

"No! Please, no!" cried Jack as Reg stood over top of him.

"Shut up, Jack!" said Reg. And he landed more expletives upon Jack as he prepped for the kill.

Then it happened. Though Darion had tried to avoid it, he couldn't stop. One of his discs came alive, rising up from out of his pocket and latching itself upon his wrist. It swiftly transformed from circular plate to elongated pistol; whirling and buzzing like it were capable of unleashing a rocket from its tiny cannon. Then – as though the weapon were thinking independently of Darion – the pistol pulled Darion's arm to a line of sight and lit itself from the base of his wrist until it burst at the end with sharp light. The purple and black cloud of Darklight subsided and a golden beam cut the air, hitting not Reg, but another behind him. To the surprise of Darion, the light struck one of Reg's men. A man whose hand was holding a pistol, ready to fire on a Lawkeeper– a revelation unknown to any who were watching the scuffle till that moment. The gun flew through the air and landed somewhere behind the bar as the light rifle moved Darion's arm again, turning its interests on the Lawkeepers. Darion tried to stop; he wanted to resist, but he stop. The power running along his arm won Darion over and he was already channeling the rifle of light's next shot. From here on, he had little, if any control of what would happen. It was always like this. As much as he wanted to stay hidden, the weapon would not allow it.

"*Don't move!*" shouted Darion, but it was not just his own voice that said it. His words were assisted by something, like his voice was being amplified. "*Release the weapon and step away. Step away. Now.*"

The pub fell under a hush like one were standing in a graveyard. No one breathed, blinked, or moved. The inside of a coffin would have been livelier. Jack turned his head towards Darion as Reg backed away, staring down Darion like he'd witnessed a man rise from the dead.

"What the hell is that thing…" muttered Reg and the rifle changed abruptly, transforming into a rotating blade. It clicked and whirred and Darion's eyes glowed with yellow light. Then it fired flares of light everywhere, tiny balls of gold looking like miniature suns, perched themselves in every corner of the room.

"*Olivia*," said Darion, voice still booming. "*Cover your eyes!*"

The swirling blades released from Darion's wrist. They hovered a moment and then latched upon Darion's face, becoming something that more closely resembled goggles than weaponry. Olivia closed her eyes as commanded. She'd been through this before. *Now comes the part I'm not allowed to see*, she thought. The balls of light crackled and burst into strobes of yellow and gold. Everyone in the room cried out; light pummeling them with beams of energy They pushed into one another, hiding away their faces but nothing seemed to stop the light from forcing itself upon them.

"The light!" they cried. "It's *Darklight*. Darklight magic!"

"My eyes! It's under my eyelids!"

"Stop it! Stop it, please! If you're from *Mars*, please, stop! We give up! You can have whatever you want!"

Darion picked up Olivia and fled. He kept his head low; the goggles firmly planted on his face.

"Show me the way out of here," Darion said under his breath and a path appeared before him in the streets. Through the goggles, Darion saw a blue line appear. It traced down the sidewalk and out of the old city, leading into the hillsides. Darion kept Olivia in his arms, walking quickly. Why did that have to happen? Why does that *always* have to happen to us? He knew the answer, but he hated it all the same. These discs - these alien discs in his possession. They specialized in this sort of thing, working against his desires. Yet if it hadn't been for the discs, that man might have met his end. But, again, he and Olivia might have escaped without all the commotion. No matter, he had to be gone now; disappear like always.

Darion held Olivia for a time, using her hair to block the goggles on his head until they were far enough away. They came the edge of the city and Darion saw another merchant standing under his canopy. He was seated in his chair, body glowing through Darion's lens. But, Darion didn't stop to analyze why. He'd seen these phenomena happen before when he wore the discs upon his face.

"Sir? Sir?" said the merchant, rising to stand. "Would you like to come see what I have here?"

Darion's goggles dropped and fell into his chest, changing back to a plain silver disc. Then they snapped in half, falling onto the ground.

"No!" said Darion. *Not again. Not another one.*

"No, thank you," said Darion, hastily. "I have to be going."

"Are you sure?" asked the merchant. "I can help you with – "

"Get away from us!" yelled Darion and the merchant fell backwards.

Darion heard voices behind him. Were they coming for him? But, the disc? It had broken. Another of his discs had broken in two.

"Here," said Darion. "Take this, if you like. Now go away!"

The merchant's eyes beamed when he saw the broken disc and picked it up like it was solid gold.

That's no good to anyone now, thought Darion. Go ahead and sell it if you like.

The merchant shouted a 'thanks' to Darion, but he and Olivia were already well down the road by then. At which point, Darion slowed his steps and looked to his daughter.

"I'm sorry about that, Liv," he said. "Did you at least get enough to eat?"

Olivia nodded. She was still hungry, but she didn't want to be a bother. Her father was angry, though he was hiding it now. So it was better to go on than complain while he was like this.

"Okay," said Darion. "Let's get out of here before we're forced to do anything else against our will."

* * * *

Back inside the building, people were thrashing about from the light flare. But, Jack – whose hands were over his face – gazed into his palms and saw nothing. He looked up and saw that the others, whose eyes were closed tight or had their arms covering their faces, were struggling like someone had put fire in their eye sockets. Jack saw Reg and the two other men – big and powerful as they were – behaving in the same manner. Even the Lawkeepers were screaming to the heavens. They all looked ridiculous. Was this a cruel joke? Jack stood and grabbed the knife Reg had dropped. He watched them suffer a while longer, admiring their pain like he had been the one who caused it.

Now what to do? Jack looked out the cafe's door and then back again. Run now? Or be certain to never be followed by Reg or any of these men again? Jack turned the knife upside down like he was about to plunge it into Reg's throat. It would feel good to do it. He knew it would. He'd done it plenty of times with less thought. But, he also knew what would follow *after* he'd done it. That feeling would be worse. So in spite of this opportunity, Jack turned the knife the other way around and stuffed it in his back pocket. He retrieved the fallen gun and even stuffed a few scattered coins into his pocket as well.

Why not? Jack thought. *I deserve something after all that, don't I?*

Outside, Jack couldn't see Darion or Olivia anywhere and cursed for having lost them. He knew there was something strange about them, even if he'd only originally followed them for their backpack. But, now he had proof of something else: that *weapon*. What was it? He wandered the surrounding streets looking for their trail, but had no luck. He didn't even know what he was looking for, really. He just knew he had to find them.

Jack passed the cafe again, but this time there were several more Lawkeepers standing outside. Jack kept his distance, watching as the people outside the cafe pointed fingers and spoke of a 'bright light' and a man with a 'gun like no other.' The Lawkeepers seemed to take mental notes and nodded their heads like they understood, but Jack could see they were handling it like the witnesses were ignorant children. They'll never believe them. They never believe *anything* unless mercs or the Hunt say it. So when the other Lawkeepers emerged, Jack knew their thoughts would change.

Jack squinted, reading lips for any mention of him or the hired mercenaries. But, there was none.

Whatever, he thought. *Guess I'm not popular enough for ya, eh?*

A sharp pain returned and Jack clutched his chest, wiped his face. Stupid mercs. The Lawkeepers he had less trouble with. It was those hired guns that made Jack weariest. They talked about the Hunt like they were part of it, but Jack knew they weren't. Reg was no member of the Hunt. Just a stooge out to make some money if he could. Jack hated them even if they were just hired gunmen, nothing like the Hunt itself, and he cursed under his breath. More of the city's Lawkeepers came up on horses and Jack knew that was his sign to leave. He took a few deep breaths, hacked, and tried to breathe again. The cough hadn't gone away, but being struck across the face and stepped upon hadn't helped either. Hopefully by tomorrow it would all be gone. He turned round from the cafe and started walking as quickly as he could in the opposite direction. His walk was staggered so he took calculated steps to appear as normal as possible.

When he was far enough away, he found his thoughts back on the pair. The ones he'd followed all the way into the old city. Who were they anyway? But more importantly, what was that thing on the guy's arm? It stopped everyone. What were the lights? Old technology? No, that was impossible. Everything that beamed light, aside from the sun itself, had been wiped out by the Pulse. Jack knew that to be true. Martians then? Were they people from Mars? If so, maybe they could help him. So Jack kept on searching. No idea where he'd go, but he kept on going.

He gazed upward and saw that the sky was breaking open. A small overcast was breaking and in response, the old city was starting to wake up. People were coming out of the buildings by the droves. There was activity on their lips, seemingly aware of the morning's happenings. It's like everyone *knew* something strange had occurred, but they weren't sure what. Or maybe they didn't. Jack didn't know, didn't care. But, news would travel of the man with the star gun quickly; Jack was sure of it. Already he imagined conversations stirring about a Martian come to Earth, a lone representative with a little girl at his side. All the while Jack's story of being attacked by the mercs, mauled by Lawkeepers; these things would be forgotten. At least he hoped they would be.

Still, those men might come for him. He needed to be gone from this place. That was lucky back there, an act of God, even. He'd escaped similar situations, but that was the closest yet. If it hadn't been for that man and that gun, he might be dead. This thought, this quiet revelation, brought Jack to a stop in the street. And he hunched over, clutching his chest. Should he be thankful? No, that was lucky. Luck always seemed to favor him for some reason. He never questioned it, or why, he just knew it to be true.

After a few deep breaths, Jack stood and looked to the sky. If only he could fly, he'd get out of the city and find them right away. Then he laughed at himself for even thinking it. People can't fly on their own. Nothing human can fly anymore, can it? Why do we even think about doing it if we can't? Then he coughed and cursed the mercs and Lawkeepers for having hurt him. *At least I'm alive*, he thought. *That's something, isn't it? To be alive is to lucky, right?*

* * * *

Darion and Olivia left the city like wandering ghosts and did not stop until Darion felt the weight of curious eyes leave them. He stayed off the main roads and took to the side trails, places less likely to be filled with people.

"How are you doing, Liv?" he asked and Olivia squeezed his hand softly. "No worries. Another day or so. We're almost there, sweetie."

She'd heard that same phrase days ago. She didn't mean to question her father's words or even his credibility, but her feet were tired and having heard the same thing promised over and over was now as exhausting as the walk itself. Olivia wanted the trip to be over, but she didn't want to make her father worry. When he worried, he became angry. And ever since they'd escaped the danger in the city, it was best not to give him one more burden to bear. So she held onto to his hand loosely; being careful not to distract him from the road ahead or the plans he had for them.

The dirt roads were younger than the stone streets of the old city and wore the marks of horse tracks and carriages. Sometimes, they'd find the tracks of an off-roader, a truck or something bigger. Darion would point to the tire treads and explain to Olivia what they meant. Olivia knew what they were, but she enjoyed hearing her dad talk about things other than the Pulse or Mars or people.

They eventually stopped and rested a while. Darion took out a canteen from his bag and handed it to Olivia. There was a little water at the bottom and Olivia drank it down. Then a rumble came on the dirt path and Darion took Olivia deeper into the woods. A caravan? No, *bigger*. A vehicle carrying people and livestock was coming up the hillside. Darion couldn't believe it.

"Hard to believe they got one of those running around here, Liv. Must be somebody rich. This one looks custom made too. Not like the Old World's...."

Olivia watched her father's eyes flutter like he was staring at silver. He nudged Olivia, wanting her to share in his delight but she didn't understand. The machine lumbered and clanked like a rusted bucket with wheels. It was not as impressive as Darion made it to be.

"Back in the old days, those were everywhere, Liv," explained Darion. "Only they worked a lot better. The Pulse eats up energy and electricity if things run for too long. It's why so many people are looking for alternate power sources. You know what I mean by that, right?"

Olivia nodded. She did understand and was glad her father could at least acknowledge that.

"Darklight eats light," said Darion. "It eats just about anything worth a darn to us, Liv..."

Darion's voice trailed off and he looked to the sky. His body trembled, like he was reminded of the events of the morning.

"Now nothing works long," said Darion, somberly. "Nothing can fly long enough to leave this place. And so it goes, I guess. But we found ways around it. We have. We had to."

Olivia tried to imagine the Old World, but it was difficult to know for sure. The thought of riding in one of these vehicles did not seem enjoyable. She stroked her father's arm as if to say so.

"Don't worry. You can have one of those when you're older," answered Darion. "But, only when you're old enough to drive, okay? I'll bet Mars has vehicles now that would make Porsche and Chevy lose their minds."

Olivia grinned, but only because her father did. When the caravan had passed, Darion led Olivia out of the woods and back onto the trail. They followed the tracks closely, heading towards what Darion believed might be an exit or another town. All the while, he kept his eyes on the clouds. Over the next hillside, he could see where the caravan was headed: a small plaza on the edge of the city.

"I'll bet you're tired," said Darion but Olivia didn't answer. That meant 'yes.' "We can stop a while, okay?"

Olivia was relieved. Her patience had been rewarded. This would be nice. No problems here. There were no clouds of Darklight in the air. There were no signs of distress. Maybe they could finally rest. Maybe the Shepherd really *was* just a day away.

Chapter 3
Looking for Truth

"Are you discouraged to hear what I'm telling you?"

"No, I am only saddened by what is ahead of me."

"I told you, don't look at what is on the *outside*. That will only deceive you. Instead, see with your other senses. That is the only way you can pierce the veil. Your eyes, good as they are, are flawed. Men do not see with their eyes alone."

"Good men don't."

"Yes, you are right. Good men see with their heart."

* * * *

The inside of the plaza diner was inviting. A stark contrast to the one he'd visited that morning. Darion appreciated its simplicity. No big, open rooms like those in the old city. No big, useless rooms that couldn't house more than a few people when the sun went down and the light disappeared. Sure, people *could* light torches; they could light matches, or they could burn something, but who wanted to do that sort of thing indoors? That would be savagery. The world was not what it used to be, but the memory of a time when expansive rooms and bright lights seemed to echo in the bones of every structure, calling people back to an agreement made long ago: we know how it used to be; and thus, we deserve better.

Darion smirked, thinking of the stubbornness of people as a whole. An older man at the bar turned towards him and looked him over. Darion pretended not to see him. Why does everyone suddenly care about us today? Or, does he know about what happened this morning? This quiet epiphany made Darion extra weary. Was there no place he could rest until the Shepherd was with them?

"Hello there," said the old man. "Traveling alone?"

Darion nodded, still trying to avoid this conversation. "Just me and my daughter."

"What of your Mrs.? Where is she?"

Darion raised an eyebrow. This guy was no fool. He saw my wedding band. But, what's more, he wants to know why I'm alone yet am here with a little girl. The thought of having to defend himself to a total stranger disgusted Darion. As if he'd have to prove that Olivia was his daughter. That was ridiculous, but Darion felt like he ought to. In as few words as possible.

"She's waiting for us. Up north," said Darion. "Just another day or so."

"Well that's good news," said the old man, but his tone was distant. He was still unsure of Darion and he looked at Olivia with a quick glance. She kept her eyes to the floor. Darion felt his pocket. The silver disc wasn't stirring or shaking; that was a good sign.

"My daughter doesn't really talk that much," said Darion. "If that's what you're wondering about."

Olivia looked up, exchanged glances with the man, and the two appeared to share in some secret conversation Darion couldn't hear. The man grinned and she grinned back, then he turned and looked at Darion.

"My name is Abe, or Abraham, if you prefer," he said, sounding more pleasant. "I suppose it's better that we know each other's names before we get into anything else. People still do those things nowadays, don't they? You know - greet each other by name and what not."

"That's fine by me," answered Darion. "My name's Darion Wallace. And this is Olivia."

Abe nodded with approval. "Do you work?"

"I'm a doctor. And Olivia here is a professional 10-year old."

Abe chuckled softly and Darion was glad his humor was met approval. "I work too, you know," said Abe. "You wouldn't believe it based on what I'm doing today though. It's the weekend for me. At least that's what I like to think of it as. We used to have weekends, you know. Back in the Old World. Now, the weekend comes whenever you're too tired to move and you have to stop moving altogether. Ha, what a concept, right?"

"So, this is what you do on your 'weekends', then?"

"Yeah. I hang out here in between jobs. I'm a Runner for the old city, a goods transporter. So I stop here as much as I'm allotted to. And I haven't seen anyone like you before so just thought I'd ask who you might be and what you were doing. Can never be too sure, you know."

"About people?"

Abe nodded, took a sip of his drink. "Yes. *Those* things."

There was a short pause in the conversation, like Abe was evaluating Darion from head to toe. And Darion, who knew it, was doing the same to Abe. Both men, despite the pleasantries, had adopted his own style of dealing with the occasional stranger. And they were testing their strategies upon one another. Seeing where it would go before the other flinched. *I wonder if he hates doing this as much as I do?* Darion thought. Always needing to vet out new people for survival's sake.

"Well, it's not a problem to us," said Darion. "I'm sure it's tough figuring out who the weird ones are."

Abe chuckled again. "The weird ones, eh? As if I'm some kind of glorified gatekeeper out in these parts," said Abe. "I guess that's my unofficial job title these days, too. Check on who is coming and who is going. That's not a bad gig for someone my age, is it?"

Based on appearance alone, Darion could make the assumption Abe was older than he. But, since the Pulse, people did not always reflect age like they did in the Old World. Coarse, drooped or worn faces could merely be signs of hard times, not years of life. And Abe seemed sprier than someone who looked to be well into his sixties. It gave Darion a small hope that he could actually have a decent conversation with this man, but then Abe looked away from Darion and leaned back on the bar.

"Well, I'll let you back to it," said Abe. "She's a pretty little girl. I'm sure her momma is beautiful too, wherever she is."

Darion grinned. He looked at Olivia; his little girl was a carbon copy of his wife, Lydia. And though it was good to hear that Olivia's beauty reflected that of his wife; the words reminded him of other things and his heart felt heavy within his chest. So he turned his attentions back upon the mission. Back upon the Shepherd and whether they would find their quarry by nightfall.

Back at the bar, Abe began to talk with the younger man next to him, Jeff; a man whom Darion learned was a Runner and only about 19 years of age. The poor soul; he's never known anything other than the world, post-Pulse. Then there was Craig, the eldest man in the shop and clearly a drunk. He kept trying to interrupt Abe and Jeff's conversation, an act that both men tolerated so long as Craig didn't speak for too long. Still, things felt calmer now. Even with Craig in the corner, rattling on about nonsense and everything in between, Darion felt some relief in this place. Anything to keep his mind off of the morning's run-in was welcome. Eventually, Craig got up and walked out and the room was quiet for a moment.

"Somebody bolt the doors," said Abe. "I can't take much more of him today. Honestly, I can't."

Jeff laughed and Darion couldn't help but grin too.

"Oh, he'll be back," said Jeff. "You know he will. Just going for a smoke probably."

The men at the bar took another sip.

"When do you have to run your next round, Abe?" asked Jeff.

"Too soon."

Jeff grinned. "I hear that."

"You know something else?" said Abe. "If I really think about it, I'd say I'm one of the few people who could brag about having the same job before the Pulse and after. Never really thought of it, but I'd swear I'm right."

Abe peered over his shoulder and looked at Darion. "What about you? Were you a doctor before the Pulse?"

Darion didn't feel like answering. This guy still wants to know more about me and I don't care to talk to him. He should have recognized that by now. Is he a Lawkeeper, maybe? Somebody in disguise? Darion shook off the notion. Quit being so paranoid.

"I was too young to have a job," said Darion. "Can't you tell?"

Abe looked him up and down. "Yeah, I suppose so. How old were you?"

"I was eight."

Abe chuckled. "Nowadays, that's the age boys get put to work. And if you ask me, that's when it should've started back *before* the Pulse too."

Jeff laughed. "Back in the good old days, right?" said Jeff.

Abe suddenly got very serious. He took a long drink and stared at Jeff like he wanted Darion to hear it too. "There *are* no good old days, Jeff. There's just *days*. Don't matter what time you're born in – things are the same no matter what year it is. People just kid themselves, talking about how it 'used to be' and how it 'ought to be.' What's behind them is garbage though. They never look ahead and think that's what in front of them might be brighter than what's behind."

Jeff only nodded. "Thanks for the encouragement, old man. Nice to know you're such an optimist."

"It's not meant to be encouraging," said Abe. "Times change, but people don't. That's all I'm saying. Don't matter if you'd been born 500 years from now or 500 years in the past – it'd still be the same old story. Just be thankful you didn't have to live through the Pulse. Now *that* – that was scary as hell. You know what I'm talking about, don't you?"

Abe turned towards Darion, half-expecting his brother-in-arms to speak up and voice the same opinion. But, Darion only nodded cautiously.

"I remember the morning," said Abe. "Don't you? I woke up, got dressed, and got ready to go to work. I was 15. Middle of summer and the year was 2049. Good Lord, that was a long time ago. A media outlet was reporting about an action to contact Mars. Everyone on the Internet had his own opinions, of course. You know about the Internet, right?" Jeff nodded like he understood, but he didn't fully. Darion did, but wouldn't say.

"Well," continued Abe. "Apparently Mars knew that we were up to no good. And because they knew we weren't about signing a truce, they prepared themselves. But, since the Earth was so afraid of Mars by then, we went ahead and attacked them. And they struck back. In the worst way imaginable, they struck back. What a bunch of idiots...."

Abe stopped talking a moment like it was hard for him to continue. Like, he felt the sting of such a decision even after so many years.

"They should have known we'd be screwed if Mars ever decided to retaliate," said Abe. "They were light years ahead of us. They had every brilliant mind sitting up on that rock, what did we think would happen? Idiots. Well, thanks to them, the clouds turned gray ... the sun stopped shining for a time... anything with electricity running through itself, turned *off*. Planes fell out of the sky, cars stopped running and phones shut off. Then there was *nothing*. An eerie silence. You wouldn't understand, Jeff, but it was like someone had turned a switch off on the whole world. One giant strangeness. But then that strangeness got confusing and then it got really *bad*. People got crazy. Grown men and women acting like children, or worse. Their favorite toys had been taken away. It's terrible to see what people really rely on when you take away a few comforts. Then the *really* weird things came."

"The living shadows?" said Jeff and Abe nodded.

"Yeah, *those* things," said Abe. "Living shadows. Like the devil himself knew his time was drawing near, they came. You hear what I'm saying?"

Darion was mute but he nodded in agreement. *The living shadows,* he thought. Darion knew of them. He knew of them very well. The demonic, walking nightmares that sprung up in the wake of the Pulse. It was bad enough when the chaos of a worldwide EMP struck, but when it was clear that more than electricity had been pulled from human control, the world got worse. Those 'living shadows' came next: apparitions that struck every house and home like ghosts with a vengeance. What were they? Why had they come? Darion drifted in thought for a moment, thinking of these things as Jeff and Abe resumed their conversation.

"I've never seen'em," said Jeff, with relief in his voice.

"Heh, consider yourself one of the fortunate ones," said Abe. "I've seen them though. And I know plenty others who have too. With so many people claiming to have seen them, they can't all be wrong, can they? With so many witnesses, how could it be a farce?"

Abe took another long breath like he expected Darion to chime in, lay more foundation to his argument. But, Darion was mum. And Abe took the silence as a sign that Darion *did* know what he was referring to. So he grinned and faced Jeff again.

"And that's what it was like," said Abe. "You happy to know that, now?"

Jeff didn't hesitate. "What did you do when it happened?"

"My family and I stuck together," said Abe. "Who knew the apocalypse had come? Nobody, I guess. And how do you even prepare for something like that? Thankfully, a lot of the nastiness took place inside the cities, so if you lived on the outskirts, you were safer than most. But, not for long. The ones who stayed by themselves, the isolated ones – they didn't last too long either. The shadows came and got them. Luckily, we had family."

Jeff looked away like Craig might be returning. "So it *was* Mars that did it, right?" asked Jeff. "They threw it at us?"

"Well – "

"Course it was!" said another voice. It was Craig's, like he'd been waiting for the exact moment to jump back into the discussion. "Course it was those bastards up there! What kind o' question is that? Mars is the only one who could've done something like that. They're the ones who had all the technology. They're the ones who left us like this. It's no secret how no jet or plane or shuttle can breach the atmosphere before the Darklight sucks up all the energy, leaving the pilots for dead. So we're stuck, son. Who else could have done such a terrible thing other than the ones who came down here with that god-awful weapon in the first place? Answer me that!"

"I remember that," said Darion, to the surprise of Abe and Jeff. "It's why nothing flies anymore. At least not for very long. The Darklight sucks all the energy out of whatever leaves the ground. Anything that goes up, doesn't stay up very long. So like you said...*stuck*."

"Stuck is damn right!" shouted Craig. "And it's all their fault! All Mars' fault. Ain't I right, Abe?"

But, Abe didn't answer. He looked annoyed with Craig so he took another sip and stayed quiet. *This guy's one of the smart ones*, Darion thought. He'll tell a story in hopes of helping someone. That's his way of dealing with the world. But, this Craig? He was a product of everything wrong and Darion knew his kind well. Craig was more interested in being heard; being seen. These two men couldn't have been more different in the way they saw the world. And Darion appreciated Abe for his stance.

"Well?" asked Craig, hands out and waiting for an answer.

"It's like I said before," replied Abe, finally. "It's not the times – it's the *people*. I know you might have missed that part, but it doesn't really don't matter who struck first. In my opinion, anyway. The fact is: we're stuck like this. Till something changes, we're stuck here so there's no use in debating it anymore."

"Stuck is all we are!" yelled Craig. Olivia winced like his voice hurt her ears and Darion rubbed her back. After a few more outbursts, Darion didn't want to hear it anymore from Craig.

"I think that's enough," said Darion. "Keep it down, alright?"

Abe turned round suddenly towards Darion. "You can't be making demands like that," he said. "You don't know who you might be talking to."

Darion was surprised to hear Abe defending the old man. "It's not a demand," said Darion, almost shaking. "Or perhaps you don't know who *you* are dealing with."

The altercation from the morning had Darion feeling brave. Or foolish. So he gripped the inside of his coat pocket, hoping the disc might come to life, but it wouldn't. It wasn't clicking or turning at all. He wanted it to though. He wanted it to come to life so he could silence them. But, it wouldn't. Even as Abe stood up and walked towards them, the disc didn't budge or even make a sound. That was good, but it was also bad. Imminent danger could be masked from the disc. Darion had seen it happen before. He knew it could happen.

So Abe approached, stopping within an arm's reach of Darion's table, peering down. He was a bigger man than Darion had calculated. When he'd been sitting down, Abe was short, but now that he was on his feet, Abe's size was impressive.

His shirt, a tight fit for a man his size, could scarcely conceal the spike-like tattoos rising up from underneath. The scruff of his hair was curled like he had horns, and his eyes - to Darion's surprise - pierced Darion like a wolf might; light blue and crystal clear. Abe looked like an angry ghost; a big angry ghost with horns and tattoos. Darion shivered.

"You're either really brave or really stupid," said Abe. "People out here leave their hearts in steel boxes, son. That way, they can take their hearts with them and then take them out when it's safe. So if you want your little girl to survive in this world, then you need to find a steel box for her heart and teach her to tuck it away. You hear me?"

So much for Abe being an optimist, a fellow brother-in-arms. Darion swallowed and stared back at Abe. "I hear you," said Darion. "Is that all you want to tell me?"

"No," said Abe. "Just what *are* you doing up this way anyway? Where are you going with your daughter and no mother at her side?"

"Even if I told you," said Darion. "You wouldn't believe me."

Abraham leaned over, his supernatural eyes looking straight through Darion. "Try me."

Darion swallowed again, feeling the disc in his coat. No movement. Maybe it was okay to tell this man? Maybe honesty was his best policy now? He looked up at Abraham and spoke as confidently as he was able.

"We're headed to find a *Shepherd*," said Darion and he paused. "We're going to find a Shepherd from Mars. That's what we're doing out here."

"A *Shepherd*?" said Abe and he leaned back again, surprised. "I haven't heard talk of one of them in a long time. So that's what you're after, is it?"

"It is, yes."

Abe shot a glance at Darion's pocket and then at Darion. Does he know what I have? Did he know all along? Then Abe turned round and walked back to his chair and sat.

"Don't waste your time with that, son," said Abe. "The Shepherds aren't worth your time. Take it from someone who's seen'em up close."

"You saw one up close?" asked Darion. "How? When?"

"Because I was a *Red Fellow* once," said Abe. "I'm sure you've heard of them."

The Red Fellows? Darion knew of the name; knew of the group. He understood them to be some kind of organization, yet they behaved more like a cult than anything else. They were interested in bringing things back into order. Yes, that's what they wanted most. They wanted the light to come back too. They had all sorts of big plans, big ideals for Earth. A few of which Darion could find himself believing in. But, the rest of their platform? Darion always thought it was pure propaganda. Another group with hidden agendas; so he stayed away as far as he could. What's more, the Red Fellows were known for having either great or putrid reputations. Abraham was claiming to be a reformed member. What did that mean?

"I have," said Darion. "Though I'm not as familiar - "

"Heh," said Abe. "That's a good thing, then. The less you know of them, the better, I'd argue."

"Nonsense!" shouted Craig. "Show'em what you can do, Abraham! Let'em see what *Gifts* the Fellows gave ya!"

Gifts? thought Darion. What were those?

"Not necessary, Craig," said Abe and he took another drink.

But, Craig insisted. As did Jeff and Darion felt like he were at a rally for a close friend. Eventually, Abe gave in. He turned towards Darion and peered at him with those light blue eyes. Darion wondered what Abe might be doing.

"An alley," said Abe, finally. "You woke up in an alley this morning, didn't you? Somewhere outside the city?"
Darion nearly gasped. Even Olivia looked up at Abe like what Abe was saying was improbable.

"How..." muttered Darion. "How did you - "

"I'll take that as a 'yes'," said Abe and the others laughed triumphantly, proud of their friend and his 'skill.'

"But how?" asked Darion. Olivia was tugging on her father, also asking, 'How, Daddy? How?'

"I'm a *Seer*," said Abe. "It's my gift as a Red Fellow. For good or for bad, it's what I was given. The Red Fellows cultivated it out of me when I was one of them. I'm grateful for it, but I'm also not grateful. I can't help but see things on people. I don't know how else to explain it. The Fellows think it has something to do with light and how it transmits data between people. And older traces of light follow us around, leave their imprints on us for a time. And as for me, I can see those traces and tie them back to where you've been. How does that grab you? Or better yet, here's my question for you: what the hell were you doing in an alley?"

Darion was stunned. What Abe was saying, it reminded Darion of the powers the discs granted him. Only he *needed* the discs to do these things. Abe didn't. What else could Abe see? Were the discs blocking the other events of the morning? Surely, they must have been. Or else Abraham would be interrogating him on *that*.

"We don't like staying in hotels," said Darion. "It's easier this way."

"To keep from getting noticed?"

"You could say that."

"I suppose that makes sense," said Abe. "Considering what you're after."

"It does," said Darion. "You never know what people want from you. Especially when you're chasing down a 'lost cause' like you put it. Something that's 'not worth the effort.'"
Abe smirked. "I guess that's true also."
Darion didn't want to linger on the topic, so he quickly changed it.

"So," said Darion. "That's your *Gift* then? You can see messages on people? And they're made of *light?*"

"More or less."

"How is that even possible?"

"Heh," chuckled Abe. "That's a bigger question than you realize, son. And it's something the Fellows and even the Martians don't know completely. They just know we *can* do it. Like breathing, or when someone takes their last breath. Nobody knows when that'll come or when it'll be. It just *happens*. The same can be said for the Gifts."

"Interesting," said Darion, officially curious.

"I guess so," said Abe.

"You make it sound like a curse though"

"That depends upon your perception."

Darion sat forward, showing Abe his interest. "Like being a Red Fellow?"

"Yes," said Abe. "The Red Fellows figured these Gifts came as a side effect to the explosion of Darklight on the world."

"So these Gifts then?" said Darion. "They were a mistake?"

"Don't know really," said Abe. "The real mistake was bringing down what they had on Mars."

"Tell'em, Abraham!" shouted Craig. "Tell'em what those idiot Martians did!"

Abe waited a moment, letting Craig settle before he went on. Then he said, "It was *Solfire* that Mars wanted to give us; the opposite of Darklight. Though I don't know if that's the best way to describe Solfire either, considering what Darklight can do: how it eats up light, save the sun and fire."

"Solfire?" said Darion, feigning ignorance.

Abe nodded. "Yeah, the *good* stuff. The resource that apparently gives Mars all their fancy powers."

"How is Solfire different from Darklight then?" asked Darion. "You have your 'Gift' and Mars clearly has theirs. What's the difference?"

Abe raised an eyebrow like Darion was revealing too much. Like Darion knew more than he was letting on. So Darion backed down, looked away. *Don't look too eager, Darion,* he thought. *This guy is smart. Maybe smarter than you, even.*

"For one," said Abe. "Solfire doesn't *eat* light. It makes *more* of it. Wherever it goes. Whatever it touches. And it takes information with it too. Sounds great, in theory, don't it? But, Darklight seems to do the same thing, passing information but only the kind that strips people of their perceptions. But all things considered, Darklight is bad, but maybe there's just one thing worse. And that thing is Solfire."

Darion's disc clicked like it knew it was being talked about.

"Mars should have kept it for themselves," said Abe. "If God wanted us to have it, then he would have given it to us from the start. But, Mars didn't bother to worry itself with the details. So they moved things along at their own pace. And look what that did to us. Maybe one day people will get it right. But until then, I'll have another drink."

Abe stopped and chuckled. It wasn't a laugh of spite or contempt, but rather out of frustration. Jeff and Craig didn't comment. It was obvious to Darion who the ringleader in this place was. Craig was a man barely clinging to sanity; Jeff was the young sponge yet it was Abe who'd seen it all, done it all. His words were like honey and above all, *truthful*. He didn't indulge, embellish, or conjure up new concepts. He merely told it how it was. And how it was, was *hard*.

Abe grinned and looked at Darion. He seemed relieved to find someone like Darion in the café. Like, every person who had come previously was only a potential deviant or armed murderer just needing a place to hide. Evil always looked for dark corners or abandoned locales. That way it could root itself, grow and stay undetected. Darion sat up, convinced that's why a man like Abe chose this café to bide his time. A silent guardian sitting on the outskirts of the old city, making use of his talents or whatever he had left of them. This was Abe's self-appointed purpose, it seemed. Guard the gates. Watch for trouble and do what you can to ward it off. But tell people what truth was available in the moment. .

Abe took a look at Olivia. "She takes after her mother, doesn't she?" asked Abe.

"You're right about that," said Darion.

"Course I am. You're not that pretty."

Darion chuckled. It felt good to laugh. He hadn't bantered with someone in a long time, he realized. The two men grinned, somehow glad to have encountered one another.

"Why not we drink to your ugliness then?" said Abe and Darion raised an eyebrow. Again, Abe's tone had changed and he was highly excited. This man was unpredictable. And as obvious lover of alcohol, too.

"I don't really know if that's - "

"A good idea? I told you I'm a Seer, son! I can tell when someone needs a drink. Milly, bring us a round, will you? It's on me, okay?"

A woman appeared and Darion looked to Jeff like he needed help. Jeff only shrugged. You're on your own, friend.

"Don't worry," said Abe. "Jeff will finish whatever you can't. There's no drinking age out here, you know. Thank the people of Mars for that small blessing, right, Jeff?"

"So long as none of it goes to waste!" said Craig. This man, too, was surely a drunk, Darion figured. All of them were and Darion wondered what he ever had to fear from them in the first place. Alcoholic breath, perhaps?

"In vino veritas, son," said Abe. "In vino veritas. Do you know what that means?"

Darion shook his head. He knew what it meant but didn't want to indulge Abe's poetic and forthcoming alcoholic analogy. But, that didn't matter though. Abe went right on talking like he wanted to make a point.

"It's a shame," said Abe. "A damn shame how it's the only way people can find what they're looking for." He motioned to his glass. "The bottom of a bottle: that's one thing the Pulse didn't change. No different before the Pulse. No different after either. People still need a little bit of comfort. And there's always a good brew to comfort you so long as God himself allows it."

"What bottle?" asked Jeff.

Showing your age now, aren't you? Darion thought. Just a kid, aren't you?

"What bottle?" said Abe. "How about the one in front of your face, boy!" Abe bellowed like his jokes were impossible not to laugh at. "Now, raise your glasses." They did. Abe hesitated. He seemed to forget what they were toasting to, but he went on with what Darion believed to be something of a mish mash of old drinking songs and familiar prayers. "A drink for our new friend, Darion Wallace. May we, as former members of the Red Fellows, toast to beauty. May we look upon the days ahead with good eyes and a clear mind. May we not be drawn into idle conversation – the kind that makes a man both stagnate and uneducated. May we know that whatever this old Earth throws at us, we're going to throw something right back. In Christ, I say this."

Throw something back? Darion imagined what he would throw back if he could. A bomb for Mars, perhaps? That would suit. A weapon meant for Mars would be more than appropriate. Penance for the days without light. Penance for the people who went insane, maddened by their losses and who took their lives in the chaos. And penance for the days that have light, but are taken by the people who crave it only for themselves. The sun's rising is not enough. Not for any one person, Darion decided. He saw Olivia raise a pretend glass and smile. The world is big, but like what it was. Tiny pockets of people exist everywhere; each with his own version of the Pulse and how to manage this thing called 'life.' It would have been the same with the Pulse or without it. For those born after, their naiveté was probably just as well served as any who might have been born before the Pulse too. People don't change, do they? They only adapt. Unless they can leave this world; leave it forever and never return, none of these human experiences will ever change. I can drink to that. That's a human experience too, isn't it? And I'm human also. Unlike the Shepherd I seek, *I* am human.

* * * *

"So, do any of you guys know anything about *Darklight?*"

Jack waited for an answer but no one in the room replied. No one even acknowledged him. Was it his face? The bruise on his cheek perhaps causing them to reject him? He decided to power through the anxiety of that being true.

"It's what you find on Mars, right?" asked Jack.

Abraham, seated an arm's reach away, hadn't liked Jack since Jack arrived at the cafe. Something about Jack made Abe uneasy and it was taking Abe a long time to figure out just what the source of that uneasiness was. When Jack had come in, pronouncing aloud how he'd lost a fight with some Lawkeepers over some food, Abe could only assume it was a lie. For there was a haze over Jack, blocking Abe's Gift and keeping him in the dark. Why couldn't he see? Had he drank too much?

"Yes, it might be on Mars, " said Abe. "And no, it might not be too."

Jack looked at the others there. Craig lie prostrate on the bar, head rested on his outstretched arm; passed out and of no use to

Jack. The young one, Jeff, held his mug loosely, pretending that he wasn't listening yet Jack knew he most certainly was.

"Interesting," said Jack. "That's an interesting answer."

"It's a resource though, ain't it?" said Jeff, eager to chime in. "Right, Abe?"

"So they say," said Abe.

"Who is *they* exactly?" asked Jack.

Abe didn't respond. He raised an eyebrow, sizing up Jack. "Why do you ask?"

"Just curious is all."

"Just *curious?*"

Jack nodded. Craig slumbered in the background with a snore. Abe kept on smoking. Ever since Jack had come to the café, he sensed a strange discord about the young man. Like, he was looking for trouble or something worse. "What else are you curious about, son?"

"Ha, a lot of things, I guess. Like, why no one talks about Darklight – like how it's not a real thing, but it is. Really gets me, ya know? I mean, if Mars has it and brought it here, then shouldn't more people know about it? All those floating lights that come around – that's Darklight, ain't it? It's what made the Pulse go off and everything, right?"

Jeff looked to Abe. He was unresponsive. "Everybody knows that though," said Jeff. "That the Pulse was made up of Darklight. Mars bombed us with it. And that's where the monsters come from. That's why – "

"The monsters, eh?" said Jack. "You mean to tell me that you've seen monsters?"

Jeff swallowed and shook his head. *Didn't think so*, thought Jack. Abe took another sip from his mug while Jack leaned closer to him. "He's seen his share," said Abe. "Just not the type you're referring to."

"What about you then? Have you seen one?"

"What's it to you?"

"Just curious, remember?"

Abe turned towards Jack. By now, he must know I want more than information on Darklight, Jack figured. But maybe now, he'll get serious with me and give me what I want.

"Why don't you ask me what you really want to ask?" said Abe. "Then we'll go from there. How's that?"

Jack leaned back. "All right then. What's Darklight?"

"Wrong question."

Jack sneered at him. "What do you mean 'wrong question'? That's what I want to know."

"No, it ain't, kid."

Jack seethed. He hated being called that. Where he'd been willing to play along with this man before, he wasn't anymore. Something about him was smug; like, he was better than Jack. And Jack began to hate Abe with every second that passed after that comment.

"Kid, is it? Is that what you think, I am?"

"Compared to me, you are."

No, I'm not, old man. Jack imagined taking Abe down by the collar and pummeling him right there. He imagined holding the nape of his neck, pinning him to the bar stool and demanding a better answer. He imagined kicking out the stool and shoving the mug into Abe's face – an act that would certainly get his point across. Wouldn't think of me as a kid anymore, would you?

Jack volleyed the scenario in his head, eyeing up Abe like he were moments away from doing just what he'd conjured up. But, then he calmed himself and thought of another alternative.

"Well, you sure got me there. You're old. Older than me. Congratulations."

Abe smirked. "I didn't want a congratulations, just an honest question out of you."

"Here's one," said Jack. "I saw someone who could wield Darklight as a weapon. He used it to attack some people at a pub this morning. I was following him up this way but I lost track of him. So I just wanted to know if any of you had seen him."

Abe and Jeff exchanged glances.

"What did he look like?" asked Jeff.

Jack described a man with a little girl. He depicted him as being in his 40s, with a backpack full of unknown items and a weapon that could shoot beams of light that looked like small bombs. He detailed every aspect of Darion and Olivia as best he could remember and watched as Abe and Jeff's faces began to change. *Yes*, he thought. They'd seen him. Seen him here. Abe, especially, looked like he'd seen a ghost. But, neither Abe nor Jeff seemed eager to speak about Darion. Jack finished his description, but when he received no such response, he realized they might know this man. They might be his friends.

"You guys know'em or something?" asked Jack. Oh well. He could still act like he wasn't aware he'd just stuck his head in a hornet's nest.

Abe took a drag and pivoted in his seat, towards Jack. "What you described," said Abe. "isn't Darklight at all. It's called something else."

Jack perked up.

"It's called, Solfire," said Abe. "Sounds to me like a weapon made from Solfire."

"Solfire?"

Abe nodded. "What's the difference?" asked Jack.

"Ha, you figure that one out and you could run the world, son," said Abe and he turned back around.

You know something, thought Jack. You just won't say it. "That's interesting stuff, chief," said Jack and he looked at Jeff. The youngster was playing with his mug, eyes down at the bar like this was an adult conversation. He'll want to say something if I ask him properly, Jack figured.

"What about you?" asked Jack. "You know anything about what he's talking about?"

Jeff looked up, surprised. His face seemed to say, 'oh, me?' "No, not really," answered Jeff. "Just the purple lights, really. You know, the clouds that come when something really bad is about to happen…."

Jack imagined them, and then dismissed the image. He'd seen them enough and he needed to stay on task. Must be friends with that pair, he concluded. Jack saw Jeff glance briefly at Abe like he wanted permission to say something. Abe was stone-faced and close-lipped so Jeff put his eyes back on the bar counter.

"That all?" inquired Jack.

Abe put down his mug and faced Jack. "Look, kid," said Abe. Again with the kid comment. *Do it again*, thought Jack. Say it one more time. "I don't really know what you're getting at, but nobody here wants to talk about it anymore. Nobody can tell another person what he's looking for if he himself doesn't know. Even if it's something alien or foreign like Marts' Solfire, alright?"

Jack tapped his fingers on the bar counter. "You're friends with them, aren't you?" asked Jack. "The ones who came in here. Probably less than an hour ago, I'd say?"

Abe and Jeff were silent. "Again, I don't – " said Abe.

"Yeah, you do. Quit playing me off, chief. You saw them here. They friends of yours or not?"

"Not exactly."

Jack reached into his pocket and pulled out a few of the coins he'd stolen He had only a few left, but it was enough to make a small wager. He laid them on the countertop and slid them closer to Abe. Jeff peered at them like they were solid gold. He'd never seen the currency before.

"Then, let me ask you something else," said Jack. "since they aren't your friends or anything – where'd they go? Do you know where they went off to?"

Abe looked at the coins on the table and smirked. "Boy, you don't even know what you're asking."

That was it. Jack jumped from his seat, taking out the pistol and holding it to Abe's head. Jack grabbed the tuft of Abe's shirt and pressed downward. Jeff yelled and jumped out of his chair. Jack ordered him to stay back or he'd fire. Craig roused from slumber; saliva caked on his mouth as he tried to assess the situation quickly. A young man, Jack, was standing over top of a slouched Abe, and he was shouting obscenities; threatening Abe's life if he didn't tell him what he wanted to know.

"What the hell is going on?" shouted Craig. "Abraham!"

Jack pressed the edge of the pistol against the back of Abe's head. Despite the sudden attack, Abe was not defending himself. He held his arms to his sides and didn't budge. He acted like this was common protocol, like he had experience in being held at gunpoint. This surprised Jack, for there was no struggle in Abe at all. Jeff yelled. Jack yelled back. The owner came out ready to defend her territory, but again, Jack ordered her to stay back. Beneath the madness, Abe's voice arose.

"Take it easy, son," said Abe, coolly. "Nobody's gonna do anything, alright?"

"Shut up," said Jack. His temper was soaring. He knew this might have been the wrong decision, but he couldn't stop now. This will show them.

"Fine," said Abe, boldly. "Seeing as you have all the power now, what's that question of yours?"

Jack almost didn't ask. He felt insulted. Like, *he* should be the one making the demands, not this man.

"The pair of travelers," said Jack. "Where did they go? Where were they going?"

"I don't know. I didn't ask them."

"I need more than that."

"I didn't - "

"Shut up!"

Jack dug the tip of the gun into Abe's head, cutting him and Abe flinched. Craig jumped out of his seat.

"They're going to find a Shepherd!" shouted Craig and Abe sighed. Jack, however, was confused.

"What is that?" asked Jack. "What's a Shepherd?"

"They're from Mars," said Craig. He felt rushed and tripped over every word as he got every last detail out. "Messengers. They're messengers from Mars. They come here, looking for people. People to go to Mars!."

"What's that got to do with Darklight? Or Solfire?"

"They harvest it!" shouted Craig. "Like corn or crops, you understand? It's their main resource on Mars. It's what they use to make everything! It's how they travel back and forth from Mars to Earth. It's what made the Pulse go off. What else you wanna know? Let him go!"

Jack loosened his grip on Abe. This was unexpected. The old man spoke with such fervor that Jack was inclined to believe him. But, he wasn't convinced. He looked down at Abe, who didn't seem afraid. But, he *should* be. I'll make sure he is.

"That all true, chief?" said Jack, but Abe didn't answer. "Is it true or not?"

"You told me to shut up, remember?"

Arrogant prick. The way Abe said it – that didn't bother Jack. It was his own words, lashing back at him that angered him most. Jack cursed himself for having said that earlier. "Talk then."

"Why not put away the gun away and let me get up?" asked Abe. "Then we can have the conversation you want so badly, okay?"

"You're not going anywhere."

"Then, I guess we're at an en passé', son."

"You can talk just fine from where you are."

"But, are you going to listen?"

Jack didn't know how to answer. The way Abe showed no fear was unnatural. He should be crying, screaming for a savior. Someone to come and help him, but he didn't. He just took the attacks and didn't budge. It's like he wanted Jack to torture him; to come at him with everything just so he could show him how weak Jack really was. And Jack hated it.

"I'm not gonna let you up, " said Jack. "Alright, chief? So, tell me about the pair, tell me about the Shepherd. Tell me everything you know about them both."

Abe took a long breath. He spoke calmly to Jack, making certain every word made a point to alleviate any confusion. "It's just as he said," said Abe. "They're going to look for a Shepherd. They stopped in here a good hour before you did. Where they were going, I don't know. I just know that's what they were looking for. We never saw any Darklight weapon you're talking about. We never saw anything like Solfire either. All I had was a drink with the guy and then he left. Okay?"

Jack heard the words and though they sounded genuine, he still didn't want to believe them. They were still protecting this man and little girl; he could feel it. It had to be that weapon. It would be worth a heavy coin. Perhaps they were splitting the profits with these people?

"Fine then, chief," said Jack and he eased up, slowly pulling away the weapon. Abe raised his hands and pivoted in his seat.

The way Abe looked at him, it made Jack feel like he'd made a serious mistake. Abe wasn't frightened; he merely appeared to be *disappointed.*

"You're not gonna shoot me, son," said Abe.

"How do you know that?"

"I know when a man looks prepared to do something he'll regret. And you don't have that look about you."

Jack backed away from Abe, pistol in the air. His mind returned to the thoughts of punishing Abraham. It was pleasing in his head, but then when he considered the action, he felt only remorse. A certain kind of regret Abraham alluded to. He lowered his pistol and took another step away.

"Look," said Abraham. "whatever it is you *think* you're after, son. It's not that. It's not what you imagine or what you want either. I don't need to know anything else about you to see that plain as day. Just go home."

There was a soft silence in the room, like the storm was over and everyone could rest again. Jack looked at Jeff - frightened, gripping the bar counter tight.

"Still scared?" asked Jack and for a split second, Abe turned his attentions on Jeff. That's when Jack lunged forward. He took the butt of his gun and smashed it across Abe's face, knocking him off the stool and onto the floor. Abe landed with a thud and Jack held up the gun to Jeff and Craig, ordering them to stay back. That's when the beating started. He kicked Abe several times, stomping on his side, shoulders and even on his head. The owner cried out, but Jack ordered her to 'shut up' and he made one last kick into Abe's side. Then it was silent, save the groaning of Abe, face to the floor.

Jack wiped his face, the gun still high in his hand. He peered down at Abe. "Tell me what I want!" he yelled. "Can you do it now! Can you?"

Abe tried to roll over. He spit on the ground, red mixed with clear saliva splattered on the wood and stuck like glue. He cursed out Jack under his breath and Jack leaned over slightly.

"Say something, chief..." said Jack, taunting him. "Say something that's worth me remembering."

"You...".

"Me what?"

Abe struggled. He couldn't make the words. Jack felt for a moment like he'd beat him too badly. Jack had no intention of killing this man, but he also needed them to know that *he* was the one with the power. Not them. And now, they all knew it.

"I didn't think you had anything else to say," said Jack. "You said you could see something in my eyes. You should have just answered me when I asked nicely. Now, look at you."

Jack turned Abe over and shoved the gun in Abe's face like he was going to split Abe's brain in two with a bullet. Abe cried out, 'don't shoot!' and he closed his eyes. Jack's teeth gritted and his eyes blazed like fire. Jeff and Craig shouted to stop and Jack shouted to stop them. That was *it*: the moment Jack had been waiting on. That moment of unpredictability – that second of power he desired. Every person broke eventually. This guy was no different. So Jack removed the weapon and when Abe opened his eyes, Jack pointed his gun at the wall and took one shot.

"See what I can do if I want to?" said Jack. "Did your intuition tell you I was gonna do that? See? It doesn't matter if you think you can read me or not. I can always change when I want to. I can do whatever I want, when I want. Do you understand me?"

Jack walked out quickly. He'd shown them all and he'll show them all yet. He's good at finding people. But, he's even better at getting what he wants.

So Jack made for the woods and where he believed Darion and Olivia to be.

* * * *

"That piece of garbage…" said Jeff. "I'll kill him!"

Abe couldn't stand. The owner put a cloth to Abe's face and he pressed it against his temple. The swelling had started already.

"We need to take ya to the old city," said Craig. "Get ya to a hospital or a doctor."

Abe shook his head. "No…" he sputtered, at last. "I'll be fine."

"What?" said Jeff. "Are you crazy? I'm gonna kill him!" He stood up like he was ready to charge outside and tackle Jack, but Craig called him back. Abe sat up and leaned against the bar, replacing cool towels with new ones for several minutes. Jeff, meanwhile, paced the bar like a man possessed, cursing Jack up and down and shouting out reasons to call the Lawkeepers or maybe even the Hunt to trail Jack.

"Let it be," said Abe. "Stupid kid…. He doesn't realize how terrified he is. Of everything. Of every *one*."

"You're too forgiving, Abe," said the owner, Milly. "Thank God you're okay."

Abe smirked, still straining to keep his anger from getting the better of him. It's no good getting pissed about this. It's over. I'm alive. And the world has another idiot running amok. What's changed really?

"So you'll do nothing, Abe?" said Jeff.

"That boy has a demon inside of him, Jeff," said Abe. "I used to smell the bad in men easily. It's why I couldn't stay with the

Fellows. After a while, you see *all* the bad in men. Guess my Gift isn't what it used to be. But you know what? I'm okay with that."

Milly grinned. "Stop your talking. It'll only make the pain and the healing worse for you."

She pressed another towel to Abe's face and he winced, pain settling in just as she said it would. The cool of the towel was nice, but it didn't help that much. Not enough to erase the nasty things and the cruel things Jack had done.

So Abe thought of Darion and Olivia. And though he hadn't done it for some time, he said a silent prayer for them both. *God willing, I hope you don't you find them, boy. But, if you do, treat them better than you treated me. You're right though. You* can *do what you want, when you want. Stupid kid. I wonder if you've ever known anything worth holding onto your whole life. Probably not, right?*

It was then that Abe felt strangely sympathetic for Jack. *Fear feels like truth, but it's not. I messed up today. If I hadn't been so apathetic, this could have been avoided. I could have helped that boy rather than giving him more reason to hate the world. Stupid.* Abe rose up, stood under his own power and sat back at the bar.

"Bring another one for me, Milly," said Abe. "While I can still drink, I'll have another. I need to think. And pain doesn't help a man to think at all."

Chapter 4
Come, the Shepherd

"They don't know I'm coming."
"They know someone is. Just not you necessarily."
"Will they be afraid to meet me?"
"Are you afraid to meet *them*?"

* * * *

Darion and Olivia were deep in the woods when night settled in. Darion's pace was fierce, making Olivia tire quickly, so he threw her onto his shoulders to keep going. The pair crossed over several streams and eventually came upon one too wide to cross. Darion cursed under his breath at having to take an alternative route. Olivia shuddered. She didn't like the cursing, but she knew it wouldn't last once he'd found another way.

"Sorry about that, dear," said Darion. "I just hate all these stupid delays. We should be there already. We should be where we're supposed to be. Don't worry, we'll get there…"

His words were for Olivia, but Olivia felt like they were more for him. She didn't mind though. Either way, the cursing was over and her father was back to solving the task at hand.

With Olivia on his shoulders, Darion walked farther upstream until he found an acceptable crossing. He stepped on a few rocks, trying hard not to get his feet too wet. But, Darion slipped on one of the smoother stones and landed almost backwards on his side. Olivia toppled into the water also.

"Liv, are you alright?" asked Darion and Olivia nodded. She had landed awkwardly but she wasn't hurt. Every bit of her clothes were wet, however. "God, I'm so sorry."

Olivia splashed in the inches of water and Darion lifted her out. They walked across the last few stones and reached the other side.

"I'm sorry, baby. You're soaked now and so am I. And this bag too…."

Darion filtered out the curse words out as much as he could, restraining himself as a water-coated Olivia looked up at him. He chuckled, seeing her wet hair stuck like Velcro to her neck and shoulders.

"We'd have been better off just swimming across, huh?"

Olivia grinned. This was the dad she enjoyed, making light of things despite their circumstances. Together, they saw a rocky outcropping on the hillside and they walked towards it. It poked out like an Earth-made shelter, giving the impression that it might be a good place to hide out. So Darion inspected the insides for anything that might say otherwise and when he found nothing abnormal, he called Olivia up to him and unpacked.

"Good Lord..." he said, checking through his things. "The inside of the bags are just as wet too." Olivia crouched under the ledge, keeping close to her father. Darion sifted through everything until he got to the bottom of the bag. Then he panicked. The silver discs. They were *gone*.

"Liv? Have you seen the discs? Do you see them anywhere?"

Olivia shook her head and Darion's panic increased. Olivia wanted to help but she didn't want to get in her father's way either. Darion searched frantically, pushing leaves and dirt aside like the discs had hidden themselves on purpose. He peered down at the stream and motioned to Olivia to stay where she was. They're there, right? They have to be. Darion bounded down the hillside and stood at the edge of the stream. The water wasn't very deep and he could see to the bottom easily, but there wasn't anything jumping out at him. His eyes darted up and down the stream. He tracked the outside of the stream for several yards and then backtracked the other direction. Nothing. How? They were just with me. They couldn't have fallen out.

The current wasn't strong, but still, there was no inkling of the silver discs. Darion started calling out to them like they might hear him, might come to life and respond, but he got no such answer. Farther back then? Could they have fallen out earlier? The thought was dreadful. If they had fallen out earlier, if they had left him somewhere along the trail, then that would be worse. He tried to remember when he'd last touched the discs. He knew he'd touched the smooth edges and he remembered their quiet hum, but he couldn't discern what time or when. There was the pub, the café' and the trail through the woods. How could he have been so careless?

"Don't do this to me... don't do this..." he said aloud, his voice becoming more and more desperate. He jumped into the water and rooted beneath the rocks. He checked the other side of the stream. He retraced his steps back several yards, but still, he was unable to find the discs. He returned to the stream's side and clutched his temple like his world had fallen to pieces. Then he stopped entirely.

"No... This can't be happening...."

He tilted his head to the side and saw something. The sun's evening rays had nicked the corners of something shiny and it reflected back at Darion. There they were. He bent over and saw all four of them, huddled together, just below the surface.

"Ha!" he shouted and carelessly dove his hands and arms into the water, removing the discs one by one. He wiped them off with his jacket; carefully examining each one and making certain they hadn't been scuffed or marked. When he found no blemishes, he sighed and thanked God for the miracle.

Then Darion chuckled aloud and held one of the discs to his chest. That was more than fortunate. He stood up and walked back to Olivia. Yet, she wasn't waiting for him.

"Liv? Sweetie, where are you?"

Darion heard a rustle above the ledge and looked up. There, Olivia was peering down at him.

"What are you doing up there?" asked Darion and she didn't move. Didn't budge.

"Come down," said Darion. "Don't worry, I found them. No need to worry any longer. It's going to be alright." Olivia stayed where she was, gazing down at her father. Only when he had looked away and removed the discs from his jacket did she obey.

"I should have known," said Darion, watching Olivia return. "I should have known you'd want to go exploring once we got out here."

Olivia grinned. 'Thank you for noticing me,' she seemed to say. Darion reached out and pulled Olivia close to him.
"Just don't go disappearing on me," said Darion. "It's one thing for me to lose these. It's another if I lose you."

Olivia smiled this time. That time it felt better; felt genuine. They sat down and Darion began to unpack. He placed three of the silver discs against the wall behind them and instructed Olivia on how she needed to not touch or put them anywhere her father couldn't see them. So Olivia watched her father set up the discs in the same arrangement he'd done on so many other nights. She'd seen him do it enough that she was convinced she could do it herself if she had to.

A half hour later, they were drier and the barriers were in place. Darion spoke a few words and tiny prisms of blue light shot out in all directions, eventually intersecting in a triangular formation. Darion walked through the interconnecting lights and when he was outside the den, he turned around and saw that the mirrors were working perfectly – Olivia and the encampment had disappeared altogether.

"Those discs are waterproof, too, eh? Mars has it all, I guess."

The two camped in for the rest of the evening. Olivia leaned against her father, falling asleep to the sound of water trickling by the stream and leaves brushing one another, as they each were commanded by the wind. Darion stayed awake for a long while, thinking of the day before and what the day ahead might hold. He thought about many things, but found his mind returning to the young man in the pub, the altercation with the mercenaries and the unfortunate way he had to exit. He imagined people talking about what he'd done, reliving the moment with each retelling and carefully injecting whatever part of the story they thought right to embellish upon, thus making their version the best.

Clearly, he would be labeled an outcast by now: a magician, a Mars refugee, or something worse. Any nightmare they could conjure up, he'd be it. Anything they could pin on him, they would. And if anyone were to see him again, they'd either run or try to take him down. There would be a price on his head too. That would come about as well. Darion had been through this before, but by now, he knew every outcome. He had tried to avoid it, tried to stay invisible but it seemed the only times he was truly invisible was when the barriers were set and the dark of night took hold. In the daylight, he was vulnerable. And so was Olivia. So long as he had the discs, these things would keep happening. What's more, he could never return so long as the faces were the same. It'd be one thing to be caught with the discs; it'd be an even worse fate to be caught without them. His mind wrestled with this and other scenarios until at last, he gave in to fatigue and slept.

Darion awoke with darkness around him. It was not yet the morning, but he could feel the dusk beginning its exit. He brushed his eyes and found Olivia rested upon his chest, breathing slowly. He grinned. Good girl. Slept like a rock, didn't you? He brushed her hair and looked up. They had another visitor, just like yesterday. Only this one wasn't human, it was a fawn: tiny and spotted with tail wagging. Darion grinned – a much better surprise than a bumbling drunk.

Darion watched the fawn creep closer, tilting its head to one side and looking indirectly at Darion and Olivia. It sniffed the air and peeled its ears back like it knew something was sitting apart from them, but couldn't see it. *Too bad*, thought Darion. I'm sure your animal instincts are telling you something's amiss, but you won't find me. Sorry to disappoint you. The fawn seemed to understand and it looked away, eventually leaving them both. Then Darion walked outside the barrier and turned around.

"Morning, can you see me?" He took the tip of his finger and pressed it through the invisible force field. Then he felt Olivia's finger poke back and he grinned. "Ha, there you are. I'll be right back, okay?"

Time to freshen up. He crouched at the edge of the stream. He was still a little damp, but not nearly as bad as the day before. Should've changed clothes. There'll be time for that later though, I suppose.

Then Darion heard something in the brush. He turned his head to the left, picturing the fawn to be there staring back at him, but it wasn't. His eyes lingered until he returned to cleaning his hands and again, he heard the noise. This time it was behind him. Darion pivoted and peered over his shoulder but like before, nothing. He saw what he thought to be a sliver of purple static and he braced himself. Was his fear making that just now? He reached into his pocket, looking for the fourth silver disc and grabbed hold of it. The disc was silent, as still as a stone, but Darion stayed on alert. Then something pressed against the back of Darion's head and his heart dropped into his stomach.

"Don't move, old man," said Jack, but his voice was shaky, weak.

"What do you want?" asked Darion.

"I'm not here to kill you," said Jack. "I know you got a little one with you so I just want that weapon you got. That's all."

Impossible, thought Darion, recognizing the voice. It was that man from the pub – the drunk with a death wish. But, how? How did he find them?

"Please don't shoot."

"I told you I won't," said Jack. "Just give me the gun and I'll be gone."

Darion hesitated. His left hand remained shoved deep in his pocket, his knees beginning to shake. Jack pressed again.

"Just give it over, chief," said Jack. "I don't want to sit out here like this forever."

"Okay, okay," said Darion. He fidgeted to one side, peering up at Jack. It *was* him – the young man from the pub yesterday. Darion couldn't believe it.

"You, huh?" said Darion, almost trembling. "I saved your life…"

"And I could have taken yours from 30 yards away if I wanted, but I didn't," said Jack, confidently, but with a hushed voice. "That makes things even. Show me where the gun is."

Darion felt the disc, but it wasn't activating. This guy's bluffing, right? "You don't even know what you're talking about," said Darion. "Do you even know what it is? What it's made from? What it even does?"

Darion's voice rose like a wave and Jack, for a moment, forgot he was in control. His hand shook on the trigger. Not my fear, but his, Darion realized. He's the one who's afraid.

"What does that matter?" asked Jack. "I've never seen anything like it before. That means it's valuable. Valuable to you. Valuable to me and valuable to somebody else too, I'm sure."

"Just because you've never seen it yourself doesn't make it any more valuable," said Darion. He turned himself slightly towards Jack as he spoke. Just a little farther. Just a little farther and I can maybe take him. He rubbed the silver disc like it might stir the gun to life, make it work for him, but it wouldn't rouse. So Darion kept stalling. "What are you anyway? Some sort of bounty hunter? You work for the Hunt, maybe?"

"No, I don't work for them," said Jack, contempt in his voice. He created more space between himself and Darion. "I'm not a mercenary. I don't do jobs for hire or anything like that. I just want the gun. So give it over like I asked."

"Not a bounty hunter and not a mercenary. Yet you're demanding my weapon? So you're just a regular, old thief? Is that what you are? I saved a thief's life and this is what I get for doing that."

Jack spit. "That doesn't matter anymore. And like I said – I could have killed you a while ago."

"Yeah, you *could* have."

Darion and Jack heard something stir on the hillside and Darion looked to see what it was: Olivia. She had wandered out of the invisible tent and was staring them both down with eyes wide. Jack looked too. When he saw Olivia staring at him, Jack's heart seemed to stop. That little girl. Did she see all of this? He released his finger for but a moment and Darion saw the opportunity. He began speaking strangely; his words like soft percussions of a hidden language, rubbing the disc on the inside of his jacket. Jack, hearing this, turned back to Darion.

"Hey – " said Jack and in an instant, the fourth disc emerged out of Darion's coat pocket. It hovered, changing into the weapon Jack had seen yesterday. It pointed itself at Jack and Jack raised his pistol to defend himself, but the light-weapon shot the pistol from Jack's hand with a beam of golden light.

Jack yelled, anticipating the pain of a shotgun blast, but he felt none. The blast had given him a jolt, however, like the light blast had shaken his core. In his bones, he felt the tremor of some strange energy. He doubled back, hand shaking, and brain desperately trying to comprehend the level of danger he was in. Darion stood and shoved Jack backwards to the ground as the light weapon poised for another strike.

"Olivia!" shouted Darion. "Up the hill! Go!"

But, Olivia was frozen. She waited for her father to come running up the hill and take her away. Darion hoisted Olivia into his arms and ran to the tent. He grabbed their things: the three silver discs; their packs filled with blankets they used to hibernate in alleys; and made off for the top of the hill. Jack rolled all over the ground, trying to get away from weapon. When he came to, he could see it circling him, clicking like it was reloading for a second shot: an orb of gold rotating and pulsing near its tip. Jack got on all fours. He heard a low hum; it increased like a swarm of bees chasing him. Was this it?

* * * *

What *is* this thing?

Jack got to his feet, grabbing his pistol before running into the woods. The light weapon followed, flying alongside like it was taunting him, fooling him into thinking that he might be able to escape.

"What the hell? Get away from me! Help! Help me!"

Jack fell to the ground, scrambling on the forest floor. His head felt weary, but he quickly regained his bearings and readied himself to counter. He raised his gun, but found it to be incredibly heavy. Its contents felt like it was made of concrete and Jack cursed, unable to defend himself. The light weapon hovered closer; spinning its barrel like it was about to shoot a rocket of light. Jack sensed it and braced himself. But, then he felt something else; a foreign urge came over him and he released the heavy-laden pistol from his fingers. And when he did, he felt lighter, like he'd shed heavy armament from his body. He looked at the light weapon and reached out, grabbing hold of the light gun with his free hand.

Time stopped. *What is this?*

Jack said the words aloud but he wasn't sure if he had. A flood of unknown words, phrases, and memories overwhelmed Jack's consciousness. He saw old grasslands; he saw forest; he saw an empty vehicle; and he saw a burning trail. Even his sense of smell seemed to be heightened, for he smelled the grasslands, the forest, and even the burning fragrance of torched landscape and metal. Every thought and every image was not his own. He tried to blot it out, make it stop, but the pictures were like bombs going off in his brain. They invaded every corner of his mind, recycling and repeating in a loop until Jack had to accept them like they were his own. He saw Darion, he saw Olivia, he saw them eating at the pub, he saw them talking with the old man and boy at the café, he saw them running through the woods, and he saw other pictures he could not identify.

Then a new series of images came to Jack. He saw a massive crater, concave and perfectly molded in the middle of what appeared to be outlying trees. At its epicenter, crouched over and facing away from him, was a person. It looked like a miniature doll how tiny it was in comparison to the hole in the ground, but it was certainly a person of some kind. However, this person appeared to be on fire. There was a cool billow of smoke rising up from its back and as Jack continued to watch, the more he witnessed the being come to life. It stood up and gazed off into the distance. It was tall, slender, bald, and though it appeared to be naked, he could not discern its gender. The being turned towards him, and Jack felt a sting of healthy fear shake him at his center. It was staring at him, he knew it, but he couldn't pull his gaze away or even blink. It opened its mouth and began to speak to him; its lightened eyes sparkling like the sun and its voice sounding like the coo of a mother's voice. Jack tried to scream, but found he had no voice in this place. The creature turned itself completely around and lowered its head, inciting even more fear and trembling in Jack's heart. A strange fire began to set itself all about this creature, moving inward towards the crater's center until at last, it touched the slender being and Jack finally yelled.

It was over. Whatever that was, it was over and Jack fell backwards, his body landing on the forest floor like he'd been thrown there. The light weapon closed its barrel and ceased to work. It clicked and reverted to the circular disc, dropping onto the ground at Jack's feet.

"What in the..." said Jack, heart racing. He was sweating all over and his eyes had watered up like he'd been crying for a long time. He wiped his face, touching his tear ducts with shaky fingers. He lay there for a time, looking at the silver disc like it was a mine set to go off. Once he'd caught his breath and wiped the last of the tears from his face, he got on all fours and crawled towards the disc like an infant. He extended a hand when he was within reach, but retracted quickly. No, don't touch it. What if that happens again? What if it starts all over? He wanted to pick it up, but he couldn't bring himself to do it. Maybe just a quick poke? Jack tapped the disc like it was hot to the touch, doing this several times till he was certain the effects of his earlier encounter would not repeat itself. Then he picked up the disc and examined it more closely. Again, he started to weep and couldn't stop himself.

Stop it. Just stop it already.... What the hell is going on?

* * * *

Up on the hillside, Darion pulled his disc-turned-binoculars from his face and fell to one knee. Olivia came to his side. Darion, too, was covered in a mess of unexpected tears and he clutched his chest like his heart was on fire.

"I...I'm okay, Liv," said Darion, with teeth clenched. Darion had seen Jack touch the light weapon, but hadn't expected this. He held a hand to his mouth like it might keep him from sobbing and for a short while, the strategy worked. Olivia did not leave him. What was wrong? Why was he crying so much?

"That...that was..." said Darion. What a crazy idiot. He grabbed the disc. He actually *grabbed* it. I can't believe he did that.

Darion tried to stand, but Olivia held onto him. "It's alright," he said, pushing his tears away. "I'm alright, Liv. Really, I'm fine."

He wasn't though. Olivia saw that plainly. She knew her father wanted to go back after that man, the man with the gun so she held onto him with both hands. *Please don't go*, she thought. Just stay with me and we'll leave like you said.

"I have to go get it back for us, Liv. I have to go get it."

Darion knew this would be the best time to get it back. Jack would be weak; he'd be confused. Just like Darion had been when he first touched the silver discs. He had to go now and not risk waiting for too long. So he left Olivia and headed down the hillside.

Darion followed the trail like he knew where Jack might be. He crossed over the stream and found himself staring into a thicket. There seemed to be a marking where Jack might have landed, where he'd grabbed hold of the light weapon but there were no tracks. Where had he gone? Then, a subtle fear came over him and he took off towards the hill.

Stupid. Of course Jack had seen where they had gone. Of course he'd know. The two of them had crossed minds, crossed their sight. Jack would know where they were. The disc would have told him. Stupid. Darion ran fast, deterring thoughts of Jack taking Olivia hostage or worse. The sting in his chest had lessened, replaced by the new fear. He ran across the stream and back to Olivia and when he was farther along the hillside, he stopped and heard a voice call out to him.

"Stop running, chief," said Jack.

Darion turned to his right and there was Jack, standing with the disc in one hand and the pistol in the other, raised to fire. Olivia was nowhere to be seen and Darion immediately assumed the worst.

"Where is she? Where is my daughter?" said Darion.

"I don't know," said Jack. "But what kind of a dad are you anyway? Leaving your daughter in the middle of these god-forsaken woods like she can handle herself? Some father you are."

Jack's voice was shaky, like he was on the verge of crying. He sounded like he couldn't believe what he was saying, but it came out nonetheless.

"How did you get up here so fast?" asked Darion.

"I followed your trail," said Jack. "I'm good at finding people. I think holding this thing makes me even better at it, too."

More than you even know, thought Darion. Or will ever, if I can help it.

"I'm sure you know by now that I'm not gonna fire on you," said Jack. "I can't even pull this trigger if I tried." He let his gun down and stared at Darion. "So, tell me, what happened to me? What are these things you have with you?"

"Just tell me where my daughter is, first."

"I told you. I *don't know*. And I didn't see her up here either."

Lying? Darion couldn't tell. Where was Olivia then? Why had she run off?

"Olivia!" shouted Darion. "Olivia, where are you?"

"It doesn't look like she wants to be found, chief."

"Just give me back the disc," said Darion.

"No. Tell me what these are."

"Give it back to me. Then I'll tell what you want to know."

"Not gonna happen. What are they really? Why are they doing these things to me?"

"Give me back the disc!" yelled Darion and a sudden rage rose up inside of him. "You're nothing but a coward, you know that? A coward! The kind who comes in the night when he thinks no one is watching! You have no idea what you're playing with or what you're doing! No idea!"

Jack's body twitched like Darion had been shooting poisonous needles at him. The words stung with a truth like Darion wasn't saying them for any reason other than for Jack to hear them. Exposed. Jack's eyes told the story. Had Darion been right? Jack's eyes welled and the heavy feeling of truth crushing his core returned and Jack released the pistol, dropping it to the Earth as his head hung with an unexpected shame.

Then, a noise, like twigs cracking caused both men to look away from each other. There, standing on the peak of the hill, was Olivia. She was gazing at her father with a hand on the side of a tree. She was unharmed and Darion practically leapt towards her.

"Olivia!"

Darion looked to Jack like it might not be safe to run up to her, but Jack was staring at the ground. He looked defeated, worn down. The gun was lying flat in the leaves.

"Stay there, sweetie," said Darion and he started his ascent.

Darion tread up the hillside with his eyes on Olivia but every second or third step, he'd look back at Jack. When he came upon Olivia, he kneeled down and took her in his arms.

"Are you alright? Are you okay?"

Olivia nodded. You should have never left, she thought. Then she turned away from him and pointed to the other side of the valley. Darion stood up, looking to where Olivia was calling his attention.

"My God…" he said.

Darion was in awe. So much so that Darion didn't notice Jack walking up beside him or when Jack took his place next to him, gazing upon the valley.

"Wow…" said Jack and Darion turned, aware of Jack, at last.

At the bottom of the vale was an empty crater, simmering like a hot water pool. It was massive, a hundred feet across, at least. And there, in the center, a strange, yet human-looking creature was curled up like a child. Jack swallowed. The being unraveled itself, rolling to one side as it stretched its limbs out like a newborn. Then it got on one knee, arched its back up and down and breathed huge breaths that could be heard all the way up on the hillside. The being rotated its head from side to side, gently at first, then much faster. It cracked its shoulders and neck and snapped its legs out like it was putting everything back in its rightful place.

"He's here…" whispered Darion. "He's finally here…"

Suddenly, the being turned its head towards them. It looked upon Darion like his whispers had been heard as plainly as if he'd been standing right next to him. Darion trembled.

Then, as if wanting to test its hearing one more time, Jack uttered a, "What is that?" and again, the being turned its body like it could hear Jack clearly.

"I almost forgot how impressive they are," said Darion. "My God, it can hear us from all the way out there, can't it?"

The disc in Jack's hand began to whirl, and soon, so were Darion's.

The alien in the crater twisted the rest of its body around to face them. It bent over slightly and began to run in their direction, arms pumping like an Olympian. Darion felt his heart leap. It was coming for them. And it was coming *fast*. It took huge bounds, covering a great distance as it cantered towards the hillside. It was closing the space between them quickly and Jack felt like running too, but it was too fast; he wouldn't be able to get away at this point. But, neither would the others beside him, who were frozen as statues.

Darion looked to be expecting this, expecting the supernatural, but Jack was terrified. He alternated looking at Darion and then looking at the creature, which would be upon them in a matter of seconds. The discs whirled faster, and in a panic, Jack threw his disc into the air, down into the valley away from him.

Perhaps that would deter the alien from coming to them?

But, the creature was more capable than Jack could have realized. It raised its head, took sight of the flying disc, bounded one more time, planted its left foot firmly, and jumped into the air, high above the trees and even the hillside. It snatched the flying disc with an extended arm, looked down to the hill, and gracefully landed like it had just been skipping on a playground. Jack couldn't believe it. Dirt and leaves flew into the air inside a small cloud. Frozen, Jack watched with a sense of helplessness as the being traveled the rest of the distance.

No escape, Darion thought. This thing is not human. You won't be going anywhere now, Jack.

The creature took one final leap, higher than before as if to show off what it could do, and came down within a few feet of the trio. The ground crunched like a tank had been dropped from the sky. Jack fell backwards and Olivia clutched her father's leg. It had made another tiny crater of its own and pulled its feet from the hole and stood before them.

At this distance, the life form appeared to be every bit human, yet its frame was impossibly structured, incomparable to any other person on Earth. It was at least seven feet tall and there appeared to be some sort of black and silver skin suit covering its entire body. Only the head, neck, and collar were exposed; skin a deep black. Even the feet and hands were draped; every toe and finger individually wrapped, making the line between what was the suit and what was the skin ambiguous to the perceiver. Its shoulders and chest were wider than a doorframe, but its waist was thin and somewhat disproportioned from the rest of its body. The arms were long and muscular and its legs rippled with a curved definition that made every muscle and tendon visible just under the surface.

It looked at Darion, Jack, and then Olivia with big, inviting eyes – like it was looking upon old friends. The alien's presence was overwhelming and Jack's terror turned to awe and back to terror again as it fixed its eyes upon him. Then it spoke.

"Hello," said the giant. His voice was surprisingly spry; deep, strong yet full of excitable vigor. A male? Jack and Darion stared, expecting the giant to be winded, but it was clear he was not – not in the slightest.

"I thank you," said the giant. "I believe this disc belongs to me or at the very least, one of the others who came from Mars before me. You are in Mars' debt for having kept them safe for so long. It made my descent that much easier to find you. I am a Shepherd of Mars and I've come for you both."

Chapter 5
The Hunt and the Adversary

"It's not that I'm afraid of what they'll say to me. I want to know how they will *think* of me."

"The people of Earth will act one way yet will be thinking another. It's how they are. Though we have done much to alleviate this behavior here on Mars, we can still hear the echoes of that dark past in our bones. And its power takes hold faster than you or I can even imagine when it does."

* * * *

Five years after the Pulse, the Hunt was formed. Its inception was the result of several factors, the chief one being the war with Mars. With Mars in the sky, moving forward, Earth was left to rot. Or so the people of Earth believed it to be. This is where the anger started. That bitter, hateful anger that comes when someone feels wronged by another.

Earth felt unified in its anger, but when that anger faded - as anger always does - the people of Earth looked to each other with bitter, questioning eyes. Didn't anyone know what to do? Was there nothing they *could* do? With no light other than the sun, it was impossible to read old data, impossible to communicate and coordinate as done in the years past. Computer screens had gone blank. Monitors became inactive. The energy was inside, somewhere, but the output of that energy was null. And when people couldn't see as they once did, or trace their words throughout history - the people of the Earth *panicked*.

Panic was the first good sign for the Hunt. Having lost control of something once taken for granted, the people cried for action. "Give us something tangible," the people said - like the *light* - which we can rely upon. Depend upon. Something that would even things out amidst all the anger that was stirring. Something that would make people feel like they had control again. Even if the war on Mars couldn't be won, at least the war on Earth against injustice could still be fought. And won, if possible.

At last, the Hunt was ready to be born.

Panic started it, but fear brought the Hunt to completion. Fear, once relegated to things like nuclear, biological, or cyber warfare, was now defined by a simple lack of light. So as local law enforcements lost power and governments no longer held the barrier of technology against their citizens, it did not take much for the Hunt to be accepted. *Finally*, there would be a force working *for* the people. A force that would take the public's opinion as its standard for justice. A force motivated by the desire to see real and direct results for crimes committed.

In that way, the Hunt didn't even need to push itself upon the people. They *were* the people. Acting on their behalf and doing as instructed. And whichever way the people swayed, so too did the Hunt.

For a time, this appeared to be good. Terrible acts were reported to the Hunt and the Hunt responded. Theft was the first offender. Then rape. Then molestation. And soon it was murder that fell under the Hunt's jurisdiction. Victims were vindicated. Criminals punished. News of a *real* force for good broke out. The war on Mars was no more. The Earth was being cleansed. Helped in part, by the Hunt and its commitment to justice.

Then came the public displays of punishment: electrocution, torture, mutilation – nearly all abominations of human treatment became commonplace. And every extreme measure was maintained as a "necessity." While those who did not agree with this philosophy were dealt with. Done so according to the Hunt's ever-changing moral compass.

Again, fear made these things possible.

In the present day, the Hunt operates over an ever-increasing territory. Spanning more than old Pittsburgh – the Hunt covers the entirety of the old American Midwest. Three decades of servitude and the Hunt has changed very little. Their objectives remain the same: find the target, ascertain the standard for punishment, and then carry out said punishment. The Hunt prides itself on being more than just bounty hunters or organized mercenaries. No, the Hunt thinks itself to be a *higher form* of law. The kind the Old World seemed to lack, but could now benefit from in this Post-Pulse era.

That's why Reggie, seated in a room full of known Huntsmen, was so nervous. Panic was with him, as was the fear. For positioned directly across from him was the Hunt's leader. A man Reggie knew of, but had never met till now.

"You were the one, correct?" asked the man across the table.

A pause.

"Well, was it you or was it not you?"

"Yeah, that was us," said Reggie. "That was me, I mean."

"So, you know what I'm already going to say?"

A pause, then, "Yes."

"No, you don't. Do you *actually* believe you know what I'm thinking?"

"I was just going to say – "

"You were trying to avoid talking about the incident; not the man you were after. I'm well aware of it though. It's why I called you in here. Why else would I have asked for you if I didn't want to talk about that?"

Reggie shrugged. He fidgeted in his chair, avoiding the stare of the man asking the questions. Across the table was Virgil Strathen, the Captain of the Hunt, and he was eyeing Reggie like this was an interrogation, not the interview Reggie had been told it would be.

"Look," said Reggie. "You heard what happened. I know plenty of your guys were there and they got the full story. That's all there is to be said. Besides, I could be workin' right now to find – "

Virgil tilted his head to one side. "You'll be compensated for this meeting," said Virgil. He said the words like it had never been an issue, or like he expected the defense to come out of Reggie. Then Virgil circled right back to the point he wanted to get to: "But, you see, I find something very interesting about you."

"What is that?"

"That nervous twitch you have," said Virgil and he pointed. Reggie wiped his eye. Nothing there, but the way Virgil said it, Reggie felt like a huge bull's eye was planted above his brow. "That's what I want to discuss," continued Virgil. "That twitch. What is it that makes you twitch like that? Right above the eye there. You're anxious, but it isn't me that's making you that way. Not completely. It's what you *saw*. It's still with you, right now – whatever it was. So let's talk about that, okay?"

Reggie fidgeted again, uncomfortable to know that the Captain was reading his every movement; analyzing and interpreting everything before spitting it back at him. Like Reggie was telling him everything he wanted to know without Reggie even knowing it. In that regard, the Captain was everything Reggie expected him to be. The Hunt were the ones in control – they kept the peace. Everyone knew that in the old city. It seemed suitable that a man like Virgil would be its Captain. The thin face, no hair on his head, save a thick patch of black on his chin – Virgil had a look of someone important. His regal features, pointed and sharp, seemed to echo back to a royal ancestry – not the hardened image most associated with the old city's acclaimed Huntsmen. And then there were the Captain's eyes: dark and beady. They looked more like the eyes of a dead man, staring back at Reggie with questioning glances.

"Alright, then," said Reggie. "What do you want to know?"

"*Everything*," said Virgil. His voice was flat and unsympathetic. "Everything you think is pertinent and everything you think isn't. Let's start with that."

Reggie rolled his shoulders. He began to piece together what he remembered. He and the others had stepped into the pub, took their seats, and recognized the man at the bar as "Jack", a wanted criminal. A man whom the Hunt were after; a felon, for all he knew. When he said the name, the Captain's eye lit up.

"A wanted criminal?" said Virgil. "And his name was 'Jack'?"

"Far as I know, why?"

Virgil smirked. "Go on. Finish your report."

So Reggie did. He told Virgil how he found Jack with Lawkeepers and his face was a mess. Then a fight ensued. But, Reggie and his men were winning and then –

"This man..." said Reggie. "Out of nowhere...he pulls out this gun. Only it's a gun like I ain't ever seen before."

Virgil tightened his lips, raised and eyebrow. "What did it do?"

"It...changed or something," said Reggie. "It moved through the air on its own and when the guy spoke, it – hell, it sounded like God's voice was speaking to me right there. Shook my head and my ears like I'd been punched straight in the temple."

Virgil grinned like his interest was piqued.

"And then what?"

Reggie scratched the back of his head. "*Light*..." he said. "Light everywhere. I closed my eyes and it was still there. I couldn't get away from it. I wanted to claw my eyes out."

"When did it stop?"

"I don't know. But, when it did, they were gone."

"The man with the gun? And Jack, too?"

Reggie nodded. Virgil rolled his eyes, thinking. "Then what?"

"Then, that was it," said Reggie, surprised. Wasn't the story over?

But, the Captain pressed his hands together and turned in his seat. This made Reggie even more uncomfortable. Reggie wondered if Virgil knew something he didn't. He certainly acted like he did.

"It wasn't Darklight," said Virgil.

"It wasn't what?"

"*Darklight*. It wasn't Darklight he attacked you with."

Reggie didn't know what to say. That sort of thing made no sense to him; it was sorcery for all he knew. Darklight was beyond his understanding, even if he had to live with it daily. That thing that ate light and electricity, thus leaving little for humanity to play with. It was *evil*.

"I know you lived through the Pulse, Reggie," said Virgil. He leaned forward and placed his elbows and hands on the steel desk.

Reggie leaned farther back. His muscles tensed and he gripped the edges of his chair. He looked for crackles of light, the kind that others claimed to see when something bad was about to happen. But, Reggie didn't see any. Or perhaps, he refused to see them. He hated them. He never wanted to see them ever.

"I know you've seen the worst of things, Reggie," said Virgil. "I don't bring people in without first learning something about them. Or where they come from. You understand?"

Reggie nodded.

"I know you remember it all," said Virgil. "When Darklight covered us all and the demons rushed to the doorsteps of every person on the planet. Those crackles of purple and black light – the ones you refuse to remember – well, they're still there, Reggie. They're *always* there."

No, thought Reggie. Don't make me remember that.

"You saw people hanging themselves on their front lawns," said Virgil. "Families burning their homes down because they thought they were possessed by the devil. Brothers killing brothers. Sisters killing sisters. Parents killing their children. I know you saw these things, Reggie."

Reggie's face had gone white. His body was like a hollow husk of human flesh. Beyond that, he might as well have been a cadaver, lifeless in the Captain's room. He breathed softly, trying hard to forget everything the Captain was saying to him. Why was the Captain making him relive all this?

"It was the worst day of my life," said Reggie, finally. "How can you speak to any of that though? Why would you?"

"Because I was *born* into that chaos, Reggie," said Virgil. "I'm a Child of the Pulse. I've never seen a light turn on or a working television screen. I've never seen the night sky illuminated by anything other than the moon and the stars. Perhaps I'm lucky to have that. Or perhaps I'm not. I really don't know and there aren't too many people alive who can tell me otherwise. But someone like you knows the truth."

Reggie didn't speak. The Captain spoke fluently, like every word was premeditated. It stunted Reggie, made him even more afraid to talk in the presence of the Captain.

"What has been like?" asked Virgil. "For you, Reggie? What have you been doing with your time since the Pulse? Taking jobs like this one? Hoping that things will eventually get better? Must be hard for you."

Virgil paused, turned in his chair.

"Right now, you're just a bounty hunter, but if you join the *Hunt*, you won't have to do that anymore. You understand what I'm saying to you?"

Reggie took a deep breath and nodded. Virgil smirked.

"Times only seem to get worse, don't they?" said Virgil. "I know. It's why I joined the Hunt." The Captain motioned to the others in the room with him and Reggie looked about. Reggie had ignored them till now, but all around the Captain were members of the Hunt, a half a dozen guards in brown outfits with red scarves and red patches on their shoulders. They surrounded the Captain on either side, standing at the ready like emotionless robots. Virgil leaned back in his chair and crossed one leg over the other.

"I may have never seen a computer," said Virgil. "Or a light beam made by man, but like you, I know there was a time when we had more control over our lives. There was a time when the people of this world didn't have to answer to the trap that Mars laid down for us. Agreed?"

Together, they agreed in silent.

"But, Mars," said Virgil. "They gave us something. Do you know what that was?"

Reggie didn't have an answer. He shook his head, not wanting to muddy where this conversation was going.

"They gave us *death*, Reggie," said Virgil. "They gave us no way out. It's why you see big, bright lights in the sky every once in a while. It's their 'satellites', the ones meant for keeping us grounded, keeping us from ever getting back to them. Back to the stars. Their satellites rotate the Earth, blocking any shuttle, any ship that might be able to breach the atmosphere and head into space. I'm sure you've heard of this, right?"

Reggie nodded. He knew of the satellites, he'd seen the streaks of white light in the sky as well. But he hadn't been aware they were meant for keeping the Earth a prison. This new knowledge infuriated Reggie and he clasped the arm of his chair without even realizing he was.

"But," said Virgil. "What you may *not* know is how they kept something for themselves, Reggie. They didn't just give us the Pulse and then trap us down here. No, they kept something too. That's how terrible they are. They kept something called *Solfire*, Reggie. It's what repels the monsters, Reggie. The demons that inhabit this world. But, the people on Mars don't seem to care to give it to us. Instead of helping us, they use it to travel the stars, paint the cosmos, and live free while we're stuck here. That's what they've done, you see: they've made it impossible for us to ever be like them."

Reggie felt a wave of anger swell up inside. He wanted to get up and go after the people of Mars right then and there. But, Virgil leaned forward and Reggie waited on what Virgil had to say.

"That's why we have to get this man," said Virgil. "Somehow, he's gotten his hands on Mars technology. I don't know how, but he has. I've already started the search, but you may join them in our hunt. We'll need you. The Hunt needs you. Do you understand what it is I am asking of you?"

Reggie nodded. Get the other guy, not Jack. That was crystal clear. And he would get paid for it too. He'd become a member of the Hunt. The most powerful group in the old city – maybe the whole region since the States disbanded. A community of people together, Reggie could have that. The Hunt was better than he thought. They weren't as uncompromising as he'd heard.

Then Virgil motioned for the guards to escort Reggie from the room and he left at once. Virgil remained, pondering the conversation. He touched the inside of his shirt, rubbing his fingers together as he thought on other things. Then he dismissed the Huntsmen, but one stayed behind.

"Bounty hunters," said the guard. It was a female's voice, but it was rugged and monotone. "I didn't think you needed to draw him out that much, but I guess it worked. You could have just thrown a dollar amount in his face and he would have said, 'yes.' Do you really want him as one of us?"

Virgil smirked. "He'll only be one of us if he succeeds. That's how it always is."

The soldier nodded.

"Everyone who lived through the Pulse relates to that story, Greta," said Virgil. "It's simple logic. Money does not always pluck the same strings as misery or suffering. Money motivates, yes, but add direction and purpose to the mix and you've got someone who will not give up so easily. That's what we need for this next job. Not just another hunter trying to win my respect for keeping to his contractual agreements. I need soldiers with a *purpose*."

Greta grinned beneath the scarf then removed it from her face. Despite the rough tone of her voice, she was quite beautiful. Fair-skinned with green eyes and short blond hair. "So, you've made him into another one of your watch dogs?"

"More or less."

"The whole city will be working for you if you keep this up."

"I don't want the city. It's dead. There are bigger places we can go."

"Like Mars?"

Virgil hesitated. He rocked in his chair, thinking of something but not intent on saying it just yet.

"Perhaps," he said. "Maybe that's where our old friend, Jack, is going. Or *thinks* he's going."

Virgil stood up and walked to the other side of the room. There were no windows save the one behind his chair, but he acted like he could see outside the steel walls, peering at them with a strange curiosity. He rubbed his fingers on the gray surface and closed his eyes.

"We're like animals held against our will, Greta," said Virgil. "Don't you think we deserve to break free of what's holding us?"

"Yes," she said. "It's not fair to us."

"It's more than that, Greta."

"Like a cage?"

"No."

"A prison, then?"

"Ha, worse still," said Virgil and Greta listened like the Captain was teaching. "Did you know that the prisons – the ones of the Old World – had *lights* in them, Greta? They had actual lights everywhere." Virgil paused; shaking his head like the thought was offensive to him. Greta nodded, aware of this truth also. Virgil went on: "So you see, even the *prisoners* had light. Inside their cages, their individual prison cells, they could receive light when it suited them. A flip of the switch and electricity ran throughout stone walls like it were a natural thing. True, others controlled this light, yes, but still, it was theirs. And now that you now this, what do you think that says about us? We can't even make our own light, if we try. The Pulse took all of that away. It robbed us of what was ours. So it's not a cage and it's not a prison either, is it? No, it's something else entirely. Do you see that now?"

Greta nodded. She enjoyed this side of the Captain. When he let his guard down and shared what was truly on his mind. She smiled inside, but made sure not to reveal herself. Still, she wondered if Virgil could sense her adoration. He was adept at doing so with anyone and everyone he met.

"And what does someone call that sort of place?" he asked. "What would you call a place that binds its inhabitants to the ground, surrounds them in dark walls, and obscures their light? Do you know?"

Greta knew the question was rhetorical, but she thought of answers anyway. A false paradise? A hell? There were several things she could say to describe it, but waited for the Captain to answer.

"It's called a *farce*, Greta," said Virgil. "A lie to make us think this is all we have. Like puncturing the eyes of a newborn on the day of his birth. But, I see through the fog, Greta, though my eyes have been gouged out. I know that what's been done to us is wrong and I'll do what I can to change it. The Darklight may make it impossible to get to Mars, tearing at every system that attempts to leave our atmosphere, but I'll figure out a way for us. I will. And I'll eliminate this farce we're all players in. Do you understand me?"

She nodded.

"And do you agree with me?"

"Of course, I do."

Virgil turned away from her and sat back in his chair. Did she say something wrong? Was he expecting more?

"Tell Argus to go with Reggie," said Virgil. "And tell him I will catch up with him soon afterwards. I will be giving Argus a gift when I see him. One that should help him when the time is right."

Greta nodded. "Sending out the 'Eyes of the Hunt' for this one?"

It was another rhetorical question. All within the Hunt knew the Captain's younger brother held the title of 'Eyes of the Hunt', but it was a position held solely *because* of the Captain. Argus was known to be vile and immature, hardly the strong and professional leader Virgil was. And in Greta's eyes, Argus lacked the courage of the Captain; the brilliance needed to be what Virgil already was.

"Yes," said Virgil. "He needs to do this. He is my brother but he is long overdue for a contribution."

Greta resisted a smile. "A punishment then? Should he fail?"

Virgil nodded. "Unfortunately, yes. I have heard new counsel on how to proceed and I intend to respond accordingly."

New counsel? Greta thought. From whom? There had been no one new at the Hunt. No one of higher rank she was aware of. Whom, then, was the Captain speaking about?

"To be safe though," said Virgil. "Have another squad follow Argus and have them report on how he is doing."

Greta nodded. A babysitter for the Eyes of the Hunt? Oh well. No reason to fight that. Yet the thought of outside influence worried Greta. She trusted Virgil's judgment though and did not speak up on the matter.

Then Virgil removed a piece of silver from his breast pocket and examined it. It appeared to be a medallion, like a disc, but it looked old and marred by something. Greta didn't recognize the item or even the material. It was alien. Was this the 'gift' for Argus?

"If I'm right about this," said Virgil. "Then it'll be bigger than anything you or I could ever imagine, Greta."

Virgil spun the cracked silver in his fingers. Greta felt the hair on her arms stretch and stand. The room grew cold, darkened like the sun was setting quickly. She looked to the window for a moment just to be certain until the Captain called her back.

"Go and find my brother," said Virgil and Greta's eyes locked with Virgil's. "No more time to delay this."

"Yes, sir," she said and left the room quickly.

* * * *

"Shepherd…" said Darion, forgetting about Jack for a moment. "I'd like to welcome you here. If this is your first time on Earth, I will say 'welcome' to you."

"Thank you," said the Shepherd, grinning. "It's good to feel welcomed in a new place. This is my first time on Earth. I'm glad to have found good company upon my arrival."

Jack was stunned. He eyeballed the Shepherd, taking in every inch of the alien visitor as he tried to understand how this thing might possibly be real. A seven-foot giant with the ability to jump as high as a mountain was standing before him. He hadn't dreamed it; he *saw* it happen. And what else was there he had yet to witness? Jack began to recycle any account he'd had of the red planet since he was old enough to remember. *All true*, he thought. Everything. There was no denying it, even if he had disbelieved it in some corner of his subconscious. The Pulse, Mars, the broken alliance between their people and ours – everything was *true*. Granted, some stories were probably not entirely accurate, but on the whole, the mythos that was Mars and its supposed war with Earth was no longer a blank space of doubt or disbelief. This Shepherd was living proof of all he'd heard about.

"These discs…" said the Shepherd. In his hand, the disc looked miniature, hardly the impressive saucer it was in the hands of Darion or Jack. "I understand you've been using these for some time now. They've served you well?"

Darion nodded.

"And you've been using them even for your own reasons, too, correct?"

Again, Darion nodded. But, did so uncomfortably. "So then," continued the Shepherd. "You've certainly discovered how they respond or don't respond when threatened or are in the presence of a certain intent? Can you comply with this?"

Intent, thought Jack. Is that what it was doing to me?

"Well no, but I mean, 'yes'," said Darion, nervously. "I did observe that. They're quite remarkable in the way they behave with people. If that's what you are asking."

"They certainly are, aren't they?" said the Shepherd. He spoke with an eloquence that sounded like a man from a distant land. He knew the native language, could speak it well, but it was clear that Earth English was not his common tongue. He accentuated certain words whether he was choosing to or not and his inflection was all his own. Anyone on the planet would notice the difference in dialect and perhaps find it to be a distraction. Beyond that, his presence was overwhelming; his words were the least imposing of things the Shepherd offered. He grinned like he was reading their minds, learning things without speaking. Darion only stared. Like, a nervous child he waited on the Shepherd. .

"And since you've had these with you..." said the Shepherd. "...you must be someone who is aware as to why I've come. Would that be accurate as well?"

Darion nodded. Jack said nothing, did nothing; his eyes stayed on the Shepherd. This is insane, he thought. There was still a small bit of steam coming from the Shepherd's skin. It seemed to be breathing, or was it the Shepherd beneath the skin suit that was doing that? Jack couldn't tell which was which.

"Good," said the Shepherd. "Then you must be someone who wishes to follow me? Or is that not your goal here?"

"Yes!" Darion said, emphatically. He acted like he'd been waiting for the question. "Yes, yes it is my goal. We would like to go with you."

The Shepherd smiled again. "And what about you, little one?"

Olivia nodded, clutching her father's side. *Tall*, she thought. He's much taller than Dad. The Shepherd he looked at Jack.

"And you? What about you?"

"Me?" said Jack, sputtering words out like he'd forgotten how to speak. The Shepherd was asking him a question. He knew it, but he couldn't answer. Suddenly, the Shepherd's gaze turned away from him, looking to the right and off upon the horizon.

"What is it?" asked Darion, but the Shepherd did not answer. He scanned the sky like he was waiting to see something.

"The sun..." said the Shepherd. "It'll be rising soon. I have never seen the sun rise on Earth before. I don't want to miss it."

Darion, Jack, and Olivia joined the Shepherd in viewing the sunrise over the valley. It seemed like an eternity at first, but when the trio realized the Shepherd would not budge until the first droplets of sunshine hit his face, they leaned in and waited. A small crescent of white and yellow light peeked over the hills and gave definition to every cloud in the sky and tree in the valley. The shadow that covered the Shepherd's face like a veil was pulled downward. His silver eyes shimmered with tiny refractions of crystal blue as the light enveloped his head and neck. His whole body was swallowed in light and the Shepherd took a deep breath, exhaling like he was drinking the light like food.

"Amazing…" said the Shepherd. "It's so incredibly bright here. The closeness you get to experience with our star is so incredible. It's no wonder our artists render its shape on Mars. You are blessed to see it this close. It's not like this where I come from."

There was an awkward pause among the group. No one dared to speak or interrupt the Shepherd. *Blessed are we?* Maybe it's the only blessing we have. Jack was thinking of the Shepherd's 'we' comment. The Shepherd spoke like he was one in the same. Like, Earth and Mars were the same people, but the idea seemed absurd to him now. How could that be? Clearly, there was a difference. Mars was a home for the superhumans; not people like him.

"Shepherd?" asked Darion. He felt the time was right to interject. "Did you want to leave soon? When will we be going?"

The Shepherd ignored Darion. He waited till the last bit of sunlight swept over him.

"Soon. I don't want to waste this if I can."

Again, they waited. But then, the Shepherd's eyes narrowed. A flicker of darkness seemed to intrude upon the sun's rays and it shone on the Shepherd's face. The Shepherd squinted and he focused his eyes back on Darion and the others.

"We do need to get moving," said the Shepherd. "I was hoping we'd have more time, but apparently we won't. I can see that it's become aware of my presence already. It's not far behind us now."

"What's that?" said Jack. Another Shepherd? Was another Shepherd coming?

A howl, like the cry of some tormented creature, filled the valley and pierced the ears of Darion, Jack, and Olivia. Each of them covered their ears. It felt like needles on the skin and its crescendo finished like the bellow of a bull. Darion and Olivia grimaced, but Jack couldn't help but yell in pain.

"Ah, what is that?!" said Jack.

A second howl followed and the trio saw the leaves move like they'd been brushed by a small gale. Even the sound was affecting the trees.

"This first attack against us will seem terrible and it may be the worst," said the Shepherd. "But, I assure you that those which follow will be worse yet. He will try to take you before you can come with me, but do not let him."

"What?! What's happening?" yelled Jack.

"Do not be afraid," said the Shepherd. "I will protect you."

From what, thought Jack. He looked at Darion; apparently he knew what was coming.

The Shepherd raised his right hand and the silver disc began to twirl. It expanded, filling itself with light like Darion and Jack had seen before, but this time it turned into something new – a sleeve, like a bracelet. Then it attached itself to the forearm of the Shepherd. The sleeve crackled, making sounds like it were being molded from hot steel. A golden light spun and filled the barrel at its exit point. The Shepherd gripped his elbow and paused. Then he spoke a few words as another howl began to wail and the Shepherd fired off a cylinder of golden energy with the force of a cannon. Jack shrieked, falling backward from the sheer power of the blast. He watched the column of light penetrate the tips of trees, but not breaking them, as it sailed into the sunrise. Then, the Shepherd waited, eyes atop the rifle on his arm.

"There you are," said the Shepherd.

Darion, Jack and Olivia saw what the Shepherd was gazing upon. It can't be real, thought Jack. Is it though? Encased in a golden aura, separated from the dark line of trees was a shadowy-looking beast, easily bigger than a bear and covered in black bristles. To Darion, it looked like a lion, but had feathered wings; to Jack, it was a wolf with curved horns like a ram; and to Olivia, it had the appearance of a blood-eyed stallion, mouth frothing. It was different to them all, but carried the same fear. The creature, exposed in the dark of the early morning dusk, was walking slowly towards them – no more than 40, 50 yards away. The beast – having been discovered – snarled and grunted loudly. It didn't like the light. It seemed agitated by the rifle's beam. It started to bound towards them like the Shepherd had earlier; taking long strides and leaping, albeit jaggedly.

The Shepherd focused and fired his arm rifle again, but the creature dodged the blast and disappeared into the darkness like it was a living shadow. The Shepherd sent a third and fourth volley, blasting the forest with beams of light that erupted like short cannon rounds. The trio saw that every blast illuminated the space where it struck, exposing anything within the vicinity of the blast radius. The creature, avoiding every shot, was remarkably nimble, if that were the proper way to describe it. The Shepherd's attacks continued and the trio jumped to the other side of the hilltop, moving away from the oncoming creature.

"Stay where you are or get behind me," said the Shepherd.

The arm cannon changed again – gears whirring as the brace moved down the Shepherd's arm and into his hand, forming itself into a dagger-like weapon. Silver steel created a hilt while a golden knife formed itself at the base, pressing up like a short-ranged saber. The Shepherd took a defensive stance as Darion, Jack, and Olivia searched frantically for the beast. Behind the Shepherd, they huddled like children, foregoing their earlier feud in favor of collected survival. Jack was panicking.

"Where is it? What is that monster?"

"Shut up!" shouted Darion. "You idiot! It can hear your fear!"

"What?"

Hear fear? Jack thought. How is that even possible?

There was a short moment of silence and then, the Shepherd turned its body round and stared at Jack.

"Don't move," said the Shepherd and he lunged at Jack's head with the dagger, missing him by fractions of an inch. The blade missed its target though, as the face of the beast appeared amidst the dagger's light and Jack could see its blood-red eyes staring at him from the other side. Jack leapt backward and the beast lunged forward as well, but found its fangs digging into the arm of the Shepherd instead of Jack's face. Surprisingly, the Shepherd didn't scream.

"Get moving," said the Shepherd – the creature biting and gnawing at his arm. "Head towards my landing and make your way up the next hillside. I will hold him off."

Jack couldn't move though. He watched the creature, with eyes mad, ripping and tearing into the arm of the Shepherd like a rabid dog. The Shepherd grabbed the creature's upper jaw with his other hand and pulled the beast's mouth off of him like it were nothing. The beast writhed and snarled and poised itself for another attack, disappearing slightly into the darkness of the hilltop. It slid to one side and pounced towards the Shepherd, but the Shepherd struck the beast in mid flight, knocking it to the ground.

"Let's go Liv!" shouted Darion and he picked up his daughter and sped down the embankment. Jack snapped out of the trance he was in and bounded down the hillside alongside. That thing, he thought. It could've killed me. I know it could have.

With Olivia, Darion was not as fast as Jack and he was quickly overtaken. Jack was at the bottom of the hillside and running through the crater when he heard another howl. The beast was making sounds like it was injured yet still focused on tearing the Shepherd to pieces. Jack imagined the Shepherd jockeying for position, wedging itself between the beast and him as he ran.

"Don't look at it, sweetie," said Darion, through heaved breaths. "Remember what we said to do. Just don't look at it."

Olivia did as she was told. She held her hands over her face and didn't watch. She thought of anything and everything other than the monster – the giant black horse with saliva flowing from its mouth.

When the trio got to the open space where the Shepherd had landed, Jack stopped. He wanted to look back and see what was happening. He began a slow walk as Darion and Olivia passed him. Idiot, thought Darion. What possessed you to stop? Darion ran right on past Jack. Then Jack turned and looked. He peered through the trees and caught sight of the beast doing battle with the Shepherd, locking his eyes with the blood-red iris of their pursuer. The beast, on its heels against the Shepherd, saw that Jack was watching him and with another howl, the creature disappeared. The Shepherd fell forward, digging the light dagger into the ground. Dirt and rock flew into the air and the Shepherd quickly pivoted all the way back around. He saw Jack, standing idly inside the crater and dug a foot into the dirt and pushed off with a leap like he was snatching the silver disc again. The Shepherd soared through the air, headed for the crater. In a few seconds, the

Shepherd landed, a heavy crush on the stone but a few feet from Jack.

"Look out!" shouted Darion and Jack turned. Behind him, the beast had somehow managed to appear. *How*, he thought. How did it do that? The beast jumped, mouth wide and claws extended, but a blast from the Shepherd's arm cannon sent the beast reeling. The blast carried the beast all the way across the crater until it landed somewhere amid the trees with a thud. It howled with anger and tried to steady itself but it appeared to be injured severely from the hit.

"Stay down this time," said the Shepherd and the giant sent a volley of cannon blasts at the creature, pummeling its black hide with golden bullets like shrapnel from a shotgun. The creature continued to moan, but still, it tried to stand. The Shepherd pulled back his gun and leapt high into the air. Where he landed, he struck the beast in the side like he was delivering a goliath-sized dropkick. The earth erupted with a geyser of rocks and dirt, the impact sending a fissure across the crater's edge. Jack lost his footing at the center, falling to his side. This was unbelievable. Where could he go? Nowhere would be safe.

The pillar of debris subsided and from out of the woods, the Shepherd's body flew backwards towards Jack. He ducked his head as the massive frame of the Shepherd flew over top of him and landed somewhere behind. Jack rolled over and saw the Shepherd was clutching his arm. The creature bounded out of the forest with needles of light falling from its body like broken glass. Though it was injured, it seemed to gain strength the more it fixed its gaze upon Jack.

"No!" shouted Jack, but the Shepherd came to Jack's rescue, landing a hard right hook across the creature's face.

The beast screamed and fell to its side. The Shepherd readied himself like a professional grappler and pulled out the light dagger again, prepping for a counterattack.

"Get up and go," said the Shepherd.

The dark beast came to its feet. Its mouth, dripping with ooze, looked broken: it was hanging awkwardly but even so, it looked determined to tackle the Shepherd and get to Jack. And Jack, who could not look away, felt immobilized as he witnessed the creature pulling itself up, snarling and snapping its mouth back into alignment like it were repairing the injury of its own will power.

What *is* this thing? The creature dug its claws into the dirt, faced Jack, and lunged forward once more but the Shepherd caught the beast round its mouth and held it in a headlock. Kicking and writhing to break free, the beast struggled under the Shepherd's vice-like grip and Jack could feel the Shepherd gaining the advantage. But with every second that passed, the Shepherd's arms shook more violently under the stress and Jack crawled to get away from the battle. The beast clawed, tearing up the rock like it was made of loose paper, barking at Jack.

"Quickly now," said the Shepherd, keeping a steady voice despite the circumstances. "To the other hill like before. Go. And do not look back this time."

Jack didn't hesitate. He ran out of the crater, running past Darion and Olivia again with his speed, traversing up the hillside. Darion, having carried Olivia the whole way, was exhausted and fell to one knee. Jack heard the crunch of leaves and turned to see that Darion was not getting up. His daughter, Olivia, looked helpless. She stood by her father, waiting, but he was out of breath and couldn't stand. Jack snorted and retreated back down the hillside. Like hell, if you're going to just let her die because you can't run. He reached Darion and grabbed him firmly by the arm.

"Come on, get up! Do you want that thing to eat your girl or what?!"

"Just go!"

He was surprised to find Jack with him, but the encouragement worked. Darion surged up and took Olivia's hand and the three of them ran the rest of the way up the hill. At the top, they stopped for a moment but only a moment and then kept on running. They ran together until they reached another shelter of trees in the next valley. When they stopped, they realized they could no longer hear the sounds of battle behind them.

"Is it over?" asked Jack, taking in big heaves of air. "Can you hear it? What do you think is happening?"

Darion couldn't answer. He was panting and had his hands on his knees. His daughter, Olivia, was breathing hard but her breathing was more out of terror than fatigue. She stayed close to her father while Jack sat on the dirt and put his head between his knees. The two men said nothing to one another – the labored inhale and exhale of their breathing the only sound either of them made. Then Jack slowly began to stand and move closer to Darion, but Darion reared up. He reached into his pockets, spoke a few words and one of the discs emerged, latching itself upon his wrist.

"Don't..." said Darion, barely able to stand. "Don't move ... don't do anything... don't even blink. You stay... right where you are."

Jack raised his hands. "Look, man. I don't know what you think you're..."

"They're mine. The discs are mine, not yours. They can sense your intent. I know you want them... and that you'll take them from me if you can.... But you're not going to.... You understand me? Now, give me that pistol. Drop it on the ground."

Jack paused. "Look..."

"Do it... or I'll fire..."

Darion wasn't lying. Jack hadn't a clue what a point blank shot might do to him, but he didn't want to find out either. However, he was also aware of what these things were capable of. Or at least, he thought he knew.

"You think I don't know better?" argued Jack. "I know what that thing does, alright? I touched one of'em. They don't fire unless something bad is about to happen..."

"It's only when dealing out death, boy," said Darion and Jack seethed. Don't call me that. Darion's accusation angered Jack and he saw the gun brighten. It's true, he thought. It senses everything you're feeling, right down to the core.

"You want shot in the foot then?" Darion was still straining, but his words were fierce. "The arm? The leg? Maybe you'll lose a toe? I don't know. Don't care either. But know this: these things will feed off my intent as much as they feed off anyone else's. Now, drop the gun."

Darion's words seemed to breathe life into the weapon. It whirred and took a new form, one more dangerous than the previous and Jack backed away. He doesn't want to kill me, but he'll shoot me if he feels he has to. I can believe that.

"Okay, man," said Jack and he put one hand inside his coat jacket and removed the pistol. He pointed the weapon towards the ground and bent over and laid it on the dirt. Then he took another step away, arms raised. "Don't shoot, alright?"

Darion nodded to Olivia to stay where she was and he went and retrieved the weapon. With arm raised and the disc whirling of golden light, Darion stood up straight and faced Jack.

"Now... stay here," said Darion.

"What?"

"I said, stay there! Did I stutter? This is as far as you go, you hear me?"

"Far as I go where?"

"The Shepherd... he'll be back for these ... he'll be back for these and us but not you, you hear me? So stay where you are and do not follow us. Do you understand what I'm saying to you?"

Jack put his arms down slightly, pleading. "How do you know that? And what the hell was that thing, huh?"

"Just stay."

Darion pointed the gun at Jack. "Wha- where am I supposed to go?" said Jack, raising his arms up again. "Out there? Are you kidding me, man?! Did you not see what just happened? Have you – "

"That's not my problem. You'll find a way. You're good at finding a way, aren't you? That's what you said to me. I'm sure you'll manage."

"Hey!... Hey!"

Darion didn't answer. He kept his eyes on Jack, backing up slowly with the discs whirling on his forearm; pistol in the other hand. Olivia gazed at Jack. His face looked desperate, aching not to be left alone in the woods. She felt sorry for him somehow. She hated to see people in need. But, she knew her father was resolute.

Jack put his hands down and thought of what to do next. He turned and peered through the woods but he didn't know the path and couldn't bring himself to move away from Darion and Olivia. What now? What if that thing comes back? What am I supposed to do?

* * * *

Darion led Olivia up the hill and every four or five steps; he looked over his shoulder to ensure that Jack was not following them. Olivia tugged on her father's jacket and he looked down at her.

"Don't worry. As long as these discs have life, so does the Shepherd."

That wasn't what she was asking .The two of them kept moving and after some time, Olivia again pulled on her father's sleeve.

"Sweetie, I can't stop. We have to keep moving. Back to where the Shepherd is."

But, Olivia wouldn't go any farther. Her eyes began to well up and Darion – not knowing what else to do – took Olivia up in his arms and walked on. Every muscle hurt. He hadn't fully recovered and it occurred to him that he hadn't eaten either. Olivia, with eyes facing behind them, gazed through the woods as if she were looking for Jack. At the hill's crest, she kept her gaze there.

"Finally..." said Darion. "Where is he?"

The sun was nearly up and Darion could see the entire valley from his vantage point. He surveyed the crater, but there was no indication of where the Shepherd might be. Trees had been pushed down and there was a trail of scorched earth leading up and away from the valley on the other side. The battle might still be going on.

"He led the beast away. That's what he was trying to do."

Darion spoke to the disc and it changed into a miniature satellite, floating just above Darion's hands. It blipped like it was sending out a signal, pulsing like it were made out of jelly rather than hard steel.

"Where are you...."

Olivia pulled on her father's leg, but Darion ignored her. He watched the skyline, he watched the trees and he watched the ground. He squinted with deep concentration like the Shepherd would appear soon and Olivia squeezed his pant leg again.

"What is it?" he said, annoyed this time. Olivia was pointing down the hillside, pointing at Jack. Despite Darion's threats, he was slowly making his way up the hill.

Bold bastard. Maybe he really *does* want to be shot? Darion spoke in a strange tongue and the ball-like disc reverted back to its weapon-like form.

"I told you to stay where you were!" yelled Darion and Jack stopped, looked up.

"I know you did!" shouted Jack. "But then I remembered somethin'..."

"I don't care if you did. Stay down there..."

"No, I *won't*."

Jack moved up the hill until he was within a few yards of Darion and Olivia. Darion held the weapon upright. *He's going to make me do it, isn't he?*

"Look, man…" said Jack and he put his hands out like he was surrendering. "I know that thing won't fire on somebody unless they got 'death in their head' or whatever you said. So just cool it, all right? I'm not here to take your life and I'm not here to hurt you or your little girl, you hear me? I just wanna talk."

Darion hesitated. He felt his guard dropping as he heard Jack speak. "What do you want to say?"

"It's like I told you before," said Jack. "I want to go with you – you and your girl, both. I saw that thing coming. I saw it when I touched that thing you got on your arm. That Shepherd or whatever he is, I saw him too. So I'm like you now, all right?"

Darion sneered. *You're nothing like me.* If anything, they were as far as one end of the universe from the other. Jack retracted his hands. He saw, sensed how contemptuous Darion was towards him. *Don't do that, old man.* The weapon clicked loudly and Jack changed his thoughts. *Was it me? Or was it him that made it do that?*

"You can't follow us," said Darion. "If I wasn't clear before, I can be really clear now, if you like. I know what you are and you can't come with us."

Jack shook his head. "Well, what am I, huh? What am I to you that means I can't?"

Jack took another step and Darion raised the rifle higher like he would fire a round directly into Jack's heart. The young man's mouth hung open and his hands and arms were held out like a beggar. It reminded Darion of the merchant in the old city. A desperate fool looking for a hand out, that's what it reminded him of. But, Jack's eyes had no agenda other than confusion, a dying need for clarity. This genuine disposition, one Darion had grown to suppress or even ignore, stirred something inside of him. *He's just a scared kid. He doesn't have a clue what's going on.* Darion could feel the tip of his gun getting heavier, but he held his arm firm and readjusted himself like he was about to fire but the pistol continued to get heavier. Soon, it was nearly impossible to hold it up and his arm shook under the strain.

"What is this?" said Darion.

Darion gritted his teeth, attempting to hold the weapon but he couldn't any longer. The light weapon detached itself from Darion's arms, reverting back to a disc. Darion panted and Olivia hugged her father round his waist as if to comfort him.

"What was that?" asked Jack. Darion looked Jack up and down curiously, but couldn't bring himself to respond. "Are we okay then?"

Darion wouldn't answer. He wanted to, but something held him back. He didn't want to explain everything, but still, he felt he should. And yet, this tug of war persisted in his head, unbeknownst to Jack or Olivia, until the disc began to glow again.

"You see that?" said Jack. "What the hell's it doing now?"

Olivia jumped back. The other two discs came to life, brimming with bright light from inside Darion's pockets. The light crackled like it would explode and Darion quickly took off his jacket, pulling out the remaining discs and setting them together on the ground. Yet, they didn't stay there. They hovered up as one and began to spin. Jack took a step towards it, but Darion held out a hand to stop him.

"Don't touch."

"What's happening?"

"Just stay where you are, for once."

The discs blipped, synchronizing like they were sending a signal or perhaps receiving one. Then the discs pulsed faster, increasing in speed but never out of rhythm with one another. Faster and faster they glowed until at last, they stopped altogether and Darion looked at Olivia like he was unsure of what would happen.

"I don't understand - " said Darion and a shadow suddenly cast itself over top his head and disappeared. He looked at Olivia, who was staring above him with eyes wide and Darion felt a ripple of fear wash over him.

"Liv?"

Darion looked up to see what had caused the shadow. Jack was looking to the sky also. "Don't move, okay?"

Darion tracked Jack's gaze to the horizon and saw a dark silhouette flying towards them. It was growing larger, but only because it was getting closer. Its legs tucked themselves underneath like it was making itself ready for a landing. It was the Shepherd; back from victory or a hasty retreat. Gravity was pulling it down, or rather; the will of the Shepherd was permitting the Earth to take over. It was difficult to know and Darion stood back, gauging the impending landing area as best he could calculate. He tried to tell Olivia to back away, but the Shepherd was upon the ground in moments. The ground trembled, shaking like an earthquake had struck as the Shepherd crouched over with fists in the dirt.

The Shepherd raised its head slowly, and then proceeded to stand up straight. Again, he towered over Darion and the others. His body was rippling with the relief of having leapt the distance of a small town.

"My apologies," said the Shepherd. "The Adversary was much stronger than I had predicted. Its concentrations are greater and denser than we last projected on Mars. It would appear that there is still much for me to learn while I'm here."

The floating discs returned to the Shepherd. The first, still attached to his right arm, reverted into a chain-like brace around his wrist. The second did the same on his left wrist and the third and fourth latched themselves to the outer sides of his thighs — falling into place like they were missing pieces from a puzzle.

"So, you'll just take those back now?" asked Darion.

The Shepherd nodded. "They belong to me. They don't belong to you."

"Is it dead?" asked Jack. "Did you kill that thing?"

There was a pause. "It's no longer here," said the Shepherd. "It can't hurt you."

The Shepherd twisted the bracelets on his forearms like each needed readjusting. The discs had been made into a perfect fit, yet required some maintenance, it seemed. Jack looked at the Shepherd's arm, remembering the attack by the woods. He'd been bitten. Jack saw it, but there was no blood. No bite marks or wound to speak to. Jack licked his lips, preparing to ask the question, but fought the urge and looked to Darion. He seems to be 'okay' with this. Probably shouldn't say anything.

"But, it will be back," said the Shepherd. "The Adversary will come again, but next time, you will have at least some knowledge of how it lays down its attacks against you. I'm sure you witnessed that during the struggle."

Jack swallowed. "Adversary? Like an enemy?" he said.

"Yes. It's the beast that tried to take you. That is what it is called."

"It's what *you* call it," said Darion. "It's a demon to us. Something brought here by the Pulse 40 years ago."

The Shepherd turned his head. "It is what it is. And I am sorry that it is."

Adversary? Darion remembered the beast as it were – its sharp horns, its terrifying howl, and its unrelenting nature that seemed hell bent on killing him. Darion trembled, imagining the beast right in front of him, but he quickly dismissed the thought. The Shepherd knew this creature. Had a name for it. He spoke of it like it was something familiar; he wasn't surprised when he saw it. That means it could be beaten. That means he didn't have to fear like he used to. Right?

"Is it far away from us or something?" asked Jack.

"That's difficult to answer," said the Shepherd. "But, I know it has been subdued for the moment. And for however long that moment is, the Adversary is in submission. You are safe. We are safe. You needn't fear."

This thing didn't seem as frightening now that the Shepherd was here. Or was it the Shepherd's cool demeanor causing the tension to leave? Still, the fact that this creature was looming in the distance made all of them uneasy. More questions came. Could the Shepherd beat it again? What if it returned this instant? The Shepherd claimed that this thing was coming back. Shouldn't he have killed it then? Why hadn't he? Could it be killed?

Darion decided to focus on something else.

"The discs helped you heal, didn't they?" asked Darion.

"Yes," said the Shepherd. "They do offer some replenishment when I am reunited with them. But, it's not a permanent fix. I'll need water and food for that."

"Don't we all?" said Darion.

The Shepherd grinned. "Indeed. We all do."

There was another pause and the Shepherd scanned the valley.

"I trust you've come to the agreement that you are all coming with me then?" said the Shepherd and Darion and Jack exchanged an awkward glance. Darion glared, his eyes speaking with poisonous barbs.

Yet, Jack's distant stare answered Darion's question – yes, Jack *was* coming.

We'll see how long you last though, thought Darion.

"Yes," said Darion. "We are coming with you. All of us."

The Shepherd smiled. His bright white teeth looked perfect. Nobody had teeth like this. Not on Earth anyway. Was all of Mars this way?

"Excellent," said the Shepherd. "We need to get moving right away. I know you are tired and hungry, but we will eat soon. I promise you. After a fight like that, the body needs servicing."

Darion felt his stomach. It was true. He'd gone without breakfast. So had Jack apparently. For Jack was also rubbing his stomach nervously.

The Shepherd then nodded to the three of them and together, they followed the Shepherd into the valley. Olivia clasped her father's hand and Jack slunk close by, but at a distance. United by the tiniest of threads, their conditional needs were met, in part, thanks to the Shepherd.

Chapter 6
Survival

"Yes, they *will* fear you. They've heard little about you and the little they've heard is probably more aligned with myth than reality."

"So their perception of me is my enemy?"

"Yes."

"I hate myths. They're so completely impersonal. Like some people can be."

* * * *

The trio of Darion, Jack, and Olivia trailed the Shepherd at close proximity, but not at a pace that might overtake the one who led them. They shadowed the silver giant in silence, an uncomfortable arrangement for every party member, save the Shepherd, whose long and bold strides kept their focus moving forward; another sharp contrast to the scurries of smaller feet behind him. What's more, the Shepherd never looked back, something both Darion and Jack noted, albeit at separate times and not at once. His eyes were always ahead, his posture pointed in one direction. It made the others feel inadequate, like their presence mattered little to the Shepherd, but when Olivia coughed and broke the stillness, the Shepherd turned and said, "Let's get some water. That cough is too dry to continue."

And so, they stopped completely. At which point the Shepherd began marveling at the Earth's wonders.

"It truly is one thing to hear of a place and then to be in that place later," said the Shepherd. "Reading about Earth does the reader little justice. It must be lived, I tell you."

The others did not share the Shepherd's innocent candor. Darion offered the Shepherd some food from his pack, but the Shepherd refused.

"Those don't have enough of what we need," said the Shepherd. "I'll get you something better."

And he did. The Shepherd left and returned with mushrooms. Only they were three times the size of a normal mushroom; easily the biggest – and freshest – Jack or Darion had ever laid eyes on. Jack casually joked that these were 'made from Mars' rather than Earth but no one laughed.

"I have helped them to get this big," said the Shepherd. "They are of Earth, just like on Mars. There is no difference."

Jack shook his head. "If I could eat mushrooms like this everyday, I might be as big as you, chief."

"Perhaps," said the Shepherd, with a grin. "There is fruit too."

Jack shook his head. "Less than a few hours on the planet and you can already garden better than any of us. That's not right."

The Shepherd grinned again, as did Olivia. She enjoyed the Shepherd's banter with Jack. It was refreshing; it took her mind off of the Adversary and the fact that she had been hungry up until now. But Darion was not amused and he feigned tolerance of Jack whenever the Shepherd looked upon him. Even when Jack was silent, Darion found himself annoyed. Jack could feel it too, but Jack absolved himself of the fact that there was nothing he could do to change that. This fact didn't stop Jack though, for he would use chatter to battle the silence. As for Darion, silence would have been preferable.

When they finished eating, the Shepherd set them back onto the road again and Jack eagerly asked where they were headed.

"My ship," said the Shepherd. "It separated from me before I landed. I'll need to find it again."

"Do you have an idea of where it is?"

"I have an idea, yes."

Jack shrugged. "Well, an idea is better than none, I guess."

"Not always," said the Shepherd. "Some ideas are better left without action. Though I know mine requires action if we are to get out of this."

"Fair enough," said Jack.

They walked on. The sun continued its ascent, an act that seemed to ignite the steps of the Shepherd, give life to his feet. The giant took them through the next valley, under the shade of trees and up the next hillside. Darion anchored Olivia close to his side, keeping himself between Jack and his daughter. Jack didn't notice Darion's protective stance, however. His gaze alternated between the back of the Shepherd's head and the trail they left behind. The

Adversary could come at any time. That's what the Shepherd said, wasn't it?

Time passed slowly, painfully for Jack. He tried to engage Darion with conversation, but Darion's one-word replies kept Jack at a distance. At the next clearing, the Shepherd stopped and halted the caravan under a tree.

"We'll rest here awhile," said the Shepherd and Jack took a seat next to a tree while Darion stood.

"Why are we resting?" asked Darion.

The Shepherd scanned the clearing and surveyed the sky. Jack noted how the Shepherd seemed to operate on his own schedule. He answered questions when he wanted to and when. It would seem rude if it was any other person, but this was the Shepherd. Jack was quickly learning that's how it would go and he wondered if Darion was learning this too.

" I need to commune with my ship," said the Shepherd.

"Commune?" asked Jack.

"It means to 'talk', Jack," said Darion.

"I know what it means," said Jack, glaring at Darion. Were you just waiting to try and make me look stupid?

The Shepherd turned to face them, ready to tell them of his discovery. "I know where it is."

"Where is it then?" asked Darion.

"Far from here."

Jack chuckled like it was Darion's turn to sound a fool. Darion ignored him. "How far?"

"A week, maybe a couple weeks of travel depending on how fast we move."

"That long?" said Darion.

"I'm sorry," said the Shepherd. "Did you have something more pressing to attend to?"

Jack smirked. He was liking the Shepherd more by the minute.

* * * *

Darion rolled his shoulders with discomfort. It wasn't what he wanted to hear, but it didn't sound unbearable. A few days? I've waited for longer, he figured. What's a few more days, really? He convinced himself of the shortness of the journey and looked at

Jack, sitting with hands on his knees. A few more days will seem long, but it may be long enough to persuade him to leave.

"I suppose that doesn't sound so bad," said Darion. "Should we get going again?"

The Shepherd glanced at Olivia. He seemed to say something to her with his eyes and she grinned. "Wait here awhile. All of you need water and I'm going to attend to that first."

"Wait here?"

What? With the criminal? *Alone?*

The Shepherd didn't flinch; he pivoted on his heel and sped off across the clearing with the speed of a cheetah and the gracefulness of a gazelle. Then he took another leap, cleared the tree line in front of them, and fell back to Earth somewhere on the other side of the woods.

"Holy hell..." said Jack. "I've got to be dreamin', man. Tell me this isn't making your head spin."

Darion glared at Jack. "You're not dreaming. Watch the language around my daughter."

Jack chuckled, but when he saw Darion's face – stern and unapologetic – he stopped.

"So you think your daughter to be a fragile thing?" said Jack. "She's probably seen and heard more than you know. When I was her age, the world was no cleaner than it was now."

"Well that was *your* life," said Darion. "This is *hers.*"

"Fine, chief," said Jack. "I'll watch my mouth around her."

The three sat in silence, waiting for the Shepherd to return. Jack soon became antsy and drew some pictures in the dirt.

"So, how'd you know about this thing anyway?" asked Jack. "I mean, if none of this scares you like it does me, and it ain't new to you, then how did you know about all of this? How'd you get those discs?"

"That's none of your business, really," said Darion. "And I'd prefer not to speak about it."

"Why?"

"Because I just don't want to."

Jack kicked the dirt in front of him. Prick. If it weren't for his little girl, I'd go right on saying what I want. He crossed his legs and clicked his tongue, thinking of what else he might be able to say that would incite a conversation. He had so many questions, but each one seemed less likely to be answered than the next. Then, he remembered something.

"Alright, look," he said and Darion stared down at him. Jack took a long breath, making certain that Darion was giving him full attention. "I'm sorry, alright? I'm sorry… I know I tried to rob you earlier, but I'm sorry."

Darion didn't blink. "You're 'sorry'?"

"Yeah."

"Am I'm supposed to forgive you then?"

"We could have killed each other today," said Jack. "But we didn't. That makes us even in my eyes."

"So you're just apologizing so I'll talk to you?"

Jack shrugged. "Hell if I know," he said and held out a hand like he was saying, 'sorry, I didn't mean to swear again.' "I just know it means that we're worth something to each other now. And it doesn't mean we can't talk to each other."

Jack sounded genuine, but the memory of what happened that morning was still with Darion. No, he would not forget so easily as Jack.

"I saw the men who were after you yesterday," said Darion, his tone growing ever more serious. "Did you think I'd forget that too?" Jack leaned back like he was on trial. "I'm not an idiot, Jack; not like the ones you're used to running into. Those were mercs, weren't they? Bounty hunters – nothing like the Lawkeepers that had you. You got a price on your head, don't you?"

Jack was silent.

"That's what I thought," said Darion. "And you know what else I know?" Jack pressed his lips together, anticipating Darion to spill some hidden sin of Jack's.

"You're an idiot," said Darion.

"What?"

"That's right. An idiot. The kind who gets himself killed by taking stupid risks. But, here's the ironic part and the one thing I can't get past: I *saved* that idiot. Someone I didn't even know until yesterday. And how did that idiot go and repay the one who helped him? How does he repay the man he owes a life debt to? By *turning* on him. Dogs behave better than that, Jack. So no, your apology needs to be bigger than 'I'm sorry,' Jack. And it needs to be more than we 'mean something' to one another."

Jack smacked his lips and let out a breath like he'd taken a punch to the stomach. Darion took a breath of his own, trembling like he'd just poured gasoline on a fire. Then he realized: the Shepherd wasn't here to protect him from Jack. He hadn't even considered that. He just had his anger and the anger seemed to speak on his behalf, without his permission.

"Well," said Jack. "I get it, okay? And I'm still sorry. I can be an idiot sometimes and I was. Is that what you wanted to hear? That I'm an *idiot?*"

Darion was confused. Did he? He felt his anger subsiding as Jack admitted his faults.

"You really want me to answer that?" asked Darion.

"Well?"

"You could have killed yourself back there," said Darion. "Did you really think you could beat up all those men?"

"I don't know? Maybe? How was I supposed to know unless I tried? They were gonna try and kill me anyway. You saw that, didn't you? What was I supposed to do?"

"Not fight back? You don't have to always - "

Jack huffed. "Don't have to what?" said Jack. He stood up and Darion cowered. "You've never been on the run like me, have you?"

Jack's eyes weren't sad anymore – they were boiling. Darion could see the fury welling up in Jack, aiming itself directly at him. Only it was happening without Jack's permission too. Like the anger had leapt from Darion's shoulder and was now firmly planted upon Jack's. This boy has a demon too. Just like him.

"No?" said Jack. "Never?"

Darion was quiet, silently trying to kill the heat between them. Secretly, Darion wanted to tell Jack of the six months he'd spent living in alleys. The six months he and Olivia stayed in decrepit homes, hiding out and avoiding people as they searched for the Shepherd. Was that the same as being hunted? Or was it a refusal to be found? Darion felt like the two could be similar, but with Jack riled up, Darion didn't want to charge more of Jack's anger with another misconception.

"So you don't know what it's like, do you?" said Jack. "You have no idea how it feels to have your back in a corner. All the time. Every minute. Every day."

"Look, just take it easy - "

Jack shoved Darion slightly. It was done with more strength than what Darion could have prepared for and he almost stumbled, but even more so, it startled him. How could he have forgotten? Jack was a *criminal*. He'd fought those mercenaries without a second thought. He'd had a gun to my head. This man is dangerous. Why was I being so stupid? Shepherd, where are you? Oh God, where are you?

"Take what easy, chief?" said Jack, pressing himself closer on Darion. "What now? Do you have something else for me?"

Darion looked past Jack, saw Olivia seated on the ground, fear gripping her. What had he done? He'd let loose the monster. Then, a voice rose up inside of him: *Don't lose. Don't lose in front of her.*

Jack kept moving forward, but Darion shoved him back. It was unexpected and Jack fell backwards. So Darion dove at him, tackling Jack to the ground as dirt flew into the air. Jack grabbed hold of Darion's body and tried to remove him, but Darion held on. He realized he had no plan other than to hold Jack down, keep him down somehow. Beyond that, he had nothing. The two of them wrestled, neither able to get the advantage over the other, Olivia screaming silently inside.

Eventually, Jack rolled Darion over and twisted his arm. In this position, Darion couldn't get free and for a moment, he looked at Olivia. She was watching them, curled into a ball against the tree with eyes wide. No, I can't lose. I have to beat him. So Darion writhed with his all his might but Jack was stronger than he imagined. Jack twisted his arm again and this time it hurt so Darion let out a yell and Jack pushed his face to the ground.

"Do something now, old man!" shouted Jack and as though his words ignited a fire inside of Darion, the man Jack was holding twisted his body violently, breaking free and rolling over. Darion hooked Jack and flung him over his head, slamming Jack into the dirt, shoulder first and Jack let out a yell of his own. It sounded like a wounded animal, lending Darion a moment of victory and though Darion wanted to go for the finish, he couldn't. The pain was setting in. And fast. He gripped his arm and rolled away from Jack, who was face first in the dirt.

"How's *that* for an old man?" said Darion.

A noise in the trees alerted Darion and he looked for its source. The trees swayed back and forth, appearing as though something was swinging from one to the other. Darion could scarcely believe it: the Shepherd was pushing himself from trunk to trunk. Unbelievable. He's using those trees like they're springboards.

The Shepherd jumped from one of the trees and landed in the clearing. He had something with him under each arm. He walked the remainder of the distance and stood before the trio.

"Shepherd..." said Darion, shakily. Jack gripped his shoulder, saying nothing.

"I have brought water with me," said the Shepherd. "You may have some."

Does he not know? Darion looked at the Shepherd, guilt practically shouting from his face. Jack stood up, albeit wearily. The two of them waited. Was the Shepherd going to scold them? Did he know what happened? He didn't appear to, for the Shepherd set to doing something the likes of which neither man had ever seen.

"What is that you're doing?" asked Darion.

The Shepherd's suit was inflated around his torso.

"Parts of my suit is filled with water," said the Shepherd. "Don't worry, I have purified it for you."

"Are we supposed to drink from your rib cage or something?" asked Darion.

The Shepherd held out his hands, palms up. The sides of his body contracted and water filtered through his arms, through his wrists and into his cupped fingers. For a normal person, it would have been a small amount, but in the hands of the Shepherd, there was plenty of water. He motioned them to drink from his hands but no one approached.

"What?" said the Shepherd. "Are you too tired from that skirmish to replenish yourselves?"

"What was that?" asked Darion.

"If you want to heal properly, then you'll need water. Then you can decide to attack each other again if you wish. But, first, get over here and take some."

"Then you - "

"Yes," said the Shepherd. "You both make a enough noise, a sleeping bear would be roused from hibernation."

Darion and Jack lowered their heads, ashamed. But, it was Olivia who walked forward. The Shepherd bent low, his hands out for Olivia to drink.

"Hey, you're not going to - " said Darion.

"Going to what?" said the Shepherd. "Are you too good to drink from my hands out here in the wilderness? Or would you rather stay thirsty and beaten?"

Of course not. But, what about Jack? What about him? Shouldn't there be some repercussion for what's happened? If the Shepherd knew, why wasn't he doing anything? The Shepherd held out his hands and Olivia cupped a small bit of water. It was like dipping her hands in a fountain.

"Careful," said the Shepherd. "Only the water. For if you touch me, you will surely begin to die."

"What did you say?" asked Jack.

"My suit is comprised of Solfire, Jack," said the Shepherd. "It protects me, but if taken directly by someone other than myself, it can be harmful. My suit is useful for many things, but it also works hard to protect itself."

So that's his secret, is it? Darion thought. A suit. One that's pumping Solfire like blood through a man's veins - the Shepherd was bathing in power. Darion nearly fell over at the revelation, thinking of what it must be like to live as a Shepherd of Mars. Olivia took a sip and grinned. Perhaps this would be a 'taste' of what it was like to be a Shepherd? So Darion took some for himself and licked his lips. The water was crisp, cool, and clean. His tongue was surprised to discover how fresh it was. Like, his body would rather reject the water out of unfamiliarity than continue tasting what was better.

When they were finished and the water gone, the Shepherd wiped his hands and stood up. Almost immediately, Darion felt his own body healing. Was it the water? Or the work of the Shepherd?

"What...what is this?"

"Your body is filled with pain and hate," said the Shepherd. "The water will help expunge that feeling. Once that's gone, we can continue."

Darion looked at Jack. He appeared to be experiencing the same. Darion's shoulder creaked with new life. The water was fixing his arm from the inside out. Before Darion could utter his thanks, they were moving again. Along the way, Darion could feel his body becoming lighter. His shoulder and arm were one matter, but his spirits felt rejuvenated as well. Even Olivia was in a better mood. And Jack, he observed, seemed to be less irritable. The battle they'd had was not only not spoken of, it's like it was disappearing with every step. Erased from memory like the pain in their shoulders.

"Shepherd," said Darion, with eagerness in his voice. "Do you have water like this on Mars?"

"Yes But, not as abundantly, of course. The Earth has life-giving water. Mars' water supply is…lacking."

"I see. But, with Solfire, you could probably change that, I'm sure."

The Shepherd hesitated. "Perhaps. Solfire cannot fix a groaning world, I fear."

The thought of groaning rock and earth made Darion think the Shepherd was spinning poetry like it was meant to confuse him. How could things be better here anyway? The Earth and Mars were separate entities, balls of rock, dust, and ice floating in the cosmos. They had no personalities of their own, save Earth's abundant harbor of life. Comparatively, Mars was scorched red, smaller than most planets, and scarcely livable. Yet, humanity had found a way to *make* it livable. The fact that human intervention caused Mars to be greater than what it had been was worthy of note, wasn't it? Like, this water. Yet the way the Shepherd explained it, he made Mars sound like it was lesser than Earth, better off without human intrusion. How could the Shepherd say these things?

Darion decided to set his mind on other matters. How was Jack doing? He seemed docile since their scuffle, yet refused to look Darion in the eye. Together, they clutched their shoulders like wounded soldiers, marching on without complaining. Would this sort of thing happen again? Could Darion ever feel safe when the Shepherd left them? Darion wished the Shepherd had come earlier, without the water, and settled the fight. At least then his shoulder wouldn't have been in pain from the start. Jack winced and Darion couldn't help but smirk.

I showed that kid I'm tougher than he thought. He'll remember *that.*

* * * *

Jack walked, his shoulder aching but gradually getting better by the minute. He coughed a few times; that unnerving cough returning after that brief sparring match. So stupid. That old man was tougher than he'd anticipated, stronger than what he'd ever guessed. Perhaps being a dad doesn't immediately make you a pansy, eh? Jack rubbed his shoulder again and grimaced. This sure is taking a while to heal. I could use some more of that magic water. That would do the trick.

They walked a long time, not saying much aloud but speaking loudly in their minds. Jack wondered if the old man was already healed. But, still, why had he gone off like that? Why had either of them done it? Jack was miffed. The old man had pissed him off. But, the anger — that was the demon he hated calling upon.

Stupid. Why are you so stupid, Jack?

He looked at the little girl. She had been watching him for a long while, he knew, but he didn't know why. You probably think I'm some kind of monster, don't you? First, I'm stealing and then I'm trying to beat up your dad. Wow, what an impression. What kind of worthless person does these things? I guess that someone is *me*. But, where were these thoughts coming from? Jack felt these new convictions rushing over him like waves, and he didn't like it. So he pushed away the thoughts and rubbed his shoulder again.

"Is your shoulder improving?" asked the Shepherd and Jack raised his head.

"It still hurts."

"That's not what I asked you."

Jack swallowed. "Yes. It's feeling better."

"That's good. See how much easier it is when you say something directly?"

Jack hadn't thought of that. When you're trying to survive, you scarcely ever say things directly. You have to obscure the truth if you're going to make it. Isn't that the way things work? With the Shepherd though, and in the short time Jack had spent with him, trying to escape with your own lies seemed like a bad gamble. Jack knew it even more when they stopped again and the Shepherd decided to tend to each man's shoulders individually. With Jack, the Shepherd examined him closely, speaking softly so that Darion might not hear.

"You're lucky," said the Shepherd. "You could have torn your shoulder."

"Feels like I did."

"What we feel can sometimes be an overstatement."

The Shepherd looked over his shoulder and then at Jack. "An apology might be the appropriate action, but perhaps gaining one another's confidence is even more important at this juncture."

"What's that?"

"If you intend to go the distance, Jack, you must try to be at peace with the ones around you."

Then the Shepherd turned forward, saying nothing else.

The party of four traveled onward, Jack mulling over the Shepherd's words. *Maybe surviving this will mean I just need to play by his rules?* he thought. I'm used to hiding and saying what I need to, but with him, I'll do what I have to. Especially if I'm going to outlast the old man and his daughter. That's what I'll do.

Jack let go of his arm and rolled his shoulder. The pain was still there but it wasn't nearly as bad as before. He looked at the old man again, his face was ahead, but his daughter was looking at him. Okay, let's try being direct.

"You know, you're stronger than I thought," said Jack. The old man must think I'm crazy. "But, you're also lucky. You're lucky because the big guy showed up. I had you back there."

"Says the man with arm hanging limp," said Darion and Jack half-grinned. Olivia smiled too.

"I'm just saying," said Jack. "You're pretty strong. You might have taken me if you wouldn't have wasted all that time trying to wrap your arms around my waist. You don't tackle right. That was your only mistake."

Darion was quiet for a short while. Jack could sense Darion thinking, conjuring up just the right words for him. Was he offended? Or would he banter a bit like an old friend might?

"I know how to handle myself, thank you," said Darion. "I may have not grown up on the streets, but I've lived on them for a good while myself."

Jack smirked. "The streets don't teach you how to tackle, chief. They teach you how to *win*. And they teach you how to lose without losing your life at the same time. That is, if you can learn that lesson without experiencing the last part. Then you're really onto something."

"Well, congratulations, Jack. You beat me then."

"We both lost. My shoulder hurts like hell and I wasn't expecting that out of you. So, well done."

There, I told you what you wanted to hear. You're tough. I'm not. You're smart. I'm not. Are we square again, old man?

"I guess we know each other's limits now," said Darion. "I would hope it doesn't have to come to that again. Agreed?"

Darion peered at Jack this time, eyes filled with warning. They weren't overtly threatening but still, they carried a weight as if to say, 'do not test me like that again. Or else I may really hurt you.' Jack grinned. This guy really *was* tough. He came across as a straight-edged father, but there was something beneath Darion that made Jack think of men who'd spent too many nights by themselves. That sort of behavior made them angry, made them hard. Darion, somewhere underneath that exterior and the protective shell of being a father, was like those men. The Shepherd was right: if Jack wanted to survive, then he needed to be more accommodating. Even if the old man didn't trust him, Jack needed to give him less reasons not to. And in the process, keep Darion from hardening up even more.

"I agree with you," said Jack. "If it changes anything, I think your recovery is going better than mine. I still can't even lift my arm that well."

"That actually does make mine feel better."

"I doubt that," said the Shepherd, eyes ahead. "But, all the same, if you believe so, it just may."

At the next stop, Jack made certain to give Darion plenty of space. Just like the old man liked it. And when they were up and moving again, Jack tried raising his arm but couldn't get it all the way.

"Stop doing that," said Darion. "You need to give it time to heal."

Jack nodded. Watching me now, are you? They walked a bit farther until Jack felt Darion's eyes upon him yet again.

"My name is Darion," said Darion and Jack's mouth nearly fell agape. "Darion Wallace. And this is Olivia."

A name, Jack thought. *Olivia and Darion*. Two names. Two faces. Actual people Jack could address by name. He didn't know if they'd ever exchange *those*.

They already knew his name. But, why not just say it anyway?

"I'm Jack," he said and Darion nodded. He raised his arm in triumph like he'd healed already.

"Did I mention I was a doctor by trade?" said Darion. "And nobody heals that fast. Leave that arm down unless you intend to never use it again."

Jack lowered his arm, squeezed it tighter. You're right, old man. Still hurts like hell.

Chapter 7
The Divide

"The mind can be changed. But - "

"But the heart is a separate matter?"

"Not a separate matter. The mind and the heart are linked. And when one suffers, both suffer. Even if one is unaware of the other's suffering, they are hindered all the same."

* * * *

"I've seen a lot like him," said Abe. "They don't know a damned thing about life but they want everything that's in it. And if you push'em one way, you're liable to send'em reeling for years in the wrong direction. It's best he find out what he's looking for on his own. I want no part of that. Not anymore."

"Well, if he comes back here again," said Milly, the plaza owner. "I'm gonna whoop his ass *for* you."

Craig, positioned at the far corner of the bar, resounded with a, "I'd like to see that!" and Jeff joined in too, but did so with an uncomfortable laughter. For Jeff's thoughts were on the traveling pair, the young man, and the talk of Darklight and Solfire. Abe knew the run-in with the young man had lit a fire inside of Jeff. Made him feel helpless, unprepared, but Abe didn't know what to say or do for Jeff. So he did what he usually did. He offered the young man a drink.

"You alright?" asked Abe, blandly. "Need another one?"

"How are you feeling?" asked Jeff. "He hit you pretty good, ya know that?"

"It's not as bad as you'd think," said Abe, feigning strength. "The swelling is the only thing I'm fighting now. See?"

Abe pointed to the side of his face where a long, red mark had become evident. Jeff winced, looking at Abe.

"And your ribs?"

"Ha, now *those* hurt," said Abe and he rubbed his side.

"I'd have killed that guy if I were you," said Jeff. "I can't believe we let him get away from here."

Abe smirked. A noble notion, kid, but not worth the effort. Still, Abe watched Jeff, admiring the youth's hatred for wrongdoing.

"If I was part of the Hunt, it might have been different," said Jeff.

"No," said Abe. "And don't say those things."

The way Abe shot him down, Jeff looked insulted. An unfamiliar rage rallied inside of Jeff and burst forth from his tongue like he'd never known before.

"Then, what, huh?" said Jeff. "What are we supposed to do when things like that happen? Just take it like dogs?"

Abe looked at Jeff, the young's man's blood was boiling like a hot kettle. Abe had never seen this side of Jeff and it frightened him. That's all it takes, isn't it? A simple act of injustice to send a boy running and a man to come out of the shadows, ready for a fight.

"If you keep your wits," said Abe. "then you'll keep your life, son. That's all that matters."

Jeff turned back in his chair, still raging. He curled his lips and tapped his feet on the floor. "What about the Red Fellows? What about them?"

Abe didn't answer, at first. "What about'em?"

"Don't they do good things? You would know, wouldn't you? You were one of'em."

Abe blinked, closed his eyes, and remembered about a half dozen thoughts that were as joyful as they were incredulous. The Red Fellows were a good group, in theory. Like most organizations born in dark times, they were meant to be the answer to life's most difficult of circumstances And their roots – the Christian theology – was no mistake of choice. But when Abe reopened his eyes, he found himself reminded of what else they were: unruly, hypocritical, divided, and most annoyingly, *human*. In that respect, the Hunt and the Red Fellows were one in the same: two groups led by humans, run by humans, and driven by human concepts. Neither could survive indefinitely. Even if there were good to be done, it would be temporary. The Hunt operated in the same way. There was little distinction between them and he looked at Jeff with sympathetic eyes.

"The Red Fellows do good things," said Abe. "As does the Hunt, at times. But the way it goes, you might as well pick your poison, son. That's why you should keep your wits. You understand what I'm telling you?"

Jeff shook his head, annoyed. "No, I don't, Abe," said Jeff. "And I promise you – it won't happen to me. Not ever. I promise you that. I'm going to change things."

"You are, are you?"

"Yeah, I am. See you around."

Jeff pressed a coin on the table and walked out. His sudden exit startled Abe. A lot of strong talk and open promises, he thought. Abe wondered how Jeff might truly react if he were faced with the same conditions again. The same dangers. And Abe hoped Jeff would choose to respond as Abe had instructed him to. He hoped.

About an hour later, Abe finished his drink and left the café. He didn't bother to say goodbye to Craig or Milly. He simply made his way back to the old city; intent on seeing a doctor for the pain he had. Then he'd be back to the plaza again tomorrow. Things would be the same as always.

Stupid kid, Abe thought, this time thinking of Jack. He'll end up destroying himself. Seen it hundreds of times. Was Jeff doomed to become like Jack too?

Yet, both men possessed a similar distinction: courage, buried deep beneath. Hidden. Locked away. They both had it, even if Jack's was filled with rage. Though Jeff's was too. Now it was. Tough kids, but stupid all the same. They didn't realize their anger couldn't be used for their advantage. Not yet anyway. Hopefully they'll figure out the best way to use it. And not destroy themselves.

Abe reached into his pocket and pulled out an old pendant. It was gold, had two circles on it and was interlocked by a single line. One circle was larger than the other and there was a scuff on that larger circle. Abe rubbed out the smudge and blew on it. He entertained putting it on his breast pocket but smirked and tucked it away.

"Those days are over, aren't they?" he said aloud. *I gave up the Red Fellows a long time ago, right?*

The thought of an old life, one etched deep in memory, tugged at Abe all the way into the old city. Funny how a disruption causes a person to reminisce on either the good times or the bad. And which that person chooses must depend upon the individual.

Abe hoped he wouldn't have any other disruptions as he walked into the city.

But, when he got to the outskirts, he found himself a witness to a blockade of people near one of its tallest buildings. They were huddled in the streets and appeared to be on the verge of a riot.

What's all this? A truck had overturned on the road. A transporter vehicle, one that looked similar to Jeff's and Abe's stomach seemed to drop. He rushed into the crowd, looking and hearing for an explanation. All above the truck were crackles of purple electricity – the Darklight was heavy. Not a promising sign.

"What happened?" he asked. "Hey? Does anyone know?"

There were no answers. The haze of Darklight was thick. Abe was forced to piece together what had happened with his own eyes. The transport had been attacked, as there were pieces of glass on the road and holes punched in its side. A rescue team had placed people on stretchers several yards away and Abe pushed through the crowd to see if Jeff was one of the injured. His ribs ached, but he dismissed the pain.

One, two, three...there were three people being attended to. None of them were Jeff. He looked about and asked another what had happened. More haze. The vehicle had 'turned over suddenly', one said. Abe overheard a few people talking by the sidewalk. Witnesses, perhaps?

"Hey, you!" said Abe. They looked at him, oddly. "Yeah, you. What happened here?"

They shrugged their shoulders. A crackle of Darklight appeared over them. There would be no answers here. Either they'd lost someone themselves or their answers would be false. Abe walked farther down the street. He heard another voice, far from him that seemed to be asking him to come closer. Abe turned around. It was one of the city merchants and he was motioning for Abe to come to him.

"Yes, you," said the merchant. "Come here."

Abe approached slowly, cautious of the merchant.

"I seen it," said the merchant. "I seen the whole thing."

"What did you see?" asked Abe.

The old merchant leaned in closer, trying to protect himself under his canopy. "Many men came. They came with guns, but they hid themselves away from everyone. They were hidden in Darklight, you see. And they were lookin' for someone. But, they couldn't find'em. But *I* seen'em. I seen who they were lookin' for. I can see through the clouds, you see. I can see through'em. But, the man they were lookin' for. He'd already come and gone. But he left behind somethin'. And I got it."

Abe's heart skipped. Another man with the *Gift*? This old merchant, despite his wretched stench and crude look, appeared to have truth on his lips. And who was this man? And this 'thing' the men with guns were looking for?

"Hold on," said Abe. "What are you talking about? Who had the guns?"

"It was the *Hunt*," said the old merchant. "They came, causing trouble for the Lawkeepers. But, I found it before they could. The one who dropped it, he dropped it a long time ago. I found it when he dropped it and – "

The old merchant stopped, looking over Abe's shoulder. Abe turned and saw a group of Rovers coming up the road.

"Don't let'em find me!" pleaded the merchant. "Don't let'em! They don't know I have it! Even though they don't know they're looking for it, they are! The one they want is gone so they'll want what I have instead!"

Abe thought of running. The old merchant was more like a raving lunatic than a Seer like Abe had presumed. His story made little sense, but even so, the Rovers were headed straight for them. Just as the old merchant said they might. So Abe stayed where he was. A startled prey is a guilty one. And Abraham knew he wasn't guilty of anything. Not here.

The vehicle stopped at the side of the road and a metal door slid open. Out jumped a short, thin man covered in a heavy jacket and a bright red emblem on both shoulders. Behind him were several other men, but these men had firearms and their faces were covered from the nose down with red scarves. The Hunt. Why so many? Abe was afraid, but stood his ground. The short man approached.

"Hello there," he said, his voice sounding like a raspy child. "You wouldn't happen to have seen what happened here, would you?"

The haze of Darklight was settling over them. Abe could feel it *and* he could see it. A ripple of purple and black cloud emanated over the top of the Hunt's Rover, alerting Abe that this situation was a dangerous one. He swallowed and assessed how he might answer best. The tiny man took another step.

"Hey, I asked you a question, old-timer," said the short man and he tilted his head to one side like Abe were incapable of understanding him. "Did you or did you not see what happened here?"

Abe shook his head, 'no.'

"What are you doing here then?"

"Just passing through," said Abe. "I saw the wreck and wanted to know what all the fuss was about. Wouldn't you?"

The short man looked Abe up and down, analyzing Abe thoroughly. "Just passing through?" he said. "That sounds nice. But, I don't believe you, but I don't. You know why I don't?"

Abe didn't answer.

"It's because I'm the *Eyes of the Hunt*, you see. I see everything that happens in this old city. So don't lie to me. You understand?"

Abe was startled. The Eyes of the Hunt, was it? Abe knew of him – Argus, the younger brother of the Hunt's Captain, Virgil. Both were equally famous – no, infamous in the old city. It was someone Abe had never hoped to meet or thought he would. But, here he was. Capable of seeing Darklight clouds too, perhaps? There weren't many others who could, and even fewer that could see *through* the haze it produced. Had Argus zeroed in on this merchant? He must know there's something over here. Something important, something like the Martian disc.

"I understand," said Abe. "That the 'Eyes of the Hunt' can see everything. I know that well."

A little flattery could help me, he thought. Argus peered at the wreckage. He raised an eyebrow and looked back at Abe, conspicuously. Abe saw more Darklight forming. It was beginning to make a sharp fog about them, clouding their line of sight and Abe noticed that Argus was beginning to be affected by it also. *Yes*, he thought. Argus *can* see it. He knows it's here. That's why he's investigating me. I can't let him know I see it too.

"You look pretty banged up," said Argus. "Sure you weren't part of that mess over there?"

"I don't work in the old city, sir," said Abe. "I work to the North. My wounds are from up that way. Not here."

"What happens up north that gets you beat and bloodied?"

"Things the southerners wouldn't understand, I'd say."

"Ha," said Argus, turning his attention from Abe. "And what about your friend there? Did he see what happened?"

Argus pointed to the old merchant, hiding in his tent. "He's not my friend," said Abe, not knowing if his honesty was protecting the merchant or not.

"Then what were you talking about just now? Trading garbage from the Old World? Is that what you were doing?"

"Just asking about the wreck," said Abe. "Wouldn't you want to know if you saw something like that going on?"

Argus wrinkled his brow, licked his lips like a lizard might. He seemed nervous, jittery, and snorted like a wild animal. He didn't project the image of a smart or a learned man. Rather, he was the conglomeration of what he said he was: the eyes of an old and decrepit city. Eyes that had become as deranged and damaged as what they absorbed, driven paranoid by every crooked edge that looked out of place.

"You there," said Argus, pointing to the merchant. "What is that?"

The old merchant feigned ignorance or perhaps, didn't realize he was being addressed.

"Hey *you*," repeated Argus. "What is that there? Under all that junk? Hey, garbage picker. Eyes up."

The merchant leaned forward in his chair. "What was that you say?"

Argus walked past Abe, bumping him slightly on the way. When they met, Abe felt a strange aura come off of Argus. Argus was *scared*. This man – a lot of talk, not a lot of substance. A kid, just like Jeff or that young man from the other day. Is this whole damned world scared out of its mind?

"Let me see that," ordered Argus and the merchant did not comply. He seemed to be meditating or praying to avoid eye contact with Argus. This, naturally, did not appease Argus and he snapped at the merchant, saying, "I said, let me see that!"

Startled, the old merchant came out of his waking coma.

"What is it? What do you want?"

Argus pointed to something, something smooth and silver underneath the canopy. Abe eyed it carefully, unaware of its presence till just now. The old merchant was reluctant in retrieving the item, taking his time as he bent down and shuffled through his inventory. Ever more impatient, Argus moved in and took the artifact by force. He examined it up and down and looked at Abe. It was Darion's disc, discarded days ago.

"Were you hiding this from me?" asked Argus, but Abe didn't answer. He was still in amazement over what Argus had dug out of the tent. *Does he even know what he's holding?* Abe thought.

Argus waved the broken piece of hardware in Abe's face and another officer jumped out of the Rover. He was a full head taller, his red scarf wrapped around his face.

"Sir," he said. "Did you find what you were looking for?"

Argus turned, annoyed. "What are you doing out of the truck?" he snapped.

"I'm sorry, sir, I – "

"Sorry, are you? Get back in the Rover."

The soldier ducked his head and retreated. Abe couldn't believe it. Anywhere else, a man this size would have been torn to shreds by the bigger, stronger men. Either the Hunt's soldiers were all brainwashed into following orders or Argus really *was* worthy of his higher rank and being respected.

But, then, a new voice – a woman's – said, "Enough of this, Argus. Quit wasting our time."

"I'm not done, Greta," Argus retorted, sounding like a child. "I found something. I think it might belong to the one we're after." Another person appeared, Greta, and jumped out onto the pavement. She was small, like Argus, and had all the insignias of her fellow Huntsmen.

"I'm not -" said Argus.

"We're leaving," argued Greta, pushing back. Her voice was firm, yet feminine in every aspect of what differentiated a woman from a man. Yet her femininity seemed suppressed, pushed back behind taut lips and a tightened gaze. "Quit making us waste our time with your 'hunches.' Get yourself back in the Rover before we lose the trail."

Greta looked at Abe, her green eyes peering over top of the red scarf that covered only her neck, not her chin like the rest of the anonymous Huntsmen. Abe quivered. The Darklight lifted, the haze was cut, and the ripple of purple static disappeared. Abe felt a new sensation come over him and he opened his eyes as wide as he could, activating every sense he possessed. Then Greta looked away, focusing her attention back upon Argus.

"I'm the Eyes of the Hunt, Greta," said Argus, boldly. "I'm supposed to see and hear *everything* that happens. How can I do that when you seem to think that you're the Eyes?"

Greta looked at the broken disc in Argus' hand. She stepped forward and Argus flinched; like a dog who knows when his master has come to discipline him. This woman has authority, even if only by sheer intimidation, she has power over this man. What's more, Argus was barely as tall, if not shorter, than Greta. "Get in the Rover, Argus. Playtime is over."

Argus stared at Abe, who looked happy to be free of him soon. Argus stuffed his pocket with the broken disc and yelled at the soldiers in the Rover like it was past time to leave. Then, grudgingly, Argus jumped inside. Greta took another look at Abe and the old merchant, pulled her firearm up on her shoulder and followed Argus in. Even with a heavy weapon weighing her down, Greta had an obvious elegance about her.

"Try to stay off the streets, old man," said Greta. "Don't want you getting more hurt than you already are. You looked banged up as it is."

Abe recalled the fight with Jack and nodded, embarrassed to have received such a strong recommendation from this woman. Then the door slid shut and the Rover headed north. Two more like the first, heavily armored and likely to be full of Hunt soldiers, followed behind. Abe was left with the old merchant, pondering what had just transpired. The haze of Darklight subsided completely and Abe felt safe again. With Greta gone, his feelings changed from fear to that of longing. He watched them disappear up the road and an old memory; one closely tied to the Red Fellows came to the forefront of his mind. He closed his eyes and sighed. Just like last time, he recalled. This meeting with Greta had been just like the last one: *nothingness.*

Abe turned to the old merchant. He was retreated in his tent, bent over and rocking back and forth like he'd been caught with something. Poor old man. "Hey," said Abe. "How did you get that anyway?"

The old merchant didn't answer. More rocking. He began speaking with inaudible words and weeping.

"Hey, how did you get that disc? How did you get it?"

Rocking again. The old merchant was unresponsive and Abe knew he couldn't stay any longer. The disc was gone, but it was likely of little use to the Hunt. He hoped it was, anyway. As for the merchant, he was of little use too and Abe decided to move on, walking across the street to join more people.

There was nothing new to report on the other side of the street, however. Nobody had seen anything and it could have been a simple accident for all he knew. A disc had been stolen and Abe was still as sore as ever. It hadn't been a very good day. He walked away from the mess, deeper into the old city as he returned to his thoughts.

Along the way, Abe found himself rubbing the pendant beneath his breast pocket. He pulled it out, examined it and returned it to its resting place. The Red Fellows –the last group he felt connected to, outside of the ones he'd befriended at the café'. There was peace there, he remembered. At one time, he'd had peace. Then, he found peace at the café', but it wasn't the wholeness he once had. Something was always missing and now, that false peace was gone. The Red Fellows – they were the last group that seemed to have their heads on straight, even if the rest of the world was going crazy. Maybe that's where Jeff was going? And now the matter of this broken disc too. Where had it come from? If the Hunt had it, what did they plan to do with it?

Abe wasn't certain of any of these things. But he knew he had to follow them. He had to follow the Hunt. If nothing else, for *her*, he had to. She was leaving the city. He didn't need to stay there any longer. He could finally leave.

"Alright fine," he said aloud. "I'm coming to get you. I'll get you and Jeff out of this, if I have to. Don't do anything stupid and don't get caught up in anything till I get to you either. Do that for me, would you? I'm going to make things right for once. I'm going to stop sitting on the other side of this divide."

* * * *

The Shepherd carved a path through the wilderness for the duration of the afternoon. Darion and Jack were silent for much of this journey, exchanging discussion that hinged between acceptance and casual acquaintance. The spectacle of the Shepherd's presence had wrapped their minds around other thoughts rather than the condition of how they'd met. And the Shepherd's words, complemented by the ultra-purified water, were having an inward effect that seemed to be spilling outwardly. Darion spied Jack periodically; curious as to why Jack was being chased by mercenaries. And moreover, just who Jack, in general was a matter of piqued speculation. But, when Darion opened his mouth to speak, he found himself fighting the urge, thus blocking any desire to connect further with Jack. However, if Jack were the one to initiate conversation, Darion would fully engage. This bothered Darion, like he'd let his guard down too easily, and he'd quickly go on the offensive, asking Jack questions that would hopefully unveil why Jack was a wanted man.

This man is a criminal, he'd remind himself. He's broken the law and is a criminal. I can't forget that.

And then there was the incident before the diner. That drunken sloth who had wandered into the alley and stopped like he'd seen Darion and Olivia. Had Jack *actually* seen through the shield? No. That would be impossible. Yet, the impossibility of their later meeting seemed to point to that conclusion. If Jack had seen them, he would have made mention of that, right? No. Why would he? Jack may be a reckless idiot, but he's not naïve. Thus, Darion's paranoia of Jack grew, even with every casual exchange they shared; Darion could not shake the coincidences that led to their inevitable meeting.

How do I get it out of him though? How do I get him to admit to me what he's searching for? Running from. Convicted of.

Conversely, Jack's thoughts were less about discerning Darion and more about believing the unbelievable. He rubbed his belly and cleared his throat, finding himself to be less hungry and less agitated than normal. His shoulder still hurt, but that was going away rather quickly. Very quickly. And any need he had to shove alcohol down his gullet was also gone. Subdued, to a point.

Calm. That's what he felt. There was calmness in following the steps of the Shepherd. Or rather, he enjoyed these new sensations in comparison to what he was accustomed to feeling. He could concentrate on other things in the silence of his own thoughts. Hunger, water, even sex – each of these needs were less prevailing as new desires began to surface in their place.

Where had Darion and Olivia come from? How they'd come to have the Shepherd's discs, and how did they know so much about the Shepherd's imminent arrival? The mystery of the Shepherd seemed like a far off place, incapable of being fully understood. But, perhaps through Darion, Jack might gain some insight. So Jack would ask Darion specific questions, searching Darion for new information as best hew as able to do with a man he deemed smarter than he.

"You been in the old city a long time?" asked Jack.

"No," answered Darion. "Was just passing through."

"Where were ya before that?"

Darion paused. "We lived outside of what was originally Pennsylvania. We're not from there though. We're from the southern states. At least, what used to be the southern states, anyway."

Jack eyed Darion intently. "Really?"

Darion nodded.

"You don't sound like you're from the south, chief," said Jack. "I've met people from the south and they don't sound like you. How long ago was that?"

Darion stared ahead. *That question was intentional,* he thought. Seeing if I'll lie to him. "It was a while ago," said Darion, finally. "We've been traveling a lot. Just the two of us. It's been a long time, really."

"I hear that," said Jack. "You ever been through Fairlawn?"

Darion shook his head.

"That's a nice town," said Jack. "I mean, it's not exactly friendly for children, but it's nice enough, I guess. There's plenty to do there and there's work too. You can find work there and stay for as long as you like."

Darion didn't respond, but that didn't stop Jack.

"I had a few jobs there," said Jack. "I was a Runner for a while, transporting goods to local stores. Mostly beer and wine, of course. That's what people love down there and Fairlawn loves to accommodate the need. Good ale in the stomach helps a person sleep at night. I think that's the motto in that town."

"Is that a motto you adopted too?"

Jack chuckled uncomfortably. "Yeah, I suppose I did."

"Everyone can enjoy alcohol nowadays," said Darion. "Doesn't matter how old you are. Nobody cares about that kind of stuff anymore. The Pulse made sure of that."

"What do you mean?"

Darion took a breath like he had a rehearsed answer waiting.

"The Pulse added new fears," said Darion. "It brought terrible thoughts we didn't even know we had inside of us. So naturally, any of the old fears didn't go away. They just got magnified. People who'd only been mild drinkers became drunkards and people who were only partly abusive, became monstrous and terrifying. The Pulse compounded the things in people that were otherwise less obvious. What was already there, just became *more*. That's why there are less people in the world now. The ones who had too much fear destroyed themselves because they were already on the edge. It's the ones who only had mild fears that survived all the days that followed."

"And that's why nobody cares how old you are to drink anymore?"

Darion couldn't help but grin. *Smart kid.* "Yes."

"And that's what all the Darklight is about too?" asked Jack. "That's what causes it? The fear?"

Darion waited. He expected the Shepherd to answer, but the giant was walking with a purpose on the path ahead.

"Not necessarily," said Darion. "Darklight clouds show up in places where fear has been. Or even where fear *will* be. It all depends on the person, really. And what is happening within that person too. Or so they say it's that way."

"Who is *they*?" asked Jack.

"Anyone who experiences it."

Jack nodded, piecing together this new information. It surprised Darion. He didn't expect Jack to be a thinker, the inquiring type. Even so, Darion liked how Jack asked *him* these questions and not the Shepherd. It gave Darion a small bit of power over Jack, he felt. A position Darion hoped to maintain as long as he was able. Keep the balance of power tipped in his favor.

The group came out of the forest and into a large clearing. Darion noticed that he hadn't been paying attention to where the Shepherd had been leading them. He anticipated a break, but the Shepherd only surveyed the clearing like a human lighthouse before walking headlong into the high grass. There were young flowers scattered about, but it was clear the weeds were overpowering them in number. Dandelions were everywhere. And when the wind blew, seeds sprung up like it was snowing. Jack hacked inside of the tiny storm.

"God, I hate this crap," said Jack.

Darion ignored Jack, at first, but then Jack hacked even harder and Darion looked him over.

"You all right?"

"Yeah. I do this all the time when I see this stuff. Long as I can remember, I do."

"Sounds like an allergy, but it could be something else too," said Darion.

Jack wiped his mouth of any excess spit. "I've had this cough a long time," said Jack. "Doesn't seem to ever want to go away. The change in seasons don't make it any better either. You're a doctor, right? What do you think it is?"

"I'd say it's a really bad cough," said Darion, but he wondered if Jack had an affliction, maybe asthma or some something worse. He could never know for sure. That would require more of his time and perhaps a stop altogether. But, again, they might be close to the Shepherd's ship. Darion quickly changed the subject.

"So were you born in the old city of Pittsburgh?" asked Darion.

"Yeah, far as I know anyway," answered Jack, still recovering. "And that's all I know."

"Why's that?"

"Cuz it just is, chief," said Jack, annoyed by the question. "One of the first things I remember is fighting another kid – twice my size – for some food in a street. Man, I think he knocked about half my brains out, too so if there was anythin' else to remember, I don't."

"You were an orphan?"

"Yeah."

Darion paused.

"How were you educated?" asked Darion.

"What?"

"How'd you get educated then if you didn't have any parents? You speak well enough and you seem to know quite a bit."

Jack felt, looked offended and Darion regretted having worded his question that way. He looked away from Jack.

"Well," said Jack and Darion turned, surprised. "You just learn while you're out there, I guess. You go and take something that's not yours and if someone stops you from taking it, you either leave it alone or you just try to be faster next time. You get better. You have to get better or you just don't make it. That's how it is."

"I'm sorry to hear that," said Darion. Then he searched for something that might relate. "That's not always how it is though, is it?"

"Heh, what other way is there, chief?"

Darion hesitated. They were getting to the end of the clearing. Then he said, "For starters, there used to be organized schools back before the Pulse. They'd house anywhere from 100 – 1,000 kids. People were trained to educate and teach children about what was right and what was wrong, but mostly it was about teaching them history, the world, and how to problem solve. So when they got older, they'd know about the world before they had to learn it the hard way. You would have been in one of those schools. Does that make sense?"

Jack seemed to be imagining Darion's picture of the old world.

"You make it sound like I was robbed of something," said Jack. "Schools were made to avoid the life I've had. Is that what you're telling me?"

"That's not entirely - "

"It makes sense, chief," said Jack. "I've had it hard. I know that. But, if I'm honest with ya, that whole thing sounds terrible. I mean – you've seen the kids in the city, right? You mean to tell me, they'd put all of them together? In the same building? How'd that work for everybody?"

Darion raised an eyebrow. A valid enough point, considering Jack's lack of knowing any better.

"I suppose it went well enough? I'm not sure, really," said Darion. "But my parents said it worked. I grew up in communities that were fashioned after the schools but they weren't completely the same. People were always fighting about the best ways to do it though. And there were hundreds, thousands of schools everywhere before the days of the community teachings. And they all operated independently of one another but still had the same basic rules and principles and – "

"Yeah, I know," said Jack. "I lived through that part, remember? Lucky me."

Jack paused.

"People are always fighting over the best way to do somethin'," argued Jack. "Then, just when things are working, something will happen and the whole system breaks down. That's nothing new to me, chief. Before the Pulse or after I guess, judging from what you've told me."

"It wasn't that the system 'broke down.' It just couldn't go on that way. Not if things could be better."

"How?"

Jack's tone had gotten slightly hostile.

"Because if something wasn't working," said Darion. "Then people needed to fix the problem. Even if the problem was affecting just one person, it still meant it could be a problem for others, later."

Jack spit. "So the whole system - this whole method of teaching kids in schools - that was learning how to work as it went along too, eh?"

"Well, if you look at it from that perspective, then yes. I'd say you are correct."

"Thought so."

Darion smirked. Jack must love and hate to hear how things used to be. *He'll look for gaps before he'll look for bridges*, Darion figured. *If Jack were to hear something was* better *in the old world - before the Pulse - then he'd be angry with it. No one wants to hear things are better before his time. It makes one long for the past and gives no room to enjoy the present. Or look to the future with eyes wide and arms open.*

"And who says that the new way is the best way?" said Jack. "Or that one person should set the standard for so many other people?"

Smart kid, Darion thought. He hadn't realized it, but Darion was becoming fond of Jack. *He thinks as I do. He sees the world with a gray veil. Clouded it may be, we are alike in this way.*

Wait, thought Darion. *What am I saying?*

"The system worked for what it was meant for, Jack," said Darion. "And without a standard, there'd be disorder."

"But if the standard is always changing - "

"It's not changing, it's just refining itself. There's a difference."

"Yeah, if you say so."

There was a silence. Their feet trampled over many dry rocks and several yards of cracked dirt before someone uttered another word.

"You know," said Jack. "I guess it's just hard to sit and contemplate the world when you're always hungry, chief. That's what I learned. Eat first. Decide whether it's right or wrong, later. I don't think anyone before the Pulse understood that. They had the time to sit and think about these things. But, in a way, it makes me think I know more about the world than any of them ever did."

Darion was caught off guard yet again. Maybe you're right, Jack? Maybe you're on to something there.

They walked a bit farther, the Shepherd maintaining his cool silence as Darion and Jack volleyed with more conversation.

"It is what it is though, right?" said Jack. "I've gotten along. I've taken what I've had to, but I've survived."

"How so?"

Jack paused like Darion were asking too personal a question. Darion didn't know if Jack were upset or surprised to still be talking. He looked at Darion, probing his eyes to see if the inquiry were genuine.

"It's a long story, chief," said Jack, finally.

"So start at the beginning."

Through his eyes, Darion saw Jack drifting into his thoughts, remembering days of his youth. But, those memories were foggy and lacking time stamps. Jack would find it difficult to remember specific details. He saw faces; people who would probably not recognize him now while others he preferred not to identify with. And there was hunger in most, if not all of these memories. Some kind of hunger seemed to accompany him with every smell and image he pulled at. He shook his head, brushing aside his reflections and rubbing his face. The Shepherd looked over his shoulder and Jack paused like he'd said something aloud by accident.

"What?" asked Jack.

"Your school systems," said the Shepherd. "I've read a lot about them."

"What about them exactly?" asked Darion.

"It's always been a curious area for me, I suppose," said the Shepherd. "How does a child learn best if not from his mother and father?"

"Is that how you learned on Mars?" asked Darion.

"Do you even have parents, chief?" asked Jack. "I mean, a mom and a dad?"

The Shepherd grinned. "Yes, I have both. I wasn't made in a lab or cooked up in a stew like so many people here on Earth believe, or have persisted with believing but have no proof of. I was made in the only way people are made: through the union of a man and a woman."

"Heh," said Jack. "You can certainly make something sound romantic, chief. I still find that difficult to believe though."

"Why?"

Jack chuckled. "You're not like any person I've ever seen. Or been around."

Jack looked at Olivia, then back at the Shepherd.

"And best be careful," said Jack. "Some of us here may not be completely aware of the 'union' you're talking about."

The Shepherd chuckled, as did Olivia. "My daughter knows what he's talking about," defended Darion.

Jack shrugged. "Hey, was just sayin' is all," said Jack. "At her age, I'll bet she knows more than you think."

Olivia peered at Jack, agreeing with him in silent. She knew much of her knowledge was hidden from her father. But it was more opinion than fact – things she wouldn't share, if ever, with Darion. She didn't feel it necessary to do so unless the situation called for it. And it rarely ever did.

"I've told her as much as she needs to know, Jack," said Darion.

"What does she need to know exactly?" asked the Shepherd.

"I'm her father," stated Darion, like the words held weight. "And that means you need to filter out what isn't necessary for your child. You have to protect them, as best you can. That's what a father does. That's what a mother would do too."

Jack didn't answer.

"And the schools did this also?" asked the Shepherd.

"Yes," answered Darion. "I wasn't old enough to know, really. You'd have to talk to somebody older than me for that answer, Shepherd. I can only tell you what was spoken to me. But I know the teaching communities were similar."

"I see," said the Shepherd.

The group walked in silence. The discussion felt open, but no one seemed eager to continue it. Then, the Shepherd stopped abruptly, turned and spoke:

"Where the child lies his head at night," said the Shepherd. "Is where he finds the most influence. On Mars, we have educators, teachers, and mentors, but we are encouraged to go to them when we have questions, not as a prerequisite. The responsibility – the filtering– lies with the mother and with the father. They are the ones who must teach the child what is most important. They are the filters, a filter that must be modeled by them both. There is no other that this responsibility may fall upon. The family is *everything* on Mars. Without it, our children could never become what they were meant for."

"Just what are they meant for?" asked Darion. Captains of a star fleet? Miners of Solfire? Xenobiologists, perhaps? Darion's mind fluttered, conjuring every possible foreign or alien vocation he could think of. But, when the Shepherd gazed back at him, the answer was less than underwhelming.

"What they are meant for," said the Shepherd. "Is to one day become mothers and fathers themselves. What else is worth more than that? When the future is coming and cannot be stopped?"

Neither Darion nor Jack knew what to say. It appeared to be more than a belief, but a truth the Shepherd was speaking to. The Shepherd stood firm, looking them over a while - waiting for an answer. Then he spoke again, but this time, with sadness in his voice, "I am sorry that you've had to endure such hardship not knowing these joys. I envy your courage."

The Shepherd turned back around and led the trio out of the forest. There was nothing more to say, it seemed.

Chapter 8
Man, Mars, and Machines

"I have asked you this before: what makes an honest person? Is it what he does? Or is it based on what he thinks?"

"The only thing that matters is if his thoughts become action. And a dishonest mind can only live inside an honest body for so long."

"Yes. This is true."

"Is that why our machines are incapable of making that distinction? Is that why we don't allow them to be intuitive like us? That they must always be honest?"

"Do not think it is intuition that we deny them. It's *free will* — the single most dangerous thing we possess."

* * * *

Darion's profession, even post-Pulse, was a position of reverence and influence. It's why he chose it. He'd never been particularly fond of people, though the job often called for a special tolerance of those who thought themselves the harbingers of every foul illness or debilitation under the sun. But, Darion was willing to put up with that. Because the common person was incapable of being a doctor and Darion refused to be common.

To many, it was messy business. Something a person with a weak stomach might avoid at any cost. Yet, it wasn't Darion's ability to disassociate the human body from the person that made him *good*. It was his ability to diagnose the issue at hand — to analyze the situation for what it was and ascertain the best means for action.

Before the Pulse, Darion understood doctors to be respected but he also knew them to be ridiculed. Medicine and technology sometimes mixed dangerously, which is why the Pulse changed the scope of everything as it pertained to the doctoral vocation. Nowadays, the term 'witch doctor' was more ordinary. Young shamans performing 'miracles' on the street, becoming local heroes in the process was more the norm. This circumstance, when observed, made Darion *sick*. To know that ignorance was prevailing brought about a special kind of fury inside of Darion. How can anyone be respected – rather, how can anyone trust the right authority – when there are so many claiming to *be* that authority?

The gap in technology is what caused it to be this way. Darion knew that. And hated it all the same. Which is why Darion decided to ask the Shepherd something his analytical nature longed to have an answer on:

"Do you believe in miracles, Shepherd?" asked Darion.

The Shepherd paused, turned round to face Darion.

"Miracles?"

"Yes, do you believe in them?"

"By definition alone," said the Shepherd. "Miracles are merely unexplainable phenomena. An event that defies the normal laws of nature."

"Do you always avoid the questions you're asked?"

"I'm still answering it," said the Shepherd and Jack shuddered like thunder had boomed over their heads. The Shepherd continued:

"But, the problem with that definition is that we cannot describe what is indescribable. We cannot know what we don't know. So, being that humans don't know all things of the universe, a miracle could merely be the difference between ignorance and knowledge. A lack of possessing all the necessary variables to comprehend the reason for the result. For if you had all the variables, then you could come to a conclusion eventually. Isn't that right?"

"I'm a doctor," said Darion. "Having all the variables is usually something I *don't* have. It's why I have to ask the right questions. I have to learn what I haven't learned so I can fix the problem. Sometimes you don't have everything you need, you just have to make due."

"Or maybe you *do* have all that you need?" said the Shepherd. "Maybe your intuition does you better than you know? And by strengthening that muscle of intuition, you can become better at seeing the variables without actually knowing they're there."

"You're just talking about intuition now," said Darion. "Not whether you do or don't believe in miracles."

"Or maybe, what I'm referring to, is a skill all humans have so they won't *need* every variable."

"That's not intuition then. That's *faith* – to be confident in the unseen. Are you trying to say that faith is a barrier to knowing the true nature of a miracle?"

Darion took a quick peek at Jack, whose eyes faced the ground. *Feeling left out, are we? Sorry, this is a big boy conversation, Jack.*

"I don't see it as a barrier," said the Shepherd. "I would rather see faith as a door to greater understanding. Life, as you know, is a miracle. Life stands as a testament to that. And since I am standing here with you, opening my mouth and communicating openly, then I would say that I too, believe in miracles. Because I cannot give you every last detail as to how that is possible without eventually giving in to a limited explanation. Though the mechanics can be explained, the very reasons why and where they are going, cannot. Does that answer your question, Dr. Wallace?"

"I suppose it does," answered Darion. "I just thought that miracles might not be as impressive where you come from. I can only imagine the kind of technology you have on Mars by now. I mean, by this time, it must be even further along, right? The stuff we use on Earth must look like the work of savages, am I right?"

The Shepherd grinned. "More questions from you. I like this."

Of course you do, thought Darion. It gives you the opportunity to assert yourself. But, in truth, it makes me look better in front of Jack. Lets him know how much I know and how much he doesn't.

"I'll answer your first question," said the Shepherd. "And then I'll answer the second."

The Shepherd paused, took a breath.

"Naturally," said the Shepherd. "I am familiar with the machines and their history on Earth. My ancestry is here, you remember? We are the same in this way. I have also spent many years in study, attempting to better understand man's relationship with the machine and the machine with the man. And the light that was birthed when man and machine became entwined across the divide."

Man's relationship with the machine? Darion thought. He looked at Jack, whose face was a mixture of intimidation and confusion. If my head's spinning, then that boy's must be upside down.

"However," said the Shepherd. "Mars' history is different than Earth's history. Man and machine are practically as one on Mars, but never equal. Man must always be superior. That's the only way the machines can function perfectly."

"What does that even mean?" asked Darion. "To 'function perfectly'?"

"Too many on Earth were controlled by their creations," said the Shepherd. "It was not the other way around. Like, a mother who bends to her child's every whim in adolescence, then wonders why he will not leave her as an adult – the machine's makers were like this. They gave authority to lesser things. Humanity became a slave to the child it made. It's what made many machines into monsters. And thus, the light doesn't come about any longer."

Darion shook his head, not following the Shepherd this time. That frustrated him so he tried hard not to let Jack see his confusion. Olivia, conversely, did not try to comprehend while Jack – not knowing the better - took the Shepherd's words as truth. But, Darion kept analyzing the Shepherd's observation, comparing it to his own experience and measuring its weight and accuracy. Had the people of Earth been careless with their technology? Had they been reckless? Darion felt a subtle rage swelling, begging that he defend the Earth if he could. Was the Shepherd attempting to pass the blame on Earth for its predicament? If anything, this was all Mars' fault. It was the red planet that threw the first stone. Darion wouldn't stand for that sort of accusation and Olivia sensed her father's anger, squeezed his hand tight.

"I don't even know about half this stuff, chief," said Jack.

Of course you wouldn't, Darion thought. The Shepherd could tell you floating toilets were important on Mars and you'd believe it.

"Just because you don't know much of it now," said the Shepherd. "Doesn't mean you should *never* know."

"If I do, then *that* will be a miracle."

Jack chuckled, as did Olivia. But, Darion was sullen.

It's easy to make these kinds of statements when you're not the one living through them, Darion thought. Jack then nodded like he appreciated the Shepherd's words. Go on then. Keep playing dumb, Jack. I'm sure it'll earn you bonus points with the Shepherd.

"As for your second question," said the Shepherd, as though everyone had forgotten but him. "We have made several more advancements on Mars since our nation's inception. This is due in part, to the discovery of Solfire. And its sister, Darklight, here on Earth. There is much to learn from both parties, we've found."

"I'm sure you've learned plenty about Darklight from your time on Earth now," said Darion. "Not so fun, is it?"

"It's stronger than we originally calculated," said the Shepherd. "The effects have been more than regrettable."

Darion huffed. Your 'gift' has given us plenty of surprises, Shepherd. Too many to count.

* * * *

Jack heard the words, 'Solfire' and 'Darklight' and more questions were birthed. They were like new languages in his head, floating phrases impossible to comprehend outright. He wanted to ask more, but he was unsure as to how he might do so without sounding like a fool. As for Darion, he wondered what the Shepherd meant when he said 'what else it has affected.' The words seemed to be directed at people, places, even events. The Shepherd had been on Earth less than a day, yet was already claiming to have a greater understanding of Earth than the two of them. Jack felt Darion's anger on this matter and shied away at every mention. It was a not a fight Jack wanted any part in.

The group came to the end of the woods and the Shepherd held up a hand. He took a few steps into the next field and scanned about.

Ahead of them was an open plot of land, filled with half-grown stumps and ground littered with gray and white ash. The deadened colors and burnt foliage stretched for several acres, partially unseen because of the hill they had crossed over. There was an animal, a dead carcass, lying prostrate against one of the logs several yards away from them. Its body was split open and strange wounds had festered by the openings.

"Well…" said Jack. "Might be a good time to sprinkle some more of that water if ya got it – eh, chief?"

"Was it a fire?" asked Darion.

"Probably," answered Jack. "Maybe a few days old, too."

"You an authority on fires too?"

Jack didn't answer.

"This fire was made to clear land for something," said the Shepherd.

"Who did it then?" asked Darion.

"Someone hoping to make way for something," said the Shepherd. Then, with a serious tone, "Be careful. We shouldn't waste too much time here."

Darion hoisted Olivia up into his arms and the group walked across the ash-covered landscape. Jack ogled the carcass until they were nearly upon it and stopped to see it up close.

"It's just a dead animal, Jack," said Darion. "I'm sure you've seen one before."

"," said Jack. "Not this close though..."

Jack thought he heard something like a low hiss and backed away. With all this death around, did that mean someone was trying to call that monster out? Is that what the Shepherd meant?

"We are almost through," said the Shepherd. "Over this hill side and we'll be closing in on the highest point for us to make camp for the night. I think you've all traveled enough for today."

"But, we aren't that tired," said Darion. "Why would we need to take a break?"

"The water I gave you may grant you endurance and give you strength," said the Shepherd. "But your body will still need food by the time the evening arrives. That's where we'll make camp and I'll hunt for you."

"We still got plenty of mushrooms though," said Jack. "Remember?"

"We'll need to save those," said the Shepherd. "We won't eat those unless absolutely necessary."

"Sure," said Jack and Darion and Olivia nodded.

They followed the Shepherd out of the burnt woods, down a small slope and up a hillside. It was rocky and jagged, with large boulders protruding from its base like spears to thwart an oncoming enemy. The Shepherd motioned to make the climb and the trio did as he said. And just as the Shepherd had predicted, the three of them found themselves growing hungrier near the top.

"Alright, ya got me," said Jack. "I'm hungry now. What are we gonna eat?"

"I'll hunt once we find a good spot to settle," said the Shepherd.

"Are you sure this is safe?" asked Darion. "Why do we have to go up the mountain side? My daughter – "

"Will be fine," said the Shepherd. "I won't let anything happen to you. Or her. We just can't stay on the ground. We need to go up."

Darion mumbled under his breath, but kept moving. The trio worked to get their footing while the Shepherd moved like a mountain ram on its home turf. He waited for the group to achieve a new level on the mountain trail then he'd leap to the next outcropping, pointing out the spots that had the best footing. Jack was glad to have the guidance – he hated the heights, but the Shepherd's reassurance eased any and all of his previous apprehensions.

But, Darion seemed annoyed. Jack took note of how Darion might ignore one of the Shepherd's suggestions, lifting Olivia over an area where the Shepherd told him to land or place his foot.

"The terrain is going to get harder," said the Shepherd. "Listen to what I say to you. And you will not fall."

"My daughter and I have traveled mountains like these before, Shepherd," said Darion. He lifted Olivia onto a rock, struggled, but eventually pulled himself up as well. "I happen to know my own land. We may not have planes that can fly, but we do have feet that can carry us just fine."

Jack observed Darion's method for climbing, but didn't follow it. The Shepherd didn't appear to be upset with Darion's defiance, but he wouldn't stop telling Darion where to step either. Between the two, it was hard for Jack to tell who was more stubborn.

When they arrived at a large shelf of rock, big enough for several people, the Shepherd instructed that they stop altogether. It felt like they were seated on a platform; one that was overlooking the valley and Jack and Darion could see for miles from where they were. Darion set his pack down towards the back of the flat rock, telling Olivia where they'd be lying for the night as he gave instruction on how and where to sleep. Jack moved within a few feet of where they were and sat down.

"What are you doing?" asked Darion.

"I'm just taking a seat here."

"You're not going to sleep there, are you?"

"Uh, I don't know. I was thinkin' I might, but – "

"I'd prefer it if you were farther over there, okay? I don't want you sleeping near me or my daughter."

"What? I'm not – "

"Look, just do it, alright? Or do you want me to hurt your other shoulder?"

Jack hesitated like Darion were joking, but Darion's eyes were fiercely serious. So Jack stood and walked to the other side of the platform. He didn't want to sit so close to the edge, but it didn't seem like he had a choice. With nothing to unpack, Jack took a seat and put his hands atop his knees. The Shepherd walked to the edge and looked out across the valley. Then he stood on the balls of his feet, like a jumper prepared to dive among the green tops of the trees below and held himself still like a statue.

"Yo, that's not safe, chief," said Jack. "I've seen you jump, but that's a long way down too."

"There are deer coming our way," said the Shepherd and he pointed to his left. "Look there."

Jack, Darion, and Olivia followed the long arm of the Shepherd and saw a herd of deer coming upon the burnt field. There were so many, traveling like a herd of buffalo and Jack and Darion stepped as far to the edge as they could.

"Wow…" said Darion. "Liv, come see these."

The herd was moving as one but when they got to the edge of the burnt woods, they slowed and splintered into separate groups, proceeding cautiously. Jack started to count them. Thirty, forty, his number stopped at 43 as he watched the herd.

"There's a little one there," said the Shepherd and he pointed to the single fawn trailing. The Shepherd squinted and said, "Its heart rate is heightened… I think it's afraid."

You can tell that from where up here? Jack thought.

A thin haze had come over the field below, but it was not like the storms of Darklight Jack might have known. It was like transparent paper, touching his face like a thin sheet stretched across the horizon. Jack raised a hand like he was going to touch it and shook his head, reminded of how those who have been touched by Solfire take time to get accustomed to their newest senses. The fawn, meanwhile, hung by the edge of the forest, sniffing curiously and slowly losing more ground with the other deer. Then it found the carcass and walked closer, lingering by the lifeless body. It flicked its tail and raised its head up and down, motioning to the dead deer like it might spring to life at any second.

"So, ya think that dead deer is its mother?" asked Jack.

"Do you think it is?" asked Darion.

"I don't know, man," said Jack. "Could be, right? It's obviously alone. And it's pretty interested in that dead one there."

Darion wrinkled his mouth. "I suppose the chances aren't great, but it could be. Why do you care if it is or not?"

Jack felt the cold in Darion's voice and realized Darion had failed to make the connection. "Because he's *alone*. He's alone and he's afraid. I know what that feels like. Know what it looks like too."

Darion stayed there with Jack a moment and then turned, headed back for the safety of the back corner of the platform. Jack faced the Shepherd.

"Do you have deer on Mars?"

The Shepherd grinned. "Yes. And many other creatures as well."

"Wow. Anything other than what's here?"

"All that you see on Earth is on Mars now."

"So why all the interest then? The way you're acting – it's like you've never seen anything like'em before?"

The Shepherd gazed upon the horizon like he needed time to give Jack a suitable answer. The sun had moved itself in the time they'd been climbing; it was getting close to sunset. Close to the time when they'd have to rest.

"The first houses and lands held many beasts," said the Shepherd. "Deer, hawks, wolves, bears – most every creature that exists here, now exists there. That was the goal of Mars when it began. Large domes filled with fertile land were the precursors for a more balanced planet. But, the gravity wasn't set yet. And it took many years for the first inhabitants of Mars to get everything right. And so, for a time, we kept animals in separate holding areas, preparing them for the new fields we were making. Because as you know, a bear cannot sit with a tiger no more than a deer can sit calmly with a bull. Territory and predation were problems, naturally. But, after those several years – after we discovered Solfire – everything changed. The pens could be reopened and animals could mix with one another without the fear of one feeding on another. With Solfire, the beasts were no longer beasts at all. They became companions to many on Mars and the pens ceased to exist in certain places. Still, we must be careful. As the lion still feeds on the deer; the tiger on the bull. These things simply cannot change. Not in this lifetime, they cannot."

Darion looked up, gazing at the Shepherd curiously. "So animals can feed on Solfire too?"

The Shepherd didn't have a chance to answer.

"So, does that make them immortal or something?" asked Jack. Then he hated himself for asking the question. He probably sounded absurd. Or stupid.

"No. We don't know the tragedy of living forever on Mars."

"Tragedy?"

The Shepherd nodded. "We only experiment with the thrill of living finitely, for however long that might be."

Jack shook his head like it was too much information. "Well, alright then, big guy. That's enough for me tonight."

"It's all right, Jack," said the Shepherd. "Let me explain it to you this way: you see that fawn, there?" The Shepherd pointed. "It's afraid. I can feel its fear even up here. Its loneliness may be temporary, but no one knows that. Not you, not me and especially not the little fawn who is experiencing that emotion right now. It saddens me, knowing this is what that animal is going through. And it also makes me long for the companionship of my friend, Bandalon. I miss him dearly. For I know I don't have eternity to spend time with Bandalon. All things pass and are gone before we often get the chance to truly soak them into ourselves and never forget them. Both sadness and joy can have this affect on us."

"*Bandalon?*" said Jack, incredulously, and ignoring the Shepherd's moment of teaching. "What is that?"

"Not what – but who," said the Shepherd. "He is a lion on Mars. I miss him."

"You have a pet lion?"

"No, Bandalon is my friend. There is a difference."

"How is there not a difference? It's a lion, chief."

"Bandalon is not dependent on me for survival. He is not like a dog or a cat or a parrot like you have on Earth. We learn new things from one another, he teaches me about himself and I teach him about me. That is how and why I consider him a 'friend', Jack."

Jack didn't bother asking any more questions. He pondered the notion of having a pet lion and laughed. "Mars keeps sounding more and more strange to me. Pet lions; big domes full of animals; weird stuff called 'Solfire' – sounds crazy. Would be weird to live there. Forget having or not having machines like we used to here on Earth. I don't know how I feel about any of this other stuff you keep telling me about."

The Shepherd smiled, this time with teeth. "It may be weird to you, but it's good. I must hunt for you three now. Stay here. I will return shortly."

A gale of cold air swept across the group like the onslaught of rain was on approach, but Jack's head perked up like the Adversary were coming instead.

"It's not *him*," said the Shepherd, calming their anxieties. "Do not worry yourself with that, but the temperature will drop tonight. Did you want to warm yourself?"

"You want us to make a fire?" asked Jack.

"I don't think that will be necessary," said the Shepherd.

"Why?"

"Because of the discs I have. They'll take care of that."

The Shepherd smiled once more, a big grin of enthusiasm and calm that made Jack relaxed again. Then the Shepherd jumped from the stone's edge, flying with arms outstretched down the mountain's side, bouncing from rock to rock like they were made of foam, not Earth and stone.

"You know," said Jack. "He tells us to keep quiet, but I'm pretty sure anybody can hear that noise from a mile away."

"You'd be surprised what the Shepherd can choose to conceal from others," said Darion.

And you would know this how, old man? Jack thought, resisting the urge to ask the question aloud. It wasn't the right time to barrel in with more inquiries though. So he walked to his side of the plateau and sat down, waiting for the Shepherd to return.

* * * *

When the Shepherd returned, he had berries and fruit cupped in his arms, and this time, he had fish too. Jack was amazed. Had the Shepherd gone and made a garden out of that water? The Shepherd didn't bother to explain. He detached a disc from his thigh and placed it in the middle of the stone cliff. It whizzed like a top and when the Shepherd placed the first fish over the disc, the slimy body levitated within a glowing yellow light. Then it started to crackle and sizzle. The fish was *cooking.*

"You smell that?" said Jack. "That thing is actually cookin'. My God, that thing is really cookin'."

Darion and Olivia moved in closer. Olivia inhaled and smiled. It did smell good. Like how her father used to make when he made the time. But, the meals were never made like this, of course.

"I had no idea it could do this," said Darion, speaking as though he could read Olivia's mind. He examined the floating fish with great interest. The Shepherd grinned.

"Did the discs 'choose to conceal' that from ya?" asked Jack.

"This is unbelievable technology, Jack," said Darion. "I'm sure there's plenty I didn't know."

"I'm sure..."

The Shepherd then set to placing the other discs in a triangular perimeter about the cliff. Darion recognized the arrangement and silently applauded himself for understanding the nature of the 'invisible tent' – an ability of the discs he'd discovered early on during his ownership. When the Shepherd was done, the three discs fired with interlocking blue lights, each compounding atop one another until there was a solid pane of blue atop them. Then the blue coloration disappeared and the night sky could be seen again.

"What the..." said Jack. He raised his hand to the clouds–new warmth was filling the space they were in. It started near the edge and made its way in, then up. "Heat?" asked Jack. "How in the – "

"I think it's ready, Liv," said Darion and he removed the fish from the levitator. He took out some utensils from his knapsack and cut the fish into several slices. The three of them feasted in silence as the Shepherd maintained his vigil on the cliff's edge. And when they were filled, Darion went to his corner with Olivia and Jack to his. There was no talking for this too.

From his corner, Jack observed how the Shepherd had not moved in all the time they'd taken to eat. He shook his head as though he were still in shock.

"Tell me I'm not dreaming..." said Jack and he stared up at the sky. He thought of other nights where he'd fallen asleep with nothing to cover him and no warmth to hold him. This night was foreign to him on more than a few levels.

"It's not a dream," said Darion. "This is really happening."

Jack smirked. "Thanks. That's real helpful."

"Isn't that what you wanted to hear?"

Jack spit. "I guess I didn't think you'd answer me."

The two men stared down each other while secretly Olivia reveled in the tension. Father hardly ever talked to people. This was good that he'd chosen to speak without restraint. Jack looked back to the Shepherd.

Jack coughed softly and Darin's eyebrow couldn't help but rise up, curiously.

"Don't worry," said Jack. "I ain't gonna die. Not yet anyway."

That's what you think, Darion thought. And for a second, Darion thought something terrible – he imagined killing Jack. He imagined grabbing one of these rocks and smashing Jack's head under it. That would be rid of him. That would leave only Darion, Olivia, and the Shepherd. But, then Darion blinked, looked to the Shepherd, who turned his head like he'd been watching Darion during that dark moment.

Reading my thoughts? Darion thought. God, I can only hope not. That was unexpected. Where had that terrible thought come from anyway? And why had it come on so fast?

"Why not take a rest for a while?" asked Jack and Darion almost jumped. The question was for the Shepherd, however.

"It's been a long day for you, hasn't it? Or do you not get tired like us normal human beings?"

"My legs are conditioned to endure gravity that's much stronger than this, Jack," said the Shepherd. "I won't sit unless I am tired and I am not tired enough to sit just yet."

"Well, you're making the rest of us feel pathetic over here."

"Don't misunderstand me," said the Shepherd. "I do not mean to make you feel incapable or inadequate. My capabilities are a product of what I've chosen to endure. The same applies to you."

Jack smacked his lips and scratched his forehead. "Again, you're not helping me here, chief. Are you sure you're not part machine or something like that?"

"I am not," said the Shepherd, his tone revealing himself to be offended. "I am human, like you, but I am also not like you. I was born on Mars. You were born on Earth. That is all."

"That's as much a difference as any, I'd say," said Jack. "How'd you get so tall anyway?"

"How is it that you ask so many questions, Jack?" asked Darion, interrupting the conversation.

Jack held out both hands like he'd been accused of thievery and stared down Darion. "Well, what do you want me to do, man? Sit here in silence? Not sayin' a damn word to nobody?"

"Yes, actually."

Jack huffed. "Why?"

"Because I like silence."

Olivia hated it.

"Well I don't," said Jack. "So you're just gonna have to deal with me. Alright?"

Darion arched his back and inhaled like he was about to argue. He looked at the Shepherd like there might be an intervention, but to his surprise, the Shepherd was still. *Very well then,* he thought and started to rise, but Olivia put her hand on her father's shoulder and Darion ceased. He took another deep breath and looked at Jack. Not worth it. It's not worth it. Remember the goal, Darion. Remember why you're here. Remember what you can control.

"Alright then," said Darion. "I'm sorry if you feel like I'm not talking to you enough."

Jack crossed his legs and peered at Darion.

"Look, chief — you're never alone," explained Jack and he nodded to Olivia. "You might like stillness and silence but that's because you got *her.* Probably makes you feel safe too, don't it? Knowing you have somebody with you all the time. Well, good for you, man. Me? I hate it. That's all I ever get is silence and I don't wanna deal with it tonight, alright? Not anymore. And I know you don't give a damn about that because that's not your problem, is it? And it probably never has been. But seeing as how we're stuck here together, I'm gonna ask you - just this one time, chief– to please, *please* put up with my needs for a night."

Both men were quiet. Jack was fuming, but it was controlled, directed, and most of all, *real.* Darion felt a sliver of fear creep inside his being, pointing Darion back to the realization that this man was dangerous. He'd tried to kill me. Earlier today, he'd tried to hurt me. Darion remembered it, but felt like he'd forgotten it somehow. Or rather, their circumstance had not permitted him to remember. A scared kid with too many issues to count. That's all you are, aren't you? But, that didn't matter as much as the fact that Darion needed to keep the peace. Keeping the peace would keep him safe. Keep Olivia safe, most of all.

"Okay. What do you want to talk about then, Jack?" asked Darion.

Jack sat back, debating. Then, "Hey, Shepherd, how did you get so tall?"

"My mother and father were tall."

Jack chuckled. "Well, isn't that the best damn response I ever heard."

Darion didn't laugh, though some part of him wanted to. There was a long silence after that, but Darion kept his eyes on Jack, who was fidgeting and twitching like a nervous child.

Nothing else to say, eh? All that penned up emotion means nothing even now that you got what you wanted. Just a child with a temper. That's what I thought.

Olivia laid her head upon her father and closed her eyes. It reminded Darion of how long the day had been.

"Ya know," said Jack. "There was something I wanted to ask you."

"Yeah?"

"What do you think about?" asked Jack. "To keep the Adversary from finding you? Is there anything you can do? The way I've been told, the monsters only come around because we can't make the light anymore. But what else can we do? What did you do?"

Darion stroked Olivia's hair and smiled. Then he looked at Jack, who was eagerly waiting on an answer.

"I think of something beautiful," said Darion. "Something to keep the monsters out of my head. That's all anyone can do, Jack. We may not have the same tools we once did, but we do have each other. I guess you were right about that."

"About what?"

"Not liking the silence. Not wanting to be alone. That's something no person wants, I'd imagine."

Jack chuckled. "Well, thanks."

"You're welcome."

Then Darion and Jack exchanged light conversation again. They talked about the old city, the merchants, and the several places Darion and Olivia liked to go. Jack recognized most, if not all, but couldn't appeal to the descriptions of the people. The common ground they'd had was not as easily tread, but at least the silence was gone. And each of their stomachs was full. As for the

Shepherd, his peaceful watch went on into the darkness of evening. The silver giant did not budge from his toed stance, his figure becoming a pillar of black within the half crescent of the setting sun. Darion watched him, as did Jack, each man wondering different things about the Shepherd and what he was meant for, if not for the sole purpose of befuddling normal human beings.

"Still feel like you're dreaming?" asked Darion.

"If it's a dream, I want a few answers before I wake up," said Jack and he looked up at the night sky.

"Like this, for instance," said Jack. "Can you believe that right now – right this very minute – there's people sitting on the surface of another world? Someone could be looking back at us and we'd never even know the difference. I don't know, man. I know it's true. I know it's happening right now. But, still, I can't really believe it."

Darion looked up at the sky. It was the same as it always was: a thin layer of clouds and a black with blue outer shell, painted with tiny white dots. There was nothing spectacular about it. He'd seen hundreds of thousands of night skies, and not once had he ever considered that another person was looking back at him. The people on Mars weren't 'normal' people, were they? The Shepherd was proof of some higher existence. No, only humans lived on Earth. The rest of the universe held other beasts, other marvels, it seemed. Earth was a place for people seeking an escape. Why would another face be looking upon theirs at all? Whoever they were, they'd see this place and ignore it. Because, as far as Darion believed, that other place was certainly better than here, whether it filled with Martians, machines or whatever existence had been favored more than humans. It was surely better than this place.

Eventually, Darion and Jack succumbed to fatigue, Darion drifting last. When they were all of them asleep, the Shepherd exhaled and took one more look upon the trio.

"This sun," he said, looking back upon the horizon. "One cannot see a sunset like this on Mars."

Then the Shepherd grinned; small tears covered his eyes until he blinked, and again, his eyes returned to normal.

Chapter 9
The Broken Signal

"My differences. They do not make me greater or lesser?"

"No, they do not. Your differences do not grant you an advantage nor do they give you a disadvantage. Yet, in the eyes of the ones you will meet, your differences will be seen as a threat. In which case, this will be your *disadvantage*."

* * * *

When Darion awoke the next morning, he panicked. His body was caked in sweat and his mouth was dry, but his temperature was cold, like he'd been submerged in ice water. He'd hardly noticed Olivia shaking his arm or how she was wiping his hair of the sweat that had beaded upon his brow. He clutched his chest, heaving in and out till he knew he was good and safe.

"Oh…God…" said Darion.

Olivia looked him over. What's wrong, she asked with her eyes. Did you have a nightmare again?

Thank God, he thought. Only a nightmare. But, this one was different. Not like any he'd had before. And far worse, at that.

Jack and the Shepherd were there – Jack, standing at attention on the other side of the stony plate; the Shepherd poised by the cliff, high upon his toes like the night before. The Shepherd locked eyes with Darion like he was reading Darion's thoughts and stepped away from the edge.

"A dream of warning?" asked the Shepherd, but it was more a statement than a question.

"What?" asked Darion.

"You've just had one. What was in it? What did you see?"

Jack looked at Darion suspiciously. "A bad dream, you mean?" said Darion. "That's all it was. People have those on Earth, you know."

"More like a nightmare, man," said Jack and he pointed to Darion's soaked undershirt.

"No one will force you to share it with us, Darion Wallace," said the Shepherd. "But I will tell you this – any encounter with purified water or fruit can and *will* affect you in ways your body is not accustomed to. You will be given insights you may have not seen before or presented with opportunities you may have not recognized either. And oftentimes, these are manifested while our conscious rests and the subconscious is awake. Do you understand what I have told you?"

"Yeah, chief," said Jack. "Do ya?"

Darion eyed Jack. "I've had similar dreams before, Shepherd," said Darion. "I've held the discs for close to six months so I know the dangers of having things like that near me."

"It is one thing to be near something and another to be immersed within it," said the Shepherd. "I know that you have imagined coming to Mars, but still, you have never been there so how can you claim to know all that there is to know about it?"

"Yeah," said Jack. "How can ya?"

The Shepherd glanced at Jack this time. "Sorry," said Jack and he bowed his head.

"And how did you sleep, Jack?" asked the Shepherd.

"Fine enough. My head hurts from lying on this stone all night but it sure beats the hell out of sleepin' on the streets. I wasn't expecting to be out here with any of you, but this was better than most nights, I suppose."

"Well, I'm glad to hear that then," said Darion and he stood up. Olivia tugged on Darion's coat again and Darion patted her head. "It's alright, sweetie. I'm awake now. No more bad dreams, okay?"

Olivia nodded, pressed her face into father's jacket.

"So what now?" asked Darion.

"The Adversary is on the move again," said the Shepherd. "He's going to be more active in his pursuit of us today. You'll all need to stay close to me."

"Where is it now?" asked Jack.

"It's...close," said the Shepherd, like it was calculating the distance in his head. "It's gone elsewhere for now. It's veered from our path and is searching in earnest for another target. It's very hungry though. So very hungry."

Jack stepped to the edge of the stone cliff and looked around like he expected to see the Adversary somewhere close by.

"Well, let's not sit around and wait for it, alright?" said Jack. "I'd prefer not to let it get our trail again."

The Shepherd nodded. "Yes," said the Shepherd and the discs that surrounded the trio clicked and flew to the Shepherd, reattaching themselves on his thighs and forearms. "Come, this way."

"Can we eat first?" asked Jack.

"You may eat on the way. There is still much leftover from yesterday." The trio ate the fruit they'd taken and to their surprise, nothing was spoiled. Nothing had gone to waste. When they were all full, they followed the Shepherd down the mountain's edge and into the woods. The Shepherd took them to an old roadway, staying just inside the cover of the trees to remain hidden. Darion kept Jack at a safe distance, shielding Olivia on his other side again.

"Hey," said Jack. "Were these roads full of cars in your day?"

"I remember them to be, yeah," said Darion.

"Do you think you'll ever see'em again?"

"I doubt that, really."

"Why?"

Darion sighed. More small talk, is it? That's fine. Talking to Jack would keep his mind off of the nightmare. And that hideous creature he'd seen.

"The Darklight makes that really hard, Jack," said Darion. "Any bit of light we try to create gets killed or swallowed up by the Darklight. Electrical outputs, man-made generators. A lot of things don't last long with Darklight around. Didn't you know that?"

Jack spit. "Yeah, man...I just wanted to know what you thought is all."

"Well, it doesn't really matter what I think or believe, really. At the end of any day, that's just how it is. No artificial light. No big power lines giving people energy. Nothing. We can't make it or else we can't see it. Either way, it doesn't work like it used to."

* * * *

Jack had never seen artificial light before, but he'd been told it existed. At one time, it had, anyway. He looked to the old road and tried to imagine teams of cars driving along it. He tried to picture a road without the weeds and high grass; a difficult task as he'd only ever seen Rovers and other diesel-powered vehicles traveling in mid-day for the transport of goods or people. Their engines pushed out smoke or other toxic fumes from old, or rather, what Jack had heard to be, 'outdated engines.'

He saw thick patches of grass cracking the pavement, nature planting itself by the edge; a visible sign the Earth was angry and was actively reclaiming territory against its human architects.

Light or no light, the fact that grass was growing in these places was proof of how much the Earth didn't *need* people, Jack figured. It simply accommodated them. If the Earth was a thinking creature, it would have made grass as sharp as knives and cut the heels of every person who tried to walk on its surface. It would have brought poisonous fumes to every corner of its forests to suffocate its human visitors. Or it would have heated its waters to boil any human who tried to drink or enjoy the coolness of a summer swim.

These were all strange and new thoughts to Jack, but they came quickly and without warning. This wasn't going to stop, was it? Ever since he'd met the Shepherd, touched those discs – pieces of him were changing. And Jack wondered if Darion had had the same experiences.

Maybe Darion felt the same sort of resentment for Earth's mistreatment? Maybe Darion thought the Earth needed to refuel, replenish itself and thus, would welcome the notion of a few people going to Mars so it could take the time to do those things?

Jack pondered until another thought came to him. One he realized he'd been wanting to ask Darion for some time.

"Hey, Dr. Darion," whispered Jack. "Do you think the Shepherd slept last night?"

Darion didn't answer. He stared ahead at the Shepherd, believing the Shepherd could hear every word they were saying.

"When I woke up, he was still standing there," continued Jack. "On the edge of that cliff. Standing there like it was nothing at all. I don't think he moved all night." Jack waited as if he was saying, 'what do you think of that?' But, Darion didn't care. However, he knew Jack would persist if he didn't at least say something.

"It doesn't matter if he did or if he didn't," said Darion, finally. "What he is –what he can do – it's not up to us to figure out."

"Why?"

"Because that's just how it is, Jack. Don't get lost in trying to figure everything out. Especially something like the Shepherd."

Jack eyed the silver giant, long legs carrying the Shepherd as if he were walking on clouds. Treating the Shepherd like a person seemed to be an impossible task. Yet, for once, Jack felt like a scientist: studying, examining – surveying the landscape. There was sure to be plenty of new things to know. He only needed to figure out how to get the answers he sought.

"You're not at all curious how he does what he does?" asked Jack, his voice dropping to a light murmur, barely audible to even Darion, who backed away slightly when Jack moved closer.

"Aren't you?"

* * * *

No, I'm not, Darion thought. And that's close enough, kid. Darion remembered he still had that pistol in his pocket and imagined having to use it if necessary. Then, his thoughts abruptly changed – but, why? The effects of the purified water, the vibrant fruit – these all felt like a life age ago. Everything had worn off in less than a day, it seemed. Everything except Jack's curious nature and persistent questions. The rest was history. Still, Darion wanted to keep things friendly. Keep Jack's attention on other things. So long as it was friendly and not intrusive, he could endure it.

"I'm just not as curious as you, Jack," said Darion. "That's not a bad thing."

"I've never seen anything like this guy before. Nothing comes to me. But, you? You don't seem to even care. I mean, come on, man. What else do you think he can do besides what we've seen already? Or have you, but you just won't tell me?"

There it was, Darion thought. Jack was still playing, wanting to dig deeper and figure out who he really was. Not today though. Darion turned to face Jack, shielding Olivia from him.

"Look," said Darion, his eyes serious and cold. "I understand how all of this might be impossible to believe, but if you really want answers, then why don't you just ask the Shepherd himself?"

Jack paused. He looked at Darion like he'd been betrayed. "Alright, chief. It's your world I live in, isn't it?"

"Yes, it is. And quit acting like I'm supposed to forget what happened yesterday. I don't forget so easily, Jack. That may be how you like to make friends, or maybe that's what you're used to, but I'm not. Most people aren't either. And nobody makes friends with somebody the day after they're held at gunpoint. You understand me?"

Jack raised his eyebrows. He seemed to be filtering through some terrible words for Darion, holding them back behind his teeth and pressing them under his tongue.

"Look, man, I told you I'm sorry, alright?" said Jack. "I didn't know any of this was going to happen, okay? If I had, I might have done things differently."

"Might have? Now, you're making me feel so much better, Jack."

"It's not like that."

"Then what is it?"

Jack hesitated. "It's like I told you. It's just how it is when you're alone. You can't depend on anybody for anything. Just yourself. All you have is you."

And you want me to feel bad for you?

"Yeah, I understand that," said Darion. "But that's not good enough, Jack. You could have handled *everything* differently. You could have asked me what the discs were, who made them, why I'd helped you, even. But you didn't. You did something just because you convinced yourself that it's all you could do. You keep asking me things, but it all comes back to what I told you, Jack. And you behaved just as I would have expected someone in this world to behave."

That one stung. Darion could see it on Jack's face. A mistake to have been so harsh? No, the boy deserved it. He needed to be put in his place. That was the way it had to be.

"Come up here," said the Shepherd and Darion about leapt with joy. The ship?

"What is it?" asked Darion.

"I'm not certain," said the Shepherd. "The path has become blocked from my sight. The signal to my ship has all but disappeared."

"Are you sure we're going the right way?"

"Yes, I am sure," said the Shepherd. "It's just…. Something is blocking me."

Jack swallowed. "It's that thing isn't it?" Olivia held close to her father.

"The Adversary is not the only thing that can – or will – block our path, Jack," said the Shepherd. "Do not believe the Adversary is solely capable."

"What do we do then?" asked Darion.

"We search until I can feel it again. What else?"

* * * *

It would be a longer wait than any could have predicted. The Shepherd and his party wandered for several days, searching for the missing signal. They circled about many sections of uncivilized ground, eating the rest of their food and staying full, but their path seemed to have no direction. The Shepherd would stop and check the wind with one hand, raising it to the sky like a hidden signal from Mars might help lead them to their destination. However, there was never a clear answer. So they walked until they were tired and rested.

In the nights, Darion and Olivia slept close to one another, while Jack kept to himself. As days passed, Jack felt the hunger returning. Something needed to satiate old desires. So he tried conversation with Darion to distract himself, but it was always limited. Darion continued to maintain an uncomfortable distance, and thus, Jack tried conversation with the Shepherd. However, Jack found every interaction with the Shepherd to be equally difficult and Jack wondered if Darion was silently judging him, eyeing Jack with condescending stares whenever discussions ceased at the end of the Shepherd's tongue and not Jack's. To Jack, the Shepherd was never completely direct and was never directly complete either. It was as if the Shepherd never wanted to give Jack a full answer on anything. He wanted Jack to come to his own conclusions, a personality trait which frustrated Jack with every new response.

For instance, when Jack asked about Mars' people, the Shepherd described them as 'like him' but that his people varied 'like the stars.' And when Jack inquired about Bandalon, the lion, the Shepherd recalled days spent climbing trees and running through the fields of Mars – hardly a picture Jack could believe or even comprehend. Mars sounded like a fantasy, not an actual place. And though it frustrated him, Jack kept on trying to find pieces of humanity so that he may understand the Shepherd better, and not marvel at every aspect of their leader.

On one night, Jack tried staying awake as long as he could, seeing if the Shepherd would give in to exhaustion and sleep, but he wouldn't. Jack continued this routine for the next two nights until on the fourth night – and still without a signal – the Shepherd addressed Jack's growing obsession with his sleep patterns.

"I do sleep, Jack," said the Shepherd and Jack looked away, embarrassed. "But, not like you."

"I got that already, chief," said Jack. "What are you doin' anyway? Looking for the signal, right?"

"Not at the moment. I'm taking in the scenery presently."

"What? Why?"

"On Mars, there are huge spheres of open landscape, protected under the domes that were made by my forebears. They are spacious and accommodate our lives on Mars, but the spheres are made with limitations, Jack. One cannot travel the entire surface of Mars and not be met without an invisible line or a door that requires you to open and get to the other side. You have to understand, it's not like that here. On Earth."

Jack pondered the image of giant bubbles on Mars – these holding pens the Shepherd often spoke about. It seemed like too large a concept for him to grasp. "That doesn't sound horrible," said Jack and the Shepherd looked at him.

"It's not a matter of horror, Jack," said the Shepherd. "But of freedom. The Earth was made without limitations, Jack. On Mars, we actually have to make boundaries just so that we can have the illusion of freedom. Do you understand the difference?"

Jack nodded like he understood, but he honestly didn't. The Shepherd went on explaining like he knew it might help Jack to understand.

"At times when I am walking ahead of you, I imagine myself running into one of those sphere barriers and having to unlock it before I can continue. And when I don't, I am reminded how Earth has no fences. I'm reminded of why my fathers speak of this place with a reverence that I could never understand until I visited it for myself. Do you understand?"

This time, Jack related. He'd always wanted to be in a better place than this. And the thought that such a place existed gave him that subtle hope he needed to keep going. The way the Shepherd described his experience; it made Jack feel like this alien monster actually was human. Like the boundaries they had between one another had been peeled back a few layers and Jack saw the Shepherd for more than a freak that went without sleep or performed acts that were otherwise inconceivable to his own inventiveness. The Shepherd was a human being. Or at the very least, some inkling of his original design made him appear to be that way.

Jack looked at Darion, already asleep a few yards from him. He doesn't wait for me to pass out first anymore. Another layer, Jack felt, was peeling away. Just like the Shepherd. And Jack thought of recent conversations he and Darion shared. At one point, they had stopped and bathed themselves by the creeks, washing their faces and hands even though the Shepherd told them it was 'unnecessary' due to their eating of the purified food.

"The dirt will come off you on its own," explained the Shepherd. "You needn't do that."

Jack had silently recognized the phenomenon over the days, but Darion went right on with cleaning himself.

"Hey, look at this," said Jack, and when he said it, he realized it was the first he'd spoken to Darion in nearly a day. He showed Darion his arm; skin glowing vibrantly and Darion shrugged.

"Don't get used to it, Jack," said Darion. "That food and that feeling won't last forever."

Darion was right, but that didn't shake Jack's disbelief. "Come to think of it," said Jack. "I can't even remember the last time I took a piss. Hey Shepherd, am I peeing through my skin too?"

The Shepherd grinned and Jack saw Darion suppress a chuckle himself. Jack recorded the image of Darion's almost-laughter and then filed it somewhere under 'times-Darion-doesn't-seem-to-hate-me'.

"The fruit is enhanced but there are still nutrients that your body will have to discard," said the Shepherd. "Soon, you will have to excrete that excess material."

"Oh, good," said Jack. "I was worried I might never shit again either."

That next morning, Jack awoke and saw that Darion was sweating all over. This was the fifth day of their continued search for the signal. And as Jack had counted, the third time Darion had woke with bad dreams. Feeling bold, he decided not to let this go any longer.

"So, another nightmare, eh?" asked Jack and Darion nodded.

"I hate bad dreams," said Jack. "This one the same as the others?"

"What others?"

"Come on, man. You sweat like that all the time when you sleep?"

Darion didn't answer. He got to his feet and walked away from Jack.

"This way," said the Shepherd. And they followed.

"Find that signal yet, chief?" asked Jack.

"If he had, he would tell us, Jack," said Darion.

Don't know if I don't ask, Jack thought. "I am hoping to discern where it is soon," said the Shepherd. "Please be patient."

Darion seethed. "It's been five days," he said. "How can you not have an idea of where it is by now?"

The Shepherd didn't answer. He led the trio out of the forest and into the sight of an old road, one that Darion and Jack recognized almost immediately.

"The signal..." said the Shepherd. "This is where I lost it before. Only now, I can't sense anything. It's completely gone."

"What?" said Darion, voiced with disbelief.

"I don't feel or hear any trace of it."

Darion walked up to the Shepherd and shook a hand in the Shepherd's face like the answer was incredulous. But, the Shepherd closed his eyes and raised a hand, looking for the signal. Jack approached, arguing with Darion as the Shepherd maintained his silence. Olivia panted, staring down the road. She wanted to reach out and touch her father, but his anger was rising. She panted louder. At which point, Darion would not hear but the Shepherd became aware of.

"Darion..." said the Shepherd, opening his eyes. "Your daughter is not well."

"What?"

Olivia was inhaling and exhaling like she might faint. Darion knelt down, "Sweetie, what is it? What's wrong?"

"Little one..." said the Shepherd and he knelt down also, his massive frame casting a shadow over Darion. "Have you also dreamed in the night?"

Olivia nodded 'yes' and the Shepherd grinned. "May I see it?"

Olivia nodded again and the Shepherd put a hand up to Olivia's face, his hand bigger than her head. "Wait, what are you doing?" asked Darion. He reached to swat the Shepherd's hand away, but the Shepherd pulled back.

"Darion," said the Shepherd. "Do not touch me. If you touch me with nothing to protect you from me, you will surely die."

"What?" said Jack, perplexed. "How can that even…"

"My suit is made of a nano tech that feeds on Solfire, Jack. So my body is infused with Solfire too and this suit helps to keep it under control, locked inside. Without it, I may be dangerous to others. To touch me, as someone who has been exposed to Darklight your whole life, your body would die quickly, like an infection overtaking its host."

Jack was still confused, but he got the gist, and backed away. 'Don't touch the Shepherd and you'll live.' Got it.

"If that's true," said Darion. "Then what are you planning on doing? Wouldn't you kill her?"

"I will not touch her," said the Shepherd. "This kind of transfer does not require physical touch, but I do need to be in close proximity. Can you trust me, Darion?"

Darion looked at Olivia, her eyes pleading with her father for approval to allow the Shepherd to continue. Darion finally nodded and the Shepherd raised his hand again, fingers outstretched and covering Olivia's face in his giant palm. The two closed their eyes together.

"Do not be afraid, child," said the Shepherd. "It's quite all right. Just don't move."

Jack stepped back like something dramatic might happen, but Darion did not leave his daughter's side. He watched the Shepherd's hands closely. After a few seconds had passed, the Shepherd and Olivia both opened their eyes, the invisible transaction was over and the Shepherd smiled; Olivia's breathing returned to normal.

"Is that it?" asked Darion. "What happened?"

The Shepherd stood.

"Olivia's dream was about our path," said the Shepherd. "She saw a broken cord, like a rope, and I have interpreted this as our broken commune with my ship."

"We already knew that, chief," said Jack. "What are we supposed to do about it?"

"There was more," said the Shepherd. "The cord was broken but another of us returned and tied it back together. And it was you, Darion. You were the one who tied the cord together."

Darion's eyes widened. Me? "What? Are you sure?"

Olivia tugged on her father's sleeve, nodded and grinned. Yes, she was saying. Please believe me, she was saying. Jack was puzzled but was now convinced of the Shepherd's interpretation.

"So what did you see?" asked Jack. "In your dream."

Darion paused, forced himself to remember the nightmare he'd had several nights before. It was of a foul creature, unlike the ball of fire he'd seen in nightmares past. And it came for Darion from the woods, attacking him on the edge of a mountain. The image had been so real that when Darion awoke, he thought he'd lost his leg.

But, this image had no bearing on their journey. It shouldn't have. And Darion asked the Shepherd if the responsibility could be passed to someone else.

"I have already told you what is required, Darion," said the Shepherd. "I cannot go any farther without the knowledge you carry."

"Here then," said Darion and he bowed his head. "Place your hands near me. See into my dream and tell me what it is we have to do."

The Shepherd tilted his head to one side. "No," said the Shepherd. "That way is blocked to me. You have closed me off from that. Now, you must undo it."

What did that even mean? Darion peered over the road like the answer was somewhere out in the wilderness. He saw the road ahead. It looked like a giant snake made of stone, wrapping itself around the hillside and to its right, there were trees with dark green tops like umbrellas all the way down the hill's edge. Darion thought of the monster, the dream. It had come for him from out of the woods. Yes, the woods held danger. The roads would be safer – had to be.

"I think we should stay by the road," said Darion. "Maybe we see where that leads?"

"Ya sure about that?" asked Jack. "The roads will lead straight into a town. I'm sure of it. All that's north of here is people. You sure you want us goin' that way?"

Darion looked to the Shepherd with a helpless expression. "It wouldn't be a terrible thing," said the Shepherd. "It would be better for you to rest somewhere more comfortable if you are able. And whatever is out in these woods, it has brought fear into Darion's heart. If we can avoid that trouble, then we should."

Jack cocked an eyebrow. "Well, alright then," said Jack.

"We will stay on the road then and see where it takes us," said the Shepherd and the trio left the wooded trail behind them, adopting the roads of men.

Chapter 10
The Way Through

"Why are you going to Earth at all?"

"I am going because of the peace we intend to make. The Earth thinks us a threat. They are afraid of what we have.
I am going to amend that fear. I am going to make certain they don't fear us any longer."

"What you say is mostly true, but do not forget: you aren't going for peace, but for *rescue*. They are in need of rescue, just as we once were."

* * * *

The Shepherd's group held to the road's edge until they found themselves gazing upon the outer walls of a small town. There was a sign that said, "Glendale" in big, bold letters, made of steel and likely constructed before the Pulse. There were no fences surrounding its exterior and was interconnected by several outlying roads. Darion counted no more than a dozen small buildings, but there were probably more waiting just ahead. The Shepherd sniffed the air with nostrils aimed against the wind, looking upon every structure like he was tracing the inner workings with all his senses. This behavior made Olivia giggle, but Darion and Jack hardly noticed.

"Shepherd, are you sure this is a good decision?" asked Darion. "We don't have to go through here. Shouldn't it be more important for us to stay out of sight? Go around, maybe?"

"I am still unable to sense my ship," said the Shepherd. "I believe your counsel was correct, Darion Wallace – there is something here that is blocking the way, but we will have to enter and find it. Then we can be on our way again."

"Is it the Adversary?" asked Darion and Jack twitched. He looked behind them as if out of reflex.

"I don't see it," said Jack.

"It doesn't matter if you can see it or not," said Darion. "It could be anywhere it wants to be and you wouldn't know it."

"I was just sayin', man...."

"We have to find what's blocking me," said the Shepherd. There was a strange trepidation on the Shepherd's face. It shook Darion and Jack like this was not going to be a light venture.

"So," said Jack. "Are you ready to meet the rest of the human race?"

"No," said the Shepherd. "I should keep myself from being noticed."

"How exactly do you plan to do that?" asked Darion.

The Shepherd clicked a disc on each forearm, then on each thigh. Then his entire metallic suit began to change and flip over into tiny translucent plates, like diamond. They wrapped around every part of his body, rising up to encapsulate even his neck and head. Darion and Jack stepped away as the Shepherd disappeared, fading out of sight. Yet his presence was felt. He was like a ghost standing in the wind.

"Wow..." said Jack.

"Incredible..." said Darion and he reached out like he wanted to touch the Shepherd. "How can you do that?"

"As I said before," explained the Shepherd. "My suit is infused with Solfire and can become many things. This is but another of the capabilities I possess." The Shepherd's face was hidden yet his voice was clear. His words sounded like direct messages, uploaded to the frontal lobe of Darion, Jack, and Olivia. Darion wiped his forehead like he expected something to be there; something sticking from his body like an antenna. "Your voice... what is that?"

"As ones who have been touched by Solfire, you may hear my voice more clearly than those who have not."

"Is it like that on Mars?" asked Jack.

The Shepherd's silence was a 'yes.' "Listen for my voice as we head through this town, but do not tell anyone I am with you. I will speak in sub vocals so that only *you* may hear me."

Jack chuckled like the orders were absurd. "People are gonna think we're crazy, chief," said Jack.

"Do not think it that way. Even when immersed in Darklight, others can still feel my voice," said the Shepherd. "And they will be drawn to you because of my presence. There could be trouble too. There is something here and it has yet to reveal itself."

"What if there is trouble for *us*?" asked Darion.

"Take these with you."

Two clicks could be heard and the Shepherd raised his hands to Darion and Jack, light distorted by the sun's rays. Two discs appeared and the Shepherd extended them to his companions.

"You will see me if you possess one of these with you."

Darion and Jack took one disc each and both men felt the surge of something familiar in their bones. It was like eating the Shepherd's food or drinking from the water, but stronger and more filling. Jack shook his head and Darion inhaled. The Shepherd reappeared for a moment; a cloud of golden energy and floating like a specter. "That's...quite the feeling," said Jack. "I don't think anybody would believe us if we told'em what we could see right now. Hell, I don't even...."

Darion glared at Jack. "Just do what he says, alright?"

Better quit that, old man. Jack's eyes lingered on Darion a moment before shifting back to the disc in his hands. Though Jack had felt changed on his first encounter with the disc, this second time was not as strong. Only a familiar brush of life and then gone. He could not rely on the disc to keep him invigorated completely. Or could he? He wanted to put the disc aside, have it snatched from his hand so he could experience the rush all over again. The Shepherd seemed to be aware of Jack's feelings and spoke:

"Before we leave this place," said the Shepherd. "You may need my assistance. Do not call on me unless absolutely necessary. Do you understand?"

"How do you know that?" asked Darion, but the Shepherd wouldn't answer. The silence made Darion and Jack aware that something ominous might truly be waiting for them.

Darion clasped Olivia's hand and Jack brushed his hair coolly. "Okay," said Darion. "What exactly are we looking for?"

"Look for it on the tongues of people you encounter," said the Shepherd. "Its source shouldn't be hard to find. Whatever is out of order eventually shows itself."

They entered the town with their heads down, but their eyes peered into every building they passed. The Shepherd's glowing body stayed near, walking in front and walking beside. It was strange for the trio, they seemed eager to let the Shepherd dictate their steps, seeing as how they had for so long, but the Shepherd would not permit it. He even walked behind them at times, waiting to see if they might take a turn or head in another direction. They walked alongside a community building, and then another with several stories, old and weathered like its purpose had been a bunker during war times. There were few people moving out and around the town but the air had a quiet peace about it and Darion let up on Olivia's hand slightly.

"Hey, do ya think – " asked Jack.

"No," said Darion. "Don't speak about it, don't say anything about it; don't even allude to anything pertaining to the Shepherd. We just need to find what it is we're looking for and leave. Alright?"

Jack shook his head. "I just wanted to know if we should tell people we meet if we're friends or something. That's all, man."

Darion looked at Jack. "Friends is fine."

Definitely not brothers, Jack thought.

The trio continued up and down the strip, saying hello to no one, yet maintaining a keen awareness that any passing glance or awkward stare might alert them to whatever might be hidden in the town. Darion was uneasy but collected on the exterior; Jack was the opposite. Jack looked over his shoulder frequently. He imagined bounty hunters in windows or behind closed doors. They could be anywhere, he thought. Still looking. Still coming for him. This was a bad idea. He looked at Darion as if to say, 'let's get out of here.'

"Don't give us away, Jack," instructed Darion. "Just look for what's important."

"That's what I'm doing."

"No, it's not what you're doing. Quit acting like we have something to hide."

"We do though."

"So lie."

"To who?"

"To everyone but us. Don't let anybody know we have something they might want. You can do that, can't you?"

Jack sneered. Back to treating me like a kid, eh? Better quit that. Olivia looked apologetically at Jack. You know how hard this is, don't you? Jack thought. He gripped the disc in his pocket and thought of the strange power he held, but had little to no understanding of. He knew these discs were dangerous. Everything about the discs scared him. He didn't like having one with him. He wanted someone else to have the disc. Anyone would be better, he thought. Even Darion.

They veered into a tight alley and leaned against the stone. There was nothing to report, it seemed. The town was as quiet as a tomb.

"If you need to rest, then do so," said the Shepherd. "I will head off and look myself. I can enter these buildings without detection."

"Should have done that in the first place," said Jack.

"As much as that would please you, Jack. I still need your help."

Then the Shepherd's voice left them. The discs, planted in their coat pockets, did not vibrate or whir, but the presence of the Shepherd had clearly diminished. Darion and Jack stared at each other, not speaking and wondering what the other might be thinking. Jack looked out of the alley.

"This is more suspicious than walking through the town like drifters," said Jack.

"Then do something else," said Darion.

Jack looked across the alley. There was a chalkboard sign with white letters spelling out, 'Pub'.

"Okay, but only because you said so, chief," said Jack and he walked out of the alley, towards the sign which caught his eye.

Maybe he'll stay there, thought Darion. That would be advantageous and the best damn thing that could happen.

But, Jack stopped halfway there and shook his head. He turned and looked at Darion.

"Hey," said Jack. "Did that thing of yours just vibrate?"

"My what?"

"Your *thing*," said Jack. "You know, the disc."

Darion took Olivia's hand and walked out of the alley. He met Jack in the street, an arm's reach from him.

"Quit saying that out loud," said Darion, sternly. "And no, it didn't. Why?"

Jack felt inside his pocket. "I think mine did. What do you think that means?"

Danger, thought Darion. When Darion had the discs, they would always vibrate or stir when trouble was near. But why was Jack the one feeling the distress? Why hadn't it been Darion?

"How is that possible?" asked Darion. "Mine have done nothing."

"Fear does not always announce itself to everyone," said the Shepherd. "Often it covers itself. Makes itself invisible so that it might find its way into new places."

"That's comforting to know…," said Jack.

"Follow my voice," said the Shepherd. "I think we may be getting close."

The trio didn't argue. They followed the Shepherd up to a small café' and walked inside. Darion held the door for the Shepherd to pass through last.

Inside, it was an odd scene. There were long couches, fluffed like peacocks but dirtied like their handlers were careless. Large statues stood against the walls. Each had a thick blemish or crack in them, telling stories that only the stone knew the truth of. There was one straight hallway and several connected rooms with no doors on them. To Jack, it felt like a palace but to Darion, it was a reminder of what the Old World left behind. There was a step down into a bar ahead on the left and a long wooden table where the bartender stood at attention. Two men were sitting and talking to one another, their clothes dirt-ridden and ragged. Their conversation could be heard up the steps and was as equally perverse as their appearance. Darion covered his daughter's ears.

Jack smirked. Won't make a difference.

At the end of the room, was a large and empty space. The main dining area, Darion figured. There were several hexagonal tables and wooden platforms there. Darion led them to a seat near the wall and they sat. The Shepherd went off in another direction, inspecting the café like a specter whose intentions were unknown.

"Well, now what?" said Jack, but Darion didn't answer. "Feels familiar, don't it? Kind of like how we met. Wouldn't you agree?"

Jack propped his feet on the stool next to him. The dirt caked the top of the stool and fell to the floor.

"Put those down," said Darion.

"Why?" said Jack.

Darion exhaled slowly. Why do I need to repeat myself? Darion watched the Shepherd, his large frame surprisingly nimble as it avoided every thing in the room like a wisp of smoke. A woman walked by their table and stared at Jack, dirt clopped on the ground. Darion saw her and leaned in closer.

"Do not draw any attention to us, Jack… "

"I'm just tryin' to relax, man. Quit trying to be such a hardass. It doesn't suit you. Even if you *can* throw me around."

"I'd relax if you'd quit. Try to remember what we're doing here is bigger than whatever you're used to doing anywhere."

Jack glared, fuming underneath. "Is it now? Tell me what it is I used to do then that was so different than this? I'd like you to take a shot at it, chief. Please. I'm eager to hear it."

"I have to protect my daughter, Jack," said Darion. "What have you ever protected aside from yourself? Anything? The 'bigger thing' is what I take with me. And what I take with me is my daughter. So if you put us in any danger, I'll put a stop to that immediately. Even if that means putting a stop to *you*."

* * * *

Jack stared at Darion. He searched his mind for things he'd fought for, fought to protect, but came up with very little other than himself. Anger. *I hate this man*, he thought. Jack hated Darion for reasons he couldn't even pinpoint or describe. He pressed his lips together, thinking of a strong retort but knew he had none.

Then Darion pushed Jack's feet off the stool and Jack let them fall before he pulled his boots back up again.

"Be careful, old man," said Jack. "You underestimate me too much. You shouldn't do that… do ya hear me?"

Jack eyed Olivia, who was cowering in the seat next to Darion. *You're lucky*, Jack thought. If she weren't here, you'd be on the floor right now, old man. I promise you that; only it wouldn't be like before. I'd really hurt you this time. I would. You'd be hurt and on the ground, wishing you hadn't pushed me like that. Jack imagined the entire scenario. It wasn't hard to do. He would pull Darion to the floor, hit him across the face and then back away in victory. It'd be that easy. Darion was strong, but Jack was smarter.

Jack moved in his chair and grabbed hold of the disc in his pocket. The rage inside of him seemed to settle, or at the very least, place its hatred toward something other than Darion. He heard the Shepherd's voice; felt the tingle of something odd in his fingertips and looked out the door.

"Look," said Darion. "I'm not trying to - "

"Yeah, that's about enough for me too," said Jack.

Then Jack stood up and walked out of the café quickly. He didn't even know if he wanted to go to the pub, he just needed away from the situation. He found himself in the pub anyway, seated at the nearest stool he could find and talking aloud to himself about how he could still beat Darion to an inch of his life if he wanted. The disc lie dormant in his pocket; his anger swelling on the surface.

stay here, Jack thought. Maybe now you'll be rid of me, eh, old man?

* * * *

In the pub, Jack gritted his teeth and called on the names of every vengeful spirit he could think of that might assist him in heading back and putting Darion's face in a hole. That would show him. I could still go do it. I could still show him who I am. The anger boiled and seethed inside of Jack until he was unaware of how much time had passed or even who was with him.

But, when he cooled, a younger woman arrived and sat near to him. Jack peered to his left and saw that it was the same woman from across the street. He drank her in; she was rough on the edges, but emanated the signal of one whom desperately wanted companionship. This too, was a familiar feeling for Jack. His thoughts shifted instantly, thinking how he might attract her to him and fill his spirits.

Jack leaned slightly and caught her eye. Just as he predicted he might. He spoke a few words to her like he held a magic ticket to a better place and the woman laughed. *She believes me*, he thought. Jack imagined how old she might be, where she'd come from, and what had brought her to this place. She answered most every one of these questions for him, but Jack only recalled those that might bring him closer to his goal. He created her entire life story and put it in a bottle of his making, holding it till he would be ready to open it and enjoy what was inside.

This one takes without asking. Just like me. We are the same.

"Are you traveling alone?" she asked.

"No," he said, not even thinking twice about the answer.

"I can meet you later," she said. "But, first I have to go get something. Can you wait here?"

"Sure," he said. Should he tell the group? No. Of course not. And certainly not the Shepherd. No one need know about this side venture.

The woman walked out. Jack felt good, but then the disc rattled in his pocket and his stomach turned. A firm hand landed upon his shoulder and Jack shuddered.

"You really shouldn't be doing that, Jack," said another voice.

A thin, regal-looking man sat himself diagonally from Jack – it was Argus, the Eyes of the Hunt. His long face and slicked hair made him look like he'd been dipped in slime. He grinned and Jack stood up quickly but was caught behind by the concrete hands of a larger man, Reggie, the bounty hunter.

"Hey there, Jack," said Reggie and he shoved Jack back into his seat. "Don't go anywhere."

No. Why? *How?*

"Hi, Jack," said Argus. "You ought to know that a woman like that probably don't have much interest in a man like you. Probably not ever either. Not with your hair like that or with your hands so dirty or – wait, have you smelled yourself? You must know you smell, right?"

It's *you* that smells bad, Argus. Nothing stunk until you arrived. Still, Jack bit his lip and tapped his foot. How'd they find me? Were they always in this town?

"No hello?" said Argus and he rolled his sleeves up. "No, 'nice to see ya'? I don't want this to be all drawn out but I'm hurt by that, Jack. Really, really hurt by your lack of affection towards me. I thought we were still friends. We are, aren't we?"

One of the men shoved Jack from behind. "Hello, Argus," said Jack and Argus grinned with a smile so big that it wrapped right around his face.

"That's better," said Argus. "We shouldn't be that way with each other. Not like that. You and me – we have history, don't we? And people with history don't act that way towards one another."

Jack didn't move. He couldn't look at Argus either. He hated the way Argus talked, hated how he moved, how he smiled. Yes, he had history with Argus. But, that was before Argus became a stooge for the Hunt and his brother became its tyrannical leader. Their lives were different now. Too different. Weren't they?

"It's still 'Jack' these days, ain't it?" asked Argus. "Or is it Mark now? Brad? Rico? I figured you might have taken on something new by now. Well, did you or didn't you?"

Jack shook his head. "Just 'Jack.'"

"Then it hasn't been that long, has it? In which case, it'll make this that much easier."

"And what's that?"

"It's time to come home, Jack. You been gone far too long."

Jack didn't answer. He pictured Darion, Olivia, and the Shepherd coming to his rescue. He imagined sending a distress signal through the disc. Was that even possible?

"So, why'd you run from us, Jack? Were the laws of the Hunt just too much for you? You do understand the penalties for being a coward, right?"

Jack didn't answer. He gripped the silver disc tighter in his pocket and Argus glanced at Jack's arm; then back at Jack and Argus smiled.

"What's in the pocket, Jack?" asked Argus. "You got something you wanna share with the rest of us?"

Jack shook his head. "I don't know what you're talking about..."

"Shut up, Jack," said Argus and he leaned closer. "My eyes...they see *everything*, Jack." Argus opened his eyes wide, pointed to them, but Jack didn't look. He'd seen them plenty of times. They were dark and lifeless. Nothing had changed since he'd last seen them, he was sure of that.

"So don't do this, alright? Don't make this hard, Jack."

You love tormenting people when you're the one in control. Jack knew he could take Argus if it weren't for the mercenaries. It'd be no problem. But, then Argus looked out the window, into the cafe' and grinned.

"If you don't give it over," said Argus. "We can always just take it from you. Or, we can take it from you and then we can check on your companions across the street. What do you say now?"

Jack tightened. "I don't travel with anybody. You know that, Argus."

"Not from what I seen," said Argus and his eyes got wide again. "I think you got some company with you. What do they have? What they got, Jack? If it's something worth stealing, then I could see why you're with them."

Jack was still.

"Maybe that little girl has something we want, eh, Jack?"

Don't you dare, Jack thought and he squeezed the disc in his pocket. It started to buzz and Jack's senses went into a blitz. Time itself slowed and Jack felt the disc latch onto his wrist, emerging from the insides of his jacket completely on its own. He couldn't stop it, nor did he try to. The disc, transformed to a weapon, behaved as if it were a guard dog set loose by its owner. Jack's oppressors couldn't respond: Argus' eyes widened once more - this time out of fright - and was shot backwards in a flash of light. The weapon twisted quickly, but not hurting Jack, and blasted the others as well.

Jack's eyes, alit with golden energy, saw and felt everything. His senses absorbed the room, anything within his line of sight was amplified. He saw visions of old ghosts at the pub, estranged words that did not find the ears of those who needed them, and he saw a specter of his past self, red like fire, saying and asking the woman questions that had sounded well to him then but made him want to weep or vomit now that he heard them again. All of this happened at once, but could well have lasted a whole hour. Which was it? Then a voice came to him.

Run. Across the street.

The weapon detached from Jack. It floated in the air beside him and Jack grabbed his wrist; like hot coals were burning his skin where the weapon had been. He cried out and Argus stirred on the floor, cursing and panting like he'd been drowning in water. Jack grabbed the weapon, ran out of the pub and across the street to Darion and Olivia.

* * * *

"Darion! Olivia!" yelled Jack and the whole café' stirred.

Darion did not acknowledge Jack, at first, but seeing that Jack was heading straight for him, Darion stood up and grabbed Jack by the collar. Jack was howling like a madman.

"Idiot!" said Darion. "What are you doing?"

"They're here..." said Jack, pleading. "Dammit, they're here! They're after us. But, this thing. It saved me."

Darion ignored the disc. "Who? Who is after you? What is happening?"

Darion saw two men enter through the front of the café'. They saw Darion locking arms with Jack and clutched their belts as if they were reaching for a weapon. Darion shoved Jack to the side, knocking a table with several people by it. Jack tried to get his balance, but he staggered, knocking others from their seats as the disc flew from his hand. Voices began yelling and screaming, unaware of the terror down the hall. Darion called towards Olivia.

"Liv! Run!"

Reggie and his partner were not in a rush. They moved down the corridor and into the main room, looking at Darion and Jack like one might be more appealing to capture than the other. With Jack on the floor, Reggie turned his attentions on Darion. He took a gun from his pocket and raised it to the ceiling. When he fired, several people screamed and Darion ran and covered Olivia.

"Enough!" shouted Reggie. "No more running! Get up and get over here! Now!"

The other man took the pistol from his pocket and held it towards Jack. Jack looked for the silver disc, but it was several yards from him, pushed against the wall of the café. He'd shoot me before I could get within a foot. I need time. No time. Jack stood slowly, ordered again by the bounty hunters.

"I know one of you has that weapon on him," said Reggie. "Slide it over."

Darion turned around slowly, blocking Olivia from view. "It's alright. It's alright," he said. "I'll give what you want. No need to shoot. Please."

"The weapon. Slide it."

"Okay, okay."

Darion reached into his pocket and removed the single disc. "This what you want?"

Reggie nodded. He took two more steps; feet hitting the floorboards like his boots were filled with concrete, not flesh. "Give it."

Darion knelt down and slid the disc across the floor. "Get it, Matt," said Reggie and the other man walked forward, leaned down, and grabbed the disc. But, at the point of contact, the disc flashed and Matt went flying backward. He writhed on the ground for a moment like a grenade had hit him. Darion and Jack froze, equally aware that the disc was not about to be taken or subdued by ill intent. Reggie watched his partner squirm and then turned back towards Darion.

"What did you do to him?!" he said, shaking the pistol at Darion. "What the hell are you anyway, huh? What did you do?"

"Please…" said Darion. "Please don't.…" This is bad. Darion could see clouds of Darklight appearing in the room. Tiny clouds of fear. Death was coming. But, who was it coming for? Darion looked for the Shepherd. Where was he? Abandoned? He's abandoned us. That abomination abandoned us after all of this. Jack was looking for the Shepherd also, but the visage of Darklight had him distracted.

"I said, what are you!" shouted Reggie and he took two more steps closer to Darion, pistol aimed at Darion's head. Darion closed his eyes, screaming but not realizing it. Jack struggled to get to his feet. More people screamed and Reggie yelled for them to stop. Confusion was everywhere. Darion opened his eyes, saw the clouds of Darklight getting thicker. *Not like this,* Darion thought. Not like this.…

The other henchman got to his feet in a fury. He was gripping his hand like it had been burned off. He raised his weapon, aimed it at Darion and shouted, "Sonuvabitch! Die, you freaks!"

"No!" Jack yelled. He jumped to his feet, thinking he might be able to run for them, but he was too late. The bullet was already on its way, as were several others in rapid succession. Jack stopped, watching and waiting for Darion and Olivia to fall to the ground, dead.

But, they didn't. There was a soft pause in the room and no one moved – including the bullets. Round and black, every one of Matt's bullets was stuck, hovering in mid-air; a foot from Darion's face and body. Olivia peeked out from behind Darion, unharmed. Then, each of the bullets disappeared like they'd been sucked through an invisible tube. Vanished.

"What the hell…" said Matt and he opened fire again. Darion jerked and Olivia hid again, yet each bullet behaved the same as the first. Four bullets floated freely; suspended in space before disappearing in the order with which they'd been fired. Matt lowered his firearm.

"Satan's children…" said Matt. "That's what they are…"

"Enough!" shouted Reggie and he turned his own pistol on Darion. "Dodge this then."

Reggie tried to fire, but a flash of white light filled the room, stopping time and Reggie too, it seemed. Jack heard a soft voice amid the light and he closed his own eyes to shield himself. When he opened them, he saw Reggie's eyes bulged and body shaking with short convulsions. He'd gone catatonic, his entire body dangling in an upright position.

Then *he* appeared.

Those in the café witnessed as Reggie's bullets reappeared, dropping to the ground as they were dislodged and discarded like empty cartridges. They fell from the long arm of a slowly materializing giant – the Shepherd – who was now standing at the center of the café. His body, wrapped in the transparent plates, was returning to normal, the silver uniform returning to its original state. Darion swallowed. So *there* you are. Were you there the whole time? How didn't we see you? It was clear the Shepherd could do more than become invisible. He could be gone, then appear in an instant. Nothing hindered him. He could act as he pleased and the thought of it, the realization, hit Darion with a new fear that caused the Darklight to swirl about him slightly and then dissipate in the presence of the Shepherd. This man - this *being* - is truly terrifying.

Fully visible, the Shepherd's left arm reached and ended with his pointer finger poised at the center of Reggie's forehead. The Shepherd looked past Reggie for a moment, peering at Matt, who had dropped his gun like God himself were staring back at him. The Shepherd's helmet then pulled back and merged with his suit, uncovering his dark-colored face and bright, silver eyes, which now looked like swords glistening in the darkness. He was looking intensely at Reggie. The glowing grin and cheerful demeanor was not there. Next to the Shepherd, Reggie looked like an adolescent; the silver giant stood tall like a mountain overlooking a tiny hilltop. He was bigger than ever, Jack observed. And Darion was standing just a foot behind the Shepherd, staring up at the Shepherd's back, fully shielded from the onslaught.

"You will not fire any more bullets," said the Shepherd. His voice was stern and affirming. This was the Shepherd at his most serious, thought Darion. Reggie continued to tremble. "Give me your gun."

Reggie was shaking everywhere but still managed to turn the gun around; raised a hand to the Shepherd and the Shepherd took it from him. The Shepherd's finger, looking like a butcher's knife, maintained its steadfast nature like a steel beam. The clouds of Darklight, once thick and heavy, dispersed.

"You will not be getting this back," said the Shepherd. "Do you understand?" His voice sounded like it was on the verge of mourning, like a parent saddened at having to scold his offspring.

"You are like an unruly child," continued the Shepherd. "Pointing this around like it's a toy for your amusement. I'm here to tell you that it *isn't*. You will only hurt others with this and in turn, you will only be hurting yourself. That cycle cannot continue. Do you understand me?"

Reggie did not answer. He was comatose, eyes wide, but quivering still. Argus came through the door, announcing his entrance with hair disheveled and angry curses on his tongue. But, when he saw the Shepherd, he ceased everything and stood like he'd been turned to stone.

"What the hell is that thing?" said Argus. "Reggie? What are you doin'? Shoot it! Shoot that thing!"

Argus saw Matt and ran over to him, shoving him towards the fallen pistol. "Shoot it! What are you doing?!" Matt leaned down and reluctantly picked up his weapon. He took aim as the Shepherd peered back at him. The Shepherd released Reggie, who fell the floor like his legs had been cut off. Matt shakily tried to raise his pistol, but the Shepherd dashed over to Matt like he were bending time, pressing another outstretched finger upon Matt who couldn't respond in time. And like Reggie; Matt immediately began to tremble, gun falling away from him.

"Did you not learn anything?" said the Shepherd and Argus jumped back. "Your bullets. They will not work against me." People began to stand and take refuge in the room. Darion and Jack watched as the Shepherd continued to teach more witnesses about the limits of his power. Or lack thereof.

"Did you not realize that even if you hit me, it would not hurt me?" said the Shepherd. "Didn't your eyes tell you that just now? Or do you still fear him more than *me*? Even when I am this close, do you still not trust your eyes?"

Matt started to cry. His lips quivered like he was staring at a guillotine about to drop. "How would you react if you knew I was always this close to you? How might you live your life with this knowledge? Ask yourself this question. Ask it always and you can walk away from this a better man, Matthew."

The Shepherd released Matt and the bounty hunter's body fell to the ground like his every bone had melted. The Shepherd turned towards Argus, who was backpedaling on the floor.

"And what do you say?" said the Shepherd. "Will you give me what I am seeking?"

Argus scrambled to an upright position and ran out the front door, screaming. He tripped and fell on his face near the outside. Argus cursed himself for being so clumsy and stood again. But, there he was. Waiting for him. The Shepherd was already in the street. "Impossible," mumbled Argus. That's impossible....

"Give it to me," said the Shepherd. "Give it now."

"Piss off, ya freak!" said Argus and he turned to run.

The Shepherd paused, then leapt at Argus and took him by the jacket, paralyzing Argus. Then the Shepherd held a hand over Argus and closed his eyes. A disc flew from out of Argus' pocket and into the hand of the Shepherd. It was small and looked like one of the silver discs the Shepherd had, but it was damaged. The Shepherd examined it for a moment and dropped the disc. It came to life before hitting the ground and attached itself to the Shepherd's body, his silver leg twitching like he'd been shocked with a live wire. The Shepherd shook his head and released Argus, who fell to the ground, limp and lifeless.

Argus wheezed and the Shepherd took one last glance at Argus before returning inside the building. It was quiet there. People moved about cautiously, save the unresponsive Reggie and stupefied Matt. The Shepherd nodded at Jack and Darion like it was okay to come out and they did, albeit slowly and with much restraint in their steps.

Olivia left her father's side, running towards Jack. "Olivia..." said Darion, calling her back to him, but she refused. She retrieved the silver disc for Jack and returned it to him. Jack nodded with a 'thanks' and stood upright. He looked at Darion, their eyes meeting with relief, yet neither man was willing to embrace the other in victory. Were there any words needing to be said? It didn't feel like there were. Olivia returned to her father.

"Come," said the Shepherd and the trio exited in silence, heads down like scolded children. The few that were still inside the building did not follow them. No one dared to. When they were gone and near the edge of town, the Shepherd spoke again.

* * * *

"I am sorry."

Darion huffed like an apology hardly felt suitable. "Are you even aware of what could have happened back there? Where were you? What were you doing?"

Jack was shocked at how bold Darion had become. Darion charged the Shepherd like he were the authority of their group. And yet, the Shepherd did not dismiss Darion. The silver giant looked sullen, perhaps even disappointed that he hadn't stepped in sooner, responded with fervor. But, the Shepherd did not stay on that topic. He moved swiftly to the next like his defense, no the reason they'd come to the village, had been what kept him at bay till the last moment.

"I discovered the source of the signal's disruption," said the Shepherd. "And I've taken it with me."

"What was it?" asked Darion.

"Something I thought my predecessors might have taken from this planet," said the Shepherd. "But again, I am reminded of our humanity and what people will do to survive. By any means necessary."

Darion looked away, upset. Jack concluded that 'humanity' was a way of saying they – Mars – still made mistakes. Difficult as it was for Jack to believe, it was a hint of the Shepherd's embedded weakness. He's human, isn't he? As much as I don't want to believe it, this giant thing is a real human being. Somewhere underneath everything, he's human.

"Don't worry," said the Shepherd. "I will explain everything later. Once we are far enough away from this place, I will. But, I have already done too much here. The road ahead will be more treacherous now that I've made myself known in this place. Please forgive me for what is liable to follow."

The words came as gently as the Shepherd could say them, but their delivery dropped a feeling of inescapable dread upon Darion and Jack. What did that even mean? Jack was inclined to ask, but was too frightened of the answer. Was there even one? The Shepherd would not have said it if he didn't already know. If he did not see ruin in their immediate future, he wouldn't be throwing around things that could only be left to chance. No, the Shepherd was as deliberate and purposeful as any person could be. Wasn't he? Darion appeared to be apathetic, ignoring the prophecy so as to keep it from being self-fulfilled. The less talk of such a thing, the better. Jack decided to follow the example and did not speak.

They followed the Shepherd out of Glendale and into the forest. The new path was unknown, but it was no longer one that had to deal with people from a strange town. And when they were far and away on the dirt road, the Shepherd pulled them all aside and let them eat fruit from the knapsack. The trio ate quickly, and they were cured of their anxieties as speedily as they were able to eat.

In Glendale, people were recovering, but not nearly in the same manner as Darion, Jack, or Olivia. A storeowner rushed into the street and spoke to a maddened woman about what happened.

"A man..." she raved. "A giant man of light with the power to kill by touch..." Her words were broken into fragments and the owner asked her to repeat what she'd said. When she did, he was even more confused. He shook her like she was delirious or had been drugged to the point of not knowing the truth of her own words. He questioned her several times, and with each retelling, the owner became more convinced that what she had said was a fantasy drawn up in her mind. However, two others overheard the conversation and came over. They reciprocated the woman's story of the 'giant man' and the 'light weapon.' Yet the owner was still not convinced. But, more people came, each speaking of what had transpired and rehashing their own versions of the Shepherd. Their vantage points were all different, but the common thread was the same: an alien, they said. A demon, an angel – something not of Earth had been here. Had it been Mars? Had Mars sent one of their own to Earth simply to torment us? The people rallied together in the square as more came forward with new stories of the Shepherd. Some terrified. Others excited by the prospect of Mars' return to Earth.

Meanwhile, the Shepherd, seated with the trio outside of Glendale, had his head tilted back towards the town. His eyes squinted like he was recording something, or was hearing a conversation inaudible to anyone who wasn't a Shepherd.

"What's wrong?" asked Jack.

"Finish what you can and then up the mountainside," said the Shepherd. "There is much we have to discuss."

Chapter 11
The Signal

"So are we *not* like them?"

"No. We *are* like them. *You* are like them. But you are also *not* like them. There are things they will do which are not like us, but are reminiscent of the wound we all carry."

"Which is?"

"To be exposed. To be trapped by death."

* * * *

When Argus finally came to, he didn't wait for the bounty hunters. He ran from the crowd that had formed about him and did not stop until he was practically out of breath. He ran down the old stone road; towards the old city, back for the encampment, back to the Hunt. He stumbled many times, the Shepherd's paralyzing touch affecting him more than he realized. He felt like a newborn trying to walk. How was it so?

Argus ran until he came upon a single traveler on horseback. Argus took a gun and waved madly; threatening to kill the rider if he didn't give Argus the horse. The traveler conceded and when Argus had his horse, he turned and fired on the former rider. Yet Argus' aim was incredibly poor. He could not keep himself steady and the man dodged his errant misfires at close range. The rider ran off, zigzagging until he was out of eyeshot and Argus could no longer follow him.

Forget him, he thought. Means nothing. Need to get back. Need to tell Virgil everything.

Argus tracked the huge tires of the Rovers until he came to an open road. Good, they must have gone this way. He was surely going to find them soon.

Eventually, he found three Rovers. Like primeval tanks they occupied both lanes, moving like the roads were made solely for their transport. Argus ran around front and waved an arm to them. The Rovers came to a halt. The middle Rover's hatch opened and out of it came Greta. She peered at Argus like he was a stranger.

Her blond hair wrapped around her face and neck, looking more like a helmet than hair as she glared at him. Argus was disappointed to come upon her first and not another of the Huntsmen. But, this was good too. Wherever Greta was, Virgil was also.

"Where is he, Greta?" said Argus. "Where is Virgil? Brother! Are you in there? I have to speak with you!"

Greta raised a rifle from inside the Rover and pointed it at Argus.

"Do the Eyes of the Hunt need ears too?" she said. "Or can I clip them off?"

Argus hid his face behind the horse and screamed for Greta not to fire on him. "Stop it! What, have you gone crazy?"

"Do not refer to the Captain in that way, Argus. Or I will shoot your ear off."

Argus danced in place. He knew Greta was a sure shot. She could clip the wings off a fly with the skill she possessed.

"Greta! Enough!" shouted Argus and the horse whinnied like it knew it were in danger. Greta kept her hands steady and her eyes poised like she was intent on shooting Argus. She could do it. She wanted to.

"What have you brought with you, Argus?" asked Greta. "Besides a horse and no bounty?"

"Let me speak with him first! Let me speak with the Captain! I will tell him everything if you let me. Stop! Stop it, please!"

Greta let down her rifle and disappeared inside of the Rover. A door clicked and the side opened. Greta emerged along with several other members of the Hunt and Argus counted them: eight in all. And then there was the Captain, his brother, who was last among them. Looking as regal and as important as always, Virgil sniffed the air and looked over the tree line. Argus dismounted and bowed his head to the Captain, looking at Greta. She was petite compared to the rest of the Hunt's soldiers, but hadn't lost her intimidating gaze. Her eyes glared at Argus and he looked away. She hated him. He hated her. No need for pleasantries.

"Captain," said Argus. "I have a report for you."

Argus then told Virgil everything he'd encountered in Glendale: the runaway Jack, the father and daughter with the discs and lastly, the Shepherd. Argus talked of the Shepherd and how he could make himself invisible and catch bullets and stop men – men like Reggie – with a single finger. Argus made himself sound like a true soldier, one who had stayed to the last before ultimately realizing he needed to retreat. Virgil was straight-faced. When Argus was finished, the Captain took a moment to digest everything before speaking.

"And you're absolutely certain then," said Virgil. "That you saw what you saw?"

Argus nodded nervously. "Why would I make that up? My eyes don't miss anything, Virgil. They don't miss anything. They don't!"

Greta stepped forward and slapped Argus across the face. Argus reeled backwards, cursing Greta and looking to Virgil for reprimand but none came. The Captain was stoic, as were the rest of the Hunt. No one moved unless the Captain moved. And no one spoke out of turn unless spoken to.

"And where are the others?" asked Virgil. "Where are the bounty hunters – our 'Huntsmen in training.'? Where are they?"

Argus spit on the ground. "They're back there. I think that thing killed one of'em. Maybe Reggie. I dunno. I ran out of there before that thing could get to me and – "

"And what of the weapon?"

"What?"

"The weapon. The pistol that shoots light. Where is it? Did you see it?"

Argus stammered. He gazed around the circle of Hunters, thinking about how he'd explain everything.

"I didn't get to see it really," said Argus.

"Why?"

"I-I found Jack and I – "

"I don't care about any of that, Argus," said Virgil. "Jack's good as dead to us. Why didn't you get the weapon?"

"I couldn't…" said Argus and he cowered. Greta slapped him and Argus moaned. He cursed her again but still, he did not retaliate.

"Why didn't you get the weapon?" asked Virgil. "Why didn't you get it for me?"

"Because of that thing!" Argus yelled. "That silver monster! It killed Reggie and it killed Matt. I'm sure of it. It didn't even need that weapon either. It just touched'em and they fell to the ground. Dead. Twitchin' and screamin' like they'd been paralyzed by its touch!"

"Dead people don't twitch, Argus," said Greta. "Maybe your eyes have gone bad?"

Argus was too flustered to argue. All he wanted was for Greta to shut up. Take her down so he could talk to his brother openly. Talk to him like he used to. Before *she* came to the Hunt. Argus looked upon his brother with desperate eyes, but Virgil was apathetic, his jaw unhinging and eyes cold.

"And what of the item you had with you? Did you lose that?"

Again, Argus cowered.

"What item?" asked Argus. "What – "

"The one you took in the old city," said Virgil. "That lowly merchant had something with him. Did you keep it for yourself? Or did you lose it during your mission?"

Argus looked confused. How did Virgil know about that? Had someone told him? All of the men with Virgil, they'd come along in the Rover. None would have known and yet, Virgil *knew*. When Argus wouldn't answer, Virgil motioned to Greta for another beating. She complied with fervor.

"Stop it, please!" squealed Argus. "Brother! I swear to you! That thing was too much for us! All of us – Reggie, Matt – I didn't know what to do so I came back here. I thought we could take'em alone. I thought we could do it for *you*! I'm sorry. I'm so sorry…Please…please have mercy, brother!"

"He's the Captain," said Greta and she whipped him again. This time, Argus fell to one knee, covering his face with his arms. "Stop it. You're embarrassing yourself and the Captain."

Virgil tightened his lip. "I believe his story is true," said Virgil. "Even though he lost something that may have helped us, he's gained some respect for telling the truth. For my part, at least."

Greta smirked. "A *silver monster*?" said Greta. "A Shepherd from Mars? Sounds like a fantastic story to help save himself."

"No, it is the truth, Greta," said Virgil and he gave Greta a look like she'd disobeyed him. "Mars has great power and they've sent one of their own here to demonstrate that. I like that. I like this new *challenge*. Anyone capable of taking out those men is certainly not to be underestimated. Not again, anyway. Argus, you've failed, but you've also brought some valuable information to us. I thank you for your report."

Argus grinned as best he was able, looking upon Greta, who was scowling at him. *Dog*, Argus thought. What will you do to me now that I'm being honored?

"However," said Virgil. "Our scouts already discovered what you've told me, Argus."

"What?"

"I had several of our people track you when you left. They followed you into the town and watched everything for me. And they returned not a half hour ago with the news of what you just said to me. Incredible as it was to hear, I am glad to have a second voice to confirm their findings."

Argus felt betrayed. He wiped his mouth, peering at the other Huntsmen like one of them was a traitor. Their faces were hidden behind their red scarves. They all looked the same. Any one of them could have been the one. Any one of them could have betrayed him and he'd never know the difference.

"Why?" asked Argus.

Virgil nodded at Greta and the secret was out; it had been *her*. She had sent someone ahead, been part of this somehow. And Argus hated her even more. A few soldiers came forward and took Argus by the arms as another smashed him across the knee with a beat stick. Argus howled like an animal and the horse kicked up, breaking free of a Huntsman and running away. The soldiers gripped Argus by his scalp and pulled his head back.

"No!" cried Argus. "Brother, no!"

Greta hit Argus again, but she used the butt of her rifle this time. Argus spit and blood ran like a faucet from his face. The red drip increased under the weight of Argus' head, hanging loosely between his shoulders. Virgil bent down on one knee and looked at his brother. He held Argus' chin up, staring at Argus from a few inches away.

"You failed, Argus," said Virgil. "You failed the Hunt, but most inappropriately, you failed *me*. Not just anyone, Argus. Me. How do you think that makes me feel, Argus? I didn't want to send someone to watch after you, but in the silence of my own mind, I knew I should. And now, I'm sorry for being right. Always, I am regretful to be in the right about you. Your eyes are not as useful as they should be, Argus. I can't ignore that any longer."

Argus tried not to look at Virgil as the verbal assault continued. By now, the other Rovers had emptied many of their passengers and a good dozen of the men and women of the Hunt had gathered to hear Argus' public shaming. It was a cruel display, but not uncommon among the Hunt's most inner of circles. If someone did not pull his weight or perform accordingly, then he was made a mockery of until he could rectify his mistakes. No one was an exception to the rule, not even the brother of the Captain.

As this went on, Argus' vision became caked with a red fog. He was in pain, but he didn't cry or moan. He heard and ate his brother's hurtful words, swallowing them like he deserved it. That's when he saw it: a strange object, maybe an animal, creeping up behind the Captain and the Rovers. It looked like a spider, but it was the size of a dog and it was growing. Its appendages seemed to separate and arch upward. Then each of them landed down like spider legs, stretching out with serrated teeth on the tips of its newly made limbs. And then the eyes appeared; red like blood, opening and shutting independently of one another all over its dark frame. Argus quivered. Is this real? Was he imagining this thing? Its eyes blinked and settled upon him, alerting Argus that this was not an illusion.

"Argus," said Virgil and he shook Argus' head violently. Argus looked at Virgil; eyes filled with terror. Then he looked away to find the creature – it was still there. But, it was on the move. It was crawling over the Rover now, pressing its legs along the hood and traveling like it could go anywhere without restraint. Argus heard a noise like a low hiss as Virgil shook him again. Virgil pulled Argus close, eye-to-eye, and whispered, "This is your last chance, little brother. Your last chance, do you hear me?"

However, Argus was not listening. He could only hear the hiss of the beast: coarse and deafening. Virgil released him and Argus frantically scanned for the creature. Had it had crawled into one of the Rovers? It was gone now, but where was it? Was it somewhere inside? The soldiers pulled Argus to his feet, blood running down and mouth swelling.

"Clean his face," said Virgil. "Give him something for the pain. And put him in back."

"What about the others still in that town?" asked Greta. "And what about the item Argus lost?"

Virgil gave Greta a look like she'd said something wrong. She'd beaten his brother to the edge of his life, yet a claim that he'd lost a valuable item was too much, it seemed.

"We'll head north to the town and retrieve them," said Virgil. "We'll retrieve the bounty hunters too, if we can. I'd like to see just what the Shepherd did to them."

"Yes, sir."

Argus was carried into the nearest Rover and Virgil and Greta followed. The caravan left, moving faster down the road towards Glendale. Inside, Argus kept babbling about a terrifying creature. That something was in another Rover and was terrorizing one of their own. That something evil was upon them. But, the Huntsmen laughed and called him a fool. They dabbed him with washcloths to stop the bleeding, but Argus went on with his rambling. None listened to him. Or rather, none cared. The public beating had taken Argus' authority from him; and his paranoia worsened with every apathetic expression he saw.

"Look at him," said one of the soldiers. "He's gone mad. Now, his eyes really *are* seeing something."

* * * *

"What did you do to them?" asked Darion.

The Shepherd, still silent, reattached the four discs to his forearms and thighs and stood over the stream. "Shepherd, what did you do?" repeated Darion.

"I must replenish myself," said the Shepherd. "Then I will answer your questions."

The Shepherd had paused the group's progression next to a slow-moving brook. They washed their faces and hands at the water's edge, but the Shepherd was taking longer than the rest of them. He stooped down, cupping water with his hands and letting it drain through his fingers. Jack watched closely. He observed the captive water move up the Shepherd's hands, flowing through external veins on his silver suit, glowing brightly and then vanishing inside his silver suit. It was as if the water was seeping through his skin, only to have the water reappear, pouring back into his hands. At which point, the Shepherd would drink. Jack rubbed his eyes like he'd imagined it.

"I stopped them from hurting you, Darion," said the Shepherd, at last.

"Yes, you did," said Darion. "But what was that? What made them that way?"

The Shepherd didn't answer.

"You touched them, didn't you? I thought you could kill someone if you touched them. Isn't that forbidden? Isn't there a code of some sort you have to follow?"

"Forbidden by whom?" said the Shepherd, as if his authority were being challenged. And Jack thought, *who indeed?* Who made the rules if not the Shepherd?

"I did not touch them," said the Shepherd. "The proximity of my touch was enough to stop them. Their intentions were to kill you both."

Jack took a long breath. Their lives had been saved but the level of danger they'd been in had not been fully realized till now. The Shepherd spoke bluntly on the topic, as if he wanted no 'thank you' but at the very least, a bit of silence as payment for his guardianship while he rested and gathered himself.

"They were evil men," said Darion. "I could have guessed that myself. And they surely got what they deserved. But, I think I'll speak for all of us when I say this: where were you?"

Darion stood up this time and faced the Shepherd like he weren't afraid. Jack trembled; eyeing the Shepherd like heaven's angels might come down to smite Darion. The Shepherd, meanwhile, was mum.

"Where were you?" repeated Darion. "Did you wander off somewhere? Or did you just stand there? Waiting for the last possible second to come and rescue us? It was horrific, in case you didn't know. Olivia was terrified. *I* was terrified. And you allowed all of that to happen. And for what? It's clear you could have stopped all that before it started. So why the wait?"

The Shepherd stared down Darion, not speaking.

"Look, chief," said Jack. "Maybe you ought to…"

"No, Jack! Stay out of this! Where were you, Shepherd? Tell me now!"

The Shepherd hesitated, but stood firm like a mountain weathering a cool breeze against its side. "Your daughter called on me and I came," said the Shepherd. "That was all."

Darion looked at Olivia, who was crouched beside the stream. "*She* called on you? She doesn't even speak! How is that even possible?"

"I saved all three of you," said the Shepherd. " What more needs to be discussed, Darion?"

"Ha, I don't believe this," said Darion. "Any one of us could have been killed back there - "

"I *told* you," said the Shepherd, firmly. "I would not intervene unless absolutely necessary. And the time hadn't come for that yet. But, when I heard the cry, I responded."

"Yes, but – "

"Are you safe now?"

Darion did not answer.

"Do you have any injuries in need of my attention?" asked the Shepherd.

Darion, again, did not answer. He had words but they were all blocked by the questions of the Shepherd. *He's beaten you*, Jack thought. Let it go, old man. Darion paced the edge of the stream before taking a rock in hand and skipping it across the water. Then he squatted next to Olivia and took a deep breath. *Who's the child between the two of us now?* Jack thought.

"So what next?" asked Darion, out of the silence. "What about that signal? You said you found the source. What was it?"

Jack shuddered at the turn in conversation. Was it him? Had he caused it?

"That man," said the Shepherd. "He followed us to the town. He had a weapon with him."

"A weapon?" asked Darion.

"Yes," said the Shepherd. "Remnants of an old technology, but it was marred and broken. A disc, like mine, only it was shattered into smaller pieces. Though it had potential to come alive again, it won't. It can't."

"Why?"

"Because the will has been drained," said the Shepherd. "But, I have transferred it to my suit and am slowly augmenting it to my levels. It will soon be safe again for usage."

The information broke upon Jack and Darion like a complicated puzzle; one that both men struggled to piece together. Somehow, the Shepherd's explanation *did* sound logical; sounded relatable, but it was only because of the sureness in the Shepherd's voice that made it clear. And if the Shepherd understood the problem, then none of them need worry about solving it for themselves. None, but Darion, who was still racked with anger.

"Are you sure it's safe?" he asked.

The Shepherd removed the tattered disc from his thigh and pushed it into the air. It hovered at eye level, rotating slowly about. It was three quarters of the way restored, healing like a wound might, stitching itself together slowly. Darion and Jack couldn't conceal their amazement. Metal and thread were behaving organically. The Shepherd then used two other discs to hover about the broken one. Each shone a light on the broken disc, illuminating a purple and black cloud. It flashed like a miniature thunderstorm, circling the broken disc.

So this is it? thought Jack. This is what causes everything to go black. Is this what eats away our light? The kind we make?

"This is *Darklight*," said the Shepherd. "In its purest form, Darklight appears to us like this — a gas, but if you are wanting to understand it better, it is more like a black hole, sucking away light and energy. These discs, made of iron, are able to contain Darklight within itself. And that same iron does the same for Solfire."

"Everyone knows that, Shepherd," said Darion though Jack was not aware whatsoever. "The real question is *why* does it do that? Why does it like to eat electric charges? How can it break down heat, interrupt wireless signals, while leaving the likes of fire, lightning, and the sun alone?"

"*Energy*," said the Shepherd. "The answer can be found in energy. Light behaves and operates within several realms of the physical universe. It is not only a force to help us perceive our world, but light also *provides* energy, transmits data from one location to another, and it pushes against all other forms of matter it encounters. Darklight just so happens to tread along those same pathways, intercepting light and its energy where it sees fit."

"Where it sees *fit?*" said Darion. "That sounds like a convenient answer for someone who doesn't seem to know the truth."

"Not convenient, Darion," said the Shepherd. "But *the* truth. Mars has worked for many years trying to ascertain the reasons for why Darklight infects the Earth in the way it does. All answers seem to revolve around energy, and its output as influenced by humans. Still, it is not as simple as telling you black is black or white is white. There are mysteries we have yet to uncover. Darklight's involvement on Earth is one of them. We may perceive our world through light, yet Darklight seems to know which to intercede upon and which not. And while it hinders Earth's perception in some areas, Darklight only compounds or enhances them in others."

"Such as?"

"Through connections," said the Shepherd. "Between yourself and Jack, for example." The Shepherd pointed to Darion and then to Jack and back again. "As you have already experienced, touching these discs, made of Solfire - Darklight's cousin, if you will - it has created a connection between the two of you. And with *me*. Light is no longer being used for sight alone, but for creating a relationship between two points. In your case, between two living things."

Darion laughed, but did so like he was amused with the Shepherd's elementary explanation. "Thanks for referring to us as 'living things'," said Darion. "That makes me feel all the better."

"You asked for an answer," said the Shepherd. "And I gave you one. Do not mock me or you'll receive less from me when you'll need more."

The Shepherd's subtle threat made Darion stop in his tracks. Meanwhile, Jack pondered the enormity of this conversation. He found he was unable to rationalize the Shepherd's answers but somehow, understood at some basic level. Had the Shepherd tried to explain further - diving deeper among the details - then Jack would have been lost. He thought of the Pulse, thinking how insignificant this tiny cloud appeared before him yet was somehow responsible for the most mysterious and elusive power on the planet. Then the cloud pulsed like it could feel Jack's confusion so he quickly looked away.

"So this disc?" said Darion. "Where did it come from?"

The Shepherd's face turned grim, rotating several thoughts and emotions in a few seconds. He seemed to tell a story just through his eyes. "That man we encountered today," said the Shepherd. "He had Darklight all around him. I knew he had something with him. I had to find its source and when I did, I found this disc. Broken and torn in two."

Darion eyed the disc suspiciously. "But how... "

"I took it from him."

"Yes, I know, but how was it broken? Where did he get it? Why was it torn apart like that?"

The Shepherd paused. Darion had high interest in where the disc came from. And Jack noted that as unusual.

"Only another Shepherd would have possessed one of these," said the Shepherd. "But, this is not to say a person on Earth could have been trying to unlock its power. Tried to tear it open by force. Perhaps the disc recognized it was being violated and rebelled? I won't know until it's completely healed."

Darion walked away for a few moments and then returned. He wiped his face, put his hands on his hips and paced like he had too many words and not enough time to say them all. Jack watched him closely, trying to stay as close and as far from this conversation as he could. Best to observe and let the two of them have out their differences. This was not a place for Jack to give his input now. Especially with Darion on edge like this.

"So how was he able to block your signal?" asked Darion, suddenly. "I mean, this probably needed to be close to us, right?"

"Yes."

"Then what? Was he following us the whole time?"

Jack quivered and Darion saw him do it.

"You said they were after you," said Darion., now focusing on Jack. "How'd they find you back there anyway?"

Jack looked to the Shepherd. The giant's silver-blue eyes pierced Jack like they were pulling truth from Jack's insides. But still, Jack didn't want to say. He wanted to block the truth from coming forth if he could.

"They just jumped me, man," said Jack. "What else do you want me to say? They tried to take my money but I didn't have any on me."

Darion chuckled, but it was out of disbelief. "I've seen this to be a common thing with you, Jack. We both know they were after you in the old city. So what did you do, anyway? What did you say or do that made these men come after you, Jack?"

"They're just after me, " said Jack.

"Not good enough, Jack."

Jack was silent.

"Who do they work for, Jack? It's not just the Law that's after you, is it?"

Jack hesitated. "The Hunt..." said Jack and Darion's eyes widened.

"The *Hunt* is after you?" said Darion. Yes, there it is. Was this the proof you needed, chief? Proof that I was even worse than you first thought?

"You must be big game, Jack," said Darion, triumphantly. "Are you hearing this, Shepherd? That was them. The ones after us. After *him*."

Jack shook his head. "Not entirely. Those were just some hired hands. Their leader though – the guy the Shepherd took this from. He's a bigger deal than them. He's one of the Hunt."

"Who?"

"His name is Argus," said Jack. "They call him the 'Eyes of the Hunt', but he's nothing but a coward who got there because of his brother, Virgil. Argus' brother is the Captain. He's the one who puts the marks on people when there's a reward. And yes, I'm one of those marks. There, ya happy now, chief? Are ya happy to know that I'm a fugitive with a bounty on his head?"

Darion laughed, but it was a mocking laugh. "What would make me happy, Jack, is you being honest about why you're a mark in the first place. All this time we've been in real danger and you didn't seem privy to share it. You're unbelievable!"

"I didn't think ..."

"Exactly!" shouted Darion. "You didn't *think*. So let's try thinking now, shall we? What should we know about you that we don't already? Say it."

Jack paused. He debated what parts of his story were worthy of mention and which were better served in secret. Darion's anger was red hot, uncontrolled. If it weren't for the Shepherd, Jack would have turned and run. Or tackled Darion, force him into an agreement with his fists.

"I stole from them," said Jack, finally.

"Stole what?"

"Resources," said Jack. "I was an orphan, remember? I needed food. I needed shelter. And the Hunt is always recruiting; looking for anybody who doesn't have either. They take kids off the streets and make'em into soldiers. Did you know that? I was one of those kids. And worse yet, I grew up with Argus and his brother, Virgil. It was long time before Virgil became who he is now. Even if Argus has always been a coward, I thought his older brother might have done something better. But..."

"But, what?" said Darion. "You know these guys personally, do you? Well, that's just...just perfect, Jack!"

"What do you want me to say?" said Jack.

"Whatever else you need to tell us," said Darion. "If there's anything else we ought to know, then say it."

Jack hesitated. Then he said, "We grew up in the orphan houses. But, when I got older I didn't want the life of a Huntsman. I didn't wanna be one of their soldiers. So I left. And in their rulebook, that's stealing. You understand now?"

There was an awkward silence shared by every person. Jack was exposed, but his face lent everyone to believe he was relieved. He'd never told anyone these things before. It was liberating, but also terrifying. The Shepherd looked to be absorbing everything. Darion opened his mouth to speak several times but didn't say anything. He looked to the Shepherd and then at Jack.

"You... " said Darion, pointing a finger at Jack. "You need to leave here... get away from us."

"What?"

"They are only going to keep coming for you – for *us*," said Darion. "And when they find us, it'll be on your head as to why they did. Not mine. Not Olivia's. *Yours.*"

Jack couldn't believe it. Did he not hear what he said? What they did to orphans? What they did to anybody too young to know better? You ignored all these things I said. You passed them over and went right back to your own agenda. Jack felt more than hurt – he felt *betrayed.*

"And once they find you, Jack," said Darion, then turning and pointing at the Shepherd. "They're gonna want to take him too. You can't do that to us, Jack. You have to go. You have to leave."

"Jack cannot leave us now," said the Shepherd, speaking at last.

"He's endangered everyone here!" said Darion. "Not to mention my daughter! I won't allow that any more! I won't! Do something about it, will you?"

"You could always leave," said the Shepherd. "And not follow me, if you wish, Darion Wallace. Is that something you want?"

Darion stared at Jack. His eyes burned with rage for the young man.

"Maybe you're not understanding this, Shepherd... " said Darion. "The Hunt is an organization that specializes in search and capture. They take down outlaws, murderers, thieves – everyone with a hit on their head. They don't follow rules; they *make* the rules. If he stays with us, then this will only continue. They're going to keep coming for him. And us."

Darion pointed at Jack like he was a criminal, and suddenly, both men were aware of the warning the Shepherd had given them at the edge of Glendale. 'The path will become more treacherous', he had said. Was this a part of that premonition?

"I will defend him if they return," said the Shepherd. "And I will defend you as well. You forget, Darion Wallace, that those who have been touched by Solfire are forever affected by it, regardless of how you may feel personally towards that person."

The Darklight inside the disc started to swirl, alerting the Shepherd. "Such as this," said the Shepherd and he plunged his hand inside the purple and black cloud. The Shepherd gripped the cloud like it was made of something tangible and by all measure, it appeared to be. His hand shook violently inside the storm like the cloud was trying to escape, but the Shepherd held on. The cloud started to settle, reverting to a smaller size. Then the Shepherd removed his hand, the disc sealed shut and returned to his suit.

"What the hell?" said Jack. "Is it *alive*?"

"These disagreements will only attract the Adversary," said the Shepherd, ignoring Jack. "He has already been alerted to our presence here, even though I have contained this Darklight inside. Now, what is your desire, Darion?"

Olivia stood up and took her father's hand. Please. No more. No more, please.

Darion's rage was not so easily cooled though. He took several long breaths, clenched his fists and laughed aloud like the circumstances were incredulous. Jack stood in silence. Had it finally come to this? How much do you resent me now, Darion?

"Fine," said Darion, his voice sounding as reluctant as ever. Darion's tone cut at Jack, hitting and pulling his thoughts into dark places. He hates me more than ever. He *hates* me.

"Lead us to wherever it is you think we should go," said Darion. "We'll follow."

* * * *

Darion grumbled. If his body were capable, it would be pushing steam out every orifice on his body. The anger made his muscles tighten and, unintentionally, tilt his head to one side under the stress. This feeling, of complete frustration, made him vulnerable. He knew this. But, even so, he couldn't control it. It simply rose up inside of him. Without any sense of letting go either.

Even when he spoke the words, "we'll follow," he hated it. It meant he had to give in. He had to relinquish himself once more. And what brought Darion such anger only seemed to make the Shepherd all the merrier. The giant grinned, elated to hear Darion's agreement. No matter then. His anger didn't matter. He needed time to quell that anger. And an agreement with the Shepherd meant he could move forward again.

Yes, anger would hinder their progress. Darion knew this. So he retreated into himself and waited for the next instruction.

"My ship is still far from here," said the Shepherd. "Unfortunately, we've been rerouted. The detour was necessary but it also increased the distance between my ship and us. I will determine the fastest route. Stay close."

Good, thought Darion. Things will soon be back on track.

As for Jack, Darion had all the confirmation he needed. A wanted criminal. Yes, he knew that all along. But, to be wanted by the *Hunt*? The one group more powerful than the Law itself, the Hunt were as infamous as much as they were revered. Jack was no small fry. He was big game. Big enough to follow all the way outside of the city and traverse broken roads for the sake of finding him. Guess that's how the Hunt treats its deserters - by running them down until they're exhausted and *have* to come back.

Darion kept a close eye on Jack as the the Shepherd led the trio out of the woods. The evening was slow to arrive and there was no talking amongst anyone. Darion persisted with looking over his shoulder; the delicate paranoia attacking him like the Hunt was nearby. Jack did the same, unaware of what to do or how to act now that all members knew of the bounty on his head. His former allegiance was like a scar across his soul. Where he had covered it well, he couldn't anymore and there was no veil thick enough to shield him from the hateful eyes of Darion or the Shepherd. But, it was only part of the story, Jack thought. The rest he hoped to keep hidden completely. From the Shepherd, too, most of all. Don't any of you want to know how hard it's been for me?

By evening, they had found another break in the woods and a long stretch of open farmland ahead of them. The Shepherd stopped at the edge and looked about.

"We will stay here tonight," said the Shepherd. "I would prefer not to venture in the open as the night draws in."

"That's fine," said Darion. "But, it's still early. Don't you think we could just go to the other side now?"

"We could," said the Shepherd. "But I think it would be unwise to make ourselves known while the Adversary has our scent."

"It has our scent?" said Darion and the Shepherd pointed behind them, into the woods and beyond.

Darion, Jack, and Olivia slowly pivoted around, half-expecting to see a terrible creature right on their heels, but there was nothing there. Nothing at all.

"I don't see anything… " said Darion.

The Shepherd's arm fell to his side and both of his wrists clicked. Two of the silver discs appeared and floated over to both Jack and Darion. Then the Shepherd nodded and both men touched the floating orbs and the discs changed again, transforming into binocular-like devices. Darion pulled the new apparatus to his face and Jack did as Darion, but slower, and both men's eyes were filled with a strange light.

Through the lens, Darion and Jack could see farther than ever; nothing new for Darion, but not for Jack, who's mouth hung agape. This was surreal. The curvature of the Earth had been flattened out and Jack could see for miles. With each concentrated gaze, Jack and Darion gave wings to their eyes, looking deeper into the woods. Across the town, over the stone path and into the mountains they viewed the world and neither stopped until they caught glimpse of a black creature, skulking the wilderness. Jack nearly screamed, as did Darion. The Adversary was frothing at the mouth and Jack pulled away before it might see him. He didn't know if it could, but he didn't want to risk it either. Darion maintained his gaze upon the monster.

"That thing… " said Jack. "I felt like it was right on top of me."

The Shepherd asked for the discs and Jack complied, but Darion held onto his.

"When I had these, I could never see this far," said Darion. His disc returned to its original shape and Darion shook the disc in his hand like he couldn't believe it was capable of doing what it could. "Tell me, how is it that I can now? Is it because of you? Is that it?"

"When a signal is no longer interrupted," said the Shepherd. "A man can hear farther than what his eyes allow. We learn to trust our eyes first, but it is our ears that we should trust with the same level of importance. A man who listens intently can see across vast spaces if he is diligent in his listening."

"So I'm listening through these binoculars? Not *seeing*?"

The Shepherd nodded like this was an easy concept to grasp.

"Whatever, Shepherd," said Darion and he gave the disc back. "I listened for close to six months but I never saw or heard anything that far from where I was. It has to be because you're letting me do it. I couldn't do it on my own."

"In some respects, you are probably right."

The three of them made camp and the Shepherd walked the edge of the woods, pacing along the invisible fence before ultimately stopping for the night. Darion and Jack took seats across from each other, like always. Darion sang to Olivia and thought of what it would take to convince Jack to leave. This man will only bring us more problems. There must be something I can do. He tried to sleep, but his mind would not allow it.

Jack, conversely, watched the Shepherd intently.

Wondering if he'll keep his word, are you? Darion thought. Darion pondered if the Shepherd might be calculating the risk, weighing the option of having Jack in the group or out. But, he knew the Shepherd would protect Jack. He'd even said he would. And when Jack rolled to one side, Darion knew the Shepherd's words had seeped into Jack completely. The Shepherd meant what he said. It wasn't an empty promise. Right?

Jack rustled in the dirt, investigating his arms and legs for bugs that might wander inside the encampment. "I don't think I smell good anymore," said Jack, aloud and to no one in particular.

None of us smell nice, Darion thought. Except the damned Shepherd, I'm sure.

Chapter 12
The Order and the Chaos

"What if they have questions I cannot answer?"

"Do not worry yourself with that. Have the gift ready upon arrival. The rest will work its way out. Mars is ready to share with the rest of the universe. With our brothers and sisters on Earth."

"And if they refuse?"

"They *won't*."

* * * *

Darion waited till Jack was asleep to speak with the Shepherd again. He had to wait a long while too, but it was good that he did. For he needed time to think of how he might address everything that had happened during the daylight hours. The moon was nearly full, serving as a distraction for his thoughts since moonbeams penetrated the treetops and snuck into every corner of the forest floor. This made it difficult for Jack and Olivia, also. Light was not a gentle commodity and any excess, such as a full moon's, did not pass to Earth without being ogled by its human audience. Jack tried to stay awake to watch everything. Olivia too. But, it was Darion who feigned fatigue long enough to coerce Jack and Olivia into a slumber. And when both were with eyes closed, Darion stood slowly and made his way to the silver giant.

He found the Shepherd standing at the forest's edge, eyes to the open field ahead of them. His metallic frame glistened under the night's sky; statuesque and planted like a scarecrow to ward off invaders. The Shepherd almost didn't seem real. And what's more, everything, including the Shepherd, was emphasized under the moon: Olivia's hair shone blonder; Jack's skin twinkled under the dome. The night was good at hiding what was dirty while accentuating the clean. Even Darion's senses felt heightened within this new darkness. He approached the Shepherd with caution, feeling his intentions were already being judged.

"Enjoying the moon?" whispered Darion.

"I am actually," said the Shepherd. "As you know, this is my first time to Earth and could be my last. Seeing the moon like this is something I don't want to miss."

"Well, it'll be there tomorrow night too if we don't make it to your ship," said Darion. "Might be full by then too."

The Shepherd did not answer him. Alright, no small talk, it is.

"The Hunt won't stop looking for us," said Darion, abruptly. "You know this, right? If any one of them discovers that you are here – if any one of them knows who you are and what you are doing here– then that means they'll be after you too."

The Shepherd wouldn't speak.

"The Hunt is dangerous," said Darion. "They're known throughout the region for being peacekeepers but peace is relative to them. Only once the dust has settled and people have been crushed under their boots is there 'peace' again."

No answer.

"The old law keepers used to be in power," continued Darion. "Did you read about this in your studies on Mars? Are you even aware of what's been happening on Earth while you've been living there? Many of the old governments fell. New powers rule here now. That includes the Hunt."

A pause. More silence. Fine then. I'll tell you how things were. How they *are*.

"They have prisons, Shepherd. Not like what you have on Mars, I'm sure. The ones we have on Earth – they're meant for caging human beings; holding them until they can be bought or sold for their crimes. Not exactly like the prisons we used to have. Are you aware of this? And this man – the one you are defending – he was one of those men. A member of that same group that does these things. I can't let my daughter be in that kind of danger, Shepherd. Do you understand what I am telling you?"

More silence. Darion wondered at this point if the Shepherd were even listening. Maybe he was sleeping? Far off somewhere in an eyes-open dream only Shepherds or those of Mars could achieve.

Then, with a fiercer tone: "Are you even *listening* to me?"

The Shepherd turned his head and looked at Darion.

"Why are you not telling me what's on your heart?" asked the Shepherd.

"I am."

"Convince me of that. Then I will listen to what else you have to say."

The Shepherd looked away from Darion. Darion took a moment to gather his thoughts. His heart? What else did he need to say? Darion snuck a peek at Jack, sleeping against a tree with head on the ground.

"I don't trust him," said Darion, softly.

"Why?"

Weren't you listening to me? Do I need to explain myself again to you?

The Shepherd turned again towards Darion. His silver-blue eyes looked to be searching, filled with empathy.

"Because of what he's done," said Darion. "I saw him in the city before you arrived. Those same men attacked him. I didn't know why at the time, but you heard him earlier, didn't you? You heard how he's been affiliated with them."

"Yes, I did."

"Alright then," said Darion. "So here's something else you don't know: if it hadn't been for me – if I hadn't have acted back in the city – Jack would have been *dead*. Do you even know that? It's why he came after me in the first place. He came to steal the discs from me. *Your* discs. After he saw what I could do with them, he wanted them for himself. Tell me: what do you think of that? Do you still want to trust him?"

The Shepherd turned away. He seemed to be evaluating Darion's retelling of the incident in the old city, an event that, according to Darion, was proof of Jack's dark nature. The Shepherd stayed silent for a while, permitting time for Darion's words to seep in and knock his resolve or be washed away as inconsequential. As Darion stood there, he realized that he hadn't expressed or explained himself to the Shepherd during the days they'd been together. This was the first time he'd tried to reason his case, left his daughter's side, or made an argument for what he thought to be the greater good of their group. He felt like he'd been let out of a bottle. And it was good. Good to be open with someone other than his own daughter. Sharing his thoughts without first needing to filter what was inside. The Shepherd turned his head.

"That was before he found me though," said the Shepherd. "Before he came to know all of us. Do you think he is still the same?"

"How can a man change in a few days?"

"Men change from moment to moment."

"Yes," said Darion. "And many of them change right back to what they know. Unless something comes along that will suit their needs better, men go right on acting in their best interest."

The Shepherd eyed Darion, looking him up and down.

"Are you judging me, Shepherd?" asked Darion. "Because if you are, then yes – I *am* also acting in this way. I am acting out of self-preservation. Because I know what I know and what needs to be done."

"I am still thinking of your last argument," said the Shepherd. "You think change is impossible?"

Darion practically huffed. "For people?" said Darion. "It's damn near impossible. Impractical, really. People just aren't like that, Shepherd. Not on Earth, they're not. I'm sorry if that disappoints you."

"It doesn't," said the Shepherd. "But, if you come to Mars, Darion, will you think it impossible *and* impractical to become as I am?"

Darion was taken aback. Is that the expectation on Mars? Darion shuddered, hearing this new information. Become like *him*? Is that what was required to live on Mars? To become a silver giant like the Shepherd? Was everyone a Shepherd on Mars? Darion hadn't thought of the possibility, it seemed, till this moment. It was unlikely to be true. Or was it?

"Is that what I'll have to do?" asked Darion. "Do I need to become a Shepherd?"

"Only if you want to."

Only if I want to? Darion could never become like the Shepherd – this epitome of human evolution. The two of them were clearly different. Separated by a gulf more than a thousand miles wide.

"I don't understand what you're saying," said Darion. "Only if I 'want' to? I thought you said that everyone on Mars stuck to order. Every person knows what he is meant for, knows his purpose and so on. Isn't that what you said?"

"Yes, and it's the same here."

"How?"

"Because not every man knows what he is meant for on the day of his birth. That purpose is always waiting to be revealed later."

"You make it sound like it comes naturally."

The Shepherd grinned like it was a joke. "It can be," said the Shepherd. "Given the proper environment. A man becomes whom he is when the weight of his circumstances clashes with the weight of his core. The more extreme the situation, the quicker the purpose is revealed, I find."

Darion sensed a moment of vulnerability in their conversation. He felt as though the Shepherd were opening a door on his own life, pointing Darion to a question he wanted to be asked but Darion needed to find the proper words first.

"Is that how you became a Shepherd?" asked Darion. "When your circumstances clashed with your core?"

The Shepherd paused. Then, the Shepherd said, "I became a Shepherd because of my desires, Darion. I wanted to bring hope, if I were able to do so. I find that to be one of my greatest joys. I was fortunate to find that desire very early on. Some are not as fortunate as me. Their paths were hidden from them and they had to discover what that path was much later. For me, it was a passion for the people of this world. My purpose was found in that pursuit."

Darion was the one who fell silent this time. He thought of how the Shepherd might have lived on Mars, growing older until that moment of clarity struck. Darion imagined teachers and historians on Mars, showing the next generation of Mars how the Earth had been their home; how they'd left Earth years ago like a foreign country, looking for better soil and a fresh beginning. Yet, the place they left behind was in peril. Then came a human voice. A sympathetic voice with a solution: the Shepherd's purpose was born. Darion saw training grounds and tests being taken, training the Shepherd for his journey to Earth and the education he'd need to commandeer the voyage successfully. Darion projected all of these events into his mind and compared them to his own. His life's work of becoming a doctor was connected to the Shepherd now. That momentary happiness, perhaps even joy, for discovering fulfillment must have been a great day for the Shepherd. But, most importantly, it was a *human* experience; something Darion and the Shepherd could share together. This epiphany hit Darion and for a moment, Darion felt to be on even ground as the Shepherd. He *was* human, after all. Only a human could speak to these things and know the depth of what they would mean to the soul – the human condition of needing purpose above most anything else in life. Darion took a long breath.

"Do you have children, Shepherd?" asked Darion.

The Shepherd grinned again. "I have many waiting for me on Mars," answered the Shepherd. "They have yet to be born, but they are waiting for me there."

"How can you be sure of that? Do you have a wife? A fiancé' or something?"

"No, but I have seen it."

Darion took another deep breath. He thought what kind of certainty the Shepherd operated under. It was nothing like the chaos that functioned on Earth. People scrambled and scattered themselves here. Mars sounded more like an incubator – a place of enlightenment where only monks, the wise, or heavenly priests might exist. Darion folded his arms, thinking of these and other things. The discussion was veering away from its original topic, he realized.

"So, he's staying then, isn't he?" asked Darion and the Shepherd brought his eyes back upon Darion.

There was no answer. Darion expected that, he felt, and found himself not nearly as defeated by the answer as he would have first thought. The Shepherd won't be persuaded, he concluded. He won't allow himself to be persuaded. Everything was predetermined with the Shepherd. Intentional. Had purpose attached to the action. Even the Shepherd's barreled chest moved in and out like there was a superior method for achieving the optimum level of oxygen. Nothing was wasted or committed in excess. Darion, at first, had been in awe of the Shepherd's attention to perfection. But, now, at the height of their disagreement, found every nuance pertaining to the Shepherd as indescribably annoying. The impenetrable life the Shepherd had led; the easy path he'd had on Mars was frustrating to Darion. He cursed under his breath thinking of the difficulties he'd faced on Earth in contrast.

And yet, Darion wondered what the Shepherd thought of him. Is he annoyed with me? Does he find my company to be a bother?

"I have my own doubts, too, Darion," said the Shepherd and Darion's eyes became excited.

"Doubts?"

The Shepherd nodded.

"What kind of doubts?" asked Darion.

"I don't possess knowledge of all things, Darion," said the Shepherd. "Nor will I ever, I imagine. But, I still long to have it, if I can. I find myself longing for absolute understanding. And this frustrates me more than I can explain. The not knowing - this is the chaos of my soul."

Making yourself vulnerable again, are you? Why was the Shepherd doing this? Is he trying to appeal to me? Make me forget about Jack?

"And yet," continued the Shepherd. "I feel like that is the condition of any human being. We want order, but not just the kind of order that is external. We want order on the *inside* of our souls. And if we can have that, we will feel right. We will feel in control, won't we? And that is something you... your daughter... even *Jack* wants. Wouldn't you agree?"

There it was: the appeal to Jack's membership; the quiet persuasion waiting to unveil itself. It annoyed Darion, to think the Shepherd had been building to this conclusion all along. Is this what Mars was like? An entire society made up of condescending giants? Is that what really awaited him and Olivia on Mars? The prospect he'd dreamed of was no longer as attractive as he'd once imagined. The image of golden halls atop red rock was replaced with the upturned noses of manipulators. How was this *good*?

"If you don't desire these things," said the Shepherd, interrupting Darion's thoughts. "Then you are free to believe as you wish. That is also a human thing, Darion. Just as I am not inclined to bring you to the ship if I don't want to. I can still make that choice. You know I am capable of this too, don't you?"

The Shepherd's words were serious and it stopped Darion completely in his thoughts. True, the Shepherd *could* leave them whenever he wished. He could jump off into the darkness and never return. They'd have no way of finding him or tracking him if he did. The journey would be over. Done. A tremor, one filled with utter fear and abandonment, came over Darion. What was he doing – bargaining with the Shepherd? Why did he think this could be accomplished? He glanced at the Shepherd, silver-blue eyes staring back. No longer were they vulnerable or sympathetic – they were disciplined, focused. And unmoving. Darion felt himself shrink. Was this a threat? A promise? An apology suddenly felt necessary.

"I do," said Darion. "I know you are capable of these things. And I'm sorry if I've made you question everything. Made you question Jack."

The Shepherd squinted. "I am more sorry, that you have yet to tell me what is on your heart, Darion."

Darion eyed the Shepherd. Hadn't he done that? This entire discussion was based around Jack, wasn't it? The lack of trust Darion had for the thief and Darion's open desire to depart from Jack as soon as possible. What was left to say? Darion peered at the field before them like there was an answer lying somewhere among the tall grass. The landscape was littered with weeds and brown grain, and beyond that, a dark patch of woods on the other side. Darion couldn't see what was in there, but he knew they'd be going there tomorrow. However, if they'd left now, he'd be frightened to go there. That was it, he figured. That's what the Shepherd wanted to know.

"I'm scared…." said Darion.

"Of what?"

Darion felt like this was the right thing to say. It was what he was feeling, but hadn't known how to express it. How it had come so simply made him resentful, bitter to a point and he struggled to get out the rest of what he had inside.

"I'm scared of what's ahead," he said, but it felt like an admission, not a statement. "I don't have ultimate knowledge like you said, Shepherd. And I don't have the powers you have either. But, I *do* have my experience. And I have my mind. I have my own knowledge to work with that experience. But, still, I'm afraid. Afraid for my daughter. Afraid for what might happen should something not go as I had planned. So there, you have it now. I'm scared, Shepherd. And I don't know how to deal with that fear other than what I've told you."

The Shepherd grinned. "A human dilemma," said the Shepherd. "I think we can agree on something now."

Darion didn't smile, but he did recognize a burden being lifted in his spirits. Was this all he could do? He'd voiced what he felt, knew it was right but hadn't gotten the answer he wanted. Maybe that wasn't the end of this struggle though. Maybe it'll take longer to get the answer I want. A 'no' does not mean 'never', he figured.

202 | J.C.L. Faltot

This could do, for now. I will wait to see what happens next. And trust the Shepherd in doing so. But, Darion had one last thing for the Shepherd. If the Shepherd were human, as he claimed to be, then this would appeal to his humanity even more. Darion looked to the Shepherd once more, his words focused and deliberate.

"Tell me what I have to do then," said Darion. "If we are in agreement now. Tell me what I have to do if I'm going to protect my daughter. How do I manage the fear of things I can't control? Can you at least tell me that if you aren't willing to listen to my other requests?"

The Shepherd paused. This habit of the Shepherd – not talking when asked a serious question – made Darion wonder if the Shepherd was thinking of a good answer or if he was cycling through reasons that could change the subject. Darion waited anyway.

Then the Shepherd said, "If you want to protect her, then you needn't change a thing you're doing, Darion. Trust your knowledge. It will speak to your experience. Trust your instincts. It will speak to your wits. But, moreover, do not trust either when I tell you that you need to trust *me*."

Trust him? Darion had a hard enough time trusting himself. How could he trust this alien? No, the Shepherd was more than alien – he was a human parading as some godly alien.

There was another long pause between them. The wind seemed to know the conversation was ending and kicked at the leaves and stirred the grass. *Trust the Shepherd?* Wasn't this something he had been doing all this time? Darion trusted the Shepherd would lead him to his Martian ship. He trusted the Shepherd could protect them. He trusted the Shepherd wasn't a liar. Was this what the Shepherd needed from him?

"Is what I'm telling you," said the Shepherd. "Enough to calm your frightened heart?"

"What you're asking of me," said Darion. "Is something I've never been good at. I don't trust anyone unless they're first proven themselves to me. But yes, the thought of trusting someone whose power is greater than mine is something I might be able to do."

"Power shouldn't fuel trust," said the Shepherd. "Power can be taken and given to another. Trust cannot exist in such a fickle environment as the delegating of power. No, trust asks more than that."

"What does it ask exactly?"

"*Everything*," said the Shepherd, with finality in his voice and Darion stood in silence.

There was no swaying the Shepherd at this point. Jack would have to remain. At least for now. But, that didn't mean Darion couldn't act. He'd tried his hand at convincing the Shepherd. But that still left room for Darion to do something. He just didn't know what. Not yet, he didn't.

"So that's it then?" said Darion.

"For which? This conversation? Or the requirements of trust?"

"Both," said Darion. "I won't say that I agree with you on everything. But, I do appreciate your insights."

The Shepherd nodded like he was thankful to hear that.

"And I trust you'll be here when I awake?" asked Darion.

The Shepherd didn't grin. He looked at Darion and nodded again. That was good enough.

Then Darion took out his camera and snapped a few shots of the open field, illuminated under moonbeams. The Shepherd looked at the camera curiously, interested by Darion's device.

"Not as fancy as anything you got, but it works just fine," said Darion.

"Have you seen your pictures?"

"No. But I hope to get them developed some day. Good night, Shepherd."

Darion put the camera in his pocket and walked back inside the barrier. He crouched next to Olivia and nestled himself into a position that would be comfortable for them both. He focused on his breathing, imitating the Shepherd's like it might help him fall asleep. The Shepherd had given him much to consider and he needed sleep if he was going to navigate every plausible outcome appropriately. He needed time to analyze and investigate every last word on the Shepherd's breath. His analysis would yield how to best handle the Shepherd next time he needed something. He hadn't failed. He'd merely tested the waters. And now, Darion would trust his subconscious to do the rest of the work. A good sleep would do him well. So he drifted in thought and was dreaming shortly.

* * * *

Across the barrier, Jack was rolled on one side, looking away from Darion. But, his eyes were wide open and his mind was buzzing. It was no secret Darion had wanted him gone; he knew that to be true. But, waiting to plead his case to the Shepherd in darkness? How long had Darion been doing this? The Shepherd didn't sound to be convinced, however, and Jack was relieved to hear this, yet his thoughts returned to Darion and the infidelity in Darion's speech. It hurt Jack, but still, Jack tried to convince himself that Darion's words didn't bother him. He'd heard similar words before. Spoken to and about him. The betrayal. The self-preservation. And so, Jack reasoned Darion to be just like anybody else.

He couldn't trust anyone anymore, save the Shepherd. He wouldn't. Experience had taught him that. Served him well. He closed his eyes and dreamt of the ways he'd keep himself safe from everyone. Especially Darion.

* * * *

Virgil and the Hunt came upon the town of Glendale within the hour and immediately set to questioning its citizens. They greeted people kindly enough, but the townspeople were frightened. The Hunt was well organized. Their Rovers announced their coming from far away and they had weapons for every man and woman within their ranks. Greta was at the forefront. She asked those she found in the street about the whereabouts of a few 'strangers', but got no solid answers. Only blank stares and scared faces.

Then one came forward with information about a 'bright giant' and Greta had the people assemble into lines.

"We'll need to look around," she said. "This won't take long."

The Huntsmen filed out of the Rovers in support of Greta's directives. Virgil and Argus appeared with them. Argus, still adrift mentally, looked about for the Shepherd. One of the Glendale men saw Argus and looked away quickly. Greta saw it and pulled the man from line.

"Who are you?" asked Greta.

"My name is Marcus," he said cautiously.

"You saw this man?"

He nodded.

"Whom else did you see?" she inquired.

"Others," he said. "But they're already gone from here. There's no one here who didn't live here already."

"What others?"

Marcus hesitated. "That-that silver giant. He was here and so were your men." He pointed to Argus, who was hiding behind Virgil.

"Where did they go?" asked Greta.

Marcus pointed away from the town. "Up into the mountains."

"What else can you tell us?"

"If I tell you, will you leave?"

Greta pretended to not be offended. She kept her lips pressed together, maintaining her poise. She was good at that.

"Of course," she said.

Marcus swallowed and divulged a quick story. At the end, he stated a large man, Reggie, was comatose and the doctors were keeping him in one of the safe houses. The man with him, Matthew, was there also. So Greta took two soldiers and Marcus with her and when they came upon Reggie, they saw a large man lying on a bed, breathing heavily. His entire body was sweating profusely. He looked like a wet rag that had been squeezed too tight. Matthew was incoherent and lying on another bed. When Argus saw them, he cringed and began muttering words about 'fire' and left the room.

"What the hell happened to them?" said one of Virgil's lieutenants. "Are you sure you want to keep at this? We're pretty far out from the city now."

"Of course I do," said Virgil. "Keep asking your questions and don't stop till you find something."

"What are we looking for, Captain?"

"A trace of something extraordinary. See if there's anything that might have been left behind."

"What about them?"

The lieutenant pointed to Reggie and his partner, but Virgil didn't answer; didn't respond. He walked out of the safe house and back onto the street. Greta motioned to the lieutenants and they left with her. *On your own now*, Greta thought. If you're not strong enough then you're not fit to be with us. Farewell, Reggie. Farewell, Matthew.

In the center of town, more people were being put into lines, the Huntsmen standing at guard.

"It seems like our runaway has made some powerful friends," said Greta. "Who knew Jack could have had that kind of influence?"

Virgil heard her, but his mind and eyes were elsewhere. He looked about the town, face tightened like he were thinking deeply.

"What do you think of all this 'silver giant' talk?" asked Greta. "It sounds like an urban legend to me. Bigfoot or Jersey Devil-type nonsense."

"All legends have some truth in them," said Virgil. "You simply have to be wise enough to recognize what's legend and what's truth. And since I believe our scouts and Argus have reported accurately, I think this legend we're after isn't a legend at all."

Greta didn't answer at first. The Captain's words always carried a double meaning, made one stop and consider everything he was saying. She didn't want to sound foolish when she spoke again.

"Then the 'giant'," she said. "*He's* what you've been looking for? Not the weapon?"

Virgil grinned. "Actually, I believe them to be one in the same, Greta."

Out in the street, one of the Hunt's lieutenants was interrogating a woman. She was frightened, mumbling and stumbling over her words as the lieutenant charged her for answers. He interrupted her several times, calling her dumb and moronic before finally grabbing her by the back of the neck and pulling her down.

"Where did they go? Did you see the light weapon?" he shouted. The woman was in hysterics. She asked what was happening and why they'd come but the lieutenant kept on with the questions. She cried out and Virgil marched away from Greta.

"What are you doing?" asked Virgil and the Huntsman stopped. He looked at Virgil, surprised to see the Captain addressing him.

"I am – "

"Tell me what you are doing," said Virgil, sternly.

The lieutenant looked about. "Finding answers..."

"Did you find any?"

The lieutenant paused. He shook his head and looked to the other soldiers.

"Then why are you wasting their time?" asked Virgil. "And why are you acting like you're the one who is in charge?"

The lieutenant didn't speak. He looked away, but Virgil met his eyes and said, "Well, are you or aren't you the one in charge?"

The lieutenant shook his head, embarrassed. Virgil reached out and grabbed the lieutenant's scarf and pulled it down around his neck. Greta grinned. Show them how inferior they are, Captain. That *you* are the one who makes the rules; not them. Not any of us. Just *you*.

"What will you do now?" said Virgil, mocking his lieutenant. "Can you bully her the same as you did without your mask? Look at her. Look upon her face and tell me if you can."

Virgil pointed to the woman, crouched beside the lieutenant. The lieutenant looked down at her and she gazed back at him, frightened yet now she could discern every feature on his exposed face. He had a trimmed goatee and a thin mouth and his jaw was narrow at the chin.

"Captain," he said. "I thought this was the way we – "

"Ask your question, lieutenant! Or do you feel ashamed now that your face is uncovered?"

Virgil snatched the red scarf, the emblem of the Hunt, away from the lieutenant and waved it about in front of him. Argus, though injured, grinned watching his brother at work. It was a break from the tongue-lashings he'd received.

"Hiding one's face doesn't hide true nature," said Virgil. "Anyone can pull a scarf over his face and pretend to be one of us. But, do you possess the determination and the will to wear it like you should?"

Silence. No one uttered a word, even the people of Glendale.

"No?" said Virgil. "That's because the scarf is more than what you believe it to be. It's not a mask, it's a *symbol*, not a shield for you to hide behind and make cowardly threats. The Hunt does not make threats. We only make promises."

Virgil paused, letting the words have their way with the lieutenant. To anyone watching, Virgil was like an alpha male, squashing the upheaval of a rogue bull among his troop. This particular rebuke had been a successful one. For the lieutenant backed away and Virgil stuffed the scarf into his back pocket. Then Virgil held out a hand to the beaten woman.

"Come," he said. "I am truly sorry for that. We will be going soon. Come up here and don't be afraid."

The woman hesitated. Virgil's wide grin and open hand were inviting, but still, she feared him. There was something in his eyes – jet black and pinched tight – that made him untrustworthy. His talk of masks would have marveled even an intelligent mind, but it was this man's face that seemed to betray his words. Something was amiss, inhuman, and lacking of the typical human features that differentiated mask from true self. However, there was no one else around. No one was coming to her aid so the woman took Virgil's hand and stood cautiously.

"There, that's better," said Virgil.

Then Virgil caught sight of Argus. He was trembling, facing away from Virgil and looking upon the rooftops. The Captain walked over to his brother, dismissing and leaving the woman like he'd torn the cord that bound them from his side. *What are you doing, Captain?* Greta thought. Your brother has lost his mind. Leave him.

"What is it?" asked Virgil.

Argus' eyes were diverted, fixed on the source of a low hiss he heard coming from the rooftops. And there it was, only this time it was even bigger. Its spider legs were climbing along the top of the café, long black lances trekking across the building. Argus stared like his eyes were glued open. It was an inconceivable monster – terrifying to the point of disbelief.

"Where is it…" whispered Virgil. "Where is he?"

Greta couldn't hear so she walked towards them.

"Tell me what you see, little brother," said Virgil, closer now.

Argus wouldn't answer. The monster had opened its eyes – *all* of its eyes so Argus froze. The beast stopped at the edge of a roof and crawled down. It crept across the sidewalk and onto the dirt road. Its eyes spun in several directions, and its spider legs grasped the pavement, raking the stone and dirt with its claws. Then came the hiss. Argus nearly forgot where he was; forgot Virgil was near as the beast opened its mouth; huge fangs dropping, dripping in saliva and mucus. Argus tried to scream but Virgil grabbed him and held him where he was.

"Tell me what it is," said Virgil. "What does it look like? What does it say to you?"

Argus couldn't break free. His brother was already the stronger and he was still injured. The beast was coming. Argus closed his eyes and cried, "No, I don't want to die!" And Virgil released him. Argus fell forward and shriveled into a ball, imagining the teeth and claws of the monster digging into him from all angles. But, when he opened his eyes, the presence of the monster had gone. Virgil stood over him, a glint of excitement in his eyes.

The Captain turned to address the Hunt. They were all of them silent, each staring in wonderment. Had Argus finally succumbed to mental deterioration? The Captain was oddly pleased, if so.

"We are close," said Virgil. Several officers looked confused. They knew they were to be watching Virgil, but it was Argus who kept their attention. His body convulsed and he had begun to ramble off words like, 'don't kill me' or 'please don't let me die.'

"Are you tired of not having *power*?" shouted Virgil, calling them all back to his voice. He addressed every person who might be in earshot. "Are you upset with where you are? Are there those among you who survived the Pulse and know there are better days than the ones you live in *now*?"

The Captain paused, swung around to another group of listeners. "I miss the light too. I wish I knew what it was like to have it. To be able to walk in a dark room and turn the lights on. Turn blackness into light. Wasn't that nice? It probably gave you comfort. Gave you security. Didn't it?"

People stirred in the lines and Virgil urged them to step out. He ordered his Huntsmen down, encouraged the people of Glendale to not be afraid and approach him if they wished to. Virgil walked towards them; his gait, boastful; his saunter, confident. Greta watched his every move, taking it in like the master was at work. You're going to win this town yet, aren't you? They're all afraid, but you'll make them *unafraid*.

"We, the Hunt," said Virgil. "Are on the verge of a great discovery. We came to this town because we were looking for someone. He was a fugitive; a man who had broken the law and deemed dangerous. It is why we had to be so forceful with all of you. But, there is something else – *someone* else – that is even more dangerous than him! We have found... a Shepherd of Mars!"

The people in Glendale began to gather in greater numbers, talking among themselves. Some seemed to know what a Shepherd was, while others identified with the 'silver giant' instead. Each of them listened like Virgil had authority, as if he knew what had invaded their town and destroyed their peaceful life just hours before. Soon, Virgil had a great audience. The unknown nature of the Shepherd; the fear which accompanied the Hunt's arrival – all of this had been supplanted by Virgil's call to arms. A call to light.

"We came here looking for him," said Virgil. "And the group that follows him, but there are none among you who know where he is or where he has gone to… "

Virgil pivoted around so as to make his voice heard to the other side of town.

"*But*," he said. "The Hunt does not miss its quarry! And we will find him soon! And when we do, we will set things straight. Mars is responsible for the life we have now. For this shadowed existence we've been made to endure. We, the Hunt, will capture this Shepherd and make him pay for what he's done. No more darkness!"

More people came to the streets and Virgil could sense his momentum gaining. Like a pack of dogs, chomping at the bit, they came and Virgil was prepared to feed them. Greta sensed it also. Argus – still a mess of human emotion – unraveled slowly on the ground.

"We will get back the weapon the Shepherd has!" stated Virgil. "We will tell him to give us our light back! Earth is our home! Not Mars! And we deserve to take it *back*!"

Virgil looked about the masses like they were about to shower him with praise. Some most certainly wanted to. Many came forward with questions for the Hunt and by day's end, the Hunt had taken many of Glendale's sons and daughters; taken with the subtle coercion of Virgil's declaration for revenge upon the red planet. Their Rovers were soon overflowing with new recruits, eager to experience what the Captain had promised. And he would give them what they wanted. He would give them all what they wanted.

Chapter 13
The Calling of the Dark

"And what else is it that I want you to know?"

"To be careful?"

"Yes. But, only so you understand – "

"That you care for my return? Thank you, Father. I will return. I promise you, I will."

- end transmission, Alpha program recording, Mars Archives, July 12, 2049

* * * *

Darion and Jack both awoke as if sharing the same dream. They stared at one another until each remembered his silent vendetta against the other, at which point, it was back to awkward stares and ill-timed glances. Darion wondered if Jack had heard his earlier conversation; if Jack had gotten snippets of Darion's plea to the Shepherd to leave Jack behind. And as Darion was doing that, Jack wondered if Darion was reading *his* thoughts; confirming that which Darion feared. But when neither man spoke, each silently assured himself that his intentions were sealed and unknown to the other.

They turned their attention upon other things. The Shepherd was not with them, but the discs were active and the invisible fortress was still in place. It had been raining, yet it was hardly a drizzle. The tiny droplets of water were pelting the top of the barrier and falling outside the dome. Jack peered at the ceiling and saw that the water was not reaching them. Everything beneath the floating disc was dry.

This thing even keeps the rain out, Jack thought.

"It keeps all the noise in too," said Darion, startling Jack like Darion *had* been reading his thoughts.

"How does it do that?"

"I don't know," said Darion. "Probably something to do with the light that's being pushed around. It always did it for me."

Light? Pushing the water away? How could light do something like that? Jack looked up at his invisible umbrella and sighed, straining to understand how all this magic was working around him.

"Just try to keep it down," said Darion. "My daughter is still sleeping."

"I will, but rain is rain. It don't listen to nobody."

"That's not what I was talking about."

"I know. I just don't care, alright?" said Jack.

Still wanting to speak for me. Still wanting to treat me like a kid. Jack looked about and then focused in on Darion.

"Where do you think he is?" asked Jack. "The Shepherd."

Darion didn't answer at first. "Oh," said Darion. "I didn't know if you were meaning someone else?"

Jack curled his lips angrily. He laughed softly and said, "That's fine, chief. One snap of bitterness deserves another, right?"

"I'm not the one whose bitter, Jack," said Darion. "I just want some quiet."

Jack looked away from Darion, fidgeting nervously.

"He's fine, Jack," said Darion. "Wherever he is, he's okay."

"How do you know?" asked Jack, surprised to hear Darion answer his question.

"These discs are all lit," said Darion. "So as long as those are lit, we'll know he's alright."

"Are you sure?"

"Yes. But feel free to not believe me. Keep on worrying and thinking about terrible things, if you prefer."

That's probably what you want anyway, Jack thought. You want me to keep my mind off of what you said. You want me to stay stupid, stay ignorant. But, I won't. I'll keep pressing till you make a mistake. And then I'll catch you in a lie, Darion. I'll catch you in it so fast you won't even know what to think.

"Rain's picking up," said Jack. "I hope this thing can hold it."

"It'll hold," said Darion. "The light of these discs emits more than just light itself, they also emit matter. Do you understand what I'm saying?"

Jack shook his head. He hated not knowing.

"It's what's keeping the rain out. Light can do a lot of things we never imagined. Now, get some shut eye."

Jack reluctantly did as he was told. He was tired anyway. So he tried to fall back asleep as Darion did too. Soon, they were both asleep again.

But, Darion moved in his sleep and his backpack moved, spilling out a book and some other things. Jack awoke.

What was this? Jack thought. Jack got up slowly and walked over to Darion. He was careful to make certain that Darion was asleep when he pulled the leather bound book from the ground and sat back to inspect it. Fortunately, Jack was learned enough to read its contents, though Darion's handwriting was difficult to decipher.

The book was a journal of some sort. There were pictures and diagrams, directions and markings too. It looked like a map on some pages, while on others it was a collection of thoughts. Jack eventually came to a stretch of words that enticed him and decided to read it. *The war on Mars?* it read at top. Jack read on till the end of the page:

"No, we know that to be a lie now. The war was never real. When Marion Perriello, the King of Mars, sent his son, Cale, and chief guards to Earth, we should have known it was an act of goodwill; not a precursor to war. Cale brought with him what made Mars so powerful. He brought with him the greatest discovery of our age. But, we didn't want to believe it were possible. Our opinion of Mars was greater than the truth. Imbeciles. How is it that the ones with power are the ones so easily drawn into corruption? Into fear? No matter. We can't change any of that now. But, Mars? They can. Regardless of their earlier intentions, they owe it to us. And I believe they've recognized their error, for the Shepherds have come. They are the bridge. They are what's going to bring us out of this darkness. I know it. My dreams tell me it is true. My dear Lydia, do you believe me also?"

Jack stopped reading and shut the book. Darion was fast asleep, or if he weren't, he was doing a damn good job of pretending he was. These words - were they true? How long had Darion known of the Shepherds? This 'false war' with Mars? And who was Lydia? The mother of Olivia, no doubt. Jack looked at the camera in Darion's backpack. Should he take it? No, there wasn't anything he would find that might help him better understand this man. Without the light, the pictures were probably worthless. So

Jack slid the journal in the backpack and walked back to the other side of the covered barrier.

He sat in silence, thinking about the journal and what he'd found in it. There were more questions now within Jack, but none of which he wanted to ask of Darion for help. When would the Shepherd return? Jack hoped it would be soon. But, he fell asleep before that could happen as lightning danced about the forest and open plains, openly mocking the power Darklight seemed to hold on mankind, but not on the Earth herself.

* * * *

The Captain of the Hunt sat among his most loyal lieutenants. They positioned themselves all around Virgil, seated at the back of a small town cafe, en route for the Shepherd. His company had followed him for the duration of the afternoon, led only by the confidence that Virgil had heard a "voice" and if had not been for Argus' persistent fear of something otherworldly, the Hunt would have left their pursuit and headed home. But, Virgil's words of providence spurred them onward and when they arrived at the next town, Virgil spoke more of the conspiracy surrounding Mars' dominion over Earth and the age-old battle against the effects of the Pulse, caused by the people of Mars and their emissaries, the Shepherds.

"I tell you," said Virgil. "This is where we will take it back. No more protecting the old city from itself. This is bigger than that. Much bigger and you'll be thanking me when it's through. I'll tell you again: a large reward is forthcoming. And the biggest one will be for the man who brings me the weapon and the Shepherd himself."

The lieutenants, hearing this, barked at one another, jutting their chests out like each one of them would be the one to do the deed for the Captain. They exchanged stories of past riches and bounties won and stacked their accomplishments against one another until the standard of supreme accomplishment was all but blurred and without measure. Virgil smiled, thinking himself responsible for the renewed life in the Hunt and subtly, he could hear that familiar voice speaking plainly in the background: the Adversary was near. It moved around the outside of the table, walking quietly, mouth frothing and tongue hissing and with every new mention of the Shepherd's demise or Mars' fall, the Adversary grew and its noise only increased.

But, in secret, and when the Captain was talking or distracted by his own thoughts, the Hunt would share doubts; questions of whether their leader was in good conscience and they spoke softly to one another around the table, exchanging their fears. This enticed the Adversary even more than their claims.

"Do ya really think he sees what he says he sees?" asked one of the lieutenants.

"Who? The Captain or that idiot, Argus?" said another.

"Both, I guess."

"I dunno. But, that was weird back there. In Glendale, ya know? Just what was that all about?"

"Hell yeah, it was weird. You're askin' the wrong guy though. But, who cares? The Captain can squeeze a coin out of a stone. We'll find somethin'. And there'll be money in it like he says. Just like always."

"I hear that," said the lieutenant.

Virgil pounded the table. It surprised everyone and they fixed their eyes upon him. The Adversary, lurking in the shadows, had positioned itself directly behind Virgil, unseen to all in the room.

"Do not..." said Virgil, his voice shaking in anger. "Do not think that I am unaware of your words, gentlemen."

The two lieutenants slouched, retreating into their seats. "I have ears everywhere now. And if it's payment that you're concerned with, you'll get it. You'll get what you're after. I assure you."

The lieutenants looked around with confused, frightened expressions. Virgil motioned to the door and one on the end stood and opened it wide. Virgil called to 'send him in' and there, standing in the doorway, was Argus and Greta. Argus stared at the ground, he was like a walking corpse and Greta sneered at the Captain's brother like she was looking at a filthy rag. She spit on the ground and pushed Argus to go inside.

"I thought the Eyes of the Hunt wanted to be involved in every roundtable discussion?" she said.

Argus hesitated. He kept staring at the floor. "I don't want any of what's going on in there..." said Argus and he looked upon Greta with haunted eyes. "There's something in there with them...."

Something terrible and I don't want none of it. I can feel it. Like, it's always with me now. And I can't get rid of it..."

Again, Greta sneered at Argus. She hated his cowardice. "You disgust me," she said. "How is it that you're the Captain's brother? Different fathers, maybe?"

Argus didn't answer. He looked at Greta pitifully and the lieutenant took Argus by the elbow, escorting him inside. Greta followed.

When Argus entered the room, he could see the roundtable and Virgil, gleaming. There were a dozen or so men and women seated about Virgil and they were all of them watching Argus like he was in trouble. Like he was the topic of their most recent conversation. Argus scanned the room cautiously, looking for the beast, but when he didn't see it, he loosened his shoulders. He was safe for the moment, it appeared.

"Leave us," said Virgil, but none of the Hunt moved. They acted like the order was not for them. "I said, get out. Leave me with him."

The lieutenants looked to each other like someone had been scolded and pushed out their chairs and left. Greta remained, but Virgil motioned for her to leave and she grudgingly did so as well. *Even me?* Greta thought. She gave Argus another look of contempt. A parting glance like Argus might finally realize his own repulsive weakness. Yet Argus didn't look, and the fact that he persisted with ignoring her, bothered Greta greatly. Like something else had become more fearful than her. She would have to try another tactic later, she thought. Something to remind him that she was still to be feared above anything else he knew.

When Greta shut the door, Argus waited. He didn't look at his brother, but he knew Virgil was looking at him. Also waiting. Thinking. Together, they shared silence like either man was anticipating a first move. Argus knew better than to initiate. Virgil wanted to be heard. That's how he was. That's how he'd always been. So Argus waited, saying nothing. Thinking nothing, if he could.

"Do you see it now, brother?" asked Virgil, finally. "Do you see it this very moment?"

Argus looked about the room slowly and shook his head like he was unsure what had been asked of him. But, he most definitely knew. Argus knew but he didn't want to answer. Ignorance was his best shield now.

"Let me try again," said Virgil. "I said – do *you* see it?"

Argus kept his eyes to the floor.

"That thing that haunts man's dreams," said Virgil. "The greatest discovery of our time; or any time, really. The power of a million atomic bombs…."

Argus felt a nervousness come over him. His brother was known to drown others in deep, philosophical lectures, but this was building with a disturbing sense of force behind it. Like there was a definitive point to his open-ended statement. It made Argus want Virgil to get to it already before it became too big for him to handle.

"No…" said Argus. "I don't…I don't see it anywhere…."

Virgil sat back in his chair and pressed a finger to his lips, thinking.

"You're not lying to me, are you? Because if you're lying to me, then that would be rude. And a cause for me to do something I don't want to." Argus swallowed. "So, are you?" Argus shook his head.

"No?" said Virgil.

Virgil leaned forward. He observed every inch of Argus: his mannerisms, his stance, his breathing – everything. Argus felt like a stranger, an alien in front of his own brother. He was not family or even a close friend. It could have been anybody, really. Anybody could have seen that thing, not just him, and Virgil would have called him in for an interrogation. And that individual – whomever it was – would have been given the same treatment as him. In that moment, Argus wanted to die. He'd rather *be* dead than be treated like he was.

"You and I both know," said Virgil. "How important this is to me, brother. How imperative it is that I know what you've seen. That I understand what you understand. Do you hear my words?" Argus nodded.

"Then tell me this," said Virgil. "What does it *sound* like?"

Argus fidgeted. "I don't know, Virgil. It's just…"

"Something magical, right? Something you could never explain unless you, yourself, experienced it. Am I right?"

Virgil's eyes widened. The room darkened and Argus' lips quivered like a cold breeze had swept in. No, not now. Argus saw a leg, like a giant black spider; reach out from the corner of the room. The end of which, a sharp hook, dug into the wooden floor, slowly tugging a hairy form into view. Argus began to shake uncontrollably, alerting Virgil to the same corner.

"It's here now, isn't it?" said Virgil. Argus wouldn't answer. He didn't want to, but then the fear superseded the want.

"Virgil...Get away ... get out of..."

"What's it look like?" asked Virgil, growing ever more excited. "Tell me. What do you see? What's it doing right now?"

More legs came and soon, a head. A sick and twisted head like a doll's mask appeared and Argus almost screamed. Argus looked away from the Adversary and fixed his eyes on Virgil. He didn't want Virgil to see it. He didn't want his brother to experience it. Yet, the Adversary kept coming. And so did Virgil's eagerness to talk and speak about the thing Argus feared most.

"It's alright," said Virgil. "It won't harm me; it can't. I know it won't."

Argus didn't believe his brother. He watched the Adversary move. It was like a serpent with spider legs. It opened its eyes, red like blood, and slunk across the back of the room. It poked in and out of darkness, disappearing for a moment and then reappearing like vapor. It glided under a chair and then under the table and Argus backed away. The air became cold. How could it be cold? This creature was even affecting the temperature of the room.

"Where is it now, Argus? Where?"

Argus clenched his lips together and refused to call attention to himself; convinced any sudden effort might reveal his location. But, the Adversary was on the move again and Argus nearly gasped when he saw a single leg wrap itself up over the table. It laid another foot on Virgil's armrest, slowly climbing above him.

"Virgil..." said Argus, eyes widened with fear. "Don't..."

Virgil only grinned. The Adversary climbed higher still, its long legs pressing against the table as Argus clenched. Would it strike his brother? Argus began looking about the room for a weapon, anything that might be able to thwart the creature. Then the room rattled like the Adversary was shaking everything with its voice. It turned its head towards Argus and there, it saw him and he saw *it*. The connection made, Argus took in every inch of the Adversary's disgusting body; a collection of nightmarish entities: a spider, human, and serpent, it was. And Argus nearly vomited at the sight.

"Don't be afraid, Argus," said Virgil and the Adversary put its legs upon the back of Virgil's chair. "It won't hurt me. Just tell me what you see."

The Adversary opened its mouth by Virgil's head; white and black tar puking up from its innards. The spit slopped on the floor with a sickening thud as the Adversary opened its maw wider. Large teeth packed themselves into several rows and Argus tried to scream, but fear had him immobilized.

"It wants something from me, brother," said Virgil and to Argus' relief, the Adversary stopped its advances. It retracted its teeth and closed its mouth tight. "But I also know what *I* want, Argus. That's why it won't touch me. It knows we want the same thing. It knows. It's our bond, brother. A truce, if you will."

Argus nodded, but it was a tense and nervous gesture. Was his brother really out of danger? The monster could take him any moment, but it wouldn't. Was that good? Argus felt compelled to leave the room, but he didn't want to leave his brother either.

"I need your help, Argus. I need your help for something."

Argus nodded again. The creature didn't seem to mind. Was that keeping it at bay?

"What's that?" Argus asked. The creature didn't acknowledge him. Things seemed to be under control.

"My scouts are out there. They're looking for him – the Shepherd." The Adversary hissed like it knew the Shepherd personally. It opened its mouth, more drool landing on the floor next to Virgil. "I have heard where the Shepherd is hiding. And we are not far from them. Not anymore."

"How...how do you know?"

"With this," said Virgil and he took a strange object from his pocket and laid it before Argus to see. The Adversary howled, its blood-red eyes following the tiny artifact as it skirted across the table. It was a silver shard, much the discs Argus had seen on the Shepherd. However, this was not the same, even if it were of the same mold.

"What is that?"

"It's a weapon made on Mars," said Virgil and the Adversary growled again like it knew it was being discussed. "But, now we have it."

"How'd you get this?" asked Argus, feeling the question necessary.

"Not how, brother. But *when.*"

Argus nodded as if to say, 'tell me.'

"The old Captain, of course."

Those words held more weight than Argus realized. It was the old Captain who had given Argus his name. It was the old Captain who had rescued he and his brother, Virgil, from the orphanages. It was the old Captain who'd started the Hunt, who'd laid down the purpose of the order and set so many fates in motion that all could be traced back to the old Captain without question. The old Captain had this thing – this piece of Mars – and yet, he'd refused to use it. He must have had his reasons for not doing so. Was Virgil so bold as to ignore those reasons? Or was he this foolish? Had this creature been the reason then?

"Creatures that aren't free don't know they're not free, Argus," said Virgil. "But human beings? They know when they're prisoners, brother. Even when they're imprisoned by their own kind, they know. That's why we have to fight to be set free."

Argus looked into Virgil's eyes and a dark truth emerged: Virgil had *killed* the old Captain. Argus knew it. He recalled the laid out body of the old Captain, sprawled in the streets of the city and knew it was true. Yet, Argus had ignored the possibility. Ignored his brother having the capacity to bite the hand that had given him life. Given them *both* life. The two of them hated people. They'd always hated humanity. But, the old Captain - he was *different.* How could you, Virgil? You speak as though humans are not beasts and yet you killed the master who gave you life! Doesn't that make you less than a beast? The words came to Argus so easily that he scarcely recognized himself. What was happening? He wanted to shout at Virgil, but restrained. Where the words were coming from, how they arrived in his mind, and why they were there, felt foreign to him. Was it the Shepherd that had done this? Or was it the monster in the room making him this way? Virgil continued.

"I've been trying to figure it out for a while, of course," he said, looking at the silver plate. "How to use it properly. I touched it, rubbed it, spoke to it. Even when nothing was working, I knew it had power. I just didn't know how to get it out. Make it useful. But, that's when I heard it: this voice. I thought it was nothing, at first, but then it became louder. And I knew it was real. That's when I knew the stories of demons and monsters were real too. Now, after seeing you today, I really can say that I've seen the same monsters. Now, I can say I really believe."

Argus didn't hear a word. He was remembering the old Captain, not listening to Virgil. But then Virgil leaned forward, and the Adversary growled, bring Argus back to the present.

"Monsters hate the light, Argus," said Virgil. "But, that's how we're going to get it all back. By using the very thing that hates what we want the most. Do you understand what I'm telling you?"

Argus shook his head. All he could think of was the dead body of the old captain and Virgil standing atop him like it was the greatest tragedy he'd ever witnessed. Only it hadn't been. Virgil had been responsible and Argus hated his brother for it. Virgil, you *are* dangerous. Am I to be like you?

"Argus?" said Virgil and Argus looked up, glaring. "I know what the old Captain meant to you. I know he was a father, or whatever you want to call it. He was someone who helped us. But, you and I decided we'd never be like that, remember? We promised it to each other. We promised to never make an ally lest he become our enemy some day. Do you remember this?"

Argus nodded.

"And he was hiding this from us," said Virgil. "He was hiding something we could have used to help us. So you see, you may hate me for doing what I did. But, I did it so that I could be here. So that you could be where you are now. So that we wouldn't have to live like rats anymore. *We* were the ones with power now. *We* were the ones who could make things happen. Don't you see that, Argus? I did that for you!"

Virgil slammed the table and the Adversary, surprisingly, backed down. It looked *afraid* of Virgil. Was it though? Argus' eyes widened. For *me?* You did these things for me? My brother! You really do care for me! Was it love then? Was it love that was scaring the monster in the room? Argus felt his fear slipping and he smiled., if not begrudgingly.

"For *me?*" said Argus, not realizing he sounded like a child. Virgil grinned.

"Yes," he said. "For you."

The Adversary further relinquished itself. It fell to the far corner of the room and stayed there. "Come forward, Argus," said Virgil. "Come and take it. You'll need this for what's next."

The Captain beckoned Argus with an open hand and the Adversary crawled back immediately. It climbed up Virgil's chair, its long legs touching the ceiling, the armrest, and the ground. Its head tilted to one side and a long tongue unraveled out of its mouth like it wanted to lap up the shard on the table. Argus shook his head at Virgil and would not move.

"Come now, Argus," said Virgil, leaning forward. "This is something we are doing. Together." The Adversary pressed its face forward too, mimicking the Captain like it was connected by invisible strings. Its deformed head twisted on its deformed neck. Its whole body looked like it'd been burned in a fire. Sunken eyes, a deep black with red, peered in a taunting manner. The Adversary moaned and Argus felt his life being pulled out through his toes and fingers, feeding the Adversary. It was torturous for Argus, exciting for the Adversary. The shard shook on the table.

"Show me you can do this, brother," said Virgil. "Prove to me you're worth the title I gave you. Prove to the Hunt that you're worthy of the power we took for each other."

Argus stepped forward. He reached across the table and the Adversary snarled, tongue bouncing about. Virgil, with eager eyes, watched Argus like the mystery of the Adversary might be revealed in his brother's terror. Argus moved slower, closing his eyes whenever the Adversary made a noise, but he did not retreat. He was almost there. Then, to Argus' shock, the Adversary backed off and the shard stopped shaking. Argus snatched it up quickly and the Adversary coiled its tongue back into its mouth, turning its head in another direction. Argus felt the outside of the shard, expecting it to be warm, but it was cold like a block of ice.

"Very good," said Virgil and he leaned back in his chair. Argus' skin bristled, seeing the Adversary run its legs close to Virgil's head. "Take that with you. It will be invaluable, the closer you come upon the Shepherd, it will tell you. Just as it told me the same."

"How do you know?"

"Darklight is a special thing, Argus," said Virgil. "But, above all else, it's a *weapon*. Mars might not have known this until they shared it with us. But, now *everyone* knows. A weapon that attacks unnatural light with a vengeance, feasting on fear and draining lesser-willed people of their hope. Truly, Darklight is the most vicious anomaly of the universe. And Mars brought it down upon us. But, now we can return the favor."

The Adversary bobbed next to Virgil's ear. Again, Argus' body tingled like it was covered with insects. The sensation was revolting.

"Darklight is always looking to find the Shepherd, Argus. Head in the direction of where they are going. Take the twelve with you and some of the ones we acquired in Glendale. Find the Shepherd and bring him back to me."

There it was: Virgil's plan. The Captain was intending to give him another chance. Another opportunity. Argus shuddered and took a deep breath. He loved the old captain, but the need to appease his brother was greater. It always had been. I must succeed. I must do this. The Adversary hissed as though it could read Argus' doubts aloud.

"What about Jack?" asked Argus. "And the other two with him? There was a girl and a man with them."

Virgil looked about the room like he was debating what to do. The Adversary gave its input independently, screeching loudly. "Kill them if you want. They aren't of any consequence to us."

Argus nodded like the order was simple. He disliked Jack. He hated that traitor. Or did he? Argus found himself uncertain of his resolve. Only the fear of the Adversary, of his brother, remained. He clutched the shard like it affirmed him somehow, like he would do whatever it took when the moment arose. Yes, I can be like my brother, too. I can be powerful with this thing. Then the Adversary howled and Argus couldn't take it any longer; he turned for the door and exited quickly, the shard tucked inside his pocket.

Outside, Argus saw Greta and the other lieutenants talking amongst themselves. They turned to Argus with questioning faces. Argus was sweating profusely.

"Get an earful, did you?" said one of them. "You look like hell, Argus."

"What's that?" asked another, but Argus was quiet. He didn't want to acknowledge any of them and he couldn't get the image of the Adversary out of his head. His brother was still in there with that thing, whatever it was.

"What did the Captain say?" asked another.

Argus wiped his face and clutched his chest. He rubbed the Darklight Shard in his pocket and stared at the ground.

"What did he say, Argus?" asked Greta.

Argus seemed to come awake. "You and some of the other lieutenants are to come with me," said Argus. "We are going after that Shepherd. And I'm takin' some of the new recruits too."

They all looked at each other. "Well, all right then," said Greta. "The Shepherd it is."

Argus then gathered the twelve lieutenants, Greta too, just as Virgil had instructed and they boarded a Rover and left the town in search of the Shepherd. They rolled through the forest and up the hillside as clouds broke and rain began to settle in over the horizon. Their tumbling sound seemed to echo through the town, slowly fading until they were out of sight.

"So, what's in the pocket?" asked one of the lieutenants.

"Power," said Argus.

Greta watched Argus closely. She wanted to take it by force. She could do it if she wanted. But, what then? If Argus failed, it would be better for her in the end. So she did not act nor did she inquire as to what Argus had with him. He'll destroy himself like always. I only need to wait.

Meanwhile, the Shepherd, having traveled quickly throughout the evening, was standing at the edge of a tall tree, surveying the Rover from many miles away. He walked farther out, his toes guiding him on the branch like his body was somehow lighter than the leaves that decorated the tree. He placed a hand against its trunk and leaned.

"You're playing with toys you don't understand," said the Shepherd. "Even so, you'll still find us, won't you?"

The Shepherd jumped from the tree's edge and landed on the Earth with a thump. He ran back towards the encampment, the soft cool of rain barely catching his body as he went. He was far from camp and it would be a long while till he would be upon them. Time was his enemy now.

* * * *

Jack awoke, the sound of heavy rain battering the invisible barrier. He checked his coat to see if it were wet. But, it was completely dry and he sighed, reminded of the magic that was keeping him that way. He looked and saw Darion sleeping soundly. Guess you were right, eh? It was still dark and the Shepherd was still missing. Why couldn't he sleep? Lightning struck, just outside the edge of the forest, and a boom of thunder shook the ground. Jack trembled. Barrier or no barrier, he still felt unprotected in the wilderness.

Sure would be nice to know if it keeps lightning out too, Jack thought. .

"Normally I'd be worried if someone were out in this," said Jack, scanning for the Shepherd. "But, you're not exactly a normal someone, are ya, chief?"

Jack stood up and paced the inside of the dome, careful to not wake Darion or Olivia. The rain was steady, making visibility difficult. Still, Jack was able to catch something moving in the distance. Was it the Shepherd? He was surprised to find his heart leap at the thought. The creature knelt behind a fallen log and disappeared so Jack walked to the edge of the dome and squinted. The lightning flashed and the object seemed to move with it, rushing to another tree and halting behind, just out of sight. Jack tracked with the newcomer, waiting for the lightning to illuminate his line of sight. But, the lightning didn't come and the creature moved under the cover of darkness without Jack's knowledge.

"Where'd you go..." said Jack and the creature moved even closer to the dome. It was nearly upon Jack when the lightning struck, lighting up the forest about him. Now he could see it.

"Well, aren't you just terrifying?" said Jack and he peered down at the face of a baby deer, its eyes wide and licking water from the leaves. Jack knelt down, the fawn only a few feet from him. Its body was half enclosed behind a small bush and its head was stuck out, slurping up rain as fast as its tiny mouth would allow.

Jack smiled, watching the fawn as it drank. With the storm raging, the fawn's presence was soothing. Jack was surprised to see how relaxed the little deer was. He looked to Olivia, debating whether or not to wake her and show her what was here. Darion wouldn't allow it, he thought. All the more reason to wake her.

Jack watched the deer hobble forward. A patch of skin, on its thigh, was coated in several colors of red, orange, and yellow. The fawn was badly injured; gangrene had formed all about a wound and was eating away at the flesh beneath. Jack looked for the mother, the herd, but nothing within eyeshot. The fawn was alone, possibly abandoned or lost.

Sorry little guy, Jack thought.

Then Jack heard something: a deep hiss, like the boiling of hot water and he moved closer to the barrier.

"What..." he said and a dark blob appeared from the shadows. It didn't have a head, but twin fangs had formed in the dark and dug into the fawn's frail flesh. Jack reeled backwards as the fawn's leg buckled yet didn't cry out. It kept on drinking the water as Jack righted himself. The hissing grew louder and Jack held a hand over his mouth, watching as the blob increased in size, sharp spikes and horns jutting from its center and rising up over the deer like it were smoke leaving a factory. Then a head came next, materializing at the base with two eyes – red and bloody. From the back of the fawn's leg, another black leg struck the ground and a horned beast separated itself from the deer, growling and growing as it detached itself from the deer like it was being birthed.

"No way... no way in hell... " said Jack, panting like a dog. The creature turned its head towards the barrier, a wolf with twisted ram horns; black hair standing like needles.

No, he thought. This is impossible. How did it find us? How did it get here?

Jack alternated between looking at the fawn and the Adversary. The fawn seemed unaware of the Adversary's recent manifestation, lapping up water as the Adversary feasted upon the fawn's wound like it was kindling from a fire. Lightning struck, scaring the fawn and the Adversary howled louder, feeding on both fear and wound together. The rain fell, but the Adversary seemed unaffected, its hair glistening with sharpness that looked unable to be tainted by the falling water's heavy cascade.

The fawn struggled a moment and the Adversary seemed to enjoy itself even more. It howled and danced with its neck as Jack heard the rustling of something near him and he broke from the Adversary's gaze to find Olivia with him. She was wide-eyed and staring down the Adversary with her own personal terror. Thunder boomed and Jack turned back on the Adversary. Then Darion awoke. And when he did, he rushed over to Jack and shoved a hand over Jack's mouth.

"You idiot," said Darion. "What did you do?"

The Adversary rose. Its face pressed down towards the barrier. Its body fanned out, covering the dome like it had wings. The black of night relinquished its power to the Adversary's darkness; a clear line separating the two. Darion moved away, holding Jack.

Where are you, Shepherd? Have you left us to fend for ourselves again?

Chapter 14
The Siege and the Choice

* * * *

The Adversary walked freely about the outside of the Shepherd's barrier. It sniffed the air, if that were possible for such a creature, and growled like it ached to find its prey. It looked massive, bigger than ever. Darion held his grip over Jack's mouth and the two men followed the Adversary's methodical walk about the barrier, saying nothing and breathing as softly as their fear permitted.

"How…," whispered Darion. "How did you bring this thing here?"

"I didn't," said Jack, unlocking himself from Darion's grasp. "It just *appeared*. Out of that deer over there."

"What?" said Darion. "That's ridiculous. It must've known somehow…."

"How can it *know?*"

Honestly, Darion didn't know either. He had only assumed, spoken his best judgment, but then he realized he was treating the Adversary like it were a living thing. And yet, the thought that the Adversary was a living, breathing entity – one with the intent to find human life and exterminate it – that conclusion sounded plausible. Nothing else made sense, even though Darion knew it wasn't a true life form. Not in the least, but all the same, here it was. Still stalking them, still after them, still showing up like it wanted to taste their flesh – and their fear – for the sake of sustaining its existence. But again, the answer was *no*, this thing is not alive. Even if it acts like it is. Only a freakishly distorted form of nature, right?

The Adversary raised its head to the sky and lightning flashed, its eyes like cherry beads inside a black silhouette. Jack crawled backwards. He knocked a rock aside and the Adversary turned its head towards the barrier and growled again. Then it changed directions abruptly and walked away.

"Can it see us?" asked Jack, reared back on all fours. "Do you think it sees us?"

Who could answer such a question? But Darion attempted to. "It looks like it's trying to," said Darion. Assuming it didn't see them was not helpful. No one knew what the Adversary could see or could *not* see.

"Where are you?" said Darion, speaking aloud like the Shepherd might hear him.

The three of them waited in the silence, rain pouring down. The fawn, having exhausted itself, dropped to its knees and rested. It looked upon its wound, indecisive of what to do. Then the Adversary's tail broke free of the little deer's wound and disappeared into the woods, leaving the fawn behind.

"Where is it going?" said Darion.

More silence. More rain. The three of them paced inside the barrier, the fawn resting till a noise made its ears rise up. It strained itself to stand and Darion and Jack watched it carefully. The fawn, unknowingly, had become their eyes for the outside world. There was a crash like, logs breaking and the fawn whined. The thud came again, closer this time and another smash like a tree had been uprooted sounded. Then the Adversary roared and Jack cowered.

"Is it *him*?" asked Jack. "Do you think it's – "

"Quiet!" said Darion.

Through the rain, two figures could be seen wrestling in the darkness. Jack pointed them out, his fingers waving nervously.

"There!" said Jack and Darion quieted Jack again.

The two silhouettes grappled and parted from one another. They disappeared under the guise of falling rain and the evening's darkness. The ground seemed to shake, but whether it was from the thunder or the struggle of the Adversary and the Shepherd was unknown to them. Was it even the Shepherd? More trees broke and there was an explosion of golden light – the Shepherd's weapon had been let loose.

"Did you see that?" shouted Jack, pointing out the obvious.

Golden energy ignited the forest like it was being bombed from above. And when the explosions ceased, Darion and Jack stood with equal silence.

Then, "Is it over?" asked Jack, but he feared the answer. There was no sign of the Shepherd. The golden light had either vanquished the Adversary or the dark had overcome the

Shepherd's light. They were forced to wait. Then the lightning flashed and the silver disc that powered the barrier clicked like its energy source had been cut off and the invisible fence that encapsulated the three members of the Shepherd's party, ceased. Jack looked at Darion, his eyes feeding the desperation of the moment, speaking to Darion as it to say, "Did he lose?"

The rain breached the broken wall and their heads and shoulders became drenched in the water that broke the cover of trees. Darion held Olivia to his side and Jack waited to see what Darion might do. The rain was noisier without the barrier. Its heavy droplets soaked the Earth, making it damp like the rest of the forest floor. They heard the sound of leaves crunching beneath something in the distance, something big and unfamiliar.

"Run, Jack..." said Darion. "Run for your life...."

Darion peered into the woods. The night was dark, but the pitch-black shadow of the Adversary was darker. It was coming and Darion could sense its cold aura.

He lost? How could the Shepherd have lost?

Darion took Olivia into his arms and darted for the open field. Jack took to the fields with them, grabbing a silver disc first. The rain had caked itself on every blade of the high grass and the ground was soggy and uneven, making it even more difficult to run on. Jack caught up with Darion and passed them both. He looked back and saw that the Adversary had broken through the edge of the woods and was surveying the field. Its head jerked from side to side, sniffing the air like it was honing in on Jack and Darion's scent. Jack turned again, but not before being tackled from behind by Darion. They fell to the ground, Olivia beside them, crouched like they were hiding in a bunker.

"Don't move, don't talk," said Darion and he put a hand over Jack's mouth with surprising strength. "Drown it out, Jack. Drown out the beast till it goes away. It may just go. It may leave us...."

Jack wriggled underneath Darion. The Adversary's heavy paws could be heard, could be felt.

"We can't outrun it now," said Darion. "Just wait it out."

Jack removed Darion's hand. "Let me go!"

The Adversary's shoulders sailed above the grass line. Darion had Jack pinned, but Jack's panic had granted him a newfound strength.

No, thought Darion. You won't do this to me! Not again, Jack!

Without a second thought, Darion grabbed the silver disc and bashed it against Jack's head. The young man didn't fall limp immediately, so Darion hit him several more times. He hit Jack until blood escaped Jack's temple and all movement had ceased. When Darion pulled away, he saw Jack's eyes were closed and his mouth was agape, blood mixing with the falling rain.

Dead? Had he killed him? The Adversary drew nearer so Darion stood and hoisted Olivia into his arms. They ran for the cover of the trees, Jack a heap of flesh and loose blood behind them.

Just run, Darion thought. Don't look behind. Leave him where he is. You need to survive. You need to run!

But then Darion felt Olivia squeezing him, but not out of fear. She was alerting him to what was transpiring behind them. And he stopped, turned, and saw what it was his daughter was witnessing: the Adversary; it was poised atop of Jack, but it was not feasting. Not yet. Olivia shut her eyes, moaning and crying like Jack were dead already.

What to do? Without the Shepherd, Darion was powerless. He was no match without the discs. Hell, he may not be a match *with* them either. What could he do now? If Jack perished, it would be his fault. Yet, he'd be rid of Jack too. He'd no longer have to worry about Jack intercepting his and Olivia's plans. Even if the Shepherd had fallen, another like him might come later. Wouldn't it?

The Adversary turned its gaze upon Darion and howled. Had it tasted his confusion? Did it see his anxiety? To feed upon the unconscious body of Jack might have been sweet, but Darion's current state of guilt and remorse might have been sweeter still.

"Olivia," said Darion. "Don't move. Shut your eyes."

The Adversary slunk across the plain, ignoring Jack and heading for Darion. What now? The beast would be upon them. There was nowhere to go.

But, then Jack stirred on the ground and stood, wearily. He clutched his forehead and screamed in the direction of the Adversary.

"Sonuvabitch!" he shouted. "Where you goin'? Try to kill me, huh?"

The Adversary stopped, coiling its body like a giant cobra. It turned towards Jack, who realized his error when he saw the Adversary staring him down. The beast then alternated between Darion and Jack; looking overjoyed at its good fortune. There was the little girl, innocent yet terrified; there was Jack, bloodied and full of anger and Darion, whose feet were locked with fear like the grass on his feet was made of cement. Who will you choose, monster? Which one of us is the worst and worthy of your wrath?

But, then the Adversary looked away. It squealed like it was in danger and a large vehicle charged unto the plain. It had torches on its sides, protected under transparent bulbs and huge, heavy wheels. Darion recognized the vehicle – it was one of the Hunt's Rovers. The Adversary dove into the ground and snaked through the grass like a serpent. Darion jumped away as the Rover careened carelessly forward, running over the spot where the Adversary had laid.

They found us, Darion thought, falling to the ground. The Rover turned sharply with surprising agility and came at them again. Darion and Olivia ran, Jack alongside. But, the Adversary reappeared, trapping them in the path of the oncoming Rover. The Rover narrowly missed them once more and turned quickly. So Darion and Jack changed directions but the Adversary reappeared ahead of them. *It wants us to be caught. Is that its plan?* The Rover turned back around as voices shouted from the inside of the vehicle. *They're trying to wear us down. They know we can't outrun them. Can they see the Adversary too?*

That didn't matter anymore. For at the next turn, the trio of Shepherd followers was separated and Jack ran for the woods. The Adversary didn't follow immediately. It stayed with Darion instead. With Olivia, pushing them back to the Rover as Jack made his run for cover.

No. How could this be? Darion thought. Jack was making his escape. Nothing seemed right. It was all wrong. Everything was wrong. Darion halted in the field, waiting on the next run of the Rover like it would be the last. He hadn't the strength to run any longer and the disc in his hand was dead. This was it, wasn't it?

Just then a new silhouette bounded from out of the forest. It took long leaps across the high grass until it slammed into the Rover with shoulder down, knocking the vehicle off course, but even more so, landing the Rover awkwardly onto its side. The

Rover's torches broke under the weight and were extinguished against the moist ground. Jack halted by the forest's edge. Was it *him*? Was he alive? Nothing else could have done that.

The shadowed figure lifted its head and turned towards Darion. Tiny cylinders began to glow a bright gold. It *was* him. The Shepherd *was* alive. And his suit was bubbling with orbs made of gold and yellow light, piercing the darkness like a dozen tiny suns had been sewn into his skin.

"Shepherd!" shouted Darion and he waved carelessly with excitement.

The Rover, having tumbled on one side, was kicking up grass and mud. The Shepherd stared it down like a bull defending its territory and leaned towards Darion and Olivia, Jack running back to them. The Shepherd clutched his left shoulder, pain resonating throughout no doubt.

Did that actually hurt him? Mortal, after all, are we?

"Give me the disc, Darion," said the Shepherd.

Good to see you also, Darion thought. The Shepherd seemed uninterested in celebrated reunion. So Darion tossed the disc away and the Shepherd took it, applied it to his right arm and raised his arm parallel to the Earth.

"Cover your eyes and ears. This one is going to be big."

An enormous arm cannon formed at the Shepherd's elbow and he faced it in the direction of the Adversary and fired. Golden light spewed from the barrel, every one of the tiny gold circles of gold seemed to give power to the cannon as it ripped through the high grass like a rocket. The light beam sliced the top of the Adversary's body and a large boom echoed throughout the valley. The Adversary moaned and reverted itself into a serpent once more. The Shepherd didn't stop though – he fired several times, hitting the Adversary with his new and improved weapon.

"Now, get out of here," said the Shepherd. "Head for the next line of trees! Go now!"

The trio ran, foregoing their previous altercations. The Rover's side door slid open and two soldiers jumped out, guns prepared to fire.

"It's them! It's the Hunt!" shouted Darion.

Two of the men pointed their weapons, but the Shepherd rushed them both and crushed the ends of one of their rifles with his bare hands. The other took aim and fired but the Shepherd deflected the bullet with a wave of his hand and threw his partner atop him. More members of the Hunt exited the Rover, Greta among them and four more of the lieutenants. Argus was inside, hidden but alive. They were disoriented from the crash, Greta included, but she urged them on.

"Take him!" shouted Greta. "Forget the others, take the Shepherd!"

The Hunt raised their weapons, but the Shepherd had disappeared, his body suddenly invisible among the field.

"Where is he?"

"Where did he go?"

"It's a demon! A damned monster! This is no man we are fighting!"

The Shepherd moved carefully through the grass as the Hunt pointed their weapons aimlessly. Then he struck.

One of the lieutenants yelled; was picked and flung from where he stood like he'd been swept into an invisible tornado. The others fired in the direction of the screams, but their bullets hit nothing, saw nothing. Greta pulled out her handgun and waited. She watched for the rain to land unevenly, where it was not touching the ground and when she saw the change in landscape, she took fire. A bullet grazed the Shepherd's arm and a ripple like golden electricity revealed a partial shoulder and a kneeling Shepherd, who was grasping his arm in visible pain. She'd hit him in his bad shoulder. She couldn't believe she had, but she did.

"There!" shouted Greta and she fired again.

The Shepherd rolled out of the bullet's trajectory and disappeared again, but Greta followed. She pursued the invisible Shepherd with a flurry of shots while the other members of the Hunt shot like they were wearing blindfolds.

"Follow the tracks in the grass!" she yelled. "He's injured, but he's in the grass! Take aim where the rain doesn't touch the ground!"

"How? Where is he?"

"Follow the ones you *can* see then!"

Several Huntsmen headed for Darion, Jack, and Olivia. Greta returned to the Rover for Argus.

"Argus? Argus?" she called. "Are you alive?"

Argus stumbled out. His face looked dirtied from the crash and his hands were shaking. The rain made him squint and he wiped his face. He saw the Rover's driver, unconscious inside the cockpit. Greta bent over, took hold of his collar.

"Come on, we have to follow them," she said. "Where's that thing the Captain gave you? Where is it?"

Argus stammered, "I... I don't even know if – "

The Shard had fallen from his pocket, onto the grass. Argus looked and bent down to retrieve it, but when he did, a black coil wrapped about his hand and pulled him downward. It felt like a vacuum sucking him down and Argus couldn't resist as he grasped the Shard.

"Argus!" said Greta, but Argus didn't hear her. He couldn't. His entire body was being overcome with raw, new energy; his senses accelerating beyond human limitations. Or was it that some had been dulled for the sake of maximizing the others? Argus found he had no time to contemplate the possibility. For even in the storm, where rain fell all about him, Argus could hear *and* feel every drop plainly. Every individual droplet could be distinguished from the other. Everything was in its place. The noise of a fierce storm played like the notes of an orchestra, melodies transferring from the sky to the Earth in the form of falling water. Argus could sense it *all*.

Another bolt of purple and black energy took him and the Adversary, lurking about Argus, came up from the grass and clasped him with its talons. Argus screamed and then stopped abruptly. Then he grabbed hold of the Rover and tugged on its axles. The other members of the Hunt stood back, even Greta, as Argus pulled mightily on the Rover's underbelly until at last, the Rover was back on four wheels; a thunderous quake on the dirt.

Argus examined his hands, the tools of his immense strength. His hands appeared to be on fire, charred flesh covered by black sores on the fingertips, and yet, there was no pain. Not in the slightest. And they were healing rapidly.

"*I see...*" said Argus, eyes wide. Another voice seemed to be speaking for him yet was speaking *through* him as well.

"*I see them all...*" continued Argus. "*Just like he said I would. They are afraid. All of them afraid. I feel their fear... get back in the Rover. You chase. I will chase them too.*"

Greta raised her rifle. What was this? *Who* was this? The Huntsmen boarded the Rover as ordered and the Rover roared back to life as another of the Huntsmen took the wheel.

"I can't see much without the torches," said the newest driver. "This rain's thick as mud."

"*I will tell you where to go,*" said Argus. "*I see. I can see them running.*"

Greta boarded cautiously. *What* was happening?

Outside the Rover, Darion, Jack, and Olivia had come to the next line of trees. They threw themselves into the thicket but were surprised to discover the edge was a ruse and there was a sharp decline leading down to a river. They stopped, debating what to do, but when they heard the Rover, each of them jumped and headed down the embankment at full speed. Darion held onto Olivia while Jack lumbered through like a loose fish. At the bottom, there was a tiny stretch of land before the river.

Jack waded into the water ahead of them. The water was cold from the rain and Jack winced as it rose up to his waistline. Darion saw Jack testing the water. *Hopefully that's as deep as it gets.* He was halfway through, the water at his ribs when the surface of the river broke and the head of the Adversary appeared a few arms' lengths ahead, red eyes beaming.

"No...," said Jack. "... how did he..."

The Adversary arose like a vicious sea monster, fangs curled back. It hissed at Jack, body convulsing as its eyes rotated like a saw blade. How was it so fast?

A tree broke, somewhere close to Darion and Olivia, and a hard thud on the ground followed. The golden lights of the Shepherd were soaring through the air, arm cannon firing. The laser blasted a hole in the side of the Adversary and it wailed, diving under the surface. The Shepherd landed in the river and fired two more shots, lighting up the dark with brilliant light. The water bubbled like fire were set beneath its surface and Jack saw the Adversary retreating, a black line like oil moving against the current. The Shepherd's right arm clicked and again, his arm cannon fired. Another beam of gold energy speared the Adversary, cutting through its tail and severing a good chunk of the shadow beast. The Adversary leapt from the water and onto the opposite shore. Its body looked mangled and disjointed and seemed to be struggling with what form it wanted as it crawled out of sight.

"Take this and wait for me in the brush," said the Shepherd and he removed a silver disc from his leg and handed it to Jack.

"But what'll I – "

"Go. It'll keep you safe."

The Rover flew over the edge and dashed down the hillside. It had difficulty keeping its front from toppling so the Rover slowed its progression, but still with enough force to destroy small trees and bushes. The Shepherd jumped out of the water and landed on the hillside, his left arm flaccid. The rest of his body was pulsing with gold light, but his left shoulder and part of his arm was dim. Darion ran past the Shepherd and into the water with Olivia next to him. The Shepherd waited till they were both close to Jack, and then he raised his right arm and targeted the Rover. A heavy noise, like the boom of a cannonball, rumbled from the Shepherd's mount. The beam would have punctured the center of the Rover, but its light was deflected by something unseen so the Shepherd took aim again and fired several more shots but the Rover persisted onwards; the light deflecting and breaking into particles of golden little orbs on the hill.

"Learned how to use it, did they?" said the Shepherd. He lowered his weapon and turned towards Darion and Olivia.

"Go for Jack," said the Shepherd. "I will stop them here."

Darion nodded and ran for the river's shore. The Shepherd, on the other side, fell to one knee like he was weary and bowed a head. *What are you going to do now?* Darion thought.

The Rover's rickety path made it look like a derailed train. Darion and Olivia were in the water when the Rover took the last line of trees under its giant tires and began its final descent upon the Shepherd. Olivia pointed at the Shepherd. *Help him,* she seemed to say, but Darion urged her not to look. The Shepherd raised his right arm and released the disc that had served as his cannon. It flattened into a short sabre-like object and the Shepherd waved his hand like he was manipulating it with his fingers.

"What is he doing?" said Jack, still holding tight to his forehead. "What the *hell* is he doing now?"

The Rover was only yards away, its engines roaring like a pack of lions, but the Shepherd's voice was there too. The Shepherd appeared to be chanting, speaking in a language they could not recognize and yet, the odd language was slowly becoming more familiar with every recant. The words rolled faster and soon became, "help me...help me..." The Shepherd repeated this over and over until at last the Shepherd thrust the silver sabre into the ground.

The rain stopped falling, the trees ceased to sway, and the ground itself rose up, pushing towards the Rover. Raindrops changed directions, turning on the Rover like a swarm of bees. The dirt at the Shepherd's feet upended and struck the Rover like a tidal wave made of raw Earth. Even the water from the river separated and splashed upon the shore, surrounding the Shepherd before punching at the Rover with force strong enough to send the multi-ton tank hurtling backwards.

The Rover's windows shattered as the vehicle flipped, spinning through the air as it landed on its backside with a crash. Greta was thrown from the inside, as were the driver and Argus. Several members of Hunt seemed to be pulled from the inside out too. Then the rain started to fall again and the Earth retreated to the ground, heeding to the natural laws they were meant for and not the commands of the Shepherd.

The Shepherd, exhausted, roared and fell back down to one knee, leaning against the silver sabre. Olivia pointed as if to say, 'look at this,' and both Darion and Jack looked where she was directing them.

A purple and black light, shining bright, appeared on the hillside and then disappeared. In the middle of that light was Argus. He had come to his feet, though he'd done so like something else was pulling him upright. He screamed, but his scream sounded inhuman. A smooth darkness moved up his wrist and arm and then onto his shoulder and neck. The black void overtook his entire body and Argus yelled again like his soul was being sucked out through his nose and mouth.

"What are you?" Argus wailed. "Stop it! Go away! Stop it!" The black cloud was overtaking him and when he was completely covered, Argus stopped moving. Water and leaves kicked up around him, pushed and pulled like gravity was being affected by his presence. Darion felt something pulling at his core also and he took a step backward.

A black hole, thought Darion. Is that a *human* black hole I'm witnessing?

The wisp of black cloud coated Argus in a fog of dark armor and he fell to his hands and knees. Greta rolled to her side as she tried hard to get back on her feet. The new Argus howled, sounding like the Adversary. And with his right hand, Argus reached with uncanny ability, taking hold of one of the fallen soldiers many yards away. His black fingers wrapped about the Huntsman's neck and the soldier gasped for air, trying to fight off the clasps of the transformed Argus. But, the soldier was easily overpowered and Argus picked his victim up like a marionette and, from what Jack and Darion could discern, began *feasting* on the soldier. On his body. On his *soul*.

"It's *feeding...*" said Darion. "Just like that deer, it's feeding on that man. My God, it's feeding on him like it's death itself...."

Argus' body was still changing; a swirl of black ash was swallowing up the captive soldier. Rain landed on his body and burned up like smoke on a smoldering fire. He leaned back on his knees and tilted his head towards another of the soldiers. The new Argus shrieked and arched his neck like he was inviting pain from above. Then Argus' left arm shot out and dug its claws into another soldier's back. The Huntsman yelled and Argus yelled also, but with a masochist's delight. Dark hooks appeared out of Argus and took more of his former comrades captive. From out of the Rover, Argus dragged members of the Hunt into the rain. Greta got to her feet and hobbled up the hillside, rifle under her arm. She stumbled by a bush and Argus' head turned towards her, eyes glowing a pale white. Their gazes met and terror paralyzed Greta to her bones.

A nightmare. That's what this was: a *nightmare.*

Greta screamed and kicked the dirt away as Argus' body slunk across the dirt towards her. Couldn't be real. Was she imagining these things? Argus coiled like a serpent and twisted his back like a cobra, mouth open for the kill.

"No!" she said. "Help! Someone, help me!"

Argus lunged, but was met by the fist of the Shepherd from above. The beast squealed and Argus emerged out of the black mist, regurgitated like the monster had no need for him. The silver shard landed on the ground and the Shepherd raised his right arm, blasting the soldiers free of Argus' grip one by one. The Huntsmen fell like crumpled brick, bodies lifeless and convulsing.

The Shepherd turned his attention upon Greta. His left arm was leaking a golden substance, like blood but it clearly was *not* blood. His silver-blue eyes gazed down at Greta; large and beautiful but terrifying all the same. Greta didn't move, for the Shepherd seemed to be analyzing her. And when Greta backed away, her mind and heart felt exposed, invaded by the eyes of the giant. Then he left and began tending to the soldiers.

Greta's whole body trembled. Which was worse? The thing Argus became, or this silver monster? Both were alien and frightening. Even as the Shepherd healed every last one of Argus' victims, Greta could not discern which was her true enemy. Darion too, across the river, was amazed.

He's healing them, he thought. *Why?* Why risk it?

The Shepherd finished his work and began walking towards Argus, yet was stopped abruptly when a rifle fired. The Shepherd turned, caught the bullet with his right hand and followed its trajectory towards the source. It was Greta, standing with gun poised and mouth agape. Their eyes met and Greta immediately felt like she'd disappointed him somehow; his silver-blue irises communicating that empty feeling of guilt. Then the Shepherd dropped the bullet to the ground and resumed his march on Argus. Greta fell to one knee, unable to stand of her own power.

Argus was breathing heavily. His body twitched like he'd been electrocuted or had suffered a heart-wrenching seizure.

"Hello?" said Argus, but his voice was weak. He coughed and blood came up in speckles of red. "Where is... where is it...."?

"You tried to steal their life," said the Shepherd. "And now your body is rejecting what it found. Your body can't handle it. It simply cannot."

Argus coughed again. "Where are you, huh? I hear you, but I can't see you...."

"Do not move and do not speak," said the Shepherd. "Your body is weak as it is, but now your spirit is even weaker. A side effect is your vanishing sight. The soul is retreating into itself. It has to be beckoned out again before it retreats completely."

Argus cried like a child as the Shepherd took rainwater into his right hand and washed it over Argus, speaking again in strange tongues. Argus' breathing slowed and his eyes blinked several times like he was awakening from a horrible dream.

"I...I can *see*!" said Argus. "I can see! I can see again!"

The Shepherd grinned, but Argus was overcome with fear when he saw the silver-blue eyes of his rescuer. Argus scurried out from under the Shepherd, pressing against a tree.

"Get away from me!" he yelled. "Get away!"

The Shepherd stood again, unfazed by Argus' reaction. The other soldiers rose up, watching in silence as the silver giant walked to one of their Rovers and placed a hand on its hull. Then, with the one hand, he pushed the tank back onto its side and with another push, landed the Rover right side up.

"What is he doing?" said Darion. "Why is he helping all of them?"

The Shepherd raised his good arm and blasted the Shard. A patch of incinerated dust lie where it was. Then he addressed the Hunt as a whole.

"Return to your master, if you wish," said the Shepherd. "But know that your master cannot win against me. He will not be victorious. Tell him this should any of you return to him. Tell him what you have seen and what awaits him should he continue this hunt for me. There was no victory for any of you tonight. Nor will there ever be. Take your lives with you. The next time I will not be as forgiving."

The soldiers looked about, contemplative gazes on their faces. They seemed to be in shellshock. None of them knew what to think, say, or even feel. It all seemed incredulous, too unbelievable and though Darion, Jack, and Olivia had witnessed the Shepherd and his power for much longer, they too fell into a state of disbelief over the Shepherd's latest doings.

"You are free to do as you please from here," said the Shepherd.

Then he turned and walked towards the shore, left arm hanging. The soldiers only watched. No one seemed to know what to do next. So they observed the Shepherd until he was on the edge of the river.

"Get back into the Rover," said Greta, interrupting them all. "All of you – get in there, now. And take Argus."

The soldiers of the Hunt hesitated, but soon, they were doing as instructed. Each of them piled into the side door and waited for Greta. She came to them limping and when they offered her help, she refused them all and pulled herself into the car alone. She slammed the door behind and called to the driver.

"Lieutenant?"

"Yes?"

The driver pointed to the shoreline and Greta saw four of the Hunt's members walking in the opposite direction. The Shepherd

242 | J.C.L. Faltot

had already reached the other side of the river, but these men appeared to be following after him.

"What do they think they are doing?" asked Darion.

The Shepherd turned and saw the soldiers. They were standing on the riverbank, their eyes peering at the Shepherd curiously. They were all of them young and had young eyes, but their faces looked aged and worn.

"The choice has been laid before them," said the Shepherd. "They are deciding."

"What the hell are they doing?" said Greta. "Traitors!"

She hung outside the door and raised her rifle, but the voice of the Shepherd stopped her. Their eyes met and her vision became fuzzy, confused. The voice grew louder and though she tried to focus on the three men, she could not fire. *Get out of my head!* she cried inside of herself, but the only words she heard were, 'enough, enough, enough.' It repeated over and over until Greta lowered her weapon, returned to the Rover.

"Get us out of here," she said, shaking her head.

"To where?" said the driver.

"To the camp. Anywhere. Just get us the hell out of here."

"What about the *weapon?*"

Greta hesitated. "That's for Argus to explain to the Captain. Not us. Just get us out of here. I can't..."

Enough, enough, enough....

The voice persisted and Greta winced in pain. She tried not to let the others see her. Don't show them you're in pain. Don't.

"Lieutenant?" asked another.

"Get us out of here!"

The Rover backed up the hillside, trudging through the mud and overcoming the terrain with brute force. Then it was gone. As was the voice that plagued Greta's thoughts.

Back on the river's edge, the four Huntsmen were stuck in debate. Three of them waded into the water but the fourth would not go. They spoke to him, but he shook his head and headed back for the Rover. The other three men waded across, making their way to the Shepherd and his company. Darion and Jack stood up, ready to fight, but the Shepherd raised a hand and they backed down. The three Huntsmen eventually made land and wiped themselves of the cold water.

"Take us with you," said the one in front, breathing hard. "Please... don't leave us out here. We are traitors to the Hunt now. We can't go back. Please...."

"It's all right now," said the Shepherd. "You are safe with us."

"What?" said Darion, unable to contain his shock. "How are they safe with us? What are - "

"They are safe with *me*," said the Shepherd. "Now, let me right another wrong, if I may."

The Shepherd took the disc he'd given Jack and placed it on his left arm. The silver giant flinched like it was painful and Jack backed away. With his right hand, the Shepherd reached to the sky and captured water, dipping it on Jack's wound and the cut healed almost instantly. The members of the Hunt gasped and one fell to his knees. Jack felt his forehead – the cut was practically closed

Impossible, Darion thought. The more this happens, the less I should be amazed. But, I can't. What has Mars made upon that red rock? What is this thing - the *Shepherd?*

"There," said the Shepherd. "Now that this is out of the way, let's be going."

The Shepherd then led the party of six through the woods and into the plains beyond the wood – Darion and Jack stayed ahead to keep a good distance from their newest companions. No one spoke. No one uttered a word. They were all tired, but their minds were busily trying to recreate the morning. What had happened, what was most important; what had been worth remembering – these were the things they'd want to talk about later. But, not now. Everything was too new and out of place. There would be time to discuss these things later.

Soon, the skies opened and sunlight beamed on every plot, drying the Shepherd and his party. Talk eventually started, but it was only among the parties who knew each other before the sun had risen.

"I will need to stop and replenish my strength soon," said the Shepherd. "I am getting weak."

"Why not now?" asked Darion. The Rover was gone and there was no sign of the Adversary. This was an opportune time to rest. The Shepherd's left arm dangled like meat on a hook, but even so, the Shepherd seemed intent on moving forward. They pressed on for another mile, maybe more, until at last the Shepherd decided it was time to stop.

"The next open field," said the Shepherd. "We'll rest there."
And they did.

Chapter 15
Vile Things

* * * *

Greta hadn't noticed her ankle was sprained or that her neck was badly bruised till a half hour into the Rover's retreat. She grimaced; rubbing the areas most associated with pain like some attention might alleviate the feeling. It didn't though. So she assessed for broken bones or torn tendons. There were none. Nothing major. Nothing life-threatening. That was a positive; and about the only positive thing she found herself able to report on.

The mission had been, for lack of any other way to describe it, a complete failure. Not only had they failed to take in the Shepherd, but also they'd lost three recruits in the process. There were no fatalities. No deaths on their end, yet it felt like the collective spirit of the party had been killed. The other Huntsmen exemplified the feeling, save Argus, who seemed dead where he sat. His body hung like a husk of human flesh, bobbing up and down with every bump of the ground as the Rover rolled towards the encampment. No one helped him when his head hit the wall or his neck lost all rigidity and he dangled forward in his belt. No one wanted to. They were scared of him, even Greta, who eyed him regularly from the passenger seat in front. If it weren't for his status as 'Eyes of the Hunt', they might have abandoned him; killed him. But, this was the Captain's brother. Returning without him would lead to a worse fate. Best to let the Captain bury his own. This was the best-case scenario for them all.

This is it for you, Greta thought. The last disappointment of the Eyes of the Hunt. Yet, Greta didn't have the energy to celebrate. Greta, like the rest of the men, was like a ghost. Her body was present, her eyes saw the road ahead, but her mind and soul felt empty, incapable of explaining what had transpired. Her thoughts were on the Shepherd and the ones they'd lost to him. What a monster. How did he do all those things back there? The way he called on nature to do what he wanted. The way he touched the dark spirit of Argus and stopped him in his tracks. And that voice. How? How did he do all of that?

The whole ordeal felt like a fairy tale and Greta began construing the best story she could make for the Captain. Something believable despite the impossible circumstances they had endured. But, what to say? They were only a few miles off and there was nothing that felt right, seemed right, to say on the matter. The Rover barreled on. And Argus' body drooped like a puppet, hardly the unstoppable monster he'd been just moments before.

"Pull over, would ya?" asked one of the men in back, breaking the silence. "I need to get out and get some air, all right?"

The driver stopped and the man in back jumped out of the Rover. He immediately started vomiting on the side of the road; a pink and yellow liquid carpeted the ground, prompting others to get out and avoid the smell. Greta stayed in the vehicle. She turned and inspected Argus. His head was down and his breathing looked labored.

Just what happened to you back there, she thought. Do you even know?

Then Argus looked up at her, startling Greta. Did he hear her thoughts? His eyes were glazed and he spied Greta like he was doing as she predicted. Could it be? Greta retracted and looked out the window. In the rear view mirror, Argus was still staring. His lips hung towards the Earth; his hair slumped over, wet and caked together. Still staring. Greta pushed on the passenger door and exited. She wiped her brow and stepped away from the other Huntsmen. Some time alone is what she needed. Just for a little while.

The man with vomit wiped his face and looked at her. "You're hurt," he said. Greta didn't answer. Her pain was noticeable, was it? She didn't like that. So she wouldn't answer. Ignoring the pain meant she refused to admit her weakness. That's how leaders are, how the Captain is. Don't acknowledge the pain, especially when it's your own.

"You're sick," she said, diverting the topic. The Huntsman wiped his mouth again.

"Can ya blame me?" he said. "Can anybody here tell me what the hell just happened back there? Sorcery? Magic? Damned hallucination, maybe? Huh, anybody? Or are we all just not gonna talk about that shit show back there?"

"It wasn't magic," said another. "It was a *Shepherd*. Damn thing was real after all."

"You didn't believe the Captain?" asked the other.

No one answered. Then the one with vomit said, "What about *him* then?"

He pointed towards the Rover, towards Argus. He had pulled his head all the way up and was looking out the open door. A single line of saliva was hanging from his lips. He looked drugged, but his eyes stayed fixed upon Greta.

"Why's he doing that?" said another Huntsman. "Is he infected with something? He looks sicker than you, Jonesy."

No one replied. No one knew the answer. Greta stared back at Argus, who moved at last, spitting as he attempted to say something.

"It's going... It's going to come back..." said Argus.

"What'd you say?"

"It's going to come back..."

Greta felt panic swirling about them. They'd been afraid before but now; terror had come. Argus, no longer just a man, - a monster - was handing out dark prophecies like he was mindful of some future yet to come. All of them knew that these were not the musings of a lunatic, but one who might actually have truth on his side. Even if it were a dark, twisted version. Greta knew it too — she saw the panic filling her men with every word off of Argus' tongue.

"Shut your mouth, Argus! That's enough!" said Greta and she stepped towards the Rover. "What's wrong with you?"

"I say we ditch him right here," said one of the Huntsmen.

"What would we tell the Captain?"

"The Shepherd took him?"

"Stupid. He'll send others to find out what happened. We'd be screwed."

Argus raised his head higher and Greta waited, anticipating Argus to bury himself with further insanity.

"I need..." he stammered. "I need to pee. I need to piss."

One of them laughed, nervously. "Nobody here is gonna help you with that, Argus," said a Huntsman.

"Please..."

They looked to one another like none wanted the responsibility, but Greta stepped forward.

"I'll take him," she said. "Somebody has to."

Here it was. A chance to restore order – and she'd taken it. There was too much chaos in the eyes of her men. They were slipping and needed a firm footing. Greta was more than willing to oblige. She walked into the Rover, unbuckled Argus, and led him out of the caravan. The Huntsmen kept their distance. Argus stumbled under his first few steps. His body felt and looked weak. He was like a newborn, grasping at his bearings.

"Come on," she said. "Let's go."

She nodded to the Huntsmen like she was going to end all this. Like, she was going to *end* Argus. The Huntsmen didn't object. They watched as Greta took Argus off the side of the road and down into the woods. The two figures limped out of sight, between the brush, and away from the eyes of the caravan.

Greta found a thick bedding of twigs and decided this would be the spot. Something that could hide the body; something that would keep Argus hidden from anyone who might be looking for him. She planned it all out, rehearsing it in her head like no scenario would fall beyond her foresight. Argus, she noticed, went willingly, like he knew what she was doing. A proper way to end everything. He's actually giving in to what's coming. For once, he's showing courage like he ought to.

"Over there," she said and pointed to the thicket, but Argus stalled. He flicked his hair and gazed about. Having second thoughts about that piss? She pushed him forward and put her hand on her hip. Her gun was in its holster and it had the ammunition necessary to *do* what was necessary. She could do it. She could do it right *now*.

"I know what you want to do," said Argus. "But, I know what's coming too. Because I saw it, Greta. It wants us all dead, Greta. It wants everything."

"Shut up, Argus."

"Especially *you*. It wants *you* most of all."

"I said, 'shut up!'"

"It wants *you*," said Argus. "Just like it took me, it wants you. It wants *everyone*. That thing, whatever it is. It won't stop. It doesn't know how to stop. It won't. Until it finds you."

Greta felt her fingers twitch unnaturally. Was it fatigue or fear? She kept her hand steady, reminding herself of what she planned to do.

Are you going to do this or what? she thought.

Argus started to sob. He whimpered like a child and Greta slowly felt herself sympathizing for her enemy.

"You can't see it like I can," said Argus. "You don't see the monster like I do. You never did. I know that's why you hate me. I know that's why you curse me when I'm near. But, it's not me you should hate. It's *them*. The monsters, Greta. And they're going to get you too. They're coming for you. They're coming for you like they came for me."

Unbeknownst to Greta, Argus was surrounded by several iterations of the Adversary. The spider-like creatures were in trees, they were on the ground, and they were carefully inserting themselves between Greta and Argus. They hissed and spat out blood-like mucus all across the forest floor and Argus shut his eyes, trying hard to drown out the sound. He cried, hearing their voices in his head even though he tried to shut them out. Greta pulled the pistol from her belt and aimed it at Argus.

"Stop it, Argus," she said. "Stop it now, you sick freak! What is wrong with you? What was that back there anyway? How did you even become that thing?"

"Please..." he muttered. "Please, Greta, make it stop... make them stop...."

This was all wrong. She hadn't imagined it this way. Argus was practically begging her to end his life. Wasn't this what she wanted? No, it wasn't. Not like this. Not *ever* like this. How could she take his life? How could she have thought that killing Argus was the result she longed for?

"I said, stop it!" she yelled.

Argus stood up. His eyes open, looking beyond Greta. The Adversary had conjoined into one and it was standing behind her. Its legs were outstretched like a snare about to collapse down on Greta. It hissed, mocking Argus like it was safe. Argus fumed. He bent down and grabbed the first thing he could grab hold of – a small rock – and pulled back to throw.

"Leave me alone!" he shouted and Greta went to fire, but Argus' throw distracted her, so she dodged instead of pulling the trigger. The stone landed behind her and when she turned back around, Argus was charging her. She raised her pistol but Argus slammed into her and the pistol fell, firing errantly and striking Greta in the thigh. She screamed, gripping her leg as she tumbled

250 | J.C.L. Faltot

to the ground, Argus atop her. He wriggled over her, taking another rock and slamming it into her head several times. Greta tried to resist, but Argus was surprisingly strong. Fear had given him strength he'd never known existed. He defeated her quickly, despite his smaller frame, striking her over and over again.

"I hate you!" he shouted. "You bitch! I always hated you! Because you hated *me!* Why did you hate me? Why did you hate me so much? I told you it was the monsters! Those damned monsters did this to us! It's not my fault! I told you they'd come for *you!*"

After several strikes, Argus stopped and moved off of Greta. The fight was over. But, it had been over for a while. Greta's hands and arms fell limp to the ground. She didn't move, didn't breathe for all he could tell. He looked about for the Adversary. It was gone. There was no trace of the monster, save the carnage unleashed upon Greta. Blood was dripping from her face now; eyes closed, and body sprawled out in a fencing position. Argus took several deep breaths and waited.

He'd survived, he realized. The rock he'd used, sitting in dirt, had a smidge of blood on its edge. The murder weapon. I'm a murderer now. He started crying and curled into a ball next to Greta.

He listened for a breath or a huffing of lungs but there was none. No sounds. Nothing. Argus stood up and backed away from her. He couldn't carry her. If she'd ever wake up, she'd come for him. He didn't want any of that. He wanted to be gone. He wanted to escape. He grabbed Greta's pistol and hobbled back to the Rover. When he got there, he was hunched over and out of breath. The Huntsmen were alert, expecting Greta to be with him.

"What happened? What was that shot?" they asked.

"It took her, dammit!" exclaimed Argus. "That monster! It took her! We have to go! It's comin' back!"

"What took her? Where's the lieutenant?"

Argus was out of breath, but he suffered through it. He straightened himself, addressing the Huntsmen as one. "The monster," he said. "I told you it would come back for us. It came back and tried to kill us. And it took her."

"*You're* the monster, Argus," said one of them, stepping forward. "It came back *because* of you. Didn't it? Where's Greta? Where's the lieutenant?"

Argus raised his pistol, wearily, and pointed it at the Huntsman. The others readied their rifles on Argus.

"Look at me," said Argus, his whole body trembling. "None of you can shoot me, ya hear me? None of ya! My brother will have you all killed if you do. So, get back in the Rover. Get back inside. We're leaving, understand?"

No one moved. "Get in the Rover," he said. "Get in there now!"

"Or what?"

"A *reward*," said Argus, thinking so quickly that it even surprised himself. "You'll all get a reward if you take me back. I'll vouch for you. All of you. Promotions. Money. Whatever you need."

"Anything, eh?" said Jonesy.

The Huntsmen exchanged questionable glances. No one spoke. Then Jonesy lowered his rifle and got inside the Rover.

"Come on, gents," said Jonesy. "I don't care who wins this thing. I just want to live."

Soon, they were all aboard, leaving the road and Greta behind; her fate unknown to all, save Argus.

I won, he thought. Fear was working. And it was keeping him alive. Then Argus began to create the story he'd tell his brother. He imagined the monster, sneaking up on Greta, and poisoning her before Argus was forced to turn and run. Yes, that would be it. And he'd have the Hunt back his claim when he told it. They'd all be promoted. He told them they would and they agreed to the terms without flinching. None of them wanted any more trouble. They only wanted to return home. Home was a safe place opposed to the hell they'd been thrown into. Argus knew it and he played on that like a master. Finally, I'm getting like *you*. Is this how you keep the Hunt in line? Fear is the equalizer. Fear is my ally. Too bad for Greta. No, he didn't feel bad. Why had he cried over her? She was the one who'd lost her edge and now that edge belonged to him. The monster is *with* me. I thought it was against me, but maybe it can help me. I'll let him use me how he likes. Have to tell Virgil. Have to let him know I'm like him now.

* * * *

Argus and the Huntsmen arrived at the Hunt's primary camp around mid-morning. They exited their Rover, a broken mess from their battle with the Shepherd, and with less numbers than what they'd left with. Argus called for his brother, asking for the Captain at once and when Virgil came to them, he surprised Argus with questions that were not about Greta or the lost Huntsmen.

"Where is the shard? Where is it, Argus?"

Argus didn't answer at first. His mind had to readjust, had to flush out the predetermined lie he'd prepared. When he couldn't do this effectively, he bought time and asked for a private audience with Virgil. When that was granted, Argus explained their raid upon the Shepherd, starting with the status of the destroyed weapon.

"They lost it, Captain," said Argus.

"Who lost it?"

"Them. Those other ones out there," he said. "The ones who came back with me. They lost it in the fight."

"You *fought* him? You engaged the Shepherd in battle?"

"Yes. They'll deny it, but I tell you we did. It took the shell from us – destroyed it."

Virgil sank into his seat, hands clasped against the arms of his chair. "Did you at least use what I gave you?"

Argus hesitated. He didn't want to answer that question. The memory of darkness that had overtaken him caused his eyes to flutter and repress what had happened. Virgil noticed the mental stammer and leaned forward.

"You did, didn't you?" asked Virgil. "What was it like - when our enemy became your ally?"

"I...I don't know. I don't really remember."

"Try."

Argus closed his eyes and sifted the memories that were least frightening. When he had had enough, he opened his eyes; a word of understanding ready on his lips.

"Hunger...," said Argus.

"*Hunger?*"

"Yes...."

"For what?"

Argus couldn't describe it. Either his vocabulary was far too limited or his mind was simply incapable of combining the words together that might help summarize the experience. It just wasn't that simple. But, Argus eventually found a word that might do its work for him and he sputtered out, "*Life.*"

Virgil stood up. He walked about the makeshift desk of his private tent and stood by the far wall. He seemed to be deep in thought.

"What about the others?" asked Virgil, looking at Argus. "Where is Greta? Where are the other recruits I sent with you?"

Now was the time for the rehearsed answer. Argus didn't hesitate. "She was killed, Argus. By the Shepherd. It killed her, but it took the others captive. They're with him now."

Virgil squinted. Argus took a small delight in relaying the news and Virgil knew it. He looked Argus up and down and took a breath. Argus waited, thinking his story might hold up. Then he added, "And the Shepherd is hurt, Virgil. Badly, too. His whole shoulder is danglin' like it'll fall off at any moment."

Virgil tilted his head to one side, thinking about this revelation. He searched Argus' eyes like the information might be false and when he discerned it wasn't, he continued with more questions.

"Where are they headed?"

Argus shook his head. "I don't know. They headed north. North west, I think."

"Are you certain?"

Argus nodded, but he wasn't entirely sure. Much of the trip back had been a blur. Greta's lifeless body, stranded in the foliage of an unnamed forest, made Argus' mind feel scattered. He had to focus much harder if he was going to win this conversation. And his brother to his side.

Virgil looked past Argus, outside the tent and grinned. "Of course they are headed that way," said Virgil. "They're going for a *Cathedral*. The Shepherd is going to take them to a Red Fellows hangout, I'd imagine."

"Yes, of course. You are right."

There, he'd done it. Virgil circled back around his desk.

"I envy you, brother," said Virgil. "Can't say that I ever thought I would, but I do."

"What's that?"

"You've had an experience no other person on this planet can claim. You've fought the Shepherd, the greatest of Mars' creations. But, that's not all. Do you know what else it is you have done?"

Argus shook his head.

"You've experienced the power of a star, brother."

"What do you mean?"

"Its *life*," said Virgil. "Followed by its cold death; an ending similar to a vacuum. That's what it was like, wasn't it? This 'hunger' you couldn't explain to me just now. You felt like you were incapable of filling yourself completely. That's what it was, right?"

"I don't understand, Virgil...."

Virgil huffed, angered by Argus' lack of understanding. Argus' eyes stared blankly, waiting on his elder brother to speak. Then the darkness started to fall. Argus looked about the tent and saw that the room was darkening, growing colder. Clouds of Darklight were beginning to form. Was his lie causing it?

"You never understand, Argus," said Virgil, angrily. "You never have. But then again, no one does. Not you. Not Greta. No *one*. It seems that I have to accept that, as much as I don't want to, I must. You, the one who is supposed to be the most like me, are anything but like me."

Argus heard the words, but again, he was unable to comprehend his brother's angle. Virgil went on, approaching Argus now.

"I gave you a task," said Virgil. "So that you might redeem yourself, Argus. That you might bring yourself back to a state of honorability, something a human being is uniquely offered. An opportunity even the stars are not granted. And yet, you *failed*. Do you understand what that means?"

Argus backed away from his brother. "Virgil, I don't know what to tell you... The Shepherd.... He's not like any human being I've ever known. You'd know if you ever saw one... ever met one...."

Then it appeared: the Adversary. It crawled out of from under the corners of the Captain's tent, spider legs dragging itself over the ground. A cold whirl of wind followed. The room's temperature seemed to drop instantaneously, a chill that could freeze blood and Argus turned to run. But, Virgil, being bigger and faster than his brother, grabbed hold of his younger kin and held Argus by the throat. He pushed his face close to Argus' ear and clenched tighter. Argus' windpipe was pinched and Argus found himself unable to breathe. The Adversary moved ahead of him. It circled round Argus and Virgil, rising up from the corners of the room like a serpent but with the legs of a centipede or spider flailing about. At the apex of this nightmare, a head formed: a twisted and ghoulish head with long teeth and crude blood dripping from its mouth. Argus tried to scream, but there was no air to make a sound. Virgil had him completely and whispered to Argus of what was to come.

"You aren't a star, Argus," said Virgil. "You were given an opportunity to be *resurrected*; to be born again because I gave you a second chance. That's what every human is given. Do you see the difference now? The difference between humans and stars? It's silly to even compare the two. We are so much brighter than they are yet people always persist with comparing us to them. Like they're the goal of our existence. But, we know they aren't." Virgil paused, Argus writhing. "And yet, when we fail, we don't shine anymore. We are like black holes, sucking dry anyone else who happens to be around for our failures. A person can change himself though. Stars cannot; their fate is sealed. But, your failures are like the stars which become black holes."

Argus was gagging on the inside. The air would not come, but his brother, oh, he was strong. And he would not relinquish his grip on smaller, weaker Argus.

"So, a star you shall be," said Virgil. "Not a human being."

At that moment, Virgil could hear two voices in his head: a voice egging him with chants of 'kill'; 'destroy'; 'eliminate,' while another quietly said, 'stop.' The latter pierced the others with a conviction that had force enough to slay dragons, but since the former was louder and more familiar, Virgil listened to the former instead. Having grown comfortable with the former, Virgil heeded its instructions and snapped the neck of his brother like he was punishing an enemy, not his own blood and bone. Argus' eyes widened at the last, watching as the fangs of the Adversary reigned down upon his face, killing him along with the hands of his elder brother. Argus' body went limp and Virgil carried the body of his younger brother to the ground until he was prostrate on the dirt. Lying there, with eyes open and terrified, Virgil shook off every notion that this was his kin. A disappointment. Not human. Not a star. Just *disappointing*. Yes, these are the words he would use to describe this flesh before him.

The Adversary went straight to work, feeding on Argus' death. It penetrated every cell, every tangible piece of the once alive body, tearing at internal engines used for housing Argus' soul while he'd been among the living.

Virgil stood and called for two of his lieutenants. They entered, eyed the body of Argus and stared at their Captain.

"Where are the others who were with him?" asked Virgil.

"We have them out front," one of them answered, shakily.

Virgil shut his eyes, thinking of his next play. He waited to hear the voice that had spoken to him this whole way. It had always felt so clear. He waited to see what it might ask of him, want of him in this moment. He looked down at the husk of flesh, the body of the disappointment and he looked away, displeased. There was no voice. Nothing that captured his attention.

"Captain?"

"Have them tied to the trees," said the Captain. "They are all betrayers to the Hunt for their failures. As for the rest of us, pack the tents and be ready to leave."

"Where are we going, Captain?"

"To the Cathedral of the Red Fellows."

Chapter 16
Abraham

* * * *

Abe had decided to travel by horseback as opposed to vehicle when he left the old city. He took only the essentials, but made certain to take several rabbit traps and his favorite bow and arrow. Abe wasn't much of a shooter when it came to rifles, but he loved to shoot his bow. He was good at it, too. The Red Fellows had taught him how, he remembered, and silently said a prayer of thanks for the lesson.

Traveling this way felt more natural. Abe didn't have a vehicle, not for many years, and couldn't afford the cost of keeping one. Life was harder without the light. Cars used to pass casually through the city. Abe remembered them. There were all sorts of cars, not just Rovers or carriages. They had various sizes, colors, and shapes. People chose them according to their needs or desires. But, each of them had a purpose. Smaller ones held one, maybe two passengers, at most. The medium ones held two, three, maybe four. And the biggest ones carried whole families of five or more. Size of the vehicle was determined by the size of the family. That's how every vehicle was made before the Pulse. Family was the dominant factor in building a car. Now, vehicles were made for survival. Or for conquering others.

The road out of the old city was a straight path, but Abe knew he couldn't take it. At least not the whole way. The destination he was going for couldn't be obvious. A man traveling on horseback with little other than a knapsack and a bow could be taken for one of many things. Ironically, a drifter was the best of scenarios. The worst would be a man with a price on his head. Abe didn't want to risk the chance, even if he weren't a guilty party. So he took the old city road north for several miles before veering west, off the main roads and onto the back roads long abandoned by the modern world. Here he could be safe from eyes that might be looking for someone traveling alone. He hated having to do it and imagined what it might be like to travel by one's self and not fear being cut down by anything other than a rabid bear or fierce thunderstorm. Other humans – those outside of the old city – were predators in his path.

The first couple days were easy. But, on the third day, he would need to trap game if he expected to eat on the fourth, fifth, and sixth. Rabbits and squirrels were plentiful in the woods, but if Abe could snag a deer then he'd be set for much of the trip. Luckily, more than one found him.

A herd, headed north, passed Abe on the western side of his camp. He was downwind and a single doe had broken from the herd. It was almost too good to be true. Abe readied his bow. When she'd gotten close enough, he took aim and fired. The arrow struck the doe through the shoulder and the animal buckled. It was a good shot and he silently congratulated himself for not missing a beat in many years. The animal struggled for a few moments before finally landing in a small thicket. He ran over; ready to end the creature's suffering as fast as he could. That's when he saw it: a single fawn bounding towards him and the fallen doe. Abe sighed.

"I'm sorry, kiddo," he said. "You'd best not watch this next part. I'm real sorry."

Abe chased off the fawn before coming back for the doe. She had been a healthy one, in the prime of her bearing years. She'd have been a perfectly good meal if it hadn't been for her offspring coming to check on her, tugging on Abe's conscience like he was a villain, an orphan-maker of baby deer. But, she would have to fulfill her part in this now. Abe would, too. What's done is done. No going back now.

The herd moved onward as Abe skinned the carcass and made ready the meat for a stew. A stew could sustain him for a good while. There was no way to refrigerate the meat on this trip. Don't worry; I'll make sure nothing goes to waste on her, little one. And he thanked God for sending this deer to him, something he discovered he hadn't done for a long while: thanking God. That night, he dined on deer stew and cried himself into a slumber. One that was a mixture of thankfulness and shame, neither emotion he knew he was carrying so heavily. He slept for only a few hours.

In the morning, on the fourth day, Abe took his horse into a small town and rested for the afternoon. He needed water and a change of clothes before he could move onward and found the accommodations there to be hospitable. The town reminded him of the old city plaza. And he hoped to maybe see Jeff or Craig if he could.

But, of course he wouldn't see them. He'd left them all behind. Shouldn't he have said goodbye?

On the fifth day, Abe awoke and headed out. He was just outside the hotel, ready to embark when he overheard the rumblings of a strange happening. Two men were discussing something beyond the entryway.

"I don't know," said one of them. "But there's a lot of them."

"What do they want?" asked the other.

"Someone said they could be military, looking for recruits."

"You know that for sure?"

"No, but there were a lot of them. Had big vehicles. Made the ground shake when they came through. Just glad they're gone."

"You think it could be the *Hunt*?"

There was a pause. Abe decided this was the right time to interject.

"The Hunt, was it?" said Abe. "Were they dressed in red scarves? Red insignias on their vehicles? That'd be them."

The two men looked confused, like Abe were an alien. Speaking to strangers must not be normal practice around here. Then one of them said, "I guess they could be, but the Hunt never comes this far north. They're more interested in city dealings. Why would they come all the way up here?"

Looking for more than just membership, I'm sure.

"How long ago were they here?" asked Abe.

"Maybe a day or so," said one of them. "Interested in joining up, are you?"

"Not exactly."

Abe thanked the men for the information and left. The Hunt is recruiting, eh? They're out looking for young blood. But, I'm sure it's more than just that, isn't it?

Abe made his way up the road and found the tire tracks of what he believed to be one of the Hunt's Rovers. And then he found several more. Another few miles up the road and the tracks veered away from the dirt road, headed west. Abe led his horse off the trail to follow the Hunt. Jeff, don't be there. It was late afternoon when he came to a break in the dirt road and the Rovers had steered off. Abe followed the new trail and found them.

The Hunt was camped out in a small clearing. It had all the makings of a medieval battle camp: horses, tents, and men and women sitting about talking idly as they waited for word to move again. There were more than Abe imagined. Perhaps they'd taken even more from the towns they'd passed through en route to where they were going?

Abe tied his horse on the trail and crept closer. He got as close as the tree line and listened. No one spoke loud enough for him to hear anything though. However, there was one he keyed in on: it was *her*, the woman from the old city. She was walking about, speaking sternly to the ones she encountered. Sandy blond hair, sharp features – just as he remembered. A lieutenant, perhaps? Her presence made other members of the Hunt quiver at her passing. Yes, she was certainly someone of authority. Abe observed her a long while, leaning against the closest tree to become more comfortable.

Abe ended up waiting a long time; so long that he began to drift off. The few nights of poor sleep had caught up to him and soon, he was asleep and dreaming. Unaware the Hunt was gathering their belongings and readying to leave.

When Abe awoke, he was enveloped in smoke. A brush fire. The forest was aflame and Abe was struggling to breathe. He looked back and saw that his horse was gone. The fire was on all sides. How had it started? Abe stood up and ran in the direction away from the smoke and stumbled by a log. His body felt heavy. The smoke was choking him. Was there a way out of this? There didn't seem to be. His body became heavier. The smoke was scratching at the inside of his lungs. Way to be an old idiot who can't stay awake, Abraham. Now, you'll die in a blaze with no one around to see you.

Then, a truck appeared in the brush. It was one of the Hunt's Rovers, come to rescue him. It stomped out the grass and leaves, headed directly for Abe. The Rover stopped and opened its side door and two men exited, picked up Abe and threw him into their Rover. They made off; out of the fire and onto the dirt road. Abe heaved and coughed. The Huntsmen let him have it out until he was breathing regularly again. Abe felt like thanking them, but the Huntsmen offered him no chance, strapping a cloth round his mouth until the Rover came to a stop. They then pushed him out, removed the cloth, and Abe was made to stand like a traitor before the ones who had brought him to safety. Behind them, the tree line could be seen in a billow of smoke like a volcano had erupted in the distance.

"Who are you?" one of them asked.

Abe didn't answer. He was still catching his breath.

"Who are you?"

No answer.

"Do you want to go back into the fire, old man? Who are you?"

"My name is Abraham. I'm traveling alone. I was taking a breather."

"In the middle of a forest fire?"

"I fell asleep."

"Doing what?"

"Where's my horse?"

"You had a horse?"

Abe nodded. "We never found a horse," said Abe's interrogator. "Just you. Wandering through the woods like a man with a death wish. Do you still have one?"

"The horse or a death wish?" he said.

The Huntsman sneered. Didn't like that joke, did you? Abe couldn't discern what they planned to do with him, but there were no clouds of Darklight. No sign of terror coming. However, it was dark where they were. It was after sundown. That made it harder to see Darklight. The Hunt had their torches lit and had an agitation about them like someone who'd been roused in the middle of the night. How had they found him? Had they caused the fire? There was no sign of the blond-haired woman among them. This was a different group of Huntsmen, he decided. One he hadn't seen earlier that day.

"Look, old man. I'll give you one more chance to – "

A heavy thud rocked the ground and Abe and the Huntsman jostled. The dirt road cracked between them and the Hunt raised their rifles to Abe. Two giant feet could be seen imprinted in the Earth. Then, Abe heard a voice, saying,

"Get down. I will handle them."

Abe crouched and the Hunt pointed their rifles at the cowering Abe. One of the Huntsmen was picked up and thrown through the air. The Hunt turned their guns as their compatriot sailed through the sky, landing somewhere near the edge of the woods with a crash. "What was that? Did you see that?" Then another was hoisted and thrown aside. And another. Then another. The Hunt scattered, firing rounds through the air to hit their unknown assailant. Abe stayed on the ground as ordered, but he could see huge feet moving about, directly under where the Huntsmen were being tossed. Soon, they were all of them immobilized and the road was still, without movement. Abe started to stand up.

"Hello?" he said; huge footprints making their way towards him. Abe covered his face.

"Do not be afraid," said a voice. "I have come to help you."

Abe heard a cranking sound; then a being appeared before him as though out of nowhere. It started at the feet, working its way up. Soon, standing before Abe, was a huge person of at least seven feet. And Abe knew precisely who it was.

"A *Shepherd?*" said Abe.

The Shepherd nodded. "Hello there. Are you alright?"

Abe shook his head, 'yes'. He couldn't believe it. Never had he thought he would see one again and yet, here one was: a real Shepherd. An overwhelming sense of joy overcame him. Not merely because he'd been rescued, but because something he'd found himself invested so heavily within had finally come to fruition. The enormity of the moment caused Abe to fall to his knees and he started to weep uncontrollably. The Shepherd bent down and looked him in the face.

"I have been tracking your movements for some time," said the Shepherd, inches from Abe's face. "I have seen your intentions from across space. You have many of the *Gifts* within you, but some are dormant now, untapped and unused. You must uncover these if you are going to find the one you seek."

Abe felt delirious, but still, he was somehow able to blurt out, "How do you know all this?"

"It is one of *my* Gifts," said the Shepherd. The two of them stood up. "I am able to see not only the intentions of others, but the potential they cannot see for themselves. I must apologize for not getting to you earlier. I was unaware of your mission until only a day ago and I have been leading a group of my own; one that is headed for my ship, but I feel we will not be going there anymore."

"Who? Why? Where will you be going instead?"

Abe asked the questions without even filtering. His mind wanted answers that the Shepherd wasn't even asking. The Shepherd grinned.

"There is a group I have been leading to my ship," said the Shepherd. "We are now headed for the *Cathedral of the Red Fellows*. This group is not ready to receive Mars yet. And my signal has been distorted as well. These people, the ones who captured you tonight – they are after my group. But, soon, they will be after *me* as well."

Abe looked about the carnage and agreed with the Shepherd's assumption.

"And when I saw that you were coming for one of your own," said the Shepherd. "And I saw the Gifts inside of you, I wanted to find you. Again, I am sorry for the delay."

Abe shrugged like the apology was unnecessary. The Shepherd was already leading a group of people, bound for Mars - just like Abe had seen happen before. So what now for him?

"What do you want from me then?" asked Abe. "Now that you've found me and helped me?"

"To stay the course," said the Shepherd. "Continue looking for the one you are after. I do not know her whereabouts myself, but I feel you will find her soon. I find it difficult to track intention and will on Earth. It has been...*trying*. But, I am adjusting well enough considering the circumstances."

Abe looked into the woods. The fire was still burning, spreading quickly like it was intent on laying siege to the entire valley.

"Don't worry yourself about the fire either," said the Shepherd. "I am going to extinguish it tonight. The Hunt started it and I am going to put it out before I return to my group."

"Is that how they found me?"

"They have been burning land and blaming it on the Red Fellows, on Mars, among others who would align themselves with Mars. Their tactics are clever, but not without its faults. They will be exposed soon enough. Head north up this road and you should find shelter there. I saw it on my way here. Make certain that you walk there too. Leave the vehicle for the Hunt. They will need it when they come to. Good bye, until we meet again, Abraham."

Then the Shepherd jumped high into the air and landed somewhere deep within the fire. Unbelievable. It all happened so quickly that Abe retraced the conversation several times before he could move forward. Had he asked every pertinent question? Did he know what the Shepherd meant by 'staying the course' and did the Shepherd know what *he* was after? He called Abe by name too. How did he know? He must have overheard the Hunt interrogating him. That was it, wasn't it?

Abe started walking. He took one of the Rover's torches and lumbered down the dirt road, trusting the Shepherd's words that shelter was near. The bodies of his captors were ahead, knocked out or sleeping soundly from having been tossed aside by the Shepherd. None of them moved or twitched. They appeared to be in a weird coma and Abe deduced that the Shepherd had done more than simply throw them away.

Less than a half-mile down, Abe found an old barn and rested inside. It was dirty but there were old straw beds and mattresses inside that he could lay on. To his surprise, he fell right asleep and awoke when sunlight touched his face. Standing in the door was a visitor he did not expect either. Abe wiped his mouth and saw that his horse was waiting outside. Somehow it had found him, or perhaps had been found by the Shepherd and brought to him while he slept.

"Thank God," he said. "Thank God, indeed."

Abe took his horse and left. He was slightly off course, but the Cathedral would be coming soon within the week. He went along, looking over his shoulder like the Hunt might be coming for him, but expunged the theory at every turn of his thoughts. All the while, he hoped he would find *her*.

A few days more of traveling and living off trapped game kept Abe away from civilization. He was taking the long way around. No doubt, if the Hunt were this far north, then they'd continue to come for him. And for the Shepherd too, no less. So Abe stayed in the woods, carving out paths where his horse might permit him to go and keeping one eye to his backside. On one such night, he saw a storm approaching and had to make shelter under a tree canopy. With nothing else to comfort him, he read from the book Craig had given him and penned inside of his journal. He read through it thoroughly and fell asleep soundly. The thunder rolled through but it didn't wake him and when he awoke, the storm had passed and it was the early morning. He went on.

When the evening came again, Abe found himself still outside the borders of humanity and he was tired and hungry. His horse needed water so he led her to a stream and made camp. Abe needed to hunt so he stayed in the woods for the afternoon and for the night. In the evening, he wondered if the Shepherd might return for him and each night that passed he imagined the silver giant waking him from slumber. And each morning when the Shepherd was not there, Abe did not curse or become angry. Instead he reminded himself of the Shepherd's words, 'until we meet again.' That means he'll come for me soon. He will.

After several nights of travel and staying off civilization's path, the Shepherd *did* come for Abe. The giant could be heard bounding through the woods; a noise that alerted the horse and forced Abe to stand and ready himself. A few yards away, Abe saw the trees part and the earth crunch as the Shepherd flew through the air and landed just beside his camp. Abe was elated and he greeted the Shepherd with a smile, but when he saw that the giant was injured, his mood changed immediately.

"What's wrong?" asked Abe. "What happened to you?"

"An encounter with the Adversary," said the Shepherd and Abe swallowed. The monster the Red Fellows fear most – that thing is *back*? The Shepherd went on, "It's gotten stronger since I last fought with it and it's injured my suit. It's taking longer to repair than I would like, but it will be done soon. I see that you have continued on your journey."

Abe nodded, but just behind the Shepherd was something else: a container? And a person inside. "I am still a few days out," said Abe. "Shouldn't be too much longer, I'd imagine."

"You are closer than you think. But, you are also closer to another still. There's been a terrible happening since my battle and you will need to take this one with you."

Abe seemed to know whom the Shepherd was speaking about, or rather, he hoped it was the one he was thinking of: the woman with sandy blond hair. Was it her – suspended behind the Shepherd? The Shepherd guided the device in front of him and it was just as Abe had thought: the woman of the Hunt, the one with the blond hair, Greta. She was badly injured, but seemed to be incubating inside of the Shepherd's alien technology, partially immersed in vibrant and shining water. It glowed gold like it had a heartbeat, helping to mend Greta as she lie inside the container.

"She was attacked by one of her own," said the Shepherd. "I trust you will be able to deliver her to the Red Fellows."

Abe, again, was speechless. Relieved, but angry. Angry to see her like this. Who had done this? Who *could* have done this? Abe walked up, examined Greta. The Shepherd laid the bed on the ground and allowed Abe to remove her. She didn't make a sound; her body seemed to be without life, but she was breathing. Abe bent down; brushed her hair. It was warm to the touch and smooth. He felt like crying, but resisted. Then he looked up at the Shepherd.

"How did you know?" asked Abe, practically shaking. "How did you know she was my *daughter*?"

"I am able to fully assess genetic knowledge of an individual upon seeing them up close," said the Shepherd. "And with your intention so great to find her, I was able to make the connection rather quickly. She and other members of the Hunt came after my party and me. I was able to hold them off, as I mentioned, but I also recognized her connection to you. From that point on, I began to track her from afar. Sadly, I saw her being surrounded with Darklight and when the Adversary came upon her, she was engulfed by the rage of another. One who feared her. And this happened. I knew I had to alert you to the situation when it did. So I saved her and brought her to you."

Abe wanted to cry. He had failed. He had failed to protect her again.

"When I saw her with the Hunt," said Abe. "She didn't even know it was me. I didn't think she would, but still, I hoped she might. Now, I know it was just a wish. That's what wishing is, isn't it? Hope without favor. Hope without reality. Hope without rationality."

"Hope is linked with faith, Abraham," said the Shepherd. "Do not subject your feelings to having to be pure logic. Human emotions are not so easily calculated. Nor are the outcomes from which they are placed within. The unpredictable nature of hope is not something one can attribute solely to the laws of logic."

"Even so, she didn't even recognize me, Shepherd. I don't know what to even make of that. How can a child not recognize the face of her father? There would have to be *love*, wouldn't there? A love that would open the eyes and see? Right? Is she so without love that she couldn't see me?"

The Shepherd paused. He stared at Abe like the question was absurd, or maybe, was irrelevant. Was it? Or had Abe taught the Shepherd something this night?

"I have said what I need to," said the Shepherd. "With regards to human understanding and love." The Shepherd then became deathly serious. "Leave now and take her with you. If you travel through the night, you will reach the Cathedral by early morning. She will remain in sleep until you make it there. I will give your horse water to make it there. And I will see you there soon as well. I promise."

"Thank you," said Abe. "I can't thank you enough."

The container, which held Greta, transformed and reattached itself to the Shepherd as four separate discs. The Shepherd held out his hands and fed the horse water as promised and then left as promised, too. Abe held Greta close, weeping for a time before hoisting her atop his horse. Never again. I'll never let you out of my sight again. They walked through the night, exiting the woods by a large clearing with a single white building in the middle of a pasture. It was unassuming and looked aged; a single bell, large and bronze-colored, was positioned at the apex alongside a cross. Abe patted his horse and held onto Greta.

"Well, we made it," he said. "I hope they still like me here."

Chapter 17
The Red Fellows

* * * *

Olivia awoke before anyone else. She normally did, but feigned sleep so that her father might think she slept through the night. But, in truth, she rarely slept through *any* night and could scarcely recall the last time she had since they'd found the Shepherd. Her mind was tired and her body was tired yet she kept any and all of her tiresome thoughts to herself. She was good at hiding things from people, save the Shepherd, whose watchful eye seemed to follow her carefully, and would periodically call the group to rest when he knew Olivia had gone too far. In this way, she appreciated the Shepherd. He was not just an otherworldly giant with magical powers, but was also a gentle soul with real human compassion; a rarity, so far as Olivia knew or had known throughout her life.

But, that wasn't all Olivia noticed about the Shepherd. In the nights, the Shepherd would wait until the party was asleep before inevitably bounding off for somewhere unknown. He never explained where he'd gone or what he was doing, but Olivia sensed it had something to do with the people who were after them. For when he'd return, he'd wear a grim expression on his face. It wasn't out of tiredness, but of anxious thoughts. There were many things on his mind, yet he disguised these thoughts from the group. Everyone except Olivia, who read every twinge of the lip or cock of the eyebrow. All were signs of the Shepherd's ongoing battle to sort things out without disturbing the peace of his comrades.

However, the amount of effort the Shepherd needed in order to conceal these thoughts was minimal. Darion and Jack were more concerned with each other than with the Shepherd, making the Shepherd's worrisome spirit an easy topic to ignore. But, again, not for Olivia. For she had recognized his weariness from their first encounter and at times, wondered if she might try telling Darion of her discoveries.

But, ultimately, she decided against it. The decision was based solely on the similar kindness the Shepherd had shown her. If there were a real problem – a real threat – the Shepherd would tell them. So there was no need to make mention or call attention to the situation. They were nearing the Shepherd's ship. Things were going to change sooner than later. No need to stir up trouble. 'No decent girl stirs up trouble,' as her father might say. So she maintained her silence.

Four days with their largest party yet and the Shepherd announced a change in direction. The group would be stopping somewhere for a few days. At first, Darion was bothered by the news while Jack was apathetic. The three Huntsmen had no objections and Olivia carried no opinion either. If this new place had a bedroom with an actual bed, then she'd be happy.

Olivia observed how the news made the tension between the Huntsmen and Darion worse. More time with these reformed mercenaries caused Darion to become even more hyper protective.

"We can't trust them," Darion would tell Olivia. "If the Shepherd has to stop and heal – or leave us for any portion of time - then we can't let them out of our sight. They outnumber us and that's not a good thing. Do you understand?"

Olivia would nod in agreement, but she wondered why it had to be this way. Why these Huntsmen were so incapable of being trusted. Hadn't they gone through the same trials as she, her father, and Jack? And their faces – they were all wide-eyed, unafraid. Olivia recognized this as similar to Jack's state of being when he first met the Shepherd. The new trio was curious, less interested in Darion's paranoid scenarios and more intrigued by the Shepherd himself. And yet, Olivia's father was usually right about people so when she could, Olivia looked across the camp and wondered who might be the worst among them; who was most liable to betray their party.

There was the 'big one', according to her father; the one who talked the most. His name was Felix. He asked plenty of questions, ones that centered on Mars' history and its dealings with Earth. He reminded Olivia of Jack when they first met. How he was full of inquiries and never-ending questions. Felix seemed to speak on behalf of the other two, who were smaller, younger, and surprisingly less talkative. They reminded Olivia of herself. There was Robert, the dark-skinned and mid-sized Huntsman. He was newer to the Hunt and barely combat-trained. Darion surmised he was no more than twenty. His body was thin, still maturing, and his face had bits of scruff all about his mouth. He spoke only when spoken to, which was not very often. Then lastly, there was Tom. Tom was young, probably sixteen, and 'hardly a soldier', per Olivia's father. But, that wasn't the most interesting thing about Tom. Olivia had noticed how Tom was not who he said he was: Tom was not a boy, but a *girl*. Olivia had seen her escape from the group one night to relieve herself. Olivia was sure of it. The other Huntsmen must have not known or maybe they were just protecting her. Tom's tight cap and loose clothing had guarded her secret well, but how long would that last? Surely the Shepherd must know the difference?

As for her father, Darion, he was less observant as always.

"They're practically kids…" said Darion. "Barely older than you, sweetie. I can't believe the Hunt recruits so young. Even so, stay on alert. Don't let any of them catch you off guard. Understand?"

Olivia nodded; paying close attention to them all, but still was without any conclusion as to who might be the betrayer. Tom seemed to be the one most bent on keeping secrets, but she didn't seem dangerous otherwise.

So Olivia fixed back on Jack, who had become emotionally distant in recent days. He hardly spoke, keeping his gaze outside the group and ignoring Olivia. Before the attack, she and Jack would play games with one another. There was one where Jack would draw pictures in the dirt and she would try to finish them, or he'd pretend to eat something gross – like a worm – and she would cringe at the sight of it. But, ever since the Hunt had come in the night, and the newcomers had become a part of their group, Jack had been mostly silent. Why? Olivia wanted to ask, but she wanted Jack to make it obvious for her. Talking wasn't something she wanted to do. Not yet anyway. She hadn't since Mom had been around. It didn't feel right to do it again without her. Olivia wanted to wait till she saw her again; a destined meeting which continued to be delayed, it seemed.

Maybe now, with the Shepherd standing before them, this would be the turning point.

"We are going to one of the Cathedrals of the Red Fellows," said the Shepherd.

"Those freaks?" said Felix.

"They're not freaks," argued the Shepherd. "There will be friends there. People who are helpful to our cause."

"The Red Fellows don't just welcome anybody in," said Darion. "You might be an exception, but what about the rest of us?"

"I will speak on your behalf."

"And what about us?" asked Tom, surprisingly.

"I will speak on your behalf as well."

"Why are we going there?" asked Darion. "Haven't we taken enough time on these side tours?"

"I need to heal."

Don't you want him to get better, Dad? Olivia thought. *Isn't that a necessity?*

"Does it have to do with your arm?" asked Felix.

"Yes. This injury can't wait any longer."

At mid-morning, they came to the edge of the woods and looked upon an old road with a single building at the top of a hill. It was older, covered in white and weathered - nothing spectacular; nothing to catch the eye and make a person take a second look. If anything, this place looked abandoned. A single, bronze bell was stationed at the apex of the building. *The Red Fellows?* Olivia thought. She and her father had been to see them before. It did not go well from what she remembered.

"Is this the place?" asked Felix.

"Yes," answered Darion. He spoke like he was speaking on behalf of the Shepherd. "It's a Cathedral for the Red Fellows. Isn't that right, Shepherd?"

The Shepherd nodded. "Come, we should go and say hi."

"You act like they're expecting us," said Darion.

"Are they?" asked Robert.

Olivia looked at the Shepherd like the answer was in his eyes. *Yes*, she thought. *You've been here already, haven't you?* Just like when you sneak off in the nighttime.

"This place will be good for everyone to rest," said the Shepherd. "And good for me too. There is something here that I need if we are going to get any farther."

No one asked what that could be. It seemed none of them wanted to know.

They walked to the doors, the Shepherd in front. He knocked and they waited, Olivia hiding behind her father. A woman answered, younger and remarkably beautiful. She eyed each and every person that was with the Shepherd, bypassing the silver giant like the anomaly of human genetics could wait.

"Hello," she said. "I was wondering where you've been. How many are with you? I see six. Is that correct?"

"Yes, there are six with me."

"How have your travels been? How is your arm doing? I see that it might need attention sooner than later."

"It will. Thank you. It's barely repaired but I am in need of real curing."

"Of course. We can show you to the infirmary right away. Does anyone else need medical attention?"

"Are you a nurse?" asked Jack and Olivia nearly jumped. She hadn't heard Jack's voice like this for days. Was it this young woman sparking him to life?

"No, I'm not," she answered. "Are you hurt though?"

"No. And never mind."

The others didn't talk. Olivia wished for her father to say something. He had been limping for a day now. She didn't know why. Jack's cough had gotten worse in the nights, too. He wouldn't say anything about that either. Every person seemed overtly cautious, not wanting to share any weaknesses he might be carrying. Like, entering the Cathedral meant one had to be strong. Or *well-hidden*. But, there was also a strange feeling of betrayal against the Shepherd himself. Like, the Shepherd hadn't been totally honest with them, like he'd been communing with the Red Fellows rather than the ship he promised to take them to.

The young woman opened the door wide and welcomed them in, the Shepherd ducking his head slightly.

"As you probably know, the infirmary will be downstairs with everyone else, Shepherd."

"Thank you, I'll go there immediately once everyone else is situated."

"Oh, my apologies, Shepherd," said the woman. "I hadn't realized I was addressing you improperly. Forgive me, may I call you by your true name while you are here?"

True name? Olivia thought. The Shepherd had a *name*? What's a *true* name?

"It is all right," said the Shepherd. "There's no need for that. You may just call me 'Shepherd' while I am here."

"That works. I trust I haven't upset you."

"Not in the slightest."

The group proceeded down the corridor and into a larger room. It was much bigger inside the Cathedral than it appeared to be on the outside. The wooden frame was supported by a stone interior and the trusses that held the roof were thick and broad. Olivia had to bend her head all the way back to see the middle of the ceiling. Candles and lamps were everywhere. There were long seats, pews, on either side of the large room, made of wood and covered in red cushions. People were sitting in them and reading or talking in low whispers. When they saw that the Shepherd was with them, some of them stood and gawked. Others approached the Shepherd, their steps staggered like they beheld a Greek or Roman god.

"The Shepherd is here," they said.

"A Shepherd?"

"A Shepherd. Here at the Cathedral? We are truly blessed."

"Most blessed."

Olivia hid behind her father. These people did not behave like the ones she knew in the old city. Their eyes were wide and their demeanors, calm. It was like their souls were positioned on the outside of their faces, unsealed and uncovered for the world to see. A young boy came running up to them and Jack about did a double take. He was about Olivia's size and had fluffy, brown hair and was jumping like he were skipping on water. It was unlike the children of the old city, whose faces examined the ground and scarcely looked upward. They were never situated forward, awaiting gentle approval like this boy. Theirs was a look of both predatory and prey, offensive and defensive. This boy was different and immediately Olivia wondered if 'different' meant to be feared or invited. She decided she'd wait and see.

"Ianna," said the boy. "Is that *him*? Is that the Shepherd?"

Jack raised an eyebrow and rehearsed the name several times before he was confident he'd placed it in his personal storage of things-to-remember.

"Hello, Turk," she said and greeted him with a hug. "Yes, yes this is him. The Shepherd we were told about. The one who was coming to visit us."

The little boy's eyes widened, gawking. The Shepherd crouched on one knee and eyed Turk face to face. Turk walked forward and held up a hand to the Shepherd's face. Darion nearly reached out instinctively, trying to stop the boy from making contact, but Turk resisted, knowing what would happen.

"Is it true?" asked Turk. "That if I touch you, then I'll die?"

"Yes, it is," said the Shepherd. "Unfortunately, it is a fact. No person may touch me or else he will perish. My suit does not allow for contact to happen."

The Huntsmen exchanged glances as if to say, why *couldn't* anyone touch him? What was so special about his suit? But, none bothered to ask. They kept right on listening, strangers in a strange land under the roof of the Red Fellow Cathedral.

"Can anyone touch you?" asked Turk. "Anyone on Mars?"

The Shepherd nodded with a 'yes.'

"That's good," said Turk, smiling. "That'd be awful if you could never touch another person."

"Indeed. You are most right, Turk."

The young boy surveyed the rest of the Shepherd's group. He caught Olivia's eye and she turned from him, hiding behind Darion. Turk smiled, as did Olivia.

"What's your name?" he asked, but Olivia wouldn't say.

"I'm sorry," said Darion. "But, she doesn't talk much these days."

"What's her name though?"

Darion took a breath and then said, "Olivia. Her name is Olivia."

Turk grinned. "That's pretty. A pretty name for a pretty girl."

Jack chuckled and Darion shot him a death glance. The two looked away from each other quickly and Olivia sighed. *Why must you two hate each other?* she thought.

"Turk," said Ianna. "Why don't you go and find the one who was waiting for the Shepherd?" Turk nodded, waved, and ran off. Olivia came back out of hiding.

There was someone waiting for them? Who? Olivia imagined her mother, standing somewhere behind a curtain or a door inside the Cathedral. Oh, if only it were her! It could be, couldn't it?

"I have to heal myself," said the Shepherd. "The Red Fellows have something here that will help me do that. It's part of why I've brought you all here. Unfortunately, I have been reminded of my own mortality. Ianna, please make them at home. I will return as soon as I am able. "

"Do you know where you are going?" asked Darion.

The Shepherd didn't answer. He walked down another hallway and disappeared from the group. Olivia felt her father's worst premonitions realized: they were *alone*, abandoned and left with the former Huntsmen. However, they weren't on a dirt road or isolated in the forest. They were among other people, in a place that felt like equal ground. There were eyes here. A mutiny would not happen so easily.

"Come with me," said Ianna. "I'll take you to the underground so you can get more comfortable."

"Underground?" said Felix and Ianna nodded.

She led them down the aisle and through a different hallway. They came to what appeared to be a cast iron door with a heavy latch on it. It looked out of place, broad and thick, incapable of being opened by someone as petite as Ianna.

"Need help with that?" asked Jack.

"No, but thanks."

Ianna placed her palm on the wall next to the iron door and the entire door lit with a golden outline - *Solfire*. Had to be. Darion and the others recoiled slightly as the door opened. Ianna motioned for them to follow her.

"Sorry," she said. "This is a kind of door they use on Mars. It has genetic recognition software built in. I guess you just get used to that after a while. Follow me. You'll have to wait inside of the corridor until the airlock is finished."

"Airlock?" said Felix and again, Ianna nodded.

The hallway beyond the door was a sharp downgrade of stone steps with torches on either side. It felt like a pathway to a hidden dungeon. Olivia could see the bottom from the top, but there was another door waiting for them. They stopped halfway down and waited. The door behind them shut tight and Ianna proceeded to open the bottom door, doing so with the same hand recognition she'd done at the top of the steps. The door opened and Olivia saw silver tiles, alit with light that was stronger than a torch. A room underground? How was it this bright without torches?

The lower level of the Cathedral was even bigger than the upstairs and opened into an entirely new section that resembled a hollowed out cave. The whole hill must have been an outer shell for the underground room. The walls were thick steel and the ceilings were higher than the Cathedral's main sanctuary. What they'd seen above ground had looked old, out of date, but what was waiting *underground* looked pristine and new; a sharp contrast of setting and proportion. People were gathered at tables as long as a bus and there were rooms with see-through walls that had people working inside of them. There was a second, third, even a fourth floor that wrapped around the edge of the enormous room. It had the essence of a university, but looked like a bunker made for the purpose of sustaining an apocalypse. Yet, an even greater anomaly was present.

"What are those?" asked Felix and he pointed upwards.

Dangling from the top ceiling and every floor were dozens upon dozens of floating lights, but not torches – *lights*. Actual lights; not fire, flame or born by the light of an animal. They looked to be human made, human-crafted, even though they were floating without the assistance of a wire or some other structure. Olivia had never seen such a thing and her eyes sparkled as she gazed upon the condensed bulbs of yellow energy. They looked like tiny droplets of sun, hanging in the rafters. She wanted to touch one of them; to feel their warmth and she broke from her father's grasp and walked forward.

"How is this – " stammered Darion. "How is any of this possible? You have *lights* down here. How do you have lights?"

Ianna kept the group moving forward.

"The lights are made of *Solfire*," answered Ianna. "The Red Fellows have engineered them with the help of the Shepherds. Every iron bulb is filled with the light that Solfire emits. But, that's not all."

"What is then?" asked Darion.

"What you're standing inside of," said Ianna. "Is a *ship*. One that's been made on Mars. And brought down here."

A Martian ship? Olivia thought. Perhaps Mother *was* here? Oh, you won't have to hate each other anymore, Dad! Jack! No one will have to hate each other anymore. We're almost there. This is our last stop, right?

* * * *

Darion's heart leapt inside of him. A *ship*? They were inside a Martian ship? The Shepherd hadn't led them astray, after all. He was taking them to a place where they could take a ship to the red planet. Was that his plan? But, this was – this was *much* bigger than what he'd imagined. Or could have predicted. Were all of these people going to Mars then? There were so many.

"How did you get it underground?" asked Darion. "*Why* did you get it underground? Is the Solfire contained only to the insides of this ship? How does it work? What else is in here?"

Ianna grinned like she anticipated this storm of questions. "Why not get some food from the cafeteria first? Then, I'll explain everything to you. Deal?"

The others looked to one another like it was more than a suggestion, but an order, and Ianna directed them to one side of the underground base. There were people serving meals and sitting at tables. One by one, the group of six took a meal – soup with bread – and sat.

Apart from the Shepherd, the group found they had little reason to sit with one another. Without their common link, the Shepherd, the group became disjointed. Even Jack ate by himself; face shoved into his bowl as he slurped at the soup and broke bread in isolation. Olivia looked towards the ceiling, watching the lights hover with their incandescent glow. The Huntsmen stayed huddled together at a round table, not saying much of anything. They looked like children sitting at the wrong table with their shoulders hunched and their eyes down.

"Look at all this, Liv," said Darion. "I can't believe this was all here, right under our noses. I wonder if the other Cathedrals have this? We should have inspected these places more thoroughly."

Jack looked up. "Well, *now* you know, chief," said Jack, from another table. "Shouldn't that be enough to make you happy?"

Darion ignored him. *You shouldn't even be here, Jack,* he thought. You're lucky to even be alive, let alone be here. And where Darion would have rebuked or shared a rebuttal with Jack, he restrained himself and looked away. The time for arguing and trying to take sides was over, he figured. They'd always be this way, he decided, even if just for a little longer.

After some time, and when they were full, Ianna returned and called the six of them together. She then led them to the far end of the ship and through a small door. Again, she used her handprint to get them there. On the other side was a short corridor with a low ceiling, but beyond that was a bigger room, circular, and with several human-shaped pods stationed at the edges. There was a fierce warmth radiating from inside the room, like summer were hiding out underground. Olivia felt it and squeezed her father's hand.

"I know, Liv," he said. "It feels like my face is being pressed against someone's chest."

"That's actually not a bad way of describing where you are," said Ianna.

"Why is that?"

"I'll show you."

Ianna led them out of the corridor and into the larger room. At the center was a large ball, filled with yellow energy, levitating above the ground inside of a metal gyro sphere. It was bigger than a Rover, but smaller than a house. Its light was bright, like a miniature sun, but unlike the sun, its beam weren't damaging to the eye. And what's more, when Darion turned his gaze away, the ball of light glowed even *greater*. It was as if the ball *knew* it was being watched, and it wanted someone to be looking at it always. He circled the ball of light and further confirmed his feeling that as he was watching it, *it* was looking back at him.

"Wow..." said Darion. "That must be a – "

"A ball comprised of Solfire?" said Ianna. "You'd be correct if that were your assumption."

Ianna walked over to a control panel and punched in a sequence of keys that set the room into motion. A noise, sounding like a crank turning, called the attention of every member in the room to the top of the ceiling. High above, a human-sized pod was traveling downward. And when it finally came to a stop, it stood up straight, showcasing its contents: four-fifths of the giant Shepherd. Only his neck and head were exposed, the place where his skin and suit met and his eyes were shut and body immobile. Darion observed this to be the only time he'd seen the Shepherd with his eyes closed for more than a few moments. He appeared to be sleeping, perhaps dreaming, as the golden pod glowed intensely.

"The Shepherd?" said Felix. "What are you doing to him?

"He's in a Restoration Tank," answered Ianna.

"What's that?"

"A chamber designed for Shepherds to be refueled," answered Ianna. "That's the best way I can explain it. You see, they aren't like us. Their bodies are grafted with the millions of nano machines that run on Solfire and when that energy begins to drain, the suit needs to be recharged. The Solfire that's trapped within all of the tiny networks turns inwards and escapes. Unless it's given an external source again."

"Like a battery?" said Darion.

"More than that," said Ianna. "The Solfire acts like a healing agent too. It assists living things so that they might return to their former state."

"So, you could use it too?" said Felix.

Ianna shook her head.

"Why not?" asked Jack and Ianna hesitated.

"Because she's not a Shepherd, Jack," said Darion, acting as if he knew. "You have to possess a suit like the Shepherd to get in one of these. Otherwise, you'd fry every cell in your body from the excess energy. Isn't that right?"

Ianna nodded. "Yes. The Tanks shoot concentrated Solfire throughout the entire pod. The energy bounces off the edges and ricochets back through the center. Whatever is inside is hit not only on the outside, but on the *inside* as well. Only a Shepherd's suit can filter out the intense rays of Solfire and keep the body from overreacting when inside one of these Tanks."

"What happens when there's an overreaction?" asked Jack.

"The body is ripped apart."

"Sounds delightful," said Felix, but no one else seemed to share in his candor.

Ianna took a breath and continued. "And what's more, if the body is unwilling to receive treatment, then it makes the process all the more difficult."

"If the body is 'unwilling'?" asked Darion.

"Yes. If the will of the person is resistant, unwilling to surrender itself, then the Solfire can be rejected. Those who enter must be willing to submit."

"That sounds insane," said Felix. "How could you ever know you were ready to submit to something?"

"I hear that," said Robert, echoing the sentiment.

"No one can answer that question for you," said Darion, again acting like he knew. "You'd only know once you were in there. That's how Solfire operates. Everything it does is based on the one it's interacting with. That's how personal its relationship is to the user. That's how it works."

Ianna seemed to be pleased with the answer. She hit a few more keys and a hologram of the Shepherd's body appeared next to the pod; a complete blueprint of the Shepherd's internal structure. Ianna left the station and used a finger to flip through various outlines. She appeared to be looking for the proper picture; one that might display the Shepherd's injury. First there was a blank picture, then one with only veins, then one with only bones. It was like having an x-ray in real time, though none of them had ever known one. Darion watched Jack. He wasn't even looking at the holograms; instead, Jack was noting the delicate yet firm manner with which Ianna carried herself. *Like her, do you?* Darion thought. *Careful, boy. Not everything is what it seems in this place.*

But, then he caught himself in the thought, wondering why he cared at all what Jack was doing.

At last, Ianna arrived at the picture she was looking for and stretched the image to make it larger.

"His injuries are worse than I think he even originally thought," said Ianna. "His shoulder separated and the muscles are having a hard time repairing themselves. This could have been permanent damage if he hadn't have come here. It looks like his encounters with the Adversary have also caused him a severe amount of strain."

"You know about that thing too, eh?" said Jack.

"Anyone who is in the Red Fellows knows of the Adversary. It's the enemy of Earth *and* Mars, despite how much people on Earth think it was an agent sent from our brothers on Mars."

"People would probably stop thinking that," said Darion. "If Mars would kill it already and show some allegiance. And quit calling them our 'brothers.' It doesn't change what's happened."

Ianna didn't answer.

"Then you *do* agree with what I said."

"What I *do* agree upon," said Ianna. "Is that the Adversary is currently unexplainable. Not even the Shepherds have a complete knowledge of what they are fighting. They only know it stands in opposition to the rest of us. To mankind. The Adversary aligns itself with death, fear, despair, and hate. Shouldn't that be enough to say we're all on the same side?"

"It'll be enough when that thing is dead," said Darion and he looked at the Huntsmen. "What do you three say about all this? Anything?"

The reformed Huntsmen were exchanging glances like scared children. Everything looked and felt alien to them. It was clear by the expressions on their faces. The walls, the ceilings, the sphere full of Solfire - *everything* had a foreign nature that shook the three of them like they were babies learning to crawl. Olivia eyed Tom especially. She was huddled close to Felix with arms crossed like she was cold, but the room was more than a comfortable temperature.

"No comments then?" said Darion. "Nothing to add to that?"

"This Adversary…." said Robert. "Was that the same monster we saw in the woods? The one that took over Argus?"

Silence filled the room. Nobody seemed ready to relive the memory of Argus' demonic transformation. Or offer up any explanation as to what came of the man whose body had become a living death.

"Maybe?" said Darion. "Or maybe he was on his way to becoming like it?"

Darion walked to the Shepherd's tank and flicked it lightly with his finger. It looked like glass but he was surprised to find it was hard as stone. He pulled away, rubbing his finger softly.

"What are these made out of anyway?" asked Darion. "Or is that unexplainable too?"

Ianna smirked. "Mars diamond," she answered. "Synthetically altered from the inside of the red planet. Diamonds don't grow on Mars like they do on Earth. The pressure just doesn't allow for that to happen. But, on Mars they can be manipulated under controlled pressures to achieve the desired result. Hence what you've just experienced. And under that, is iron."

"Because iron is what holds the Solfire inside, right?"

Ianna nodded. Darion turned around, looked at his compatriots. This conversation is beyond any of them, isn't it? None of them knows what is being said, what is being talked about. How do any of them hope to get to Mars with their limited knowledge? Darion peered back at Ianna.

"Is he going to be all right?" he asked.

"Yes, but it will take some time."

"How long?"

"I'm not certain."

"You have all this technology and you don't know?"

The ball of Solfire flickered and a ripple, like a small wave, rolled across its surface.

"No, I don't," answered Ianna, firmly. "It's like I told you. There must be a willingness to be healed. Even the Shepherd must make that decision. It's not always so simple."

Darion then realized that this wasn't his final stop. The Shepherd only needed to come here so he could rest. He should have known this. Should have realized the he was still playing by the Shepherd's rules. How much longer must I wait? How much longer will this go on? Darion wanted to scream, but thought better of it and held his tongue. I can wait longer, can't I?

"Well, what are we supposed to do in the meantime then?" asked Darion.

"I'm glad you asked," said Ianna. "There is someone here who wants to see you. He's likely upstairs somewhere, up in the Cathedral."

"Then why did you bring us down here?"

Again, the ball of Solfire pulsed like it was being affected by Darion's words. This time, Jack and the others noticed it.

"I brought you down here," explained Ianna. "so you could see the Shepherd. So you might see the one who brought you here was healing. He's been through a lot, you know. And he's risked much to keep you safe."

"We've risked a lot too, Ianna."

"We've all lost something, Darion Wallace. Don't presume to act like nobody else here has. Or has nothing to gain by being with the Shepherd."

"What did you say? How do you – "

"I've lived and lost too. Just like you."

"I didn't mean *that*. How did you know my name?"

Ianna smirked again. But this time, like she knew something no one else did.

"I'm a Namer," she said, matter-of-factly. "I can read and reveal the names of people when I meet them. It's one of my Gifts as a Red Fellow. Or rather, as a Red *Lady*. Those exist here too, you know. We're not just some exclusive fraternity. Regardless of what our name implies."

"How do you do it?" asked Jack.

"I can't say for certain," said Ianna. "It's just something I've always done. Something I've always felt. So I do it. And as you can see, I do it well."

A *Namer?* Darion thought. It sounded like a fancy title for a witch or a sorcerer. Not something real. Yet, Darion had met another like this. One who claimed to be a 'Seer.' Was this another of the titles used to describe those 'gifted' among the Fellows?

"Now," she said. "As I was saying, there is someone here who would like to speak with you. You may take your daughter with you to the chambers upstairs, back in the main sanctuary. Felix, Robert, *Sophia* – " And there it was, thought Olivia. The reveal that Tom was not who she had claimed to be. The group looked upon Sophia, her face a crimson red. "The three of you will need a change of clothes too. You can't be walking around here as Huntsmen. One of our people will take you to the barracks so you may dress there. We'll catch up with you later."

"A *girl's* name?" said Jack. "You have a girl's name? What happened to 'Tom'?"

'Tom' was quiet, at first. Then, "No. I *am* a girl, Jack."

"What? You're a girl? How in the...."

Olivia tugged at her father. See? I told you, she said with her eyes and Darion shook his head with disbelief.

"I'm sorry," said Sophia and she removed her cap. In the light of the Solfire, Sophia's feminine features were accentuated. The group looked to one another as though they should have known this all along. How could anyone *not* have seen this?

"I pretended so I could join the Hunt," said Sophia. "I'm sorry that I didn't tell any of you. I really am."

"Is there anything else the three of you are hiding?" asked Darion.

"No," said Felix and he held Sophia closer to him. "Nothing we need to mention to you. Or anyone else."

The ball of Solfire flickered and everyone turned to see it. "I swear," said Jack. "I swear that thing is watching us."

"That's not possible, Jack," said Darion.

"I feel it too!" said Robert.

"Me also," said Sophia. "Do you think it is?"

"It's possible," said Ianna. "Solfire is unlike anything in the universe."

"One could say the same for Darklight," said Darion.

"Yes, but at least Solfire is actually useful," argued Ianna. "It can power ships; it can give light, and it can grant the ones who touch it with Gifts. It's no wonder its applications were able to accelerate Mars beyond Earth in such a short span of time. And we're still only scratching the surface of its potential."

"If it's so useful," said Darion. "Why haven't any of you gone off world? Why isn't anyone taking this ship to Mars so you might rescue the people you have here?"

"I thought no one could leave?" said Robert, innocently. "Nothing can leave Earth thanks to the Pulse, right?"

Darion laughed. "Not Martian ships, apparently."

Ianna was quiet for a moment. Then, with eyes directed at Darion, she said, "Not everyone is interested in running away from things. There's still some good to be done here. And this is our home. I'd rather protect my home than sleep in a stranger's bed."

"Well," said Jack. "Sleep there long enough and it's no longer a stranger you're lying next to. Right?"

"With enough time, sure," said Ianna and Jack looked away, embarrassed. He'd unintentionally helped Darion's argument – all for the sake of flirting with Ianna. And she knew it too. Stupid.

"Amazing," said Felix, creeping closer to the center of the room. Robert and Sophia followed him.

This is not good, thought Darion. This place will make them all loony; make them believe that whatever they see is truth. All these new things and alien technologies - this is the essence of the Red Fellows. So what if they have a Martian ship buried underground? Or a chamber for restoring Shepherds; or the ability to learn a person's name without first hearing it? None of these things make this place any more special than anywhere else. There's still only *people* here. People who so happen to possess a ball of limitless power for manipulating light in their basement. But, that was only part of the problem. People, organized people with power, meant agendas. And when power meets human agendas, false leaders and cults always seem to spring up. Looking at the expressions on Felix, Robert, and Sophia's faces, it only reaffirmed Darion's belief and he looked to his daughter to make certain she was not gawking with the rest of them. But, she was.

No, he thought. *No more of this.*

"That's enough talk about those kinds of things," said Darion. "You all want to scare my daughter? It's bad enough we go to sleep with dreams of the Adversary at our heels. Do you want to add an inanimate ball of light to that list of nightmares?"

No one challenged Darion.

Yet the ball blipped and no one did a thing. Darion saw it though. Was he the only one who did? There's no possible way this thing was *thinking*. Perhaps it was behaving this way due to the connection with the Shepherd? But then again, Darion knew the discs held strange powers. He could speak to them. He could commune with the discs when he possessed them. But, it was only the machine he was speaking to, wasn't it? Not the pure energy beneath its metal casing, right?

A few of the Fellows entered the room, the boy, Turk, with them. Olivia hid herself again. Don't see me. I only want to see *you* if I can. Behind her, the ball of Solfire pulsed and expanded for a moment and then retracted. Darion and Jack both noticed it this time, but did not exchange the glance of 'did you see that too?'

"Didn't you find him, Turk?" asked Ianna.

"I did," said Turk, out of breath. "But he wanted to come see them instead."

Then a man came down the corridor and into the circular room. He looked refreshed with a collared shirt and long pants. Darion knew him when he saw him, as did Olivia, who nudged her father as if to remind him. It's that nice man. It's him, Dad. The one with the nice laugh and who shared a drink with you. Jack recognized him too and hid his face immediately. Impossible. How on Earth did *he* get here?

It was Abraham.

"Hello, Darion," said Abe. "I see you've accumulated quite the group since you found the Shepherd. Ha, good for you. It's never good to travel alone, I say. Even if that's something I've been forced to do lately."

"How did you - " started Darion.

"Ha, nice to see you too!" said Abe. "Why don't we all go for a walk? Have a drink maybe? There's much you need to know and even more I need to find out from you."

They then followed Abe out of the chamber, Jack farthest behind. Darion didn't know whether to be excited, surprised or upset. Either way, he felt an overwhelming sense of unfinished business in this place. The Shepherd couldn't heal fast enough.

Chapter 18
Revelations

* * * *

Abe led Darion, Olivia, and Jack back through the main hall of the Martian ship. All the while, he pointed out the highlights of the Fellows' underground base. He didn't bother to reintroduce himself or even call out Jack on their last encounter, an act that made Jack all the more nervous and skeptical if he should be able to trust this man entirely. But, it also made Jack wonder if Abe really *did* remember him. The way Abe spoke, it was like he'd failed to recognize Jack. And in some other, more concealed way, it hurt Jack's pride to know their altercation at the plaza held little importance to Abe.

He knows, Jack thought. He just has to. But, then there was the surprising fact that this man *knew* Darion too. Had he been protecting Darion back then? What was their connection? In one regard, Abe gave no indication there were any prior allegiances. Abe treated them like distant acquaintances, soldiers in need of being briefed on the latest happenings rather than engaging with idle talk. Yet, Abraham would tend to look upon Darion like he'd been reunited with an old friend, smiling wide and inviting Darion close to him as they walked. Jack maintained his distance as much as he could without losing earshot.

"This ship was brought down here about 10 years ago," said Abe. "It was given as a gift to the Red Fellows out of several years of faithful service. Though I wouldn't even call it 'service.' You see, it was about 20 years ago that Shepherds first started showing up on Earth, but by all accounts; it was actually earlier than that. Right after the Pulse hit and Mars stopped the spread of Darklight with their satellites, Mars pulled away, and devised a plan to come back for the people that were trapped here. It was a real mess. Seems Darklight is a tricky bugger. There was worry it might have the power to 'infect' anyone in contact with it and thus, bring it back to Mars. Mars wouldn't have that, of course. Hence, this ship was brought down as a safe haven for anyone who came from Mars to Earth."

Darion tried to interject with a question, but Abe went right on without taking a breath.

"Only problem with sending out your emissaries is that reconnaissance teams don't always know how powerful the enemy is. Turns out the Darklight was stronger than anyone could have imagined and Mars lost several of its own before realizing they needed to do something better than just send soldiers. Again, it was another mess in need of cleaning. Mars' people, unfortunately, were too immersed in their own matters and didn't realize the severity of what they'd unleashed here. The monsters that came, of course, like the *Adversary*, were part of that unexpected flurry of side effects that swept over the planet. But, none were worse than those that came out of Mars' first rescuers. The Adversary fed well on the first of Mars' fallen rescuers, grew in strength exponentially. So Mars needed even better soldiers than the ones they had. That's where the Shepherds come in. Tell me if you don't think *that* is messed up."

Darion and Jack agreed, silently, but were still processing Abe's information dump. Each man took the admission from Abe with thoughts of disgust, but also with confusion. The people of Mars had been coming the whole time? For 40 years they had been sending their people to help us? Neither man understood the story this way. For Darion, Mars was an escape – a way out of the hell they were in. He blamed Mars for the Darklight and the ramifications that came with it, but he always knew of the Shepherds and their promise for salvation. In that way, he had something to hope for. Something to chase after until judgment day or the day he could be free – Mars *owed* that to him. He believed it did. But, for Jack, any knowledge of the bigger war was hidden; up until only a couple weeks ago. Survival was his only truth; not the war between Solfire, Darklight, and Mars. But when Mars became real – an Eden in the stars – something took hold of him. Jack saw Mars as the escape. He didn't care whose fault it was. He didn't even care who started it. He just wanted *out*. But, this new information about Mars, the Adversary, and their relationship to the Shepherds, made Jack feel like he was collateral damage. Like, there was always a war going on, one he'd never known about, and wouldn't have unless he'd encountered Darion at the old city and later still, the Shepherd. That felt incredibly unfair and he clenched his fists as they walked through the lower level, up the stairwell and into the old sanctuary.

"As you might have guessed," continued Abe. "The Red Fellows were established to work with the Shepherds, keep the communication pathways open so we might find a way to end this thing. End this time of darkness for everybody. The Shepherds are powered with the ability to take monsters like the Adversary head on. That's what they're made for. They're human, but they're not entirely human either. I'm sure you've discovered that much for yourselves."

"That's the understatement of the year," said Darion. "I never knew their sole purpose was for fighting the Adversary."

"And for researching the Darklight," said Abe. "Since there's no Darklight on Mars, it's impossible for Mars to study it. That's why the Shepherds take in everything they can while they're here. So when they get back, they can give their findings over. All the light they absorb is calculable upon reentry, so to speak."

"And no one has any answers yet?" asked Felix. The question felt long overdue for everyone. Yet, Abe only shook his head.

There were none, apparently.

Abe then looked over the group, stopping his gaze on Jack, whose eyes were facing downward.

"This is a lot to take in, Abe," said Darion. "You must understand that what you're saying is no easy pill to swallow."

"I do." he said. "And I'm sure it is." Then very seriously, "But, did you want the truth or did you want fluff? I prefer the hard truth myself. It has a way of setting people free."

Oh, he knows, Jack thought. He knows who I am. He's trying to bait me, trying to out me in front of Darion. I won't say a thing though. It's bad enough Darion wanted to leave me behind, practically tried to murder me to do so. No! I just won't look. That's what I'll do and nothing will happen. I just won't look.

"Everyone appreciates the truth, Abe," said Darion. "And I'm in need of a truth from you right now: how did you get here? And how did you know we were coming?"

Abe chuckled. "Sorry, I suppose I need to explain myself more thoroughly too. I told you I was a Red Fellow once, didn't I? When I met you in the plaza, I knew you were special but I didn't know *how* special at that time. I guess my Gifts aren't what they used to be. But, having come back here for a day or so, I'm starting to feel more like my old self."

Jack waited for Abe to transition to their encounter and turned away from the conversation. But, Abe kept his eyes on Darion.

"However," said Abe. "That's not nearly as important as this: after meeting you, I realized was how much I'd been running from things. I couldn't do that anymore. The whole world's gone to hell and here, I was just helping it get there faster. What a terrible existence. I had to leave where I was; get back to what was good again. I hope you've discovered something similar during your travels, my friend."

"If I say I have," said Darion. "Will you tell me how you knew we were coming? Or are you just going to keep dancing around the question?"

Abe laughed, but Darion's expression was deathly serious. Not old friends then? Jack was confused. Darion didn't appear to be the least bit interested with embracing Abe or even shaking his hand. But they clearly knew each other. That was true, but who's friend was who's? Then again, Jack had never seen Darion treat *anyone* with gladness since he'd met the man. Maybe this was normal?

"I'll answer in due time," said Abe. "But let's discuss that later, okay?"

Darion nodded. *They must be friends*, Jack thought. Otherwise they wouldn't agree to 'secret meetings.'

"We're glad you are," said Ianna. "We missed you."
"I wasn't planning on being here," said Abe. "But, things happen, plans change, and now I'm here. There's nothing wrong with that."

Ianna grinned and Abe gazed at Jack again. "And *you*," said Abe.

Jack jumped and was immediately embarrassed for doing so. This was it, was it? Abe took a few steps towards Jack and Jack looked up slowly. Abe looked different to him, dressed in a white shirt and pants; much the opposite of the hardened old man from the plaza café. He looked healthy and not hunched over and lonely. But, it was most definitely *him* – the man he'd beaten with his hands and 'taught' to respect him. Here he was: of all the people in the world Jack expected to see again, this man was not among those he would have counted.

"So, did you find what you were looking for, son?" said Abe. "Or are you still running around, giving away grief like it's your responsibility to do so?"

Jack fell silent. He felt like a different man since he'd last seen Abe. Things *had* changed. *He* had changed, but there was still an anger inside which he hadn't known was there and it came to the surface, revealing itself as he stared back at Abe. The rage was still his master and Jack silently cursed himself as Abe looked into Jack's eyes like he was looking into a child's.

Finally, Jack licked his lips and answered, "More or less, I suppose."

"You know this man?" said Darion, surprised.

"Oh, I *know* him," said Abe. "We met once before. Just as you and I did, Darion. Only my encounter was not nearly as pleasant as yours and mine was. Wouldn't you agree, son?"

Jack didn't like being called that, especially in front of Darion. And though he felt an inclination to apologize for earlier - for being a monster - Jack couldn't bring himself to go through with it. Not for everyone else to see. Yet Abe waited like Jack might. He wouldn't.

"Sure," said Jack. "I'd agree with you."

Abe grinned. Of course you'd agree, Abe seemed to say. You're in *my* home. These are my people. You'll have to do what *I* do. Jack looked to Ianna, who had a confused look on her face. Sorry. You don't want to know what I did. Not now and not ever.

"You know," said Abe. "I'm just glad you fell in with a good group, son. The way you acted before, I didn't know where you'd end up. But, this is better than any other, I'd say. You can figure out how to have a conversation with me later. Sound good?"

Jack nodded. "I need some air."

Jack walked up the aisle, through the sanctuary and out the front door. Olivia trailed him as far as her eyes could, sad to see him leave so abruptly. He couldn't stay in there any longer. He felt ashamed to even stand in that place. He didn't deserve this. He didn't deserve any of it. The war. Mars. Earth. An apology for Abe and another from Darion. He didn't deserve it but maybe what he *did* deserve was his own beating. The one he'd gotten from Darion in the plains.

He reached into his pocket and took out a cigarette. A good smoke might help clear some things. He knew it wouldn't though.

It would only delay what was going on inside of him. Distract him a while so he might calm down. That's how it always worked, but he was willing to go through the motions for the sake of letting himself know he'd tried.

Jack took a seat on the porch and stewed. Now what?

Meanwhile, back inside, Darion immediately set to inquiring Abe about Jack. How Abe knew Jack. Where they'd met. What they thought of each other. Everything.

"He beat me up," said Abe. "Wanted to know where you were and I wouldn't tell him. So he beat me up. Fool kid thought he'd intimidate me, and at the time, he did, but I needed it. A good wake up call, you know? Ha! Don't matter how old we get, we always need a good kick in the ass once in a blue moon, don't we?"

"Abraham…" said Ianna, as though scolding him.

"I'm sorry. *Butt.*"

Olivia smiled and Abe winked.

"You have no idea what that man has done," said Darion.

"I believe you," said Abe. "and I know he's probably done things to you that are similar. But, what good will any criticism or recounting of wrongs do us now? If you have a story that will give life to this conversation, I'm all ears. Otherwise, I need to show you something else."

Darion wanted to talk about Jack further, but when Olivia took him by the arm, he stopped. No reason to go down that road, I guess. Darion had already aligned himself with the fact that Jack and he were two different people. Feeding a fire wouldn't do anything. Not anymore.

"What do you want me to see?" asked Darion.

"Let me take you this way, but first, let your daughter go and play awhile."

Olivia's heart jumped. Play? With Turk? She looked at Turk, who was grinning wide.

"My daughter hasn't spoken for – "

"Well maybe today's the day, my friend! Go on, little one. A moment for joy is not one to be taken for granted."

Olivia let go of her father and ran off with Turk. At last, some fun to be had. Darion yelled for her to return shortly and then looked at Abe like he'd done something terrible.

"I trust they're going somewhere safe?" said Darion.

Abe didn't answer. He led Darion out of the sanctuary and into a new room down the hall. The Huntsmen left them, walking about the sanctuary with Ianna and some other Fellows.

This new room looked to be an offshoot of the ship underground. It had several white beds on either side, looking like an old hospital. And in the corner, hid partially behind a curtain, was a single person resting. Abe took Darion to the bedside and pulled the curtain slowly back. Darion recognized her, but he wasn't sure how or where from. Then it occurred to him.

"This woman," whispered Darion. "She's – "

"One of the Hunt's most fearsome lieutenants," said Abe. "I know. A demon with a rifle and a scorned huntress by any who fall within the Hunt's jurisdiction." Abe brushed her sandy blond hair with his outstretched hand and sighed. She had been beaten by someone and her leg had been pierced by a bullet.

"Yes," said Abe. "I understand that she's known by all these things. But, as fate would have it, she's also my daughter. I'm guessing you might have known her, maybe seen her at one time or another, haven't you? I hope not as she was before all this."

Darion tried not to gasp. "She was with the group that was tracking us," said Darion. "The Shepherd headed them off though. Took them all out as they were chasing us. I guess I just didn't know that he'd done this to - "

"No," said Abe. "This was not the Shepherd's doing, but another's. And I wish I knew. I'd...."

Abe trailed off a moment. He looked to be holding back tears. So Darion decided to speak instead.

"Those other three with me," said Darion. "That's how they came to be with us. The Shepherd beat them and then three of their own joined us. She wasn't one of them though. She went back in one of their Rovers. I figured she went back to the Hunt's base. She's one of them still, isn't she?"

"She *was*," said Abe. "But, I doubt that she is anymore."

An understatement. Or perhaps, someone had betrayed her. Or she'd been exiled. Who knew. Darion felt like leaving. He'd seen what dark secrets Abe had kept for him and wanted out. But, Abraham was saddened beyond measure and Darion found it within himself to ask Abraham about her.

"What's her name?" asked Darion.

"Greta. After her grandmother."

Darion could see Abe was beginning to become more and more emotional. It pained Abe, looking at Greta like this and Darion felt an eerie similarity taking hold. Darion saw his own future, one where he'd neglected or perhaps ignored Olivia, leaving her to her own devices. Then, only years later, discovering how the life she'd chosen was one filled with oppression, the dealing of death, and pure survival. And the weight of this possible future struck Darion with a mighty force. He took a deep breath, feeling faint as he internalized every bit of Abe's current situation. There was a short pause between them as Greta breathed in and out peacefully. Still alive, yet hanging somewhere between life and a slow death.

"I'd set out from the old city," said Abe. "Only a day or so after I met you. I'd seen her in the old city, but she was leaving to go find someone else. I could lie and say I knew it was you she was after, but I didn't. I had no clue what I was doing at the time. I just knew I had to leave and I did. After that, the Shepherd found me one night and told me to come here. Later, he brought her to me and I'm sure you can figure out the rest."

Abe paused a moment, letting everything sink in as it did before.

"The Shepherd *found* you?" said Darion, stunned.

"Yes," said Abe. "In the nighttime. He would visit me while I was traveling. It was only sporadic though, not every night. But, I came to expect his arrival when things were going bad. Strange, how that pushes a man onward. Having something to look forward to is one thing, but to receive reassurance along the way? Well, I think that's what keeps the will moving forward. Without it, we'd all be sunk, I figure. Dead where we stand with nothing to do. I'm so glad he came that night. I'd probably be dead if he hadn't come."

Incredible. Not only had the Shepherd been watching over *his* group, the Shepherd had somehow been running errands in the dead of night. Like some vigilante, he'd been aiding the desperate, like Abe. Darion had been impressed by the Shepherd's ungodly powers before, but this - *this* was uncanny. What else had the silver giant been up to while Darion slept?

"I'm sorry," said Abe.

"For what?"

"That you have to hear all of my burdens," said Abe. "I know it isn't fair to you, but I appreciate you listening. I thought I'd never see my daughter again. I thought it was better to have left her to her own fate years ago. I *truly* believed that. What kind of father am I? What kind of father says that about his own child? Maybe I'm not worthy to be a father. To be a man, even. But, now that I see her again, I know that I have a second chance to make things right."

Abe paused. Then he looked at Darion.

"Do you think she'll accept me again?" asked Abe and Darion looked away.

Truthfully, Darion didn't want to comfort Abe at all. He owed Abe nothing, other than a verbal blasting for the way Abe had abandoned Greta; left his daughter to the shredder of life without a father; a task Darion had taken without question when the call arose. How could he possibly console this man? But, when Darion saw the shame in Abe's eyes - no, the *relief* - of having Greta home again, Darion drew back. Are these the things you're still trying to teach me, Shepherd? Am I to show this man compassion even if I don't believe he deserves it?

Darion looked back at Abe. His eyes were watering up, begging for sympathy.

"Darion?" asked Abe.

"It's a good feeling, isn't it?" said Darion. "When a child comes home to the arms of his parent. It's a miracle, wouldn't you say?"

Abe grinned. "Yes. Yes it is."

* * * *

Ianna found Jack walking outside the Cathedral. She watched him from the corner of the porch, making note of every mannerism he openly displayed as he paced on the green grass. Something would give her some insight as to who he was and why the Shepherd had chosen him. There was obviously something different about him. What was it though?

He smoked his cigarette with a cool nonchalance so he'd clearly done it before, but when he hesitated to bring the tip back to his lips, Ianna surmised Jack was a thinker, not a feeler. That was her first clue as to how to approach him. Make contact and break down the walls. She knew she was good at those things. As a Namer, she was already talented in one aspect of the Red Fellow disciplines, but she was also adept at searching the hearts and intentions of the people she encountered. Jack, though he didn't know it, was another on Ianna's list of 'people to break through' with.

She waited for a long while, looking for an opening and when she didn't find one, she disengaged. Tomorrow then. And she left the newcomers to their own business throughout the evening and into the night.

The Shepherd's party slept in the barracks, but in separate bunks and apart from each other. Jack, Darion, and Olivia slept the longest. A real bed with pillows was like resting in the czar's palace. For the other three, the reformed Huntsman, it was more like training camp. Confined quarters. Less personal space, but at least it was warm.

The next morning, Ianna found each of them dressed in new clothes provided by the Red Fellows. And judging from their behavior, the group seemed pleased; all except Jack, who wore a face that seemed as confused as it was bitter. He appeared to hate the handouts, or rather, the conformity associated with wearing clothing that resembled everyone else.

Was he an orphan once? We are all of us, orphans, at one junction or another. Ianna believed Jack to be one. Those who lived on their own hated having to look like everyone else, even if deep down, they craved the acceptance. At lunch, the newcomers did not converse with one another either, instead preferring to stay invisible and talk only when spoken to.

This is what amazed Ianna the most. Having been through several battles and having experienced an ongoing relationship with the Mars Shepherd, Ianna expected more of this group. She expected them to be as tight as a carefully woven basket; a steel chain without a frayed or broken link. But, it wasn't that way at all. The three Huntsmen were an entity, the father and his daughter were another pair and then there was Jack – the one who preferred to be alone – the anomaly among them. Perhaps he was choosing to be a loner on purpose? Or maybe he was simply acting out the pattern he was most accustomed to? Ianna couldn't discern which. Even when a Fellow approached Jack and asked him to join for a fire gathering that night, Ianna was still uncertain.

"Would you like to come to the fire tonight?" asked one of the Fellows.

"What are you burning?" asked Jack.

The young Fellow nearly laughed. "The fire isn't really the important part. We mostly talk about life. How people are coping without the light, without the things we had. Things we can do to improve our lives even without the light. Normal things like that."

"That doesn't sound normal to me, chief."

This was intentional disassociation. Was Jack a victim of circumstance then? Did he really trust no one? Ianna approached Darion on the second day to see what might be the source of Jack's demons.

"You should ask him yourself," said Darion. "I don't know how much you'll get out of him but you can try. Just be careful."

Ianna turned to leave, but Darion stopped her.

"Thank you," he said. "For everything, by the way. We really appreciate you letting us stay here. Sorry if I can't be more help than that."

Not without manners, that one. Darion knew how to make nice with people, even if he didn't necessarily want to. Was Jack like Darion in this way? She decided it was time to find out. The Shepherd was still slumbering beneath the hillside. Tomorrow, she'd talk with Jack.

She found Jack outside the Cathedral early the next morning. He was smoking a cigarette and puffing mightily. It looked and felt good. A simple pleasure to ease his mind. Ianna leaned against a porch pole, folded her arms and breathed loud enough that it might alert Jack to her presence. Jack sputtered out a final smoke and then snuffed out the cigarette.

"You didn't need to do that," she said. "People smoke cigarettes. I get it."

"It's a disgusting habit," said Jack. "I never used to smoke, I swear."

"Ha, is this place bringing out the worst in you?" said Ianna. "If so, I'm sorry to hear that."

Jack grinned. "No. I mean, I don't know."

"I used to smoke too," said Ianna. "Does that surprise you?"

Jack turned towards her. It was only the second time she'd tried to talk to him and about the fifteenth he'd entertained how he might talk to *her*. Only now he didn't need to imagine. She really *was* beautiful, he thought, looking her over, but with obvious permission this time.

"Tell me you didn't smoke," he said.

"Yes, I *did*," she answered. "Why is that so hard to believe?"

Because you look clean, Jack thought. Because you don't look like someone who is dirty. Because you live in a place that's meant for clean people. Jack looked up at the bell and then at Ianna. Everything about the Cathedral felt and *seemed* like a place where he didn't belong. And yet, he *wanted* to belong too. She was here. Wasn't that enough to want to belong?

"Don't let this place fool you," she said. "There are plenty of people with disgusting habits inside these walls. And below it, too. I learned that really fast when I got here. Nobody in the world is perfect."

"Except the Shepherd, right?"

Ianna hesitated. She seemed to be evaluating how to best answer Jack.

"He's not really human, is he?" said Jack.

"No, he *is*," said Ianna. "Just like you and me. The Shepherd deals with fatigue. Deals with sadness. Deals with disappointment. Deals with joy. They deal with stress too and they get hungry just like you and me."

"I find that hard to believe, missy," said Jack. "You haven't been on the road with him so you haven't seen the things he can do. It's...."

"It's what?"

"God-like."

"Well, he's not a god," said Ianna.

"Says who?" said Jack.

"What do *you* say about the Shepherd?"

Jack kicked the dirt. He had a million and one questions about the Shepherd that were in need of answering. And yet, the only thing on his mind was how attractive Ianna was and how that attraction was increasing by the second. Where to start? Jack raised his eyes to the sky, looking to the sun as it began its slow ascent over the horizon.

"Honestly," he started. "All this Darklight and Solfire stuff. I don't have a clue how any of it works. But *he* does. He knows a lot more about it than I do. Or probably ever will. That's the difference: what he knows and what *I* know. Do you see what I mean?"

Ianna smirked. "You surprise me."

"Why's that?"

"I just thought I'd be wrong about you," she said. "But, turns out, people aren't always as good at hiding themselves as they think they are. It's rare to find someone who is good at it, but why on Earth would that ever considered to be something of worth, I have no idea."

Jack shrugged. He guessed it was a compliment.

"Well, thanks," he said. "But, as I was saying, I've seen what he does. And I've seen what you can do, too. Where does that leave me?"

Ianna stepped off of the porch and joined Jack in the grass. She looked towards the horizon and then at Jack.

"You know," she said. "They say the sun was brighter before the Pulse. Have you ever heard that?"

Jack searched his memory. He hadn't, but he didn't want to appear stupid in front of Ianna. He didn't answer but he didn't shake his head either. That felt safest.

"It's true," she continued. "The sun *was* brighter before the Pulse. After it happened and all the lights started going out, there were monsters that showed up. Monsters like the Adversary, right?" Jack nodded this time. "In the beginning, everyone thought they were demons or creatures from another planet, brought down by Mars to kill us. But, when that turned out not to be true, people came up with other conclusions. Maybe they were beings born out of the Darklight and when Darklight was around, they'd spring up and kill people. Well, we now know that's only *partially* true too. What started out as myth had some truth in it and what was true had some myth too. See how people can be? Adding little things like it'll make the truth more interesting but the truth is already interesting as it is. Not that the truth needs to be interesting at all."

Jack squinted. Ianna's words, the way she spoke – it was intimidating. "So what are you trying to say exactly?" he asked.

"The sun illuminates *everything*," she answered. "It exposes darkness for what it is: a hiding place. And that's where fear hides. People have *fear*. Even the Shepherd. The differences lie in how we learn to *conquer* those fears. And that has very little to do with knowledge of strange gifts."

Jack contemplated Ianna's explanation. She spoke eloquently now, softening her tone so as to make Jack feel more comfortable. It wasn't because she pitied him or his intelligence; her tone was deliberate – like a lover making her bed ready for her beloved.

"You make it sound easy," he said and Ianna smiled.

"It's not though," she said. "I just wanted you to know the truth."

"Heh," said Jack. "Thanks again. What else do you plan on telling me the truth about?"

"Darklight," said Ianna. "I'll tell you everything I know about it. Then you can decide if we can be friends or not. Deal?"

Jack nearly laughed. Then Ianna explained everything. She explained how Darklight feeds on light particles and energy, but since the sun produces more light than anything else on Earth – and with greater intensity - the sun remains unaffected. At least to some smaller degree, it did. This revelation of how Darklight operated was a major breakthrough when the Pulse occurred and Ianna asked Jack if he knew what it all meant.

Jack shook his head. He followed everything she had said, but still wasn't drawing any conclusions. Ianna walked closer to him. At this range, Jack could smell Ianna when the wind blew. And it was a heavenly smell, if heaven itself had one. Her dark hair moved when the wind did and her eyes reflected the sun in the corners of each of her irises. What she said next could have been the most ridiculous thing he'd ever heard, but it wouldn't have mattered. Jack would still think her the smartest human on the planet and applaud her. Beauty, he knew, was an easy trap for him. But, Ianna was different still. She wouldn't lead him off course, he felt. She'd tell him exactly what he needed to hear.

"What does it mean?" he asked.

"It means that all the light in the world – the light we *used* to see – it's only *dormant*. It's still there. It always has been. We just can't see it anymore. The haze that was left after the Pulse still covers our eyes, keeping us from seeing what we're meant to be seeing. Do you understand what I'm saying? Darklight has killed much of our power to generate energy, but it hasn't blinded us completely. When you find yourself aware that something is wrong, yet you are unable to see it, then you know you're doing the right thing. You know you're on the right path to solving the mystery. Do you see?"

Jack blinked, assessing Ianna's explanation of Darklight and what it meant to him. Stolen light? So it was like a giant blindfold? That was much different than the Shepherd's lengthy explanation in the woods.

"And the Adversary?" said Jack. "Is that thing even real?"

"Yes," said Ianna, as though reluctantly. "It's as real as Darklight and it's as real as Solfire. But, beyond that, we don't know much else other than the Shepherd fights them. They're able to interact with the Adversary because the two are similar. They both manipulate light through Darklight or Solfire. That's all I know on that one."

Jack stepped away from Ianna a moment. He needed space, as much as he didn't want to be a part from her, he needed space to think. Guess I am a thinker. I don't know what to think - or feel - about this. I just hate it. It's not fair. How is it that all these things must be stacked against him? Against anyone living after the Pulse - none of it seemed right. And Jack cursed himself for cycling back to his argument over things being 'unfair' or 'unjust' in his life. Then a hand touched his shoulder and he turned to find Ianna standing behind him. He turned round all the way to face her, his heart rising up inside his throat. It was nearing sunrise and Jack swore he could see the grass becoming livelier, getting greener; the old white paint of the Cathedral was shining with a pristine finish like it'd just been painted yesterday. The tight reflections of light focused themselves upon Ianna — her cool hair, her smooth features; the picturesque image of beauty in a small frame that seemed to brighten all things within Jack's vantage point. If it were real beauty he'd been searching for, then this was it. Ianna removed her hand and grinned.

"Sometimes finding out what's real can be scary," she said. "But truth doesn't have to be frightening. It's only frightening when you don't have the courage to share it. That's what I've come to understand."

Jack smirked. She was being sincere far as he could tell. Now, he was happy he'd come here. Jack may have felt overwhelmed by the experience, everything he'd come through with the Shepherd, with Darion, with Olivia, but all those trials had been worth this singular moment. He felt a strange peace, looking back at Ianna. And he wanted it to last until sunset and into the next and the one after that, if he could.

"I know you haven't said anything about my name," said Jack. "Can you tell me what mine is? Or are you not playing that game with me?"

Ianna grinned. "Your friends call you 'Jack,'" she said. "'Jack' is fine with me if it's fine with you. Does that make us friends then, Jack?"

Selfishly, he knew he wanted 'friend' to mean more, but he also knew she was being easy on him. Jack knew she could see his true name with her Gift. She practically mouthed it with her lips but refused to give voice to what it was. Perhaps it was better to let that name stay buried. He assumed that Ianna felt the same. The two of them shared a long gaze and spoke on other things until the sun rose. No more talk of Shepherds, Adversaries, or Mars - that's what Jack wanted and Ianna, seeming to know his desires, deflected bigger inquiries to talk about little things. Simple things; *life*.

This is nice. Is it possible to have this for as long as I want? Can I just stay here forever?

* * * *

Darion awoke in his chambers in a sweat and headed straight for the Restoration Room. He was hoping no one would be with the Shepherd but sure enough, Abe was there. He appeared to be checking on the Shepherd's vitals, punching codes into a computer screen when Darion approached.

It'd been three days and still, the Shepherd would not wake. Darion was restless, as was Abraham, whose daughter, Greta, remained in a comatose state just two floors above them. Despite it all, Abe had somehow maintained a jovial demeanor. This surprised Darion, who believed even Abe was aware that his homecoming with the Fellows was not a happy one. Or at the very least, not nearly as great as what Abe would have imagined.

Looking at the Shepherd, standing prostrate in his pod, Darion wondered if Abe were comparing the Shepherd to Greta. They were both like vegetables, rooted where they were and unable to speak or interact with whomever came to their side. But, then Darion thought of Olivia. How she also refused to speak. She was no comatose child, but Darion longed to hear her voice again. As sure as Abraham longed to hear Greta's.

"Hello Abraham."

"Hello, Darion."

Abraham hit a few more keys on the control panel and turned to face Darion. He looked tired, like he'd been at Greta's bedside throughout the night. But then he smiled and energy seemed to fill the room.

"You look tired," said Darion.

"So do you. And thank you."

"For what?"

"For not telling anyone of importance around here about my daughter's previous vocation. I'd prefer that no one else know. Only a few do. The ones I trust, that is."

"It's no problem for me," said Darion. "I just thought you could trust everyone in a place like this"

"Heh," said Abe. "Even a church is a place for caution, Darion. It's said the Devil roams the Earth like a lion, looking to devour anyone who falls into sin. Last I heard, that can happen anywhere. Inside or outside of a building. The place doesn't matter, only the person."

"That's a fair enough logic, I suppose."

"It's the truth, Darion. And truth trumps logic every time."

There was a pause between them. Then Darion tried to speak, but Abe cut him off.

"If you're here about the Shepherd," said Abe. "Then I'll have to disappoint you. There is nothing to report. He's completely healed but he's just refusing to wake up. I don't what else to tell you."

"So there's been no change?"

"None."

Darion started to pace around the room. What had he not been doing? Why was this taking so long? Were the Fellows attempting to steal the Shepherd from him?

"Don't you worry," said Abe. "He'll wake up when he's good and ready and then you can be on your way again, Darion. I can assure you of that."

"Can you now?"

"No, not really," said Abe and he chuckled softly. "I've never seen anything like this before in my life. I'm not sure if anyone alive here has either. But, that's doesn't mean I can't tell you it'll all work out."

"Is that supposed to be your 'truth trumping logic'? Because if it is, then how am I supposed to believe anything you say to me?"

"Because," said Abe. "Worrying and wondering about what you *can't* control will only give you trouble. You should go lay down. Play with your daughter. Maybe talk to the Huntsmen who joined your group. There's other things you could be doing with your time other than speculating scenarios out of a vacuum."

Darion wanted to argue with Abe. How could this man be so calm? Between the two of them, Darion thought Abe would be the more distraught. His own daughter was in a coma, unresponsive and barely breathing. Yet, here he was: performing what had to be his turn to monitor the silver giant in the Fellows' underground base. And he wasn't even the slightest bit fazed by any of it.

"I've waited a long time for this," said Darion. "I don't expect you to understand that so forgive me if I seem a little on edge. I would think my feelings are warranted considering the circumstances."

"Oh, I forgive you," said Abe. "And I'm sure your emotions are justified. At least in your head. But, again, fixating all your energy on something you don't have any control over is not going to help you. And what's more, it's incredibly unhealthy."

Abe paused, looking Darion over.

"Are you feeling alright? You look more than tired now that I've had a chance to look at you."

Using your Gift on me? Darion thought. Trying to figure out my nightmares? Abe had no powers of deduction like the Shepherd but even so, Abe claimed to have the ability to see truth in people's eyes. Darion wouldn't have believed it if it hadn't been for Ianna's naming of Sophia earlier. Perhaps Abe was doing that now?

"I haven't been sleeping well," said Darion. "That's all."

"Nightmares?"

Darion nodded.

"Are they the same one or different each time?"

"What does that matter?" asked Darion.

"It does if you plan on sleeping better."

Darion folded his arms, tapped his foot impatiently. A therapy session? Whatever happened to enjoying a beverage like the Abe of old?

"They're usually different," said Darion. "They come and they go, but they almost always leave me in a sweat before I wake up. I've been having them for a while."

"Sounds like anxiety."

"Heh, probably is."

"Then tell me about it."

Darion shrugged his shoulders and stepped away from Abe. What good was any of this?

"Someone you love go to Mars?" asked Abe and Darion turned to face him.

"That's none of your business," said Darion.

"Ha!" said Abe. "That's a 'yes,' isn't it? So who is it? Who's the one you're looking forward to being reunited with again once you get to Mars?"

"It's none of your business," said Darion. "My daughter and I are going to get to Mars. The Shepherd is the only way we'll get there. That's all there is to know."

Abe paused, licked his lips like he had something important to say. Then, "I understand that you care for your daughter," he said. "I saw that in your eyes when I first met you. You think it a noble cause what you're doing, looking out for your daughter and trying to give her a better life. It's something I neglected years ago and was reminded of when we met again. But, I warn you to be mindful of something during your time here. And that is what you can and cannot control. What you *can* control is your frame of mind, your willingness to see this journey through to the end. But, that is all. What you *cannot* control, above all other things, is the *Shepherd*. He will do as he pleases. He will choose as he pleases. And he will wake when he pleases. You cannot demand things of the one who has brought you this far."

"You talk like the Shepherd has dominion over me."

"He does," said Abe. "At the moment anyway. Because you allow him to."

Permitting the Shepherd authority? Never! Darion was, again, insulted by the thought. If the Shepherd were his master, then Darion would be bowing at the Shepherd's feet, showing him praise for every decision made, and never thinking twice about the Shepherd's intentions. But, that wasn't Darion's experience at all. He'd questioned the Shepherd at times, even criticized him. He'd done this in secret and he'd done it outwardly too. How could

Abraham make such an accusation against him? The Shepherd was no more his master than Jack was his closest friend. Absurd!

"I think you misjudge me, Abe," said Darion. "I am not ruled by any man, not even one such as the Shepherd."

"You may think you aren't," said Abe. "But, you most certainly *are*. We all have masters we bend to, even if we aren't aware of it."

Abe went back to the computer terminal and brought up a new hologram display. In the 3D image was a picture of the Earth. And next to the Earth was Mars. And all around the Earth were tiny satellites, orbiting in separate directions and independently of one another. Abe pointed to the hologram and spoke.

"This is a picture of Earth and Mars as you can tell," said Abe. "And the tiny silver dots are Mars' *Lightbringer* satellites. You're familiar with these, right?"

"Yes. They're the machines that helped build Mars' first city. They also help contain the Darklight."

"That's right," said Abe. "However, did you know that each of these satellites has enough firepower to wipe out an entire city? Are you aware of that?"

A shiver went up Darion's spine. Mars had satellites ready to strike the Earth at any moment? What was the purpose behind that? Were we really at war?

"I'll take your silence as a 'no'," said Abe and he circled the hologram. "The Lightbringers are incredible machines. They landed on Mars and made its first greenhouses so humans could live there. And when they were done, they took to the skies to monitor the Earth. But, that's not all. Even after the Shepherds started showing up and taking people back with them, the Shepherds informed us of the Lightbringers above us. They weren't just there to contain Darklight. They were also put in place to keep an eye on us, keep us in line, I imagine. Could be watching us right now for all I know."

Again, Darion felt sick. Mars had the Earth at its complete mercy, it seemed. Not only had they brought a serious calamity to the planet, they were policing it as well. *Slaves.* Was this Abe's lesson for him? Earth was just a slave, no - an *experiment* in Mars' plans?

"So, we're all under Mars' watchful eye?" said Darion. "Is that your point? That we're slaves and they're our masters?"

"Not exactly," said Abe. "At times, I feel like it's more of a parent-child relationship. They have all the tools, but they don't know if we're ready to use them just yet. I was speaking more from a personal perspective. You've made Mars into your only reality, Darion. And you haven't even considered what that could mean once you've made it there. When you blindly follow something, you make that thing your master. The relationship has no give and take, it's completely one-sided."

Was Abe right? Perhaps he was. Still, the news of Mars' Lightbringers hovering above, holding the Earth hostage was a far more pressing issue than what Abe was speaking to.

"I still can't believe it," said Darion, trying to divert the topic. "I don't understand how they could be..."

"And why *not?*" said Abe, becoming very serious. "Why is it so difficult to believe that another group of human beings, no matter how technologically advanced, would ever *not* attempt to control their circumstances out of self-interest? You must not understand human nature at all, Darion Wallace, if you choose to see humanity through such a narrow lens."

"It's not that I have a narrow lens," said Darion. "It's merely about picking the lesser of two evils. Yes, it scares me to know of Mars' power. It's disturbing to hear the things you've told me about the Lightbringer satellites and what they are capable of. But, I am also aware that Mars is the better alternative to what is here. And if those are my only two options, then I will certainly pick Mars over this world. I will always pick what is better for me. For my daughter. So, you see, I *do* understand human nature. I am living out that philosophy and will continue to do so once I get to Mars. Despite what you say or what Mars is doing to us."

Abe smirked and hit a button on the control panel. The hologram disappeared and Abe returned to his seat.

"Then I guess we're done here, Darion," said Abe. "You clearly know more than I do. So what's the point in you coming to me with questions at all?"

"Don't twist my words," said Darion. "I didn't come down here looking for answers from you. I came for the Shepherd. If you hadn't been here, I still would have deciphered the Shepherd's condition for myself. I didn't need someone telling me the obvious."

"No, perhaps not," said Abe. "So let me tell you something else that's not so obvious: you can't undo what's been done, Darion."

"What are you even talking about?" asked Darion, annoyed.

"Your nightmares," said Abe. "You said you keep having them. Nightmares are a result of fear inside us; an anxious feeling where we want to change things. Or perhaps alter what's been done already. So let me tell you this again, Darion: you can't undo the years you think you've lost. I want nothing more than to make up for the twenty years I missed with my daughter. And I could spend the next twenty trying to erase that absent memory. Only I'd never be able to do it. No man alive can. So if and when you get to Mars, remember that."

Darion smirked. "I think you've lost your Gift, Abe. You don't understand people and you don't understand their motivations either. Stop trying to tell me what it is you think I need."

Then Darion waited for Abe to retort, but when Abe only sat in silence, Darion walked away. Abe stopped him by the door.

"You and the kid are the same, Darion," said Abe. Darion turned to face Abe. "You're both scared. You shouldn't be, but you are."

Darion turned quickly back around and left. He walked the long way back to his quarters, but went outside for a walk before settling back on his bed, thinking of the conversation with Abe while simultaneously trying to forget it.

Trying to make up for lost time, Darion thought. How could Abe presume to think that's what he was doing? Mars held the escape he dreamed of. It didn't matter if they were targeting Earth or surveying its inhabitants like animals in a zoo. None of that mattered. He knew the Shepherd was here to deliver people out of this hell. That's what kept him going. Not the many months of chasing down discs to attract a Shepherd. Not the many nights enduring nightmares that brought him closer to the Shepherd's next landing. Or the times he'd faked his existence so he might not be discovered with Mars technology.

He'd risked so much that it was incredulous to suggest that all he was doing was chasing after lost years and lost time.

And yet, Darion could not shake Abe's words as the day became night. He tucked Olivia in for the evening and told her a story, something he hadn't been able to do while they had been on the road and then tried to fall asleep himself. Perhaps it was true what Abe had said. That he'd been chasing lost time and was too eager to make up for it. Perhaps this was his crutch, narrowing his sight and in turn, narrowing every other aspect of his life worth examining.

If you were here, he thought. You'd know what to do. You were always better at waiting and knowing when the time was right to say something. What else have I been missing? I need you to tell me what it is I'm doing wrong. I need you to keep me honest, keep me on the path we started. If you were here, you'd point to me what it is I can't see. What it is that's hindering everything I'm trying to accomplish. And yet, why haven't I heard from you? Why won't you answer me? I'm here. Olivia is here. Where are *you*?

Then Darion laid his head to his pillow and held back tears he didn't realize were waiting on him. Crying. He hadn't done it in forever. Not since *she* had left.

Then Darion rolled his head to one side and felt something. It was under his pillow and he pulled it out from under.

"How?" said Darion. "These are...."

There were photographs. And a note atop them:

Stop worrying so much. Especially when a friend of yours might pull some strings and get those photos of yours developed. I can see why you want to get to Mars so badly. Here's hoping you make it. Here's hoping we both do. - Abraham

More tears. Darion couldn't help himself. His photos had been printed. He didn't care who had taken his camera and done the deed either. This was a great discovery. A great gift. He smiled and sifted through them all.

Damn you, Abe. You were right about me. True, I can't control much. But, I *can* control what I am thinking. Tomorrow, if the Shepherd is still slumbering, I'll ask you what else it is I don't know. I can't keep pressing on alone, can I? Damn you for seeing that in me. And damn your Gift. But, thank you all the same.

Then Darion fell asleep and slept without interruption throughout the night. He had no nightmares, or at the very least, none that he could remember in the morning.

Chapter 19
The Captain and the Shepherd

* * * *

"What do you mean it's *dying*?"

A semi-circle of Red Fellow elders had cornered Abraham and Ianna near the back of the sanctuary. Another week had passed since the Shepherd slipped into a sedentary coma. And there were big problems in need of being solved.

Jack was at the meeting, as was Darion, who had made it his business to be part of any meeting the Red Fellows had. Conversely, Jack had made Ianna *his* business and so, was at every meeting involving Ianna. The two men sat in silence, listening to the elders debate their latest problem: the ball of Solfire. It was depleting. Or as they had put it: *dying*.

"I don't know if 'dying' is the proper term," said Abraham. "But, it has been decreasing in size. It may just be retreating for a time. Waiting to come back out when the time is right. I don't see an immediate cause for concern though. Things are still working as they should be and the Shepherd could wake any minute now. We must remain faithful that things will change soon."

"We appreciate your optimism," said one of the elders. "But, that doesn't mean you have the authority to speak on these matters, Abraham. No one has any way of knowing if that will happen."

"Yes," said another. "Who is to say the Shepherd isn't the one responsible for all this? None of this happened until the Shepherd arrived. Perhaps Mars has sent a traitor to drain us of our power?"

A few voices spoke up and denounced the idea. But, there were still some among them who believed the Shepherd might be intentionally draining the Solfire for his own purposes.

"Again," said Abe. "We can't be sure of anything. When the Shepherd wakes up, we'll know."

"And what if the ship goes out before then?" said one of the elders. "Then what? We'll have been left with *nothing*. And when that happens, will you still be saying, 'wait, things will change soon.' That sounds more like wishing on a star to me."

"I'm not saying we are to wish things away," said Abe. "I'm merely trying to present our situation as it is. The lights in the main hull have dimmed and the ball of Solfire has decreased. These may be temporary problems; not cause for panic or pointing fingers."

"And who is pointing fingers exactly?" said an elder. "Surely, no man or woman is above another inside of this circle. And what's more, no one would accuse someone else of being responsible. Prodigal son you may be, Abraham, but no person is more favored than any other in this place."

"Yet you blame the Shepherd?" said Abraham.

"His direct connection to the Solfire is an observation worth noting."

"As is your narrow mindedness and fear," said Abe. "It reminds me of why I left this order in the first place."

There was a pause among the group. Then one of the elders spoke. "We appreciate your honesty and boldness, Abraham. But, if things do not improve soon, we will be forced to take action."

"And what action will you be taking?"

A low murmur came over the group as men and women leaned next to one another's ears and whispered things like each of them had an answer. Abraham seethed but didn't speak. The bickering of old voices made Jack cringe. Is this how things are supposed to get accomplished?

"I suppose there is little we *can* do in the meantime," said one of the elders. "We will just have to wait until the Shepherd wakes, after all."

"Absolutely we will," said Abe. "Is that not what I've been saying all along? Or did it take this long for my words to finally seep into your heads?"

More murmurs. Jack was beginning to enjoy this. Abe was bold; *very* bold. Bold in a way that made Darion or any other man look like an untrained puppy.

"We get your point, Abraham," said an elder. "All of them. So we will no longer be discussing this matter." Another pause. "However, it would be pertinent for you to explain why we must wait on the Shepherd. Especially when it is clear that the Shepherd might be the cause of our problems in the first place?"

"Because if the power goes out entirely," said Abe. "He's the only one who could fix it among us. There are no others capable of dealing with the ball of Solfire that's shrinking underneath this

Cathedral. And if there is such a man or woman who thinks he *can*, then I ask him to please step forward and claim responsibility for what happens next."

Abraham's confidence seemed to have won, for no one spoke up after that. Jack was captivated but Darion wasn't surprised. Darion had been watching Abe carefully over the past week, examining the way Abe projected himself among them. Despite having been gone so long, Abe had reasserted himself as someone of influence. Though there was confusion; caused by the shrinking power source – the ball of Solfire – and the fact a real, live Shepherd was calmly restoring his body in their basement, Abraham spoke like things were going to be 'fine.' And when he said it, people believed him. If it were anyone else, Darion would have considered this behavior a clever way to mask one's own fears. But, after having spent more than a week with Abraham, Darion was convinced of an inner confidence - an authenticity - that permeated Abe and anyone else he chose to impress himself upon.

"And what of Greta, your daughter?" asked another elder. "Are you still waiting on something to change there as well?"

This time Abe hesitated. "She... is still recovering also."

"And do you still intend to put her in the tank too? Knowing that the Solfire light is *dying*?"

Abe nodded. "I'll do whatever I can to save my daughter."

Darion silently agreed. Abe gets it. There's more at stake than our own lives here.

"Very well," said an elder. "We will continue to wait. And pray to God that things get better."

Then they all prayed, thanking God for new information and a steady hand to stay together through these new developments. Darion and Jack felt like outsiders. They ducked their heads down in unison, meeting one another in silence. Neither man spoke, each waiting on the group to come up for air. But, then the boy Turk rushed in and all prayer ceased.

"Mr. Abe! Mr. Abe!" he yelled. "There's some new people here! Just outside. New people."

Abe's head popped up. "What's that?"

"There's a whole bunch of them. And they got big cars too! Cars with smoke and steam!"

An ominous feeling came over Darion and Jack. Was it *them*? Had they finally caught up? If their party had left a trail, then they'd certainly given their enemy a long enough time to find them. Abe looked at Darion, whose eyes were wide.

"Come on," said Abe. "Let's go see."

The group left the inner sanctum, but Jack and Darion lingered.

"Coming?" said Darion.

Jack didn't answer. He kept his eyes forward and Darion surmised Jack was still harboring some unsaid prejudice against him.

"If it's *them*," said Darion. "Then it won't matter if you come now or later. They'll still find you." Darion paused. He took a breath and tried something he'd been learning from Abe. "I'm sorry, Jack. Whatever I've said, whatever I've done. I'm sorry. I want the same things as you - to *live*. Can we agree on that at least?"

Jack turned towards Darion. Was that all it took? A simple 'I'm sorry' to clear the haze?

"Thanks," said Jack and Darion left, Jack following shortly thereafter.

There were several people in the sanctuary. Abe was in front, looking out the windows. Turk stood nearby with Olivia. Darion pushed his way to the front until he could see what the others were gawking at. It was as they feared - the Hunt had found them.

How did they get here? Darion thought. Their numbers were huge. There were a dozen Rovers, maybe more, seated at the bottom of the hillside. They faced the Cathedral like they were about to charge it head on. Several Red Fellows were outside, standing on the hill as members of the Hunt approached. Among the Red Fellows were some of the children. Darion looked and saw Jack's hand trembling. He put a hand on Jack's shoulder and spoke.

"Just don't do anything foolish," said Darion.

"I wasn't planning on it," said Jack.

One of the Huntsmen called for the leaders of the Red Fellows to come out, but no one moved.

"We need the Shepherd now!" said one of the elders. "What is going to happen to us? Who are these people?"

More chatter ensued and several people began running to the back of the Cathedral, hiding like the Hunt might not see them.

Darion pulled Olivia close to him. Now what, Shepherd? What is it that you're waiting for now?

"I'm going out to meet them," said Abe, but several voices protested immediately. "What do you intend to do then?" Abe retorted. "Act like no one is home? They already know we're here. There's no point in hiding. Besides, they may just be here to negotiate."

"Their vehicles say otherwise," said Darion. "We need weapons. Don't the Fellows have anything to fight with?"

"I'm hoping for a negotiation if I can manage it," said Abe. "So the need for weapons should be null and void. And I need to find out who injured my daughter too."

"Didn't you hear what I said?" said Darion.

"I *did*," said Abe. "But, the way I see it, if they ask for the Shepherd and I tell them they can't have him, they might just go home."

"I severely doubt that. And that's not how a negotiation works."

"No, but if they *do* back down, then we'll have had a successful negotiation, won't we?"

Insane! Darion wanted to shake Abe into better thinking. To be confident was one thing, but this was asinine. The Hunt don't negotiate, they take. And no words were going to win this battle.

But, before Darion could intervene with any kind of counterargument, Abe made for the door. And Ianna was following him.

"What are you doing?" asked Jack.

"I'm also an elder," said Ianna. "Or didn't you get the memo?"

With that, Ianna left and Jack was forced to wait. Abraham, along with a few others brave enough to join him, ventured outside to greet their new guests. When they were about halfway off the porch, a new figure appeared, as if wandering out of the shadows.

"It's *him*," said Felix, from behind Darion. "The Captain. He came all this way with them, after all."

Of course he would come, Darion thought. Haven't you seen what's in this bunker, beneath the hillside? Any man with some knowledge about the Shepherd would travel the country, no, the *world* to see the Shepherd.

"But where's his brother?" asked Robert. "'The 'Eyes of the Hunt' or whatever." Jack and the others scanned the Huntsmen but didn't see Argus. "He's never far from the Captain. Where is he?"

Outside, Abraham met with Virgil and the two parties stopped. "Afternoon," said Abraham. "Welcome to the Cathedral of the Red Fellows. How may we serve you today?"

Virgil grinned. "There's no need for that," said the Captain. "My name is Virgil and I am the Captain of the Hunt. I don't need to know any of your names, thank you. Just give him over and I won't be forced to play my hand."

"You'll have to be more specific than that. There are many – "

"Don't do this with me. The Shepherd is inside your Cathedral. Bring him out to us."

Abe paused, smiled and spoke. "Why don't you come in and have a drink, Captain?" asked Abraham. "All are welcome here, you know. There are no barriers to – "

"To what? God? Is that the pitch of the Red Fellows these days? Is that whom you believe the Shepherds to be acting through?"

"Who says God isn't speaking through them?"

"You're pathetic," said the Captain. "Your minds are all twisted. Miracles happen every day, but I don't see you worshipping those. Yet, when a man drops down in a spaceship, you bow down like he's one of heaven's angels. I can't help but think that's not God at work - just *ignorant* people."

"God makes fools of the wise by using the foolish," said Abraham.

"Quoting the Bible is a clever shield," said Virgil. "It might work on simpler minds, but it won't on me. I suppose that makes me one of the 'wise' then doesn't it? Does your God see that you're failing to sway me also?"

"He sees everything. He *does* everything. He made Mars and He made the Shepherds. We're all just trying to get a handle on what else God has done. What about you?"

"I'm no different," said Virgil. "If God does all these things, then he also makes the rules. Rules you aren't following very closely. For one, you've turned one of God's churches into a house made for worshipping another human being. Do you think your God appreciates that?"

"We don't worship the Shepherds," said Ianna.

"But you do," said Virgil. "Why else would you change your creeds for the sake of survival? Why else would you hide behind old words so you can treat the Shepherd like he's some sort of savior? Between the two of us, I'd say I'm the one who deserves God's favor. At least I'm honest, not mixing ideologies for my own benefit."

"You're only assuming that's the case," said Abe. "I'd wager you've never been inside one of the Red Fellow Cathedrals."

"Now, you're just stalling," argued Virgil. "Give over the Shepherd and stop with the philosophy lesson. And bring me Jack while you're at it. I've missed him."

"That won't happen either," said Ianna. "He's one of us."

Virgil only smirked. And again, there was another pause. Virgil stared at Abraham, eyes on fire. But, Abraham was staring right back, for he could see something forming about Virgil. Layers of Darklight were manifesting and with his Gift, Abraham could see the mark of death on Virgil. A shadow of Darklight shone on Virgil's hands and swept around his arms. It caused Abraham to raise an eyebrow; it was the mark of a *killer*, but it was more than a mere mark of murder. The Darklight had stains that mixed perfectly with one another. Both the foreign and the familiar came together at once and Abraham swallowed, eyes closed. He'd seen it before. And he grieved for more than one when he recognized the signature.

"You..." said Abraham, opening his eyes. "You've taken your own blood. You took the life of your own flesh."

Virgil's eyes widened; exposed. The elders were amazed, understanding they were witnessing Abraham's Gift in action.

"What are you talking about?" asked Virgil.

"I told you. God sees *everything*, remember?"

"Is he seeing things through *you* this very moment?"

"And who is to say that he isn't?"

The Darklight grew. Jack and Darion saw it too. But, who was it for? Was the Adversary close? Jack leaned over, peering into the woods to see if the Adversary were near. Darion did the same.

"Go back home, Virgil," said Abraham, holding back tears. His entire body seemed to be affected by Virgil's stained hands. "You've come all this way, but there's nothing for you here. Nothing you can take with you."

"I don't believe that," said Virgil. "The Shepherd took three of ours and my best lieutenant, Greta, as well." Abraham's lip curled and he nearly blurted out the secret of Greta being his daughter, but Ianna took a step and stopped him.

"The Shepherd has a lot to answer for," continued Virgil. "When I first heard of the Shepherd, my only intent was to take him. Take *his* life. Just enough to atone for the crimes of Mars. That was my original plan. But, now? I'd say he's done more than his fair share in mucking up everything; and not just the light we miss so dearly. So I promise you, I will take revenge for everyone who has been wronged by the actions of Mars and by the actions of any who would defend the traitorous red planet. Do you understand me?"

Abraham's hands began to shake. The Darklight clouds were heavier now. The haze of purple and gray increasing; Abraham signaled for the group to head back. Only Ianna saw the subtle twitch in his brow, the hint to move away from the Hunt as quickly and discreetly as possible. The others looked afraid, their lives in danger for possibly the first time since the Pulse hit four decades ago. They didn't move. Each of them seemed to think one of them had to say something, had to become a hero among the Fellows if only for a moment. But, then the Captain spoke and there was no time for further negotiations.

"And I will tell you this, old man," said Virgil, leaning forward. "I will have the Hunt fire on your entire Cathedral if you don't give me what I want. There won't be a pillar left. There won't be a doorframe standing; there will be *nothing*. Is that what you want? More martyrs for the sake of the false prophet you have buried under your Cathedral?"

Abraham didn't answer Virgil. Instead, he bowed his head and grinned.

"It would appear you're not welcome here, after all," said Abraham. "Good day, Captain."

Abraham turned and walked away, Ianna following close behind. The Captain watched them go, the other elders a hair behind. *Good man*, Darion thought. Get out of there. Get back to safe ground. They were nearly there, close to the front door when Darion blinked. And when he did, the Captain reached inside of his jacket and removed a small pistol. He took aim and fired in the same breath and one of the elders lurched in pain. Darion screamed, his words catching up with his senses. Blood was being spilled. And soon, it was more than just Abraham being shot down.

* * * *

"Ianna!"

Jack screamed and pressed his face against the window. If she heard him, it would have been a fleeting moment. For if her brain could function at a speed that could interpret the sound Jack made, then rationalize what his words meant and then further understand the meaning of Jack's call to her, then she may have died a happy death. She would have known that Jack had cared deeply for her, that his cry for her was a cry of loss and a cry for unjust action. So that when she fell to the ground she would know that someone had loved her right up until the end. Would have fought for her, would have protected her if, he could.

But, this was all a matter of wonder and speculation.

For when Ianna was shot from behind, the bullet traveled through the back of her skull, into her brain, and out the other side in what felt like milliseconds. And with that much shock to the brain cavity, Ianna was dead nearly as fast as the bullet had traveled. Jack's pleas were not likely heard and her soul was already departing – devoured by the Adversary – as she toppled in a heap on the hillside. More of the elders joined her, shot down by not only Virgil but by the Huntsmen who stood with the Captain. They fired with remarkable precision. These were not green recruits like Felix; they were trained enforcers. The Captain had brought his most loyal, most deadly of servants. Abraham, too, was shot but managed to barrel through the door as members of the Red Fellows shut the doors behind.

"Get the guns!" shouted Abraham, his breathing labored and clutching his ribs. The Fellows scattered, searching for weapons. Bullets flew through the windows and more of the Fellows fell as they ran. Jack didn't even see them though; his soul was on fire.

"No!" cried Jack. "You bastards!" He yelled and punched through the window, glass tearing at his flesh as blood landed on the windowsill. Jack tried to leap out but Darion grabbed him and pulled him back inside. "Filthy bastards! I'll kill all of you!"

"You'll die too, you idiot!" shouted Darion, throwing Jack backwards with surprising force. Jack landed on his back, adrenaline still pumping but when he caught himself, the pain set in. He grabbed hold of his hand and cried out. A rumble outside alerted everyone that the Rovers were on their way up the hill.

"Jack!" shouted Darion. "We've got to get downstairs! Liv, go the Shepherd!"

More bullets pierced the windows and bodies fell to the floor. Some alive but injured. Some dead where they fell. On the hill, Virgil was letting his troops do the work. Easy. This would be easy. They would have little trouble smoking out the Shepherd. And tearing down the Cathedral that stood in their way.

The Adversary, meanwhile, was gorging. It ran over those who were dead or those barely clinging to life as it split into more copies of itself, maximizing the space it could feed upon.

Jack came to his feet, hands bleeding profusely. He felt faint, blood rolling down his wrist and forearm. He began to topple over, into the arms of Darion.

"Dammit, Jack," said Darion. He pressed Jack's other hand over the cut. "Keep pressure on it. Stay awake!"

"Darion!" said Abe, shouting yet barely able to speak above the chaos. "Go for the Shepherd... He will awaken and destroy them." Abe paused, his life leaving him. Darion saw the Adversary stalking from a distance. Though the beast was everywhere, one of its copies was slowly creeping towards the fallen Abraham. Darion shouted at the beast, kicking up loose wood and broken brick like it might deter the monster, but it had no effect. Seeing this, Abe stressed another command. "Darion, save my daughter... Please....."

Darion threw Jack's arm over his shoulder and made his way to the ship. The Hunt were nearly upon the front door. Darion activated the door and led Jack down the stone steps and into the main hull of the underground ship. The booms of rockets and bullets raking the Cathedral could be heard above. Jack could scarcely recognize his bearings. They hustled their way towards the Restoration Room as the lights – the floating orbs overhead – pulsed with a dim fade like they could sense every fallen soul above ground. In the ship, some of the Red Fellows were still searching for weapons. Others hid inside of rooms while others fell to the ground and prayed like their end was coming.

"Where..." said Jack. "Where are you goin', man?"

"To the Shepherd, you idiot."

Jack's mind was drifting. Ianna. She was *dead*. He saw her die. All the beauty in the world. It was gone. Just like that. No, it had to be a nightmare. When will I wake up? What does it matter now? Why are we running away?

Jack's body became even more limp, falling farther down on Darion till Darion hoisted Jack higher.

"Your legs aren't dead, Jack," he said. "So use them!"

* * * *

Darion came to the door of the Restoration Room and placed a hand on the wall. It turned red and denied his entry. He tried again, but he received the same result.

What the?

Another boom by the steps and Darion heard more screams. The Hunt was breaking inside the Cathedral and advancing down. Darion slammed at the alien steel.

"Olivia! Are you there? Let us in! Olivia! Turk!"

Several masked Huntsmen had accumulated by the main entrance. The Captain was not with them but they were taking hostages and shooting any who resisted them. Jack stumbled, his face had grown pale and the room was hazy. It was difficult to stand. The rush of adrenaline and the loss of blood had taken their toll. The floating orbs flickered one more time and then pulsed their last bit of light and dissipated. The entire underground went dark and Darion grabbed hold of Jack, making certain he wouldn't lose Jack in the chaos.

"Jack, don't move," he whispered. "Don't go anywhere. Darklight's coming in here. It's breached the air locks. Dammit anyways!"

Jack couldn't move if he wanted. His whole body felt heavy as he grabbed his wrist, the slimy feeling of blood escaping his veins covering his other hand. He scarcely noticed when the door clicked and slid open.

"Come on, Jack!" shouted Darion and he lifted Jack under his armpits and pulled Jack inside of the Restoration Room. There were others that joined them, the small hint of light poking out from inside the room drew people in. Inside, the ball of Solfire was no bigger than an apple. How had it shrunk so much? Seated about the room were Olivia, Turk, and several other children. They were positioned specifically around the Shepherd. When Darion saw Olivia, he put down Jack and ran over to her.

"Liv! Are you all right? Are you okay?"

Olivia nodded, but her eyes were terrified. The other children were afraid too and Darion saw them huddling closer to one another in the little light they had under the ball of Solfire. Then there was the Shepherd: eyes shut and still standing inside the pod like nothing had changed. Darion heard more screams coming from inside the ship and he let go of Olivia and walked up to the Shepherd. He stood as close as he could, staring at the silver giant.

"Do you hear this?" asked Darion, his voice steadily rising with every word. "Do you? Are you *hearing* this? Do you even know what is happening right now? How can you stay in there, doing nothing! Is that all you ever do? Wait, and do *nothing*! People are dying! How can you do nothing? Don't you even care?"

The ball of Solfire expanded and retracted back into itself. It made new shapes: first a thin sliver of golden light, then splitting into a helix as it severed into several more. Then it wrapped itself back into a tiny ball of gold and disappeared. And in its place, a black hole appeared. It looked like a portal to another dimension, another place waiting on the other side. There was a subtle pull in the room, drawing every solid object towards the black orb and Jack could feel his loose blood being drawn as well. What now? What is happening? The miniature black hole transformed again into a black helix; then disappeared, shrinking as the entire room was pulled towards the spot where the black orb had been. Then the room retracted slightly and there was stillness.

The Shepherd opened his eyes, silver and blue irises piercing through the darkness.

"It is finished," said the Shepherd and the pod opened.

The Shepherd stepped out and looked around; his silver suit was glowing with several of the golden orbs again. The children, who had been sitting around the pod, stood and backed away, clearing a path for the resurrected Shepherd. The Huntsmen stormed the room, following the light of the Shepherd, torches in hand and rifles raised towards the light.

"Do not leave this room, Darion Wallace," said the Shepherd and Darion crouched next to his daughter. Jack pulled himself up against the wall and cowered. What will he do now that we're cornered?

The Shepherd leapt through the air, a trail of gold following him wherever he went. When he was traveling fast enough, the Shepherd moved with a speed that lit the entire room, jumping off of the walls and diving from the ceiling. The Hunt fired on him, but their bullets hit empty space and when they did hit the Shepherd, the bullets had no effect. Their torches landed on the ground, their guns crunched within the hands of the Shepherd and they yelled and screamed as their bodies flew off the sides of the Restoration Room. The Shepherd threw them about with a strength that looked like a leisurely stroll for the Shepherd. The long sleep had no effect on his physical nature, it seemed. If anything, he was refreshed. The ones he touched fell to the floor, shaking violently. The ones he passed twice were thrown aside on the second turn.

"More?" said the Shepherd and he moved outside the Restoration Room, into the main ship. There, more of the Hunt's army was waiting.

The Huntsmen saw him and started yelling to each other, 'There he is!' 'It's him!' and fired at the golden orbs, but their bullets missed their target. Instead, the Shepherd was catching their fire in the dark, dodging the ones he managed to *not* catch, and dropping others to the ground. He moved in close, shoving the Huntsmen with arms outstretched, dropping many to the ground while others flew through the air, landing in a seizure of confused agony.

When the room was cleared of the Huntsmen, the Shepherd stood alone, orbs radiating. He cracked his shoulder like it needed greasing and surveyed the room. The orbs clicked and left his body, flying higher into the room and burning bright to illuminate the carnage. Among the shadows, the Adversary lurked. It was feeding on the spilled blood of the Red Fellows who were injured or near death.

"Filthy creature," said the Shepherd and he raised his arm, the light cannon forming at the wrist and he fired against the monster. The Adversary squealed and slunk into the darkness. The Shepherd then tended to the hurt, healing their wounds and bringing them up. From out of the Restoration Room, Darion and the others slowly appeared. Jack hobbled, hands bloodied but drying in the light.

"I told you to stay in the room, Darion Wallace," said the Shepherd, still tending to the Red Fellows.

On the ground, there were bodies of Red Fellows and Huntsmen alike, the only difference between them were the convulsive twitches of the Huntsmen and the eerie lifelessness of the Fellows. There was a slam against the door up the steps and the Shepherd stood again.

"I will take care of the rest," said the Shepherd. "Get the children and the others out of here. The Adversary may become too many for me to handle while you are near me."

"Where should we go? There are too many of them upstairs."

The Shepherd ran up the stairs and returned just as quickly. In his arms was the ailing body of Greta, body wrapped in bed sheets so that the Shepherd might not harm her with his touch.

"Take her," said the Shepherd. "And place her in my pod."

"Shepherd, that won't - "

"Do as I say."

The Shepherd handed over Greta, turned, and ran up the stone steps. Darion went to the Restoration Room and placed Greta inside the Shepherd's former holding cell. The pod activated almost immediately, swallowing up the lieutenant like it was intent on holding her hostage. With the Solfire gone, would the Tank even restore her? Would this even work? Darion heard the groans of other Fellows and left the Restoration Room, shutting the door behind him. Greta's fate would have to remain unknown. *Godspeed*, he thought. There's nothing more I can do for you now, Abraham.

Outside the Room, Darion found Felix, Robert, and even Sophia among the injured, but alive. He was relieved to find they had made it through this first wave of attack. Meanwhile, Jack was busy cursing his ineffectiveness, his inability to save Ianna when it mattered. He had fallen to the floor in a heap, sobbing and trying not to cry uncontrollably between breaths. Darion felt sorry for him, but empathy would only slow them down. He called out to Jack with force.

"Get up, Jack," said Darion. "The Shepherd's not through yet. We have to go. We have to get to the jeeps."

"I can't go up there..."

"Get up, Jack! There's only a short walk out back and if the Shepherd clears a path then all of us can make it! Now, get up!"

But, Jack wouldn't move. He slipped into a fetal-like position on the floor and sighed. That's it then? Darion was about to leave him when Olivia came to Jack's side and touched his shoulder. Jack lifted his head. Olivia's eyes were glowing blue, the soft color of a hope that Jack had seen in Ianna. He felt rejuvenated and slowly began to rise. He labored towards the exit, refusing help from anyone who offered. Perhaps there was still some life in him?

Above ground, the Captain waited. He watched his Rovers destroy the entire Cathedral, bullets and explosives wrecking every layer of the white building. The bell and cross lie in the debris, crushed by one of the massive Rovers. One of the Huntsmen returned to the Captain's side, speaking quickly like there was urgent news.

"Captain," he said through veiled scarf. "We've sent several of our Huntsmen into the Earth. There appears to be an underground base of some kind. We think the Shepherd might be hiding down there."

Virgil grinned. "He *was* there. Now, he's coming to see us."

One of the Rovers stopped moving, its wheels stuck on something, it seemed. Then it began to flip over slowly and several of its passengers jumped out before it crashed on its backside. Another did the same and more Huntsmen bailed from their vehicle. This process repeated itself until every Rover was flat on its back, windows crushed or destroyed. Virgil walked farther up the hillside.

"There you are," said Virgil, grinning.

The Shepherd finally revealed himself. His invisible cloak clicked and rotated to silver as he stood among the wreckage of the Cathedral. His eyes burned with silver-blue as he gazed upon the Captain. The Huntsmen raised their guns to fire on the Shepherd.

"Stop! Hold your fire! We want him alive!" shouted Virgil.

But, their bullets were already in flight. And as before, they had no effect on the Shepherd, who stood at attention, allowing every bullet that was fired to land upon his suit and fall dead to the ground. When the Hunt realized their weakness, they stopped and looked to one another like a ghost had appeared. Just what *was* this thing?

"Heh," said Virgil, as though the Shepherd impressed him. "You certainly are every bit of what I hear about you."

Virgil walked towards the Shepherd, closing the distance between them.

"At *last*," said Virgil. "I have found you. Why have you run from me for so long?"

"I am not the one who does the running," said the Shepherd.

"And yet *you're* the one who has!" Virgil laughed, doing so like he expected the Shepherd to answer him this way. "Is it because you're afraid of me? I'm sure you know who I am, don't you? I am Virgil, the Captain of the Hunt. No doubt your compatriots and the traitors you have with you have told you about me."

"You presume much," said the Shepherd. "I don't know who you are. You must not know as many people as you think."

"I don't need to. People know *me*."

"But, do you know who *I* am?"

Virgil chuckled again, a disbelief and joy coming over him. This was a Shepherd standing before him. Finally, a *Shepherd*. He would not waste the moment.

"You *must* be afraid, Shepherd," said Virgil. "You must be frightened since you've been so careful to dodge me as long as you have. To keep yourself lurking in the shadows, hiding out in the woods where no one can see you. Is that how Mars tells you to live? 'A life that's meant for hiding is one that's worth living?' Is that what the red planet's teaches its children?"

"I don't hide from anyone," said the Shepherd, his voice taking on what felt like a growing fury. The Huntsmen seemed to feel it too. They took short steps away from the Shepherd while Virgil advanced.

"You *are* afraid of me, then?" said Virgil. "Or maybe it's a fear of being one of *us*. Being among those who have to live like we do; deprived of the light. Or is it guilt that outweighs your fear?"

The Shepherd didn't answer. He looked to the ground. He saw the bodies of Abraham, Ianna, and other Red Fellows scattered all over the dirt. The Adversary had feasted upon their bodies, sucked them dry of life and the Shepherd shuddered. He closed his eyes, a tear forming as he mourned them. Many of the fallen were beyond his power to heal them. Their will to live was gone, save Abraham, whose spirit twinkled beneath the dark cloud of death that hung over him. The Shepherd moved towards Abraham, ignoring the Captain and thereby, enraging Virgil even further.

"Nothing to say, Shepherd?"

Virgil came even closer. The Shepherd leaned down and placed a hand on the back of Abraham. Blood had stained Abraham's jacket like he'd bathed in red. The Shepherd closed his eyes and spoke softly beneath Virgil's voice.

"What do you think you're doing?" mocked Virgil. "You're only a man, but even then, 'man' is a term I'd use loosely with you. You see, what you are, Shepherd… is a *freak*. You are an accident. A freak that was born on a freakish world; a lab experiment. But, me? I am a *human being*, Shepherd; one that was born of this planet – our *true* home – and not created artificially by men. Men who wanted to make new gods for themselves, ensuring their legacies might be catalogued as the beginners of something better. But, we both know that isn't the truth."

The Shepherd seemed to be waiting, saying nothing.

"Do you see the difference between us now?" argued Virgil. "You're conquerable, Shepherd. An idea that will never realize its true potential because it was fashioned by imperfect people. The created can never usurp the creator. In comparison to you, I'm a *divine* creation. Don't you see that?"

The Shepherd opened his eyes, lips trembling. He could see the Adversary wrapping itself about Virgil's body, the Darklight clouds swarming about.

"The depth of hatred you have for yourself," said the Shepherd. "Is truly *frightening*, Virgil. To have required so much agony, to have spent so much time and effort to inflict so much pain – you are among the worst kind, Captain of the Hunt. Even taking the blood of your own was not enough. For what little truth you may think you know, or have acquired, you have surely given yourself over to monsters."

The Shepherd stood upright, head towering over Virgil's. Abraham's body shook with a twitch like electricity had been passed through him. Virgil saw it and reached into his jacket for the pistol, but the Shepherd reached out to stop him. The Adversary emerged, clamping down on the outstretched hand of the Shepherd, immobilizing him. He staggered back, clutching his wrist and Virgil jumped backwards too, alarmed, and unable to fully see what was happening. Virgil saw only Darklight, twisting itself around the Shepherd –the Adversary was hidden, yet its mouth was chomping and claws scratching at the Shepherd. Some of the Hunt, however, could see everything and several dropped their weapons and ran. Their collective fear only fueled the Adversary even more.

"Yes!" shouted Virgil, now understanding the situation. "Do you feel it now? Do you like being confined? Do you like feeling like you're in a cage? Like an animal?"

The Shepherd shook the Adversary from his arm and armed his cannon. He fired a blast so bright that it blinded every person above ground and Virgil and his Huntsmen fell; eyes on fire and screaming. The Shepherd turned and leapt for the door of the underground ship. He pried it open and there was Darion with more of the Red Fellows.

"Move," said the Shepherd. "Head down the hill and make for the jeeps. But, do not look behind you or else you may be blinded also. I have bought you all the time needed to escape. I will catch up to you shortly."

There were no disagreements or discussion. Darion, Jack, and Olivia filtered out, and made way for the other side of the hill, away from the writhing Hunt and down the dirt path for the Red Fellow's garages. Jack staggered, trying not to look upon the bodies that were littered everywhere. He vomited in his mouth and fell to the ground. The garage was just ahead.

"Hurry, Jack!" ordered Darion.

Darion started up the jeep and realized he hadn't driven a vehicle for a long time. Not a diesel or one like this anyway. Jack, Felix, and Olivia joined him in the nearest car. From there, the caravan of Fellows headed north, away from the demolished Cathedral.

On the hill, the effects of the Shepherd's blast had faded. The Adversary was returning, in greater numbers, and attacking the light that had afflicted Virgil and his men. The Shepherd thereby began jumping from Huntsman to Huntsman, striking the Adversary with his fists and feet, trying to keep the Adversary at bay. Yet the attacks would not completely subdue the Adversary. The Huntsmen rose up on their feet, reaching for their weapons.

"Get the Rovers!" shouted Virgil. "Get them up! They are taking off."

Some of the Huntsmen scattered, not wanting to continue, but those who did, pushed the Rovers back onto their sides. They gave chase over the hillside as the Shepherd caught up to the runaway cars, his steps at first a blur of silver and black, then turning to long bounds. He came to the side of Darion's jeep and looked in.

"Keep on ahead," said the Shepherd. "Lead them north on the dirt trail. There is a valley coming soon. We will lose them there."

"Can't you just take out their Rovers?"

"It's not the Rovers I am concerned with now."

The Shepherd's eyes pointed behind and Darion looked in his rear view mirror. It was the Adversary, but there were dozens of them. They were packed together; a conglomeration of black lions with red eyes and wings. Some were flying and others running along the ground in a cloud of black.

"Oh my God..." said Darion. "I've never seen – "

The Shepherd abruptly stopped and began fending off the Adversary. The beasts slashed and jumped at them from all directions but the Shepherd dodged and blasted back.

"Shouldn't we help him?" said Felix, looking back.

"How might you do that?" asked Darion.

"Shepherd, give us something to fight with."

The Shepherd, in mid-battle, released a disc from his forearm. He jumped ahead and handed off the disc to Felix, who took it in hand and trembled.

"Wow..." he said, the rush of Solfire filling his body. The disc clamped to his wrist and a light weapon appeared. Then Felix stood and shot at the Adversary like he'd done it a hundred times before. A golden ray struck the beast, hitting it cleanly and scattering it into many pieces. Felix yelled triumphantly.

"That's good! Keep it up!" shouted Darion.

Jack kept his head low in the jeep, Olivia next to him. Felix was doing well, but the Rovers were closing in. For being such large vehicles, they were remarkably fast and the terrain was helping them. The road was primitive so the Rovers had little trouble managing the earth-made potholes that lied in their path. Their engines were not powered by electricity so Darion knew he had little time to outrun them. He had to, lest the Darklight consume their batteries. They would most certainly catch up to them and Darion calculated that it wouldn't be much longer till they did.

"Where are you taking us?" said Darion. "They're going to catch us!"

As Darion said the words, the trail veered to the left, revealing a slanted drop and a valley on their right side. Jack and the others held tight; the other jeeps close behind. The Rovers made the turn easily as Felix continued his assault.

"Persistent bastards, aren't they?" shouted Felix.

Felix turned his blaster on a Rover and fired. The light beam cut open the Rover like paper and the Rover toppled like its front half was disintegrating into the Earth.

"Woo!" shouted Felix. "You like that?"

Then a bullet struck his shoulder and he wailed, falling back into the jeep.

"Are you hit?" shouted Darion

"I think it only grazed me," answered Felix, but the blood was escaping his body fast. Olivia breathed hard, trying not to panic. The Adversary would sense this. It would know Felix had been hit. She looked behind and saw the Adversary's face, its red eyes and fanged mouth huffing at their heels. Its head split in two, multiplying itself as it rode up to trap them between. Darion saw it and jerked to the side, slamming unexpectedly into the Adversary. The Adversary lost its footing and fell flat to the dirt.

Did I actually *hit* it?

Darion turned his wheel to the other side, knocking into the Adversary. *Yes.* This thing has mass. It's made of something, isn't it? It *can* be hit if I want to hit it. That was it. Darion resolved his will to be the key; that his desire to not be overtaken could strike against the Adversary if he wanted to. His *will* could affect the monster

"Don't like that, do you?" he shouted. "You can't have us!"

"Nice work!" said Felix. "Keep hitting that thing."

When the Adversary retreated, Darion could see there was only one jeep left with them. The others must have taken a different path. Or suffered a fate he was yet unaware of. But, the Shepherd was with them. He was still running alongside their car, battling off the Adversary and deflecting enemy fire. The last jeep, Darion noticed, had Sophia and Robert inside, with Robert at the wheel. And there was the child, Turk, with them. They had survived this, somehow, and Darion was leading the way. They could do it. They could get away. They just needed a little more time.

And yet, the Shepherd was losing. The Rovers had weeded out the Fellows' cars like wolves separating weaker prey from the herd. Or was Darion's jeep and the Shepherd their real objective? Where the Shepherd went, Virgil and the rest of the Hunt would follow. To have the Shepherd watching one's back was a blessing, but it also positioned Darion as a target. He was in more danger being *with* the Shepherd than without. He would have to save them then. Lead them out of danger with or without the Shepherd. He'd be the one responsible if they failed. So Darion pressed forward, eyeing the goal like there was a finish line waiting.

The road dipped, rose, and Darion swerved to one side. Then a bullet. As if directed by the Adversary itself, it came and hit Felix directly between the eyes and he fell limp inside the jeep. Darion lost control and hit the turn with speed that rocked the jeep and sent the car into a tailspin of dirt and dust, inevitably sending them into a barrel roll. Felix's loose body flew from the side window while Jack and Olivia hung inside by their seat buckles. Felix's body landed somewhere on the embankment and rolled steadily downward. The jeep itself was rolling towards the edge and would be crashing down the hill in moments. But, then it stopped – the Shepherd had grabbed hold of the axle and planted his feet firmly on the cliff's edge.

"Are you alright?" asked the Shepherd. His grip was firm, but his voice had worry in it.

"Felix!" shouted Jack, breathing hard. "Felix...he...."

"Are you alright?" asked the Shepherd again.

Olivia was fine, hanging inside her buckles but there was blood on the windows; possibly anyone's but hers. Then came the Adversary. Jack heard the beast rush upon the jeep, clawing at the Shepherd, who was now juggling between saving the jeep and defending his own life. The vehicle shook as Jack moved to the front seat to check on Darion.

"Darion?" he said. "Are you alright? Darion?"

No answer.

* * * *

Jack was wrong about the blood being his own. It was Darion's head that had caused the red spray on the dashboard – his head had been cut and was bleeding profusely. Jack pulled a piece of his own shirt away and shoved it over top of Darion's forehead. And there was more blood, possibly Felix's, but it most certainly wasn't Jack's.

The jeep shifted again, this time caused by the Shepherd trying to pull them back up. Jack climbed over Darion and opened the driver door. The Shepherd was there, holding on, but the Adversary had covered him. Its fangs were on his shoulders, in his legs and dug into his ribs and torso. Still, the suit seemed to be holding against the attack. But, the Shepherd was in obvious pain, trying hard not to let the jeep tumble over the edge. He looked like he was crying, like he might give out at any moment. Robert's jeep came barreling down the trail. Jack saw it. He and Robert locked eyes for a moment and Jack saw Robert's intent.

No, thought Jack. Keep going. Don't stop for us. Get away from this place as fast as you can. We have the Shepherd. He'll save us. Just *go*.

But, Robert slowed, his eyes fixed on Jack and the struggling Shepherd. Robert pressed on his brake and attempted to swerve around, but too late. The Rovers had caught them and it was the Captain at the forefront. He was seated atop his vehicle, staring down Jack. They too locked eyes and then both of them looked at Robert's jeep.

No, thought Jack. Me! Me! It's *me* you want! But, Virgil had chosen his target and the Rover unleashed a torrid of bullets upon Robert's vehicle, cutting the doors like needles through paper. The jeep sputtered and swerved, then slammed into the other side of the road.

The Shepherd looked at Jack, eyes weeping. Why didn't you help them? Why won't you help them now? Jack screamed, feeling helpless. He pulled himself out of the jeep and fell flat onto the ground. Let them all have me. Let them have me if they want me so badly. I'm sick of this. I'm so sick of everything.

"Jack," said the Shepherd "Get Darion and Olivia. I'm ending this."

There's still people alive? That's right, I know them. I need to help them. What else can I do? I can't stand to see this anymore.

* * * *

The Shepherd made one last heave and pulled the jeep back onto even ground. Then he threw the Adversary from his back and pushed the beast away from him. Darion stirred and Jack, with hand wrapped in cloth, pulled Darion out of the car. Olivia helped as best as she was able. They emerged from the driver side door, Darion's body and mind fighting for consciousness.

Then the Shepherd roared, a noise that terrified Jack and even the Adversary. Darion awoke at the sound, eyes fluttering. What was that? That wasn't human. Twin cannons sprouted on the Shepherd's arms and the silver giant began blasting at the Adversary, piercing the creature wherever it was densest. The monster howled back and slithered into the darkness of the curving road. The Rovers were turned round and headed for the Shepherd when he turned his weapons upon them. A thick line of gold fired past Jack and struck the Captain's Rover, slicing the vehicle in two. Virgil and his men fell from the Rover as it fell apart like a broken toy.

On the ground again, Darion felt half-awake. Olivia helped keep him stable beneath his arm and Jack held him for only as long as his single, working arm could. What was happening? Felix. Where was Felix? Shot. No, Felix had been *shot*. Oh God, Felix was dead. And now, there were all of them exposed, the Shepherd their only line of defense against the Hunt and its militia.

"There it is!" shouted Virgil, springing to his feet. "There it is! The power of Mars! That's what I've been *really* waiting for. How could you not want to use – "

Virgil hadn't even the time to say the words when the Shepherd fired and cut the second Rover in two as well. Jack fell to the ground in a heap. How could it do that? Was light being used like a sword? The Shepherd was showing a side of himself that was horrifying.

"You...," continued Virgil. "You have such *power*." The Shepherd's eyes turned upon Virgil. "You have all this power.... "

More Huntsmen took fire on the Shepherd, but the Shepherd retaliated swiftly and walked towards Virgil. Bodies fell to the ground, flailing like their eyes were being burned from their sockets. Virgil seemed to be unfazed.

"You put us in this place, Shepherd! A cage! A cage is what your people gave us!"

332 | J.C.L. Faltot

Darion suddenly became very afraid for the Captain. He didn't know why, or even how the emotion seemed to rise up in him, but something spoke of something horrible waiting to happen. Something terrifying was about to happen to the Captain.

"Can you experience *guilt,* Shepherd?" said Virgil. "It's a human emotion, you monster. Do the people of Mars even know it? If you can, the guilt you must feel is staggering."

The Shepherd was now within a few feet of the Captain. He stopped, looking down at Virgil, pitifully. The golden orbs and arm cannon were glowing radiantly. *Kill him,* Darion thought. And Jack thought it also. Kill him and be done with it. He doesn't deserve life. He deserves eternal darkness. And if you will, do it slowly. Make it last. Make him remember why he was so wrong. Why he was so unfit to live. Virgil continued his verbal assault, taunting the Shepherd like he wanted the worst death imaginable. The Shepherd raised his chin and looked about.

What's he doing? Why isn't he punishing him?

"So," said Virgil. "Is that how you intend to leave it? Is that how you intend to leave *me*? Truly, you – "

The Shepherd raised his hand and touched Virgil in the center of his forehead. Virgil stopped, body trembling, eyes shaking.

"I have searched your heart, Virgil Strathen," said the Shepherd. "*This* is what you want."

The Shepherd removed his hand and Virgil fell forward, catching himself just before he landed. He clutched his chest, heaving in and out with heavy breaths.

Now what? Darion thought. I've seen this before. Are you intending to treat him the same as the bounty hunters? Make him face every nightmare he's wrought while simultaneously bringing him to his knees in wonderment? What did you do this time?

Virgil slowly raised his head, a cold tremor pouring through him. Yet, it felt like someone had wandered up next to him. There was *something*. It was breathing, but its breath was not warm –it was ice-like. Virgil heard a shrill sound in the background. It grew into a murmur, then a hiss. It became more and more unpleasing, like a snake or a rabid animal was near. Virgil turned around quickly, expecting to see something there, but there was nothing. The feeling returned and he spun again. Nothing.

"What is this?" he said and stared at the Shepherd. The giant was silent. Virgil heard another noise: the trotting of feet, like hooves and he turned round to face it. Darion and Jack could see it now, as could Olivia. The Shepherd saw it too. It was the *Adversary*. And though it appeared as a wolf to Jack, a lion to Darion, and a stallion to Olivia, in the eyes of Virgil, the Adversary had become an even more hideous creation than any of the previous three's nightmares. And somehow, all three of them saw the Adversary the same as Virgil.

"Is that – " sputtered Virgil. "Is that *you*?"

Standing no more than a few yards from Virgil was a monster made of several different creatures. It had a goat's head, but the eyes faced forward and were as large as dinner plates. Its feet were like a vulture's and its body was thin and spiky. Its long neck twisted into the sky, as tall as the Shepherd and its stare - its eerie gaze - was unblinking. Yet there was one last horror upon this creature: in its hands it held the head of Virgil's deceased brother, Argus, whose eyes flickered and blinked independently of one another. Virgil tried to speak, but Argus' mouth opened and out from behind the tongue came worms and maggots. Virgil nearly vomited at the sight and stood, clutching his mouth and stomach.

"No..," said Virgil. "This cannot – "

"Be the 'voice' that led you?" said the Shepherd. "Yes, Virgil. They are one and the same. Now, you may see who you've been listening to."

Virgil took a step backward and the goat creature took one step with him. Virgil took another step and the creature followed him again. The goat tilted its head to one side, not making a sound. What is this thing? Is this the so-called Adversary? No, it can't be. But then, what else could it be? An agent of the Martian? The Shepherd's magic gone awry? Virgil swallowed and stepped away, the creature following him. He moved to the side and it followed. He turned slightly away and it hurried closer till he faced it completely again. It stood at attention, waiting for Virgil to move. *No.* It wants to be *near* me. It wants to be right next to *me*.

"Get away... get away...."

Blood and vomit spilled out of Argus' severed head. Virgil practically gagged again. He leaned over, hand covering his mouth as the anguish swept inside. His brother. My God, I killed my brother. And the others, I *killed* them too. They were like worms, maggots to him. And the maggots were landing on the ground, crawling towards him on the dirt road. They reached his leg and tried to crawl up his shin, but he kicked it away and stepped backward. The Adversary tracked with him, moving closer. He'd found the game out. If he took his eyes from the beast, then it would only get closer. He'd have to watch it. But how? Surely he couldn't watch it forever? Oh God, how do I get away?

More insects; this time centipedes and spiders, crawling towards Virgil. They each had voices, speaking to Virgil as though they were asking why he had killed them or given their lives for him. Their voices grew louder as they scaled Virgil and he tried to shake them off. They bit into his legs and arms and Virgil screamed. No, this thing *is* real? Wasn't it just a voice? Wasn't it only a *thought*? Virgil took his eyes from the Adversary for a moment and the creature leapt even closer to him.

"No!" he shouted. "Only a thought! Only an idea! That's all you are! Enough! Get away from me! I hate you! I hate you!"

Virgil tripped and landed on the ground. It wasn't ground though. It was covered with the insects and their voices were louder. 'Kill me again,' they said. 'Kill me as many times as you like!' They crawled over his legs, over his arms, and over his stomach. Virgil squirmed about, trying to stand but when he pushed against the dirt, he heard the crunch of insect shells and the screams of their voices calling out to him.

Darion, Jack, and Olivia stood in awe, frightened but in awe.

"Are you seeing this?" asked Jack but no one answered. The once proud and unshakable Captain of the Hunt was thrashing on the ground, clouds of Darklight hovering over his body, the Adversary closing in. The beast's attention was entirely set on Virgil. This was its newest prey and it was interested to see what its prey might do. So Jack and Darion watched as though they were hidden behind thick glass. They were protected, it seemed. Virgil stood and ran for the cliff.

"No! Get away from me!" yelled Virgil. "Get away! This isn't right! This isn't right! This is not the voice I heard!"

Virgil stumbled and fell again. He looked behind; the Adversary was so near. It was closing the distance. The head of Argus was spewing forth more vile creatures: half-eaten rats, decayed birds, and crabs with infectious growths. Virgil finally vomited, and the insects and other creatures scurried to eat it. They called to him, asking why he refused to give them something better than his own spew and Virgil vomited again. Virgil's eyes welled.

His whole body felt like it was emptying itself, but it would never be enough to satisfy whatever it was the Adversary wanted of him. He walked to the edge of the cliff and peered down at the valley. Virgil turned and saw the Adversary. It was right there. *Waiting.* It would never leave him. He knew it wouldn't. It would always be there. And so would these little monsters. He'd never be able to rid himself of them. He'd never be alone. He'd always be surrounded by this filth. How long had it been this way? He didn't know. He couldn't think. He only wanted to escape. It's what he'd always wanted. To escape *everything*. There were none that could help him; there were none who understood him. Only the Shepherd, though it was by his hand he'd been cursed. Surely, the Shepherd would not take pity on him now. His time was done. It was more than what he deserved; it was what he'd wanted all along. Virgil took one last look at the Shepherd, his eyes pleading for sympathy, but the Shepherd turned his gaze from him.

"Death to Mars," said Virgil. "Death to them all for what you've done."

Then Virgil jumped from the cliff. But, the Adversary followed, leaping down after him. Even in death, the creature would not let him leave. And when Virgil landed, his body did not break completely. So the Adversary's spawn, the hundreds of insects and other foul beasts that had birthed from the head of Argus, feasted on Virgil's remains, sucking up the death that was killing his flesh and ultimately, his soul. Virgil writhed, but only in his mind, for his body was broken and could no longer utter a sound that might reflect the torment that was taking place on the inside. It was here that Virgil perished along the mountainside. His burial was hardly the site of a revered Captain.

Back on the dirt path, the Shepherd was inspecting the second jeep. He found the bloodied mess that was Robert, Sophia, and Turk and paused like he was taking a moment of silence. Olivia stepped forward. She was aware that Turk had been in the other jeep, but Darion held her back. Don't look, sweetie. This isn't meant for your eyes. The Shepherd laid his hands inside the jeep and then backed away slowly.

Not even you can resurrect the dead, can you? Darion thought. Even the Shepherd must have his limitations.

The Shepherd turned, looked upon Darion and the others. They were the last, it seemed – the survivors. What would he say to them? What words did he have for them after enduring such an atrocity? Darion, Jack, and Olivia waited like the Shepherd would have some offer of consolation. Perhaps there *was* a suitable phrase or word of encouragement waiting just behind the Shepherd's lips? Something to learn? *Say something*, Darion thought. *Anything*. But, the Shepherd didn't. He simply walked over to them, body blotting out the sun as it descended on the western side of the valley. He seemed determined, almost apathetic considering what had happened.

"We still have to find my ship," said the Shepherd. "Come."

And they followed without question. The end of the journey had to be near.

Chapter 20
The Shepherd's Ship

* * * *

Darion poked at a slab of fish; its body cooking above the Shepherd's disc in the twilight.

"Do you want some more, Jack?" asked Darion.

Jack shook his head.

Suit yourself, Darion thought.

Behind Jack, the Shepherd stood on guard. He was atop the balls of his feet and scanning the horizon like always. Darion smirked. Despite everything that had happened, it was the one thing Darion could count on every night: the Shepherd would not sleep. The Shepherd would not speak unless spoken to and finally, the Shepherd would stand guard so long as he, Jack, or Olivia were awake. And for the first time since the trio had begun their journey, this truth bothered Darion in ways he could not express. The Shepherd had remained inhumanly casual; apathetic in light of the past few days. The Shepherd had hardly spoken of the Hunt's subtle massacre at the Red Fellows' Cathedral and the Shepherd seemed to offer little explanation as to why his recuperation had taken so long, thus, costing dozens of people their lives. And instead of reparation, there was only empty space between the Shepherd and his followers. Even Jack, usually so full of questions or inquiries, was relatively dull; numb, to a point. His mind seemed to have retreated deep within himself and was refusing to come out. This too, Darion found, troubled him as much as the Shepherd's emotional distance.

Have we done our part yet? Darion thought. How much longer will we have to endure this?

It was three days since they'd escaped the Hunt, but the ghost of past events lingered. For one, Darion and Jack's wounds had healed, but the Shepherd was not nearly as concerned as times prior. Where the Shepherd had helped in the past, he kept himself at bay, monitoring their progress rather than intervening with supernatural means. This was also strange. For two, Darion could feel Olivia's curiosity over what had become of her friend, Turk. Darion knew she was likely aware of the boy's death, yet Darion dared not speak of or bring the topic up. His daughter's refusal to speak had worked as a cruel favor for Darion. Though this realization pained him to admit it in the quiet of his own mind. Thirdly, there was Jack. His hand had healed, but his cough had returned. He hacked in uneven intervals and Darion began to wonder if something might be seriously wrong with Jack. So Darion thought of asking the Shepherd to heal Jack, but the Shepherd's disinterest seemed to answer the question for him. Again, this troubled Darion. Like this new behavior was something in need of investigating. Something he shouldn't miss or ignore. Was this another test on behalf of the Shepherd? He resolved himself to do so sooner than later, when the time was right and communication felt more open.

And lastly, there were the *others*. The ones they'd left behind; the people at the Cathedral and on the dirt road. Both places had no doubt become nothing more than an unsettling graveyard, waiting to be found by Runners or wandering drifters. Perhaps some of the Hunt, the ones who had survived, had gone back to the Cathedral and inspected the ship beneath the hillside. Perhaps they might find something worth cultivating there. Greta was there, the girl in the chamber. Did the Shepherd care to return and ensure her safety? Or was she doomed to stay inside Mars' tank forever? Darion had no idea. She could be dead already. Or taken by the Hunt. Every loose end played on Darion, agonizing him as their group moved forward without any regard of regard for turning back.

Had anyone survived besides them? There was one who may have. Not a full-fledge Fellow, but one of their party. After Virgil's leap, the four of them headed down the cliff side and into the valley. They looked but couldn't find the body of Felix anywhere. It was as if he'd never been with them.

"What do you think happened to him?" asked Darion.

The Shepherd was mute. He bent to one knee and touched the soil with his finger. When he stood, he looked to the horizon and stared. There was no grin or smile like usual, he merely peered off into the sunset and then turned back towards Darion.

"He's far from us now. I don't suspect he'll be returning."

Then there was the body of the Captain. Darion hid Olivia's eyes on approach. Mangled and twisted, it scarcely resembled a human any longer. The hands and arms were contorted in improbable directions and the head was bent in a position only one who had died could imitate. Even his eyes were open in a demonic posture. The beaded gray eyes of the Captain, the proud captain, were open wide like they were frozen that way, an expression that spoke of shock as much as it spoke of perverted gladness. Darion hated the sight. But, Jack hated it enough to act and when the Shepherd turned his back to the Captain, Jack kicked a tuft of dirt on one of the Captain's hands. He muttered under his breath, detailing how he would stab right through the Captain's heart, again and again, until there was no more blood left inside. Only then would the crimes be good and paid for.

"Was he ever your friend?" asked Darion.

"I don't..." said Jack, words struggling to make sense before they left his lips. "He had been, chief. Now, I don't know how. Other than we needed each other to survive. That was our only bond. Now, I wish he'd come alive again so I could kill him one more time."

"I don't blame you, Jack."

"For what?"

"For thinking that. I'd hate him too."

From then on, they walked in silence and when the evening came, Jack would cry. He seemed unable to control it, for when the night fell, it burst forth like a waterfall. Jack hid his tears as best he could, but Darion and naturally, the Shepherd, heard his silent whimpers. It was on this first night, when Jack sobbed and the Shepherd did not offer any consolation, that Darion first took note of the Shepherd's odd conduct. Had even the Shepherd chosen isolation now? Was the final leg of their journey meant for this? To strip them of community and fellowship?

Darion's goal – his endgame for Mars– began to feel secondary under the mournful sobs of Jack, who routinely curled into a ball and kept his face concealed on frequent stops. Shouldn't Jack's emotional state be dealt with? That's what the Shepherd would *normally* do. It's what Darion had learned he'd do. Yet, there was nothing. And Darion dared not engage Jack himself; fearful of what lied underneath. There could still be feelings of resentment there, a wound Darion had no bandage for and if provoked, Jack may lash out at him with. Best to wait it out. See if Jack wants to talk first, he decided. But moreover, see what the Shepherd might do; if he'd do *anything* at all.

Olivia, too, was worried for Jack. She watched him more than her father did and thought of what she might say to him if he tried to talk to her. Would she speak if spoken to?

Yet, when she took her eyes from Jack, she thought of Turk. Had he somehow survived? She drew his picture in the dirt once but her father didn't understand. Rather, he refused to. That's when she mourned for him. In silence, she did, not letting her father see; or Jack, not even the Shepherd.

But, Darion *did* notice. So it was then, on the third night, with salmon cooking in front of their faces and the Shepherd as distant as the moon, Darion decided to break the silence on many things.

"None of this is your fault, Jack," said Darion and Jack's head perked up. *There you are, kid*, thought Darion. *I knew you were still in there.*

"None of this, you hear me?" continued Darion. "Everything that's happened so far. The Hunt... the Captain... Felix, Robert, Sophia – none of it has anything to do with *you*, all right? I don't know if that's what you're thinking about, but I thought you should know that it isn't your fault. You hear me?"

Jack took a deep breath and exhaled. He wiped his mouth like he had a lot to say. "I don't know what to say to that," he said.

"Don't say anything then," said Darion. "Just know that it's true."

Jack was quiet for a time and Darion thought his words had helped Jack. Brought him out of emotional hiding.

"I was an orphan, remember?" said Jack, suddenly, and Darion nodded. "And so were *they*. All of them."

"The Fellows?" said Darion.

"No, the Hunt *and* the Fellows."

"How do you mean?"

"It doesn't matter anymore."

"It matters now that you brought it up," said Darion. "Might as well say why."

Jack hesitated. He looked away from Darion like the conversation was already over. He was through. So Darion returned to the food when Jack started talking again.

"When you're an orphan, you live for the day," said Jack and he looked into Darion's eyes. "You know nothing other than hunger and the day. That's it. There's not much else, man." Jack paused like the conversation were open-ended, but Darion waited anyway.

"So, when you find something you can rely on," said Jack. "Something that makes you think more than two days ahead of yourself, you start to see things differently. You don't think you're an orphan anymore. You have a *home*. And you make yourself believe that the loneliness is over. That you'll never be the way you were ever again. The world has finally done something on your behalf and you can stop being so angry or crossed up about everything."

Darion sensed Jack's anger rising up. He leaned back slightly.

"But, not everybody finds their home at the same time. And the ones who don't find it, they'll take yours if they can. That's the difference in people, I figure. The ones who find a home have to guard theirs. And the ones who don't, well, they have to fight for it."

"So long as the cause is noble, you may fight for it, Jack."

"Was the Hunt's fight 'noble', chief?"

Darion shook his head.

"Heh, *exactly*." Jack looked like a powder keg about to burst. Darion swallowed, afraid he'd said the wrong thing.

"Who decides what's noble anyway, chief? *Him*?" said Jack and he pointed to the Shepherd, expecting the silver giant to respond but he didn't. So Jack turned towards Darion again.

"No?" said Jack. "I guess nothing's noble, is it? My version, your version - *his* version. More opportunities for fault. That's all it is." Jack stopped and looked at Olivia. She was terrified with his rage. Her blue eyes were wide, unblinking and staring at Jack, hinging on every last word from his lips. Then Jack imagined saying how Turk had been slaughtered in cold blood. He imagined Olivia's reaction, the harsh reality of knowing her friend was no longer alive. It would be right to give her that peace, wouldn't it? Was it *noble* to tell her the truth? She still didn't know, he figured. No, she *had* to know. She wasn't stupid even if she was still a kid. No, not even a kid. She had seen and experienced things that no kid should have. But, at least she wasn't an orphan. She had her father. That was better than nothing. But, a child? No, that identity was killed a long time ago.

"I just can't take it anymore," said Jack. "I'd rather be an orphan again. I'd rather just live for the day and take it as it comes. I don't want to remember anything anymore."

Jack tucked his head between his legs and tears came quickly. Olivia reached for Jack but Darion held her back. Then he reached into his bag and pulled the photos from his bag.

"Jack," said Darion. "There's a reason I've had those discs all this time Here, look at these."

Jack raised his head. There were several photographs waiting in Darion's outstretched hands so Jack took them. He began to sift through slowly, looking at each one for a few seconds. They were of Darion and Olivia, pictures in the old city and in other places too. There were skylines, horizons, and wooded areas. There was nothing overly spectacular in any of them; nothing of special note, and it was clear that Darion was not a skilled photographer. Much of the shots looked like impulse pictures, taken because he needed to use the film or fill some space. But, then, near the end, Jack found something unique: it was Darion, Olivia, and a woman. Only she looked just like Olivia, but older. Her long blond hair was mature and thick and her eyes were like Olivia's, but again, older. Jack looked at Darion.

"Your wife?"

Darion nodded. "Yes, her name was Lydia."

Jack recalled the name from his time spelunking through Darion's backpack. He closed his eyes, ashamed of doing it.

"What happened to her?" asked Jack.

Olivia's eyes drooped and Jack immediately regretted the question. He hadn't bothered to ask what kind of person she had been; her likes or dislikes - the only thing he thought to ask was why she was in this picture and not with them now. Stupid.

"It's okay, Liv," said Darion. "I'll tell you, Jack."

Darion leaned in and told the story of his life: He talked about his wife, Lydia, and how she'd been taken by one of the Shepherds almost six months ago. He spoke of how a Shepherd had come to their town and announced that some of them would be going to Mars. On the outside, it seemed like a reason to rejoice – to know that you'd be escaping this place. But, when the Shepherd made his choice on who was to go, he only picked Lydia. There would be no one else. Darion and Olivia weren't allowed to leave. But, the Shepherd vowed to return someday and Darion decided to find every remnant of Mars tech he could in hopes of attracting a Shepherd back to their town. At about the same time, Olivia stopped speaking. There was nothing more to the story after that. Darion ended his tale and poked at the fish lying prostrate in mid-air. Jack heard every word of Darion's story, but he wanted more. The way Darion told it, the Shepherds sounded more like kidnappers than saviors. He sighed and peered over his shoulder like the Shepherd might have heard them.

"Does my story not satisfy you?" asked Darion.

"I don't know," said Jack. "I just... I don't know. I'm sorry."

"It's fine," said Darion. "It's why I keep going, Jack. She's up there right now. She's up there looking down at us. So I know it's not like I'm staring off into some imaginary space like I'll never see her again or have put all my hopes on a star that I might get lucky some day. No, this is an *actual* place I'm going to. Mars is a real haven and she's there too, waiting for me. Waiting for her daughter. I just hope she knows us when she sees us."

Jack digested the story and laid back. Darion put the photos back into his knapsack, content with ending their conversation.

But, Jack wasn't through.

"Did I ever tell you I killed someone?" said Jack and Darion about spit his food from his mouth.

"You *what?*"

"I killed someone, man," repeated Jack, this time with less surprise in his voice. "About 10 years ago, I did. I just remembered. It would be about 10 years ago to the day. I was fifteen at the time. I had to do it though. Had to."

Darion's mind buzzed. Jack? A *murderer?* The way Jack said it, it sounded like it were second nature.

"I don't follow, Jack...."

"I don't know what I'm saying, man. I just felt like I should tell you. That's all."

Darion was silent for a moment. No use in moving Olivia farther away from Jack, right? Here, a dangerous man had shared their quarters for weeks. More than just a thief - a *killer.* Darion took a short breath and then asked, "Why'd you kill someone, Jack? Why did you do it?"

Jack sat up and Darion felt like he'd asked too deep a question. Jack's eyes were watered and depressed. The 'why' was a question Jack didn't want to be asked, was it? The 'why' meant the memories and the experience had to be relived - had to be retold and remade no matter how deep they were buried. Jack could have been venting, not wanting Darion's input. But, now? Jack's vault was coming open.

"It was either me or him," said Jack, matter-of-factly. "He probably thought my life was the one in danger, but turned out, he just didn't know *his* life was in danger at the time too. Probably never crossed his mind. Otherwise he wouldn't have done it."

"Was he stealing something from you?"

"No, it wasn't even that, chief," said Jack. "He wanted my *chair*. Can you believe that? It's so incredibly stupid when I say it out loud like that. All these years and I never once said it out loud. And now that I am, God... it makes me sound even more ridiculous."

Jack paused, let out a short laugh like he was cutting the tension. Clearly, this was hurting Jack, but it was also liberating for him too, Darion figured. *Just don't interrupt,* Darion thought. There's no way in knowing what else might come out of him now. So Jack went on and Darion listened.

"I told him he couldn't have my chair," said Jack. "And he didn't like that very much so he pulled a knife on me. Only he didn't know I had a knife of my own. And when he came at me, I came at him. Then the next thing I knew, it was over."

Darion swallowed. That was it? Darion almost felt half-cheated by the story. Surely there was more than 'then it was over.' Yet Jack, the one who held all the details inside, looked at Darion like he was about to vomit. The memory seemed to be alive in his mind again. His face became pale and he rubbed his hands together like he was taking his mind off the puke settling in his throat.

"I'm sorry, Jack. I don't know what to say...."

"Say nothing then," said Jack.

"Maybe you just needed to tell somebody, Jack?" said Darion. "Get whatever it was out of you and move on."

Jack nodded slightly. "Is it so bad a thing?"

"What is?"

"Telling other people the worst parts of yourself?"

Darion paused. More than a kid. More than a thief. Jack had been a *murderer*, but only out of self defense, it seemed. Or so goes the story. Was Jack looking for empathy now - asking Darion if it were a bad thing to share after so much time? This wasn't a confessional, but Darion felt like he were in one. He knew Jack was searching, leaning on some hopeful understanding that what he'd done did not define him. And when Darion looked into Jack's eyes again, he saw that fifteen-year old inside of Jack come running to the surface, eyes wide and pleading for a response. 'Tell me why it had to happen,' they seemed to say. But, Darion didn't have a good answer.

"You were only fifteen?" asked Darion. "I remember that age myself. It's frightening when you're that young and don't know how the world works yet.."

"I knew how it worked by then," said Jack. "I just didn't want to work within it. The knife I had - that knife made me strong; made me *brave*, I guess. But when the time came to use it and I did, it made me feel weak. So I threw it away. I didn't want to feel that way ever again."

"Were you ever caught? Murder is – "

Darion trailed off. Crimes having to do with murder were handled differently depending on the district. Jack just shook his head. "No one cares about the lost boys, chief," said Jack. "I don't think I need to explain that one to you, do I? Not enough people anyway. If one of us went missing, starved, or got lost, then nobody would put forth the effort to find out the reason why. Nobody had to. God, when I say it out loud, it sounds even worse than what it does in my head…."

Darion waited.

Then, "Did you know his name?"

"No, never did. I think it's better that way too. To not know, I mean. If I knew, then…well, I don't know. Having a name attached to a face might make it harder to sleep at night. So I prefer to not know. Until I die, I'll take the price, whatever it is, for not knowing."

"I'm sorry, Jack. That all sounds awful."

"It's different than shooting someone," said Jack, surprising Darion as though Jack had done that too. How many people had Jack *tried* to murder? Darion leaned back and thought of the moments when Jack could have pulled his trigger and killed him. It frightened Darion and an eerie sense of insecurity came over him. Like, someone had informed him that someone had been watching him while he slept. Yet, why bring up the topic of shooting people?

"How many people have you killed, Jack?" asked Darion.

Jack tilted his head and cocked an eyebrow. "I'm not some mass murderer. I killed someone once. That's what I said."

"That doesn't really answer my question, Jack."

"No more than the one, if ya just have to know. Happy?"

"Not really."

Again, there was an uncomfortable pause between them.

"But sometimes I wonder...." said Jack.

"About what?"

"I wonder how many I *haven't* killed. That's a number I'd like to know."

Darion didn't quite understand Jack's logic. He wanted to stay on point. "You've made your choices just like the rest of us and you've survived. Isn't that enough to live off of?"

"Is it?" Jack retorted. "The more I think about it, the more I feel like we kill people every day. Without even thinking about it, we do."

Where are you going with this, Jack? Darion thought.

"We tell them we like them, but inside, we hate them," said Jack, his voice pleading. "Isn't that the same as killing someone?"

What is this? Are you trying to talk about *our* relationship? Or was he talking about someone else?

"What do you mean by that, Jack?"

"If someone does something to you, you'll remember it for next time, won't you? But, unless you allow that person back, they're forever murdered inside of you. They can never reach you and you can never reach them. Isn't that right?"

"Once someone is dead, they're dead, Jack. Otherwise they're not. There's nothing else to consider. That's obvious."

"But, is it? I know the difference is obvious — you know, the physical side of things — but then there's the *soul*. It's in there, isn't it? I mean, we all have one, don't we?"

All these questions. Darion wished the Shepherd to step in, say something that might answer Jack on his behalf. Surely, the deaths of the Fellows had caused something to stir in Jack; forced him to reevaluate every aspect of his life. *So this is what's been stewing in you all these days?* Darion thought. And he straightened his posture to look at Jack more intently.

"The human soul is a complicated matter, Jack," said Darion, sounding as though he knew. "Humanity has no shortage of explanations for the soul and where it comes from. Some believe the soul keeps coming back, turning into new things every time it chooses to return. Others believe souls are one-time deals, and you either go to hell or you go to heaven when you die. While others put their faith in prophets; believing as though their prophet's lives hold the key to finding the soul inside. And of course, there's the last option: no soul at all. A lot of people believe this. They believe there's nothing but the person. Nothing more underneath. That's it."

Darion paused, letting the information seep in. Then, "You just have to choose which one suits you the best, Jack. That's the best I can tell you on the matter."

Jack hesitated. Then, "Which one suits *you?*"

Darion was caught off guard. *Interesting,* he thought. Which version *did* appeal to Darion most? What *did* he believe? Darion realized he hadn't considered either for some time. Ever since the Pulse, Darion found Mars to be his only truth. He knew he had to get there, or else he would die. Soul or no soul. Did anything else matter? No, it didn't seem so. Yet Darion did not let Jack's question cause him duress.

"I suppose the one that suits me," said Darion. "Is the one that helps me get to where I'm going. I think that's the real purpose behind any religion. It's supposed to help the person in some way."

"Is there a specific one that's best?"

Again, Darion didn't know to answer. So he presented all the knowledge he had of old religions; the pros, the cons - *anything* to help Jack answer the question for himself. Darion spoke of purgatory; he spoke of 'soul sleep', and he discussed the never-ending cycle of life and death as described in Hindu ideology. Jack heard them all, internalizing Darion's every explanation as it came. But, at the end of Darion's dissertation, Jack's mind was still restless.

"What do you think of the dead?" asked Jack.

"The *dead?*"

"Yeah."

"I don't know, really," said Darion. "The thought of death frightens me more than the dead themselves. That's kid's games, if you ask me. I don't look forward to death either. Can anybody?"

Jack looked at Olivia. She was sitting there, absorbing everything. "I think that sometimes the dead affect us more than the living," said Jack. "But not because they're dead, it's because they're still alive inside us. I guess I used to fear death – fear the dead – but I don't really anymore. I don't know if I could be afraid of anything anymore. No matter what waits for me once this is all over."

It's too much for you, isn't it? Darion thought. It's just *too* much. Had it not been for Darion and Olivia's paths crossing with Jack, he'd likely be dead by now. Or drunk, ready to die somewhere, Darion figured. Jack was a survivor, but he wasn't someone who could make it to the end. This journey had broke him. And Darion knew he didn't have to worry about Jack's involvement with this trek any longer. So he reached out and touched the top of Jack's head, rubbing his hair gently. It was softer than he thought it would be. Poor kid. We're nearly there too. But, not everyone is meant to see the last scene, are they?

Darion looked up and saw the Shepherd staring back at him. *How long have you been watching us?* Darion thought. *How long have you been hearing this?* The Shepherd's eyes squinted, a glint of gladness appeared like he was proud of Darion; overjoyed to see Darion comforting Jack. But, Darion did not feel the same as the Shepherd.

You could have been the one doing this, Darion thought. *Don't you see how much he's suffered? Why have you done nothing to help him?*

So Darion removed his hand from Jack's head and held Olivia close to him. Not long now. We'll be away from here soon. Far from Earth. Far from death. Far from the confusion this place brings us.

* * * *

Jack pulled his feet close to his body. He thought of Ianna; how she'd told him the secret of the Darklight and the illusion they were all under. And he remembered her beauty. Oh, he remembered it. He thought of Abraham, staring up at him. First, as a victim beneath Jack's fists and later, as a protector; staring down at Jack this time, urging him to forget his pride and move on. They were so much better than him yet they were the ones who died. Were they just not afraid to die? Is that why death found them? Or was it because no one could protect them? Jack couldn't protect them. He couldn't save them. And young Turk - Jack had failed him too. *You failed them all, Jack*, he thought and all at once, Jack began to cry again, cursing himself over and over until he was too tired to cry any longer. Then he slept.

The next morning, Jack awoke and saw that Darion and Olivia were already up and moving about. He'd overslept, but he felt rested; eyes caked under dried tears. No matter though. It was the best sleep he'd had in days. His cough was gone too. He looked about and saw the Shepherd was missing also.

"He said he'd be back soon," said Darion, answering Jack's questioning eyes. "I guess that's supposed to mean something to us."

Olivia peered into the woods. *You're out helping someone again, aren't you? But, you're taking a long time. Don't be gone too long, please.*

"How much farther do you think?" asked Jack.

Darion shrugged, looked away from Jack. *Did I share too much last night?* Jack thought. Then the Shepherd came walking back, his body wet and covered in water or perspiration.

"Go for a swim?" asked Darion.

The Shepherd, for the first time in days, smiled. "I did," he said. "There is a large stream close to here. I had to inspect it. With a splash, of course."

No one laughed but the Shepherd's smile made everyone less tense. The silver giant closed his eyes and raised his nose to the wind. "One day left for us. I think it will be one more day."

Darion took a deep breath.

It would end up being one more day. But, first, the Shepherd led the trio up the side of the stream, following its trail for several hours and stopping only twice. He purified the water by its edge and gave it to Darion, Jack, and Olivia to drink. Their conversation began to open up again. They did not talk of the incident, preferring to reminisce on other things. Olivia waded out into the water at one point and skipped stones through the center. Darion and Jack watched while the Shepherd went out and joined her. He stood next to Olivia, towering over her like an oak would a sapling. He bent down and touched the water; a tiny ripple of gold appeared and pushed the water aside. It made a cylinder of empty space and Olivia could see her feet at the bottom. She looked up at the Shepherd and smiled.

"Do you think Mars has scenery like this?" asked Jack.

"They live in domes, Jack," said Darion, wiping his hands in the water. "It's not like what we have here. Their cities are giant domes, insulated from the atmosphere on Mars. It's nothing like Earth, but still, it's better."

"That's not so bad, I guess."

Darion shook his head. "Not bad, but not the best. Though I'm sure that by now, the people of Mars have realized that Mars isn't even the ultimate goal. I'm sure they've understood that Mars isn't the endgame."

"What do you mean?"

"It's all the planets we *haven't* touched yet, Jack. It's those worlds beyond Mars. The ones still waiting to be discovered by human travelers. They're out there, Jack. And they'll be better than Earth even, I assure you."

Jack could scarcely imagine what that would be like. He hadn't thought beyond Mars. This place was hard, but it had been his home. If he stayed with the Shepherd, he'd be getting a new home and perhaps another after that. Did that appeal to him? Perhaps it wasn't up to him to decide. Jack looked up and saw the Shepherd playing with Olivia and in that moment, tried to imagine a similar scenario somewhere else. Only he couldn't. Not even on Mars. Everything was in its place here. The image of sunlight breaking the tree line, illuminating the blond edges of Olivia's hair and darkening the many tones of the Shepherd's muscles - it was all very picturesque. and Jack was admiring its beauty. Every color and shape melded flawlessly together, made possible by the sun's advancing light. What of Mars then? Were these domes as transparent as the sky itself? Would the sun's rays trickle through layers of foliage like they did on Earth? If so, then Jack hoped it would be just like this. Like Ianna too. Then Jack sobbed again, wiping his face before tears burst forth.

Soon, they were on the move again. The Adversary was nowhere to be seen. And no one spoke of the Adversary either. The sun stayed high and the clouds were parted so it was hot but not humid. A little sliver of light gave them energy and they didn't stop in the afternoon like they normally would. When evening began to close in, the Shepherd picked a cave by a hillside and instructed the group to stay there. This would be their last night together. The Shepherd announced it, pronouncing that the time was coming. The ship was near.

"Good night, Jack."

"Good night, chief."

* * * *

Olivia hardly slept through the night. There was a strange nervousness among the group and she couldn't discern if that meant excitement or fear. She was normally adept at understanding her father's nonverbal, but tonight? She felt off. Like, Darion had veiled something from her. Even the Shepherd was strangely silent. A new type of hushed focus enveloped the silver giant and Olivia wondered what he might be thinking. And then there was Jack - sitting at the corner of the cave, drawing caricatures on the walls with pointy rocks. He loved doing that, Olivia concluded. Wherever they traveled, Jack would find time to scratch out things in the dirt or stone. Tonight, it was people or something close to it. Beneath the light of the Shepherd's disc, Olivia watched. There appeared to be four in total, one much larger than the others, which she took as the Shepherd. Jack didn't stop at that, he continued to draw more characters; huddling them on the outskirts of the Shepherd. They appeared to be sitting or standing under a hillside. Were these their friends from the white building? Olivia looked for Turk. She found him, she thought, a smaller picture near the bottom and holding hands with a larger one. They were all of them together, on the wall, written by Jack's hand. That *was very nice,* she thought. Then Olivia smiled and fell asleep.

* * * *

In the morning, Jack was again late in waking. The sun's light had already pushed itself deep into the cave and covered Jack's face. Olivia was leaning against the opposite wall yet both Darion *and* the Shepherd were missing. Even the discs had gone. Jack stood up quickly, fearing some sort of premature abandonment, and walked outside the cave. Was it safe to leave Olivia here? Outside, Jack heard a rumble coming from the other side of the hill so he moved towards it. He paused for a moment, looking back at Olivia, before deciding to investigate.

She'll be fine. Find out what's going on first, he thought.

Jack walked round the corner and came to a thick section of brush. He pushed through, seeing that there was something on the other side. The hum was growing louder. He could see a gray silhouette through the foliage. It was sharp, bright, and huge but it wasn't the Shepherd. At the edge of the brush, he saw an open field. And there, seated at the center of the open land, was it: the Shepherd's ship.

Jack was amazed. The ship hovered in mid-air, a triangular-shaped vehicle with slick edges and a shining exterior. The entire ship didn't even look metallic, it shined and reflected sunlight like it was made of glass. The low hum must have been its engine, he decided. It floated above what looked like a hole in the ground, its original landing site, perhaps. Jack looked about; there was no landing strip or signs of duress on the terrain. The ship had simply planted itself in the ground here, maybe even come *out* of it based on what he could see. But, there was no Shepherd, no Darion. There was no one anywhere. Were they already inside? Had they already begun to leave? Jack took some steps forward before he was grabbed from behind and he spun around quickly.

"Get back here, Jack," said a voice and Jack knew it to be Darion.

"What's going on? Where is the Shepherd? What are you doing?"

"Quiet!" whispered Darion, firmly. "He's underneath the ship. Keep your voice down, boy."

Jack examined Darion. He was sweating. On his wrist was one of the Shepherd's discs, transformed into a bracelet. It was strapped to his arm and though Darion was holding a part of it, the disc appeared to be hurting Darion. Like it was squeezing *him*.

"What is that?" asked Jack.

"One of the Shepherd's discs, of course," said Darion. "But, it belongs to me now."

"What?"

"I took it last night, Jack. I didn't know if I could, but since we were close, I had to try. And it paid off, Jack. Oh, it paid off." Darion's eyes were wide and red, like he was drunk or inebriated. Jack became afraid looking at Darion.

"You see," said Darion. "I figured out how these things work. They respond to the one with the greatest *will power*. That's how all of this works, Jack. The Solfire, the Darklight – it's all tied to human *will*. Every weapon, every ship, every device they've ever made with Mars tech, it all started with human will. Do you know why?"

Jack shook his head. He could scarcely recognize Darion as he was now. The cool and soft-spoken man from a night ago was replaced with this alter ego, it seemed. The *real* Darion was here. Or was this yet another alternative version of Olivia's father?

"Because human will, Jack," said Darion. "Is the most powerful thing in the universe. Will changes everything. A choice, a change in direction, it all starts with *will*. And if I can convince these discs to do what I want them to, then I can do anything. Do you understand? It's so simple, isn't it?"

Jack was confused, even if he was following Darion's logic. Then why? What was Darion doing that required him to manipulate something? Unless.

The Shepherd appeared. He rose up from underneath the ship, climbing out of the hole beneath. He scanned the horizon, staring up at the sky like he were intent on going there soon and turned round to inspect his ship. He crouched on one knee and set to working on something, but Jack and Darion couldn't see what it was. His back faced them and seeing this, Darion began to stand.

"Where are you going?" asked Jack. "Are you – "

"Stay here, Jack. Don't move and don't make a sound. You don't have to watch if you don't want to."

"Watch what? Darion, I don't know what's going on…."

"Why do you think my wife was the only one to go all those months ago? Huh? It's because the Shepherd only takes *one* back with him, Jack. That's what they always do. They come here only looking for *one* of us to take to Mars. Don't you get it? He's not going to take all of us with him. That was never his plan, Jack. Only *one*. But, I'm not going to let it be just one of us. Not this time."

Jack was mortified. Darion's proposed truth was difficult to swallow but it made sense. Darion's every motivation, every desire, every desperate measure he'd made since Jack had met him was on display. Darion hadn't wanted Jack from the beginning, but the reasons were more complex than Jack had originally imagined. Darion was intent on taking himself *and* Olivia to Mars. And he would slaughter the Shepherd to do it. No room for negotiations. No time for talk or discussing the matter. Darion's will was to overcome the Shepherd. With the tainted disc on his arm - the weapons made for the Shepherds themselves - Darion would force his new slave to kill its former master. Was this really happening?

And yet, Jack could see the ramifications of such a choice: the disc was burning Darion's arm, fighting against the murderous intent circling inside of Darion. If it had a voice, the disc would no doubt be crying, begging for Darion to stop before the deed could be done. Too late for that though, as Darion left Jack behind; creeping slowly towards the unsuspecting Shepherd. Jack was frozen.

He held his tongue; immobilized by Darion's sudden change in plans. He looked for Olivia, wondering what she might think of her father's actions or if she knew of Darion's plan all along. Had she? Jack, himself, had never known the better. Perhaps Olivia was just as innocent?

Darion was within a few feet of the Shepherd now. Crouched at the foot of his ship, the silver giant seemed unaware of Darion. Unaware to the point when Darion raised his hand and a sharp, piercing weapon formed at the base of his wrist, Jack figured it was already over. Darion was going to *kill* the Shepherd. This was actually going to happen. Despite his near invincibility, Jack had seen the Shepherd bleed. He'd seen him in pain. And if any power could defeat the Shepherd, it would be one of the discs turned traitor in the hands of one such as Darion.

So as Darion reared back and thrust forward, Jack prepared for the worst. But, when there was no cry of death or pain, Jack realized something was wrong. He ran out of the brush and stood within a few feet of them. His mouth fell agape.

"I had hoped it would not have come to this, Darion Wallace," said the Shepherd, blandly. "In the deepest levels of my heart, I had hoped."

The Shepherd's body was still hunched over, but his right arm was raised next to him, firmly holding the armed dagger of Darion in his palm. Darion's attack had been thwarted without even the slightest hint of effort on the part of the Shepherd. Darion's eyes widened as he realized his weakness against the silver giant. Then the Shepherd turned to face Darion.

"I had hoped you would not have resorted to this," said the Shepherd, gazing up at Darion. His silver-blue eyes were filled with disappointment. "I had prayed for many days and many nights that your heart would change. That you would understand what it was we were doing. What *you* were doing. That you would open your heart and your mind to the possibility that this ending was not what you wanted. And yet, you still persisted. Why? *Why* did you do this?"

The Shepherd stood up, fingers wrapped about the weapon. He was unharmed. The dagger was shaking violently, its allegiance on trial as Darion's skin burned. Darion cried out in pain, grasping his forearm as the Shepherd asserted himself.

"These belong to *me*," said the Shepherd. "You may have stolen these from the others, but you cannot steal these from me. These were given to others as a *promise*; a sign that one of us would return and rescue them, but you cannot steal from me like you stole from them. You never could. What made you think you could now?"

From the *others*? What others? Jack stood in bewilderment. More Shepherds? Jack didn't have to wait long for an answer.

"How can you say that to me?" hissed Darion. "Not one of them lost what *I* had lost... Not one of them knew pain like I knew pain... Not one of them had something waiting for them on Mars. None of them!"

"And that made it right? That gave you the right to *steal* from them? That made it right for you to take their lives, even?"

Jack's heart dropped. Darion – a *killer*? The Shepherd turned towards Jack, finally acknowledging his presence.

The Shepherd raised his other hand and a hologram appeared.

"No!" squealed Darion. "Don't show him that! I beg you, please!"

Jack watched with horror in his eyes as Darion's history of finding each disc was played out before them. Every action Darion took was replayed, showed to him so that Jack might know the depth of Darion's treachery. First, there was a man Darion had beaten over the head. And then there was another, a younger girl that he'd coerced and taken the disc by force. Then a small boy; one who'd found a tattered disc by accident in the streets and was beaten by Darion for having found it. And then there was the last, a larger man whom Darion had killed with a pistol. All had been victims of Darion's. All of them broken or destroyed by Darion's lust to find the Shepherd's discs.

Jack couldn't believe it. He didn't *want* to believe it. He looked at Darion, whose eyes were burning with tears of shame.

"Stop it..." said Darion, pleading. "Stop it already! Enough! I can't take it anymore! Stop showing me that!"

The Shepherd turned even more serious. "You mean, stop showing *him* that." The Shepherd's eyes turned upon Jack and then quickly back to Darion. "You thought you might hide these things. But, there is nothing hidden forever, Darion Wallace. Though we'd like to believe there is some corner we can hide away within. That there is some crevasse we might be able to sneak into and find shelter from; this quiet belief of ours is a lie. Our every action – our human *will* - is always at work, leaving a trail behind us. Do you see that now? Your trail of broken light led me right to every one of your victims. And I weep for them. Just as I have wept for you."

Darion's knees started to buckle under the strain of his sins. He went from sorrow to bitterness and eventually to hatred in a few moments and Jack could feel it. Darion took his other hand and grabbed hold of the Shepherd's wrist, squeezing and scratching at it like he might be able to hurt the Shepherd. But, Jack knew he couldn't. Still, Darion tried and Jack witnessed as Darion's life began to slip from him.

"Darion! Stop it!" yelled Jack, but Darion would not. He accosted the Shepherd, clawing and pounding at the Shepherd's outstretched arm.

"I hate you! You don't know loss, Shepherd! You don't! Can you even comprehend the void? Can you?! I hate you! I hate everyone of you for what you've done to me!"

Darion's words were not his own, yet the Shepherd did not move. He stood with arm extended, eyes wet with tears. Tears that flowed down his cheeks as he watched Darion slowly destroy himself. It was true what the Shepherd had said: the suit would defend itself if provoked. And it was doing just that. With every open touch from Darion, the Shepherd's suit came alive with tiny tendrils, injecting Darion with poison like it were a million fire ants stinging an enemy. The pain must have been excruciating, but Darion wouldn't stop. Eventually, his flailing became steadily weaker and his legs lost their strength but his will was not finished.

He rose up, beating at the Shepherd's forearm before slumping downward again and again. It was beyond painful for Jack to watch and he wanted to run to Darion and make him stop. *Why are you doing this? Not another one. Not another one! Don't leave me alone too!*

The Shepherd glanced at Jack briefly, his expression bleak. Darion was still fighting, but it was clear he was near the end of his strength. Even so, Darion resorted to *biting* the Shepherd's arm; an action that prompted a moan from the Shepherd, but not out of physical pain, but sadness. It seemed like the torture would never end, until at last, Darion let go and his body crumpled to the ground. His chest heaved up and down, laboring for air as his mouth gargled with spit and blood. Jack looked to the Shepherd - still crying yet doing nothing.

"Do something!" shouted Jack, but the Shepherd would not acknowledge him. Darion twitched, looking for Jack.

"Do...do you see now, Jack?" asked Darion, but his voice was weak. He was dying exponentially - his body caving inward towards the Earth. "Do you see what the Shepherd will do? He lets you *suffer*. Lets you destroy yourself. The bastards.... They'll lead you along only to let you kill yourself in the end...."

Darion wanted sympathy. His words begged for it, but Jack only felt a stark repulsion looking down at Darion. Jack wanted to feel sorry; he wanted to empathize with this man he'd shared this journey with, but Jack could not erase from his mind the image of the ones who suffered on behalf of Darion. The elderly man; the young girl, the man Darion had beaten over the head - all of them were victims. More so than Darion was now. Their promises had been taken from them, because of Darion's selfishness. And Jack took a step away from Darion.

I cried out on your behalf, Jack thought. *Yet how could you ask for my help now? After what I've seen?*

When Darion saw Jack back away, his eyes narrowed and he spit at Jack. "And you! You aren't going to Mars either! You think you are? You... you who can't even...."

Darion coughed and blood coated the dirt in red. He looked at Jack once more and sputtered out a few words as life was leaving him.

"...Lydia...cold...Liv...sorry..."

Then Darion breathed his last. His face went pale and his entire being seemed to sink into the earth. The moist soil absorbed his body, pulling him downward as life and light left him. For a moment, Jack thought he looked like the Captain: body torn and contorted in a terrible manner. Jack expected the Adversary to appear, to feast upon Darion's deceased frame but nothing came. The black beast would not appear and Jack feared this new death was a fate worse than the Captain's. Or was it? He didn't have time to figure it out. For the Shepherd had turned his gaze upon Jack and was walking slowly towards him. When Jack saw this, he fell to his knees, realizing what was liable to come next.

Darion was a murderer. So was he. This was the end for him also.

"You knew...," said Jack. "You knew *everything*...." The Shepherd stopped a stride away from Jack and looked down upon him. Jack looked up, pitifully.

"Yes," said the Shepherd. His tone had shifted almost instantaneously. He was himself again, stern yet gentle in his delivery. He seemed to have already put Darion's demise behind him and was now focusing entirely on Jack. "I knew everything I needed to know. As a Shepherd of Mars, I possess all the Gifts of the Red Fellows. Their abilities to use light are all a part of me. I have always known who you were, the moment you touched the discs and opened your memories, I was able to see into them — learn you, learn your heart. Yes, Jack, I have always known of your crimes. And your sins. They were never a secret from me."

Jack wanted to cry. He peered at the decaying body of Darion, a tuft of dirt and ash on the ground.

"Then you know," said Jack. "You know how much of a monster I am. I can't go to Mars, can I? You're not taking me with you, are you?"

"No, Jack. I am not."

Jack huffed; a sound like relief coupled with incredulousness. *All for nothing*, he thought. I've been following this path for nothing....

"So now what? Are you going to give me a disc? Is that what you'll let me have?"

The Shepherd shook his head. "No. I cannot do that either."

Jack began to chuckle. Then what? He couldn't believe this. Nothing for me, is it? Then came the *fear*. Jack felt fear come over him. If not the journey and not a disc, then what? What did the Shepherd plan to do with him? He looked at Darion's body again. There was even less of it now. Any evidence that a man had been lying in the dirt was gone. Even his blood was disappearing in the dirt. Jack breathed heavily. This was truly the end, wasn't it? The Shepherd knelt down on one knee; an arm's reach away from Jack and looked into his eyes. Jack had never been this close to the Shepherd before. His silver-blue eyes were metallic and round like marbles. They were unlike any person's he'd ever seen before; bright and filled with a strange light. Within them, Jack could see Mars because the Shepherd had seen Mars. Jack could see the stars, endless pathways of light pushing to every corner of the existent universe. What else had these eyes seen? What else had they already witnessed? Jack felt the weight of the Shepherd's life press against his own and he shrunk into himself, an unworthy husk of undesirable flesh. That's all he was. There was no way he could ever go to Mars. Why had he been so foolish? Why did he ever think it might be possible to leave this place and walk on golden roads and taste perfect, unaltered water like the Shepherd?

"I…I don't know what to do," said Jack.

"What can you do?"

"Nothing."

"You can always do *something*. So what will you do? What will you do with the power you've been given?"

Jack couldn't go to Mars, but he didn't want to stay here. The Shepherd would never come for him again. He could be sure of that. And yet, there *was* something he could do. He could end it all. Yes, he could end everything now and not have to suffer for the rest of his life. So Jack closed his eyes and raised his hand. He would touch the Shepherd. He would accept his fate; he would join the others – Turk, Felix, Robert, Sophia, Abraham, and Ianna. He could see their faces, all of them waiting for him as he reached for the Shepherd. Would it hurt? Doesn't matter. Almost there. He would be there soon. Then, a voice interrupted everything.

"Jack, no!"

Another hand grabbed hold of Jack's wrist and Jack opened his eyes. That voice - Jack had never heard it before. It was serene, clear, and crisp – the voice of a *child*. Olivia? Yes. She was standing next to Jack and breathing hard. Her eyes were wide with shock, her sandy blond hair was a mess yet still possessed that innocent beauty Jack had come to know and appreciate. She was on the verge of tears, looking him over.

"Please…" she said and she pulled herself close to Jack and held him. "Don't hurt yourself. Please."

The Shepherd smiled. "There you are," he said. "I was wondering when you might come out."

"Olivia?" said Jack. "I wasn't… I didn't know. Where were you?"

Olivia sobbed against Jack. "Please don't hurt yourself," she said, embracing him tighter. "You don't have to do that. Please don't do that. Please don't go away."

Finally, Jack hugged her back. He looked at the Shepherd, who was standing again and smiling at them both. Jack trembled, amazed to be alive at this moment. He let go of Olivia and stood, facing the Shepherd. What of Darion? There was no sign of his body in the dirt. No trace of him anywhere. *Good*, he thought. Jack didn't want Olivia to see it.

"Olivia," said Jack. "You spoke. You spoke to me."

She wiped away her tears and grinned. I did it to save *you*, she said without saying a word.

"Olivia?" said the Shepherd. "I am ready to take you now. Your mother waits for you on Mars. Will you come with me?"

Olivia, still holding onto Jack, looked up. "What about everyone else? Where is Dad?"

The Shepherd and Jack exchanged glances. "No," said the Shepherd. "They must stay here. I can only take one of you."

"What about Dad though?"

Jack took a deep breath. He's gone, Liv. He's gone forever. Gone to whatever place best suited him now that his life is over. That's the best I could explain it to you, if I could.

"He cannot come either," said the Shepherd. "He'll have to remain on Earth too."

"For now?"

"For now."

Olivia looked about, searching for her father. When she didn't find him, she looked to Jack, her eyes welling up with tears.

"I'll stay with him on Earth for you," said Jack. "I'll stay here. You go and see your mother. And when we're ready, we'll come too."

"But, I….," she said. "I don't know. What about Dad? Where is he? Why can't I – "

Olivia's voice trailed off and Jack pulled her close to him. He looked at the Shepherd, staring into the silver blue eyes of the beast that'd let Darion destroy himself. *How could you just let that happen,* Jack thought. *How could you?* Darion may have been an asshole but he was still her father. He still loved her. Still cared for her. Yet, you let him die.

But, the Shepherd didn't budge. So Jack made a decision.

"Olivia," he said. "You have to go. You have to go or else none of this was worth it. Do ya understand me? You just have to. Your daddy wanted you to make it. So you make it. And we'll come for you later, okay? He had to go away right now, but he'll be back."

Olivia nodded, eyes to the ground with tears coming down her cheeks. She asked for her father again, asked why she couldn't say goodbye to him. She pleaded to see him before she left, but Jack held onto her and told her she would someday. He lied. He lied like he had a thousand times before, only this time it felt horrible to do it. Then he held onto her one last time and then urged her on towards the Ship. The Shepherd led her to the entrance, but was stopped by Jack.

"So, are you satisfied?" asked Jack, teeth gritted. "Are you satisfied with the result of all this?"

The Shepherd pivoted around to face Jack. His eyes seemed to burn with anger and Jack suddenly realized the error of his accusation. The Shepherd could still kill him. Could still take his life if he wanted to. What was Jack's life to the Shepherd now?

"Mars' imperative is to save those who want to be saved, Jack," said the Shepherd and he looked to the ground where Darion's body once was. "There are some who wish only destruction upon themselves. I cannot change a man's fate."

Jack surveyed the ground. That could have been him. That could have been his body decomposing in the dirt. Jack took one more look at Olivia. She was scared, but she was doing as she was told. She'd miss her father always, but at least she'd be rid of this place. Then, one day, she'd know the truth of why her father was no longer at her side. What then, Shepherd?

Then the Shepherd started to turn away, prompting Jack to stop him again.

"What about me now?" asked Jack and the Shepherd turned round. "What am I supposed to do with all this?" He held his hands out like a beggar. The Shepherd walked up to Jack and stopped, but didn't answer right away.

"Where am I supposed to go?" asked Jack, eyes looking up at the Shepherd. "You said I have to stay but what does that mean? The world is still filled with Darklight. And the Adversary – it's *still* here too, isn't it? What am I supposed to do when that thing comes back for me?"

The Shepherd took a deep breath. "Go and tell others of what you have witnessed here. Tell them what you have seen. There will be many. And they will come to you and you will tell them all that you have to say. You will tell them that the light will soon overcome the dark. And the Earth will be made whole again. But it is not that time yet."

Jack absorbed his orders yet maintained his confusion. "Who's going to listen to me though? I'm no one, Shepherd. Don't you know that? And the ones who *do* know me - they hate me. Who listens to someone they hate? I'm - "

The Shepherd raised a hand and pointed at Jack. His silver extremity stopped a hair's breadth between Jack and himself. Jack shut his eyes. He could feel the Shepherd's power, like there was a bomb ready to explode at the tip of the Shepherd's finger.

"Go and tell them you are not Jack, but *Isaac*," ordered the Shepherd. "That is who you are now. And if people claim to know you as Jack, then you will correct them. You will tell them, 'no, I am not that man. I am Isaac.' For Jack does not exist any longer. *Isaac* is all there is. Where you brought pain, you will now bring peace. And where you once were afraid, you will now find courage. You are an enemy of the Adversary so he will follow you always, but now you are equipped to face him. Go and find others who have seen what you have seen. They are waiting for you, Isaac."

The Shepherd dropped his arm and Jack breathed air with new life. The oxygen filled his lungs like water satisfying a dry man's mouth. *Make the path straight*, he thought. He was tasked with showing others the road. He was tasked with finding the truth. The Shepherd was pointing him in the proper direction, awakening what purpose had been lying dormant inside. All the years of being an orphan – he'd endured it for the sake of returning to that place. Yes, this was true.

As for the others like him, they would be soldiers of the same army. The ones searching for God's fingerprint, trying hard to lift the curtain of meaning to expose what lied behind. And they would know him as Isaac, not Jack. Just as the Shepherd said they would. Jack saw this vision and opened his eyes not as Jack, but as Isaac. Jack was gone – only Isaac remained.

"Thank you," said Isaac, tears forming in his eyes.

"We will fix this someday," said the Shepherd. "But, for now, you must hold strong for the people here. One day, Mars will be ready to come and take back the Earth for everyone who lives here. But, until then, you must wait."

Then the Shepherd turned and entered his ship. It hovered for a few seconds before lifting itself high into the sky; then a loud boom sent it off through the clouds. A trail of white painted the sky and Isaac watched it till it was gone from sight. Unbelievable. The journey was over - no, it was only the beginning. For Isaac, it was only the start.

He stood idly for a moment, thinking of what to do next. He made a note of where all this had taken place, remembering everything he'd done and the road he'd taken to get here. Then he took a deep breath and felt a tingle on his neck. He turned round and saw beyond the veil of brush, the eyes of the Adversary. It was hiding; red eyes glaring like it was looking for fear to cover Isaac. Yet Isaac only grinned.

"Follow me, if you like," said Isaac. "But, I warn you - you'll only be disappointed if you do."

Then Isaac left the spot where the Shepherd's ship had landed, the Adversary following behind. Isaac paid no attention to the beast, walking with a confidence where he knew the monster could only take him if he allowed it.

Isaac walked west, looking to the sky for trails of stardust of other Shepherds. It was there he hoped to meet others who had been through a similar journey. There must have been several Shepherds. There were most certainly more of them. They had come to Earth to do more than find us, he concluded. They'd come as teachers. Or perhaps, they'd come as judges. Or perhaps they'd come as *friends*. Yes, Isaac would count the Shepherd among those he called, 'friend.' Others would feel the same, too. He needed to find them. And multiply the ones who did. His journey was far from concluded and he smiled at the challenge set before him.

Isaac wanted beauty. He wanted justice. He wanted *truth*. Were the Shepherds the holders of ultimate truths? Isaac didn't know, but he was willing to explore more of what he'd learned. Maybe this mystery would bring even more people together? People who once hated each other could unite under some new understanding? Or *old*. The Old World had known light. The Old World could control many things. The Old World was not at war with brother Mars. Was it Isaac's job to change all that?

The weight of this new burden was huge, and it nearly caused Isaac to collapse where he stood. The Adversary moved in, but then Isaac righted his thoughts and the Adversary backed off. God is watching me. I cannot let my mind become afraid. Can there be any greater burden than that? He would seek the others out - the ones who wanted truth as he did. It was time to find people who would hear him. And he would hear them too.

But, it would have to start with grace. It would have to start with forgiveness. The same kind he had been shown by the Shepherd. The same the Earth needed to show Mars.

So Isaac traveled to towns and cities, looking for the ones who would listen. And he found many that would. But, when he left and they spoke of the one who had come to them, they didn't speak of 'Jack'; they spoke of another.

"I am *Isaac*," he would say. "That is my name. You may call me *Isaac*."

And so, Isaac's name became known in every land he visited, all the while awaiting word from the Shepherds. *I will never forget*, he thought. Not ever. Till we see each other again. I won't forget. I promise you.

* * * *

High above Earth, the Shepherd's ship was breaking through the atmosphere. Olivia scarcely noticed. She was having difficulty staying awake as the Shepherd was punching coordinates into his ship's computer. It was all being done rather casually. The Shepherd simply made the arrangements and then clicked a button to change the ship's interior. A holographic map showed where they were headed.

"Look there, Olivia," said the Shepherd and Olivia opened her eyes wide.

One of the side panels turned transparent, permitting Olivia to see the Earth below. She wasn't afraid, she found, looking down at the blue and white object that was Earth. It felt more like a dream than reality. There were other ships coming up to join them too. Dozens, no *hundreds* were coming. All of them Shepherd ships, all of them leaving the blue planet and headed for the red planet. There had been many Shepherds on Earth. They'd all come for ones like her and they were leaving just as she was. That meant there were friends waiting. More friends waited where she was going. And Mom, too. They would all be there. And Dad would be too, someday. And Jack. He'd be there with them, she hoped.

The ships gathered as one, a chain of interplanetary vehicles linking together like they were made of a larger vessel. On Earth, the hundreds who had witnessed the Shepherd were gathering too. Olivia imagined Jack and her father meeting new people. It would be a great moment for them both. Maybe now they would finally get along? Maybe now her father wouldn't be so angry all the time? Maybe now he could find peace, being with others like him? Olivia prayed silently that he might.

The ship closed its window and Olivia drifted into sleep. Then the ship interlocked with many others and began to move. Time seemed to bend and space shifted with it. Soon, Olivia would be moving at a speed where God came and went as he pleased.

"My father," said Olivia. "He won't be coming, will he?"

The Shepherd didn't answer. Olivia's hands held onto the pictures of her father and mother. She had kept them since they'd left the Cathedral, stealing them away from her father so that she might see her mother's face and remember. Remember how things had been when they were *one*. Olivia didn't want these pictures to leave her ever again. So she held on and waited for the Shepherd to answer.

But, the Shepherd wouldn't. He hit a few more buttons on his control panel and looked back outside the ship. His eyes lingered on the horizon. The sun was rising up over the blue planet beneath them and the Shepherd smiled, a tiny tear of joy pushing out from under.

"Will I ever see you as what you were meant for?" said the Shepherd, aloud but not for Olivia. "Or is this really the last time we will embrace each other? I, for one, hope it is not the last. The road was hard, but it was good. All things worked together as they were meant to. I am eager to see what is next."

Then the fleet of Shepherds flew away as one. Headed for Mars, headed for the red planet. Only this time they carried several of Earth's own along with them.

The Shadow of Mars

A short preview from Book Two of the Mars series.

Chapter 1
Olivia

"What is that you brought with you?"
"A gift."
"A *gift*? What kind of gift?"
"A gift that will change the world."

* * * *

Good news, Olivia.
Your application has been accepted for research on Colony 3, Jupiter's moon,
"Europa." Please reply that we may know you have received this message and
that you are going to accept this offer. At which point, please report to the
academy within the next hour.

Congratulations,
Professor P.

The words flashed on Olivia Wallace's projector screen for several minutes before she realized they were there. She had been napping on her couch, listening to a string quartet on her Alpha player. That always helped to curb her anxiety. So when her eyes opened and she recognized the message as not a dream, but reality, her mind became alert and she sat up. Then the joy came.

Her application had been accepted. The academy had selected *her*. The news was enough to make her stand up, then sit down immediately for fear she'd read the message incorrectly. No, still the same. Still there. She was going to Europa. She was leaving Mars.

Not that she had desperately wished to depart. Her life had been good, for the most part, these past 10 years as a resident of the red planet. She had little, if any, resentment for living on Mars as opposed to her birth world, Earth. And having spent nearly the majority of her life now on Mars rather than Earth, Mars was more synonymous with "home" than anywhere else.

And yet, Olivia had always felt a unique tension during her time here. Something had been stirring in her heart for a long time - a feeling culminated by her application at the academy not three years earlier. It was then she chose to pursue a career in ecology, specifically off-world ecology. The pursuit of terraforming other planets had become, for lack of a better term, *popular.* Taking up a career such as this could someday take Olivia to the Rim: humanity's outermost point of civilization. That would be more than exciting. But, beyond that? Olivia couldn't see herself going any farther. She just knew she couldn't be here anymore.

So Olivia gathered some clothes and got dressed quickly, nearly forgetting to message the academy back with a 'thank you'.

"That would have been poor etiquette, Olivia," she said aloud, but saying the words as though they weren't her own. She'd heard them plenty of times from another. The 'other' being professor Payton: Olivia's favorite teacher and chief advisor at the academy. "If you saw what I was wearing, you'd know poor etiquette was all over this place, Professor."

The thought of Payton walking in on her while changing was comical. He was always so professional and so serious that she couldn't imagine the man ever flirting with another human being. Maybe he was asexual? That was a possibility, wasn't it?

Stop it, Liv. Stay focused. Make jokes later. Not long after, she was out the door.

"Looking especially red today," she said, looking out. No different from any other day, of course.

Outside her living quarters, Mars' translucent bubble shield was doing its job: keeping humans out of the harsh climate that was Mars' surface. And simultaneously, enhancing the sun's light, creating the optimal level of sunlight for Olivia's Earth-born body. It felt good, just like a warm sunrise on Earth. And when the rays hit at the right angle, Olivia could easily discern where the bubble ended and Mars' landscape began.

There were many like this on Mars – huge towers filled with people living on the surface. Similarly, there were the Domes: places where the atmosphere was crisp, clean, and wonderfully breathable. But, outside the Domes, there was only Mars. And Mars herself was toxic. The air alone would drain the life of anything organic within seconds and its terrain was just as hostile. True, there were impressive canyons and long stretches of rocky outcroppings. But, none held the multi-colored splendor of Earth's simplest streams or ruggedly diverse hillsides.

Strange, she thought. It always seemed odd how Mars used invisible barriers to separate places of life from places of death. Like Mars' inhabitants needed to be reminded of what was on the other side lest their walls come down. It was like saying, 'Here, see what you *can't* enjoy. But know it's there all the same.' A big, white wall would be just as useful. Or a hologram of Earth's terrain would be even better, perhaps?

Olivia shook the thought and walked on. She was no engineer so it wasn't her job to decipher to best means for surface dwellers to experience the Martian landscape. After all, she would be trading this red for blue again. Europa was covered in ice. Maybe that would keep her from criticizing Mars so much, keep her from reminiscing on Earth and comparing the two.

Still, she'd done it again. That one thing she could never seem to shake: thinking of her past life, the one she'd left on Earth. Must she always be comparing them? She couldn't help herself, it seemed. The Pulse had crippled the Earth while Mars continued to thrive. Earth was dying by the hour, swallowed up in Darklight and its fear-driven people. Olivia was fortunate to be living on Mars. She was blessed to have escaped that hell.

And yet, it saddened her to think that all she wanted to do was leave Mars behind. Not to forget Mars entirely, but somehow move past it. She knew she'd been one of the lucky ones – one of the Shepherd's Chosen: an Earthborn specifically selected by a Shepherd for relocation. Though she understood the selection process to be something governed by the Shepherds themselves – a practice rarely questioned by Mars' highest authorities – what Olivia *couldn't* rationalize was how each individual Shepherd could be held responsible for such a difficult decision.

But, then of course, there was *Solfire*. The answer always seemed to lie with Solfire. The Shepherds used Solfire to see light. Traces of light on people: past, present, and future. The light transmitted information only those with the Gift could discern. However, no one could use this Gift like the Shepherds could. It was as awesome and amazing as it was terrifying.

It made Olivia –and by default, her mother before her – an *anomaly*. Those of the Shepherd's Chosen were among the privileged on Mars and as such, were watched more closely. Like, one day their rescue might manifest itself in a way deemed worthy enough for the trouble it took to save them.

Olivia knew it to be true. She'd been treated differently ever since she came to Mars. Those of pure Martian birth glared at her in passing, fully aware of her heritage. But, there were others who treated her better than what she deserved. Like, she was a mini celebrity. And then there were those who were fair with her. No preferential treatment or royal rollout. She appreciated these people the most.

However, Olivia was playing directly into that ideal, into that stereotype of great expectations. For only a few were awarded the opportunity to travel off world immediately upon graduation. And even fewer could go to a place of their choosing. Olivia, again, was among the elite. She was getting to do *both*.

True, she could have chosen a career in Mars agriculture or AR – Adversary Research – but none of that enticed her. It was off world that she wanted. A new adventure, something far from here.

So before she stepped inside the elevator and pressed the button to head underground, her thoughts returned to the blinking message on her screen and the joy returned. She would only ruminate on good thoughts from here on.

Yes, she thought, the door closing. This was the right choice. She'd be leaving Mars, but perhaps even more importantly, she'd be seeing her mother again. Her mother, the anomaly – just like her.

And maybe, if she were really lucky, the Shepherd – her friend and protector – would be there too.

About the author

Joshua (J.C.L.) Faltot is the author of *The Road to Mars* and is a lover of all things science fiction (except for digitally mastered remakes. He draws the line there). Before writing became more than just a hobby, Joshua worked as an insurance analyst, hospital contractor, and a self-touted Walgreens photo lab expert. *The Road to Mars* is the first of three books in Faltot's Mars series, but is not his first publication. Joshua has published short stories and satirical non-fiction, available in ebook format. Joshua currently resides in Cleveland, OH and is married with one child.

You can find more info on Josh and upcoming projects at
www.jclfaltot.com

Made in the USA
San Bernardino, CA
21 April 2017